ISAAC ASIMOV

Foundation and Earth

HARPER
Voyager

Harper*Voyager*
An imprint of HarperCollins*Publishers*
1 London Bridge Street
London SE1 9GF

www.harpervoyagerbooks.co.uk

This paperback edition 2016

Previously published in paperback by
HarperCollins Science Fiction & Fantasy 1994
And Harper*Voyager*, 1996
And by Grafton 1989

First published in Great Britain by
Grafton Books 1986

ISBN: 978-0-00-811753-5

Typeset in Janson Text by Palimpsest Book Production Ltd, Falkirk, Stirlingshire

Printed and bound in Great Britain by Clays Ltd, St Ives plc

MIX
Paper from
responsible sources
FSC C007454

To the memory of
Judy-Lynn del Rey (1943-1986).
A giant in mind and spirit

Contents

The Story Behind The Foundation

On 1 August, 1941, when I was a lad of twenty-one, I was a graduate student in chemistry at the Columbia University and had been writing science fiction professionally for three years. I was hastening to see John Campbell, editor of *Astounding*, to whom I had sold five stories by then. I was anxious to tell him a new idea I had for a science fiction story.

It was to write a historical novel of the future; to tell the story of the fall of the Galactic Empire. My enthusiasm must have been catching, for Campbell grew as excited as I was. He didn't want me to write a single story. He wanted a series of stories, in which the full history of the thousand years of turmoil between the fall of the First Galactic Empire and the rise of the Second Galactic Empire was to be outlined. It would all be illuminated by the science of 'psychohistory' which Campbell and I thrashed out between us.

This first story appeared in the May 1942 *Astounding* and the second story appeared in the June 1942 issue. They were at once popular and Campbell saw to it that I wrote six more stories before the end of the decade. The stories grew longer, too. The first one was only twelve thousand words long. Two of the last three stories were fifty thousand words apiece.

By the time the decade was over, I had grown tired of the series, dropped it, and went on to other things. By then, however, various publishing houses were beginning to put out hard-covered science fiction books. One such house was a small firm, Gnome Press. They published my Foundation series in three volumes: *Foundation* (1951);

Foundation and Empire (1952); and *Second Foundation* (1953). They became known as *The Foundation Trilogy*.

The books did not do very well, for Gnome Press did not have the capital with which to advertise and promote them. I got neither statements nor royalties from them.

In early 1961, my then-editor at Doubleday, Timothy Seldes, told me he had received a request from a foreign publisher to reprint the Foundation books. Since they were not Doubleday books, he passed the request on to me. I shrugged my shoulders. 'Not interested, Tim. I don't get royalties on those books.'

Seldes was horrified, and instantly set about getting the rights to the books from Gnome Press (which was, by that time, moribund) and in August of that year, the books (along with *I, Robot*) became Doubleday property.

From that moment on, the Foundation series took off and began to earn increasing royalties. Doubleday published the *Trilogy* in a single volume and distributed them through the Science Fiction Book Club.

In the 1966 World Science Fiction Convention, held in Cleveland, the fans were asked to vote on a category of 'The Best All-Time Series'. It was the first time (and, so far, the last) the category had been included in the nominations for the Hugo Award. *The Foundation Trilogy* won the award.

Increasingly, fans kept asking me to continue the series. I was polite but I kept refusing. Still, it fascinated me that people who had not yet been born when the series was begun had managed to become caught up in it.

Doubleday, however, took the demands far more seriously than I did. They had humoured me for twenty years but as the demands kept growing in intensity and number, they finally lost patience. In 1981, they told me that I simply had to write another Foundation novel and, in order to sugar-coat the demand, offered me a contract at ten times my usual advance.

Nervously, I agreed. It had been thirty-two years since I had written a Foundation story and now I was instructed to write one 140,000 words long, twice that of any of the earlier volumes and nearly three times as long as any previous individual story. I re-read the trilogy and dived into the task. *Foundation's Edge* was published in October 1982, and then a very strange thing happened. It appeared in the New York *Times* bestseller list at once. In fact, it stayed on that list for twenty-five weeks, to my utter astonishment.

Doubleday at once signed me up to do additional novels and I wrote two that were part of another series, *The Robot Novels*. – And then it was time to return to the Foundation.

So I wrote *Foundation and Earth*, which begins at the very moment that *Foundation's Edge* ends. It might help if you glanced over *Foundation's Edge* just to refresh your memory, but you don't have to. *Foundation and Earth* stands by itself. I hope you enjoy it.

ISAAC ASIMOV,
New York City, 1986

Foundation and Earth

Part I

Gaia

The Search Begins

'Why did I do it?' asked Golan Trevize.

It wasn't a new question. Since he had arrived at Gaia, he had asked it of himself frequently. He would wake up from a sound sleep in the pleasant coolness of the night and find the question sounding noiselessly in his mind, like a tiny drumbeat: Why did I do it? Why did I do it?

Now, though, for the first time, he managed to ask it of Dom, the ancient of Gaia.

Dom was well aware of Trevize's tension for he could sense the fabric of the Councilman's mind. He did not respond to it. Gaia must in no way *ever* touch Trevize's mind, and the best way of remaining immune to the temptation was to painstakingly ignore what he sensed.

'Do what, Trev?' he asked. He found it difficult to use more than one syllable in addressing a person, and it didn't matter. Trevize was growing somewhat used to that.

'The decision I made,' said Trevize. 'Choosing Gaia as the future.'

'You were right to do so,' said Dom, seated, his aged deepset eyes looking earnestly up at the man of the Foundation, who was standing.

'You *say* I am right,' said Trevize impatiently.

'I/we/Gaia know you are. That's your worth to us. You have the capacity for making the right decision on incomplete data, and you have made the decision. You chose Gaia! You rejected the anarchy of a Galactic Empire built on the technology of the First Foundation, as well as the anarchy of a Galactic Empire built on the mentalics of the Second Foundation. You decided that neither could be long stable. So you chose Gaia.'

'Yes,' said Trevize. 'Exactly! I chose Gaia, a superorganism; a whole planet with a mind and personality in common, so that one has to say "I/we/Gaia" as an invented pronoun to express the inexpressible.' He paced the floor restlessly. 'And it will become eventually Galaxia, a super-super-organism embracing all the swarm of the Milky Way.'

He stopped, turned almost savagely on Dom, and said, 'I feel I'm right, as you feel it, but you *want* the coming of Galaxia, and so are satisfied with the decision. There's something in me, however, that *doesn't* want it, and for that reason I'm not satisfied to accept the rightness so easily. I want to know *why* I made the decision. I want to weigh and judge the rightness and be satisfied with it. Merely feeling right isn't enough. How can I *know* I am right? What is the device that makes me right?'

'I/we/Gaia do not know how it is that you come to the right decision. Is it important to know that as long as we have the decision?'

'You speak for the whole planet, do you? For the common consciousness of every dewdrop, of every pebble, of even the liquid central core of the planet?'

'I do, and so can any portion of the planet in which the intensity of the common consciousness is great enough.'

'And is all this common consciousness satisfied to use me as a black box? Since the black box works, is it unimportant to know what is inside? – That doesn't suit me. I don't enjoy being a black box. I want to know what's inside. I want to know how and why I chose Gaia and Galaxia as the future, so that I can rest and be at peace.'

'But why do you dislike or distrust your decision so?'

Trevize drew a deep breath and said slowly, in a low and forceful voice, 'Because I don't want to be part of a superorganism. I don't want to be a dispensable part to be done away with whenever the superorganism judges that doing away would be for the good of the whole.'

Dom looked at Trevize thoughtfully. 'Do you want to change your decision, then, Trev? You can, you know.'

'I long to change the decision, but I can't do that merely because I dislike it. To do something now, I have to *know* whether the decision is wrong or right. It's not enough merely to *feel* it's right.'

'If you feel you are right, you are right.' Always that slow, gentle voice that somehow made Trevize feel wilder by its very contrast with his own inner turmoil.

Then Trevize said, in half a whisper, breaking out of the insoluble oscillation between feeling and knowing, 'I must find Earth.'

'Because it has something to do with this passionate need of yours to know?'

'Because it is another problem that troubles me unbearably and because I *feel* there is a connection between the two. Am I not a black box? I *feel* there is a connection. Isn't that enough to make you accept it as a fact?'

'Perhaps,' said Dom, with equanimity.

'Granted it is now thousands of years – twenty thousand perhaps – since the people of the Galaxy have concerned themselves with Earth, how is it possible that we have all forgotten our planet of origin?'

'Twenty thousand years is a longer time than you realize. There are many aspects of the early Empire we know little of; many legends that are almost surely fictitious but that we keep repeating, and even believing, because of lack of anything to substitute. And Earth is older than the Empire.'

'But surely there are some records. My good friend, Pelorat, collects myths and legends of early Earth; anything he can scrape up from any source. It is his profession and, more important, his hobby. Those myths and legends are all there are. There are no actual records, no documents.'

'Documents twenty thousand years old? Things decay, perish, are destroyed through inefficiency or war.'

'But there should be records of the records; copies, copies of the copies, and copies of the copies of the copies; useful material much younger than twenty millennia. They have been removed. The Galactic Library at Trantor must have had documents concerning Earth. Those documents are referred to in known historical records, but the documents no longer exist in the Galactic Library. The references to them may exist, but any quotations from them do not exist.'

'Remember that Trantor was sacked a few centuries ago.'

'The Library was left untouched. It was protected by the personnel of the Second Foundation. And it was those personnel who recently discovered that material related to Earth no longer exists. The material was deliberately removed in recent times. Why?' Trevize ceased his pacing and looked intently at Dom. 'If I find Earth, I will find out what it is hiding –'

'Hiding?'

'Hiding or being hidden. Once I find that out, I have the feeling I will know why I have chosen Gaia and Galaxia over our individuality. Then, I presume, I will *know*, not feel, that I am correct, and if I am correct,' he lifted his shoulders hopelessly, 'then so be it.'

'If you feel that is so,' said Dom, 'and if you feel you must hunt for Earth, then, of course, we will help you do so as much as we can. That help, however, is limited. For instance, I/we/Gaia do not know where Earth may be located among the immense wilderness of worlds that make up the Galaxy.'

'Even so,' said Trevize, 'I must search. – Even if the endless powdering of stars in the Galaxy makes the quest seem hopeless, and even if I must do it alone.'

2

Trevize was surrounded by the tameness of Gaia. The temperature, as always, was comfortable, and the air moved pleasantly, refreshing but not chilling. Clouds drifted across the sky, interrupting the sunlight now and then, and, no doubt, if the water vapour level per metre of open land surface dropped sufficiently in this place or that, there would be enough rain to restore it.

The trees grew in regular spacings, like an orchard, and did so, no doubt, all over the world. The land and sea were stocked with plant and animal life in proper numbers and in the proper variety to provide an appropriate ecological balance, and all of them, no doubt, increased and decreased in numbers in a slow sway about the recognized optimum. – As did the number of human beings, too.

Of all the objects within the purview of Trevize's vision, the only wild card in the deck was his ship, the *Far Star*.

The ship had been cleaned and refurbished efficiently and well by a number of the human components of Gaia. It had been restocked with food and drink, its furnishings had been renewed or replaced, its mechanical workings rechecked. Trevize himself had checked the ship's computer carefully.

Nor did the ship need refuelling, for it was one of the few gravitic ships of the Foundation, running on the energy of the general gravitational field of the Galaxy, and that was enough to supply all the possible fleets of humanity for all the eons of their likely existence without measurable decrease of intensity.

Three months ago, Trevize had been a Councilman of Terminus. He had, in other words, been a member of the legislature of the Foundation and, *ex officio*, a great one of the Galaxy. Was it only three months ago? It seemed it was half his thirty-two-year-old lifetime since that had been his post and his only concern had been whether the great Seldon Plan had been valid or not; whether the smooth rise of the Foundation from planetary village to Galactic greatness had been properly charted in advance, or not.

Yet in some ways, there was no change. He was *still* a Councilman. His status and his privileges remained unchanged, except that he didn't expect he would ever return to Terminus to claim that status and those privileges. He would no more fit into the huge chaos of the Foundation than into the small orderliness of Gaia. He was at home nowhere, an orphan everywhere.

His jaw tightened and he pushed his fingers angrily through his black hair. Before he wasted time bemoaning his fate, he must find Earth. If he survived the search, there would then be time enough to sit down and weep. He might have even better reason then.

With determined stolidity, then, he thought back –

Three months before, he and Janov Pelorat, that able, naïve scholar, had left Terminus. Pelorat had been driven by his antiquarian enthusiasms to discover the site of long-lost Earth, and Trevize had gone along, using Pelorat's goal as a cover for what he thought his own real aim was. They did not find Earth, but they did find Gaia, and Trevize had then found himself forced to make his fateful decision.

Now it was he, Trevize, who had turned half-circle – about-face – and was searching for Earth.

As for Pelorat, he, too, had found something he didn't expect. He had found the black-haired, dark-eyed Bliss, the young woman who was Gaia, even as Dom was – and as the nearest grain of sand or blade of grass was. Pelorat, with the peculiar ardour of late middle age, had fallen in love with a woman less than half his years, and the young woman, oddly enough, seemed content with that.

It was odd – but Pelorat was surely happy and Trevize thought resignedly that each person must find happiness in his or her own manner. That was the point of individuality – the individuality that Trevize, by his choice, was abolishing (given time) over all the Galaxy.

The pain returned. That decision he had made, and had had to make, continued to excoriate him at every moment and was –

'Golan!'

The voice intruded on Trevize's thoughts and he looked up in the direction of the sun, blinking his eyes.

'Ah, Janov,' he said heartily – the more heartily because he did not want Pelorat to be guessing at the sourness of his thoughts. He even managed a jovial, 'You've managed to tear yourself away from Bliss, I see.'

Pelorat shook his head. The gentle breeze stirred his silky white hair, and his long solemn face retained its length and solemnity in full. 'Actually, old chap, it was she that suggested I see you – about – about what I want to discuss. Not that I wouldn't have wanted to see you on my own, of course, but she seems to think more quickly than I do.'

Trevize smiled. 'It's all right, Janov. You're here to say goodbye, I take it.'

'Well, no, not exactly. In fact, more nearly the reverse. Golan, when we left Terminus, you and I, I was intent on finding Earth. I've spent virtually my entire adult life at that task.'

'And I will carry on, Janov. The task is mine now.'

'Yes, but it's mine, also; mine, still.'

'But –' Trevize lifted an arm in a vague all-inclusive gesture of the world about them.

Pelorat said, in a sudden urgent gasp, 'I want to go with you.'

Trevize felt astonished. 'You can't mean that, Janov. You have Gaia now.'

'I'll come back to Gaia some day, but I cannot let you go alone.'

'Certainly you can. I can take care of myself.'

'No offence, Golan, but you don't know enough. It is I who know the myths and legends. I can direct you.'

'And you'll leave Bliss? Come, now.'

A faint pink coloured Pelorat's cheeks. 'I don't exactly want to do that, old chap, but she said –'

Trevize frowned. 'Is it that she's trying to get rid of *you*, Janov. She promised me –'

'No, you don't understand. Please listen to me, Golan. You do have this uncomfortable explosive way of jumping to conclusions before you hear one out. It's your speciality, I know, and I seem to have a certain difficulty in expressing myself concisely, but –'

'Well,' said Trevize gently, 'suppose you tell me exactly what it is that Bliss has on her mind in just any way you please, and I promise to be very patient.'

'Thank you, and as long as you're going to be patient, I think I can come out with it right away. You see, Bliss wants to come, too.'

'*Bliss* wants to come?' said Trevize. 'No, I'm exploding again. I won't explode. Tell me, Janov, why would Bliss want to come along? I'm asking it quietly.'

'She didn't say. She said she wants to talk to you.'

'Then why isn't she here, eh?'

Pelorat said, 'I think – I say I *think* – that she is rather of the opinion that you are not fond of her, Golan, and she rather hesitates to approach you. I have done my best, old man, to assure her that you have nothing against her. I cannot believe anyone would think anything but highly of her. Still, she wanted me to broach the subject with you, so to speak. May I tell her that you'll be willing to see her, Golan?'

'Of course, I'll see her right now.'

'And you'll be reasonable? You see, old man, she's rather intense about it. She said the matter was vital and she *must* go with you.'

'She didn't tell you why, did she?'

'No, but if she thinks she must go, so must *Gaia*.'

'Which means I mustn't refuse. Is that right, Janov?'

'Yes, I think you mustn't, Golan.'

3

For the first time during his brief stay on Gaia, Trevize entered Bliss's house – which now sheltered Pelorat as well.

Trevize looked about briefly. On Gaia, houses tended to be simple. With the all-but complete absence of violent weather of any kind, with the temperature mild at all times in this particular latitude, with even the tectonic plates slipping smoothly when they had to slip, there was no point in building houses designed for elaborate protection, or for maintaining a comfortable environment within an uncomfortable one. The whole planet was a house, so to speak, designed to shelter its inhabitants.

Bliss's house within that planetary house was small, the windows screened rather than glassed, the furniture sparse and gracefully utilitarian. There were holographic images on the walls; one of them of Pelorat looking rather astonished and self-conscious. Trevize's lips twitched but he tried not to let his amusement show, and he fell to adjusting his waist-sash meticulously.

Bliss watched him. She wasn't smiling in her usual fashion. Rather, she looked serious, her fine dark eyes wide, her hair tumbling to her shoulders in a gentle black wave. Only her full lips, touched with red, lent a bit of colour to her face.

'Thank you for coming to see me, Trev.'

'Janov was very urgent in his request, Blissenobiarella.'

Bliss smiled briefly. 'Well returned. If you will call me Bliss, a decent monosyllable, I will try to say your name in full, Trevize.' She stumbled, almost unnoticeably, over the second syllable.

Trevize held up his right hand. 'That would be a good arrangement. I recognize the Gaian habit of using one-syllable name-portions in the common interchange of thoughts, so if you should happen to call me Trev now and then I will not be offended. Still, I will be more comfortable if you try to say Trevize as often as you can – and I shall say Bliss.'

Trevize studied her, as he always did when he encountered her. As an individual, she was a young woman in her early twenties. As part of Gaia, however, she was thousands of years old. It made no difference in her appearance, but it made a difference in the way she spoke sometimes, and in the atmosphere that inevitably surrounded her. Did he want it this way for everyone who existed? No! Surely, no, and yet –

Bliss said, 'I will get to the point. You stressed your desire to find Earth –'

'I spoke to Dom,' said Trevize, determined not to give in to Gaia without a perpetual insistence on his own point of view.

'Yes, but in speaking to Dom, you spoke to Gaia and to every part of it, so that you spoke to me, for instance.'

'Did you hear me as I spoke?'

'No, for I wasn't listening, but if, thereafter, I paid attention, I could remember what you said. Please accept that and let us go on. You stressed your desire to find Earth and insisted on its importance. I do not see that importance but you have the knack of being right so I/we/Gaia must accept what you say. If the mission is crucial to your decision concerning Gaia, it is of crucial importance to Gaia, and so Gaia must go with you, if only to try to protect you.'

'When you say Gaia must go with me, you mean *you* must go with me. Am I correct?'

'I am Gaia,' said Bliss simply.

'But so is everything else on and in this planet. Why, then, you? Why not some other portion of Gaia?'

'Because Pel wishes to go with you, and if he goes with you, he would not be happy with any other portion of Gaia than myself.'

Pelorat, who sat rather unobtrusively on a chair in another corner (with his back, Trevize noted, to his own image) said softly, 'That's true, Golan. Bliss is *my* portion of Gaia.'

Bliss smiled suddenly. 'It seems rather exciting to be thought of in that way. It's very alien, of course.'

'Well, let's see.' Trevize put his hands behind his head and began to lean backwards in his chair. The thin legs creaked as he did so, so that he quickly decided the chair was not sturdy enough to endure that game and brought it down to all four feet. 'Will you still be part of Gaia if you leave her?'

'I need not be. I can isolate myself, for instance, if I seem in danger of serious harm, so that harm will not necessarily spill over into Gaia, or if there is any other overriding reason for it. That, however, is a matter of emergency only. Generally, I will remain part of Gaia.'

'Even if we Jump through hyperspace?'

'Even then, though that will complicate matters somewhat.'

'Somehow I don't find that comforting.'

'Why not?'

Trevize wrinkled his nose in the usual metaphoric response to a bad smell. 'It means that anything that is said and done on my ship that you hear and see will be heard and seen by all of Gaia.'

'I am Gaia so what I see, hear and sense, Gaia will see, hear and sense.'

'Exactly. Even that wall will see, hear and sense.'

Bliss looked at the wall he pointed to and shrugged. 'Yes, that wall, too. It has only an infinitesimal consciousness so that it senses and understands only infinitesimally, but I presume there are some subatomic shifts in response to what we are saying right now, for instance, that enable it to fit into Gaia with more purposeful intent for the good of the whole.'

'But what if I wish privacy? I may not want the wall to be aware of what I say or do.'

Bliss looked exasperated and Pelorat broke in suddenly. 'You know, Golan, I don't want to interfere, since I obviously don't know much about Gaia. Still, I've been with Bliss and I've gathered somehow some of what it's all about. – If you walk through a crowd on Terminus, you see and hear a great many things, and you may remember some of it. You might even be able to recall all of it under the proper cerebral stimulation, but mostly you don't *care*. You let it go. Even if you watch some emotional scene between strangers and even if you're interested; still, if it's of no great concern to you – you let it go – you forget. It must be so on Gaia, too. Even if all of Gaia knows your business intimately, that doesn't mean that Gaia necessarily *cares*. – Isn't that so, Bliss dear?'

'I've never thought of it that way, Pel, but there is something in what you say. Still, this privacy Trev talks about – I mean, Trevize – is nothing we value at all. In fact, I/we/Gaia find it incomprehensible. To want to be not part – to have your voice unheard – your deeds unwitnessed – your thoughts unsensed –' Bliss shook her head vigorously. 'I said that we can block ourselves off in emergencies, but who would want to *live* that way, even for an hour.'

'I would,' said Trevize. 'That is why I must find Earth – to find out the overriding reason, if any, that drove me to choose this dreadful fate for humanity.'

'It is not a dreadful fate, but let us not debate the matter. I will be with you, not as a spy, but as a friend and helper. Gaia will be with you, not as a spy, but as a friend and helper.'

Trevize said, sombrely, 'Gaia could help me best by directing me to Earth.'

Slowly, Bliss shook her head. 'Gaia doesn't know the location of Earth. Dom has already told you that.'

'I don't quite believe that. After all, you must have records. Why have I never been able to see those records during my stay here? Even if Gaia honestly doesn't know where Earth might be located, I might gain some knowledge from the records. I know the Galaxy in considerable detail, undoubtedly much better than Gaia does. I might be able to understand and follow hints in your records that Gaia, perhaps, doesn't quite catch.'

'But what records are these you talk of, Trevize?'

'Any records. Books, films, recordings, holographs, artifacts, whatever it is you have. In the time I've been here I haven't seen one item that I would consider in any way a record. – Have you, Janov?'

'No,' said Pelorat hesitantly, 'but I haven't really looked.'

'Yet I have, in my quiet way,' said Trevize, 'and I've seen nothing. Nothing! I can only suppose they're being hidden from me. Why, I wonder? Would you tell me that?'

Bliss's smooth young forehead wrinkled into a puzzled frown. 'Why didn't you ask before this? I/we/Gaia hide nothing, and we tell no lies. An Isolate – an individual in isolation – might tell lies. He is limited, and he is fearful *because* he is limited. Gaia, however, is a planetary organism of great mental ability and has no fear. For Gaia to tell lies, to create descriptions that are at variance with reality, is totally unnecessary.'

Trevize snorted. 'Then why have I carefully been kept from seeing any records? Give me a reason that makes sense.'

'Of course.' She held out both hands, palms-up before her. 'We don't have any records.'

4

Pelorat recovered first, seeming the less astonished of the two.

'My dear,' he said gently, 'that is quite impossible. You cannot have a reasonable civilization without records of some kind.'

Bliss raised her eyebrows. 'I understand that. I merely mean we have no records of the type that Trev – Trevize – is talking about, or was at all likely to come across. I/we/Gaia have no writings, no printings, no films, no computer data banks, nothing. We have no carvings on stone, for that matter. That's all I am saying. Naturally, since we have none of these, Trevize found none of these.'

Trevize said, 'What do you have, then, if you don't have any records that I would recognize as records?'

Bliss said, enunciating carefully, as though she were speaking to a child. 'I/we/Gaia have a memory. I *remember*.'

'What do you remember?' asked Trevize.

'Everything.'

'You remember all reference data?'

'Certainly.'

'For how long? For how many years back?'

'For indefinite lengths of time.'

'You could give me historical data, biographical, geographical, scientific? Even local gossip?'

'Everything.'

'All in that little head.' Trevize pointed sardonically at Bliss's right temple.

'No,' she said. 'Gaia's memories are not limited to the contents of my particular skull. See here' (for the moment she grew formal and even a little stern, as she ceased being Bliss solely and took on an amalgam of other units), 'there must have been a time before the beginning of history when human beings were so primitive that, although they could remember events, they could not speak. Speech was invented and served to express memories and to transfer them from person to person. Writing was eventually invented in order to record memories and transfer them across time from generation to generation. All technological advance since then has served to make more room for the transfer and storage of memories and to make the recall of desired items easier. However, once individuals joined to form Gaia, all that became obsolete. We can return to memory, the basic system of record-keeping on which all else is built. Do you see that?'

Trevize said, 'Are you saying that the sum total of all brains on Gaia can remember far more data than a single brain can?'

'Of course.'

'But if Gaia has all the records spread through the planetary memory, what good is that to you as an individual portion of Gaia?'

'All the good you can wish. Whatever I might want to know is in an individual mind somewhere, maybe in many of them. If it is very fundamental, such as the meaning of the word "chair", it is in every mind. But even if it is something esoteric that is in only one small portion of Gaia's mind, I can call it up if I need it, though such recall may take a bit longer than if the memory is more widespread. – Look, Trevize, if you want to know something that isn't in your mind, you look at some appropriate book-film, or make use of a computer's data banks. I scan Gaia's total mind.'

Trevize said, 'How do you keep all that information from pouring into your mind and bursting your cranium?'

'Are you indulging in sarcasm, Trevize?'

Pelorat said, 'Come, Golan, don't be unpleasant.'

Trevize looked from one to the other and, with a visible effort, allowed the tightness about his face to relax. 'I'm sorry. I'm borne down by a responsibility I don't want and don't know how to get rid of. That may make me sound unpleasant when I don't intend to be. Bliss, I really wish to know. How do you draw upon the contents of the brains of others without then storing it in your own brain and quickly overloading its capacity?'

Bliss said, 'I don't know, Trevize; any more than you know the detailed workings of your single brain. I presume you know the distance from your sun to a neighbouring star, but you are not always conscious of it. You store it somewhere and can retrieve the figure at any time if asked. If not asked, you may with time forget it, but you can then always retrieve it from some data bank. If you consider Gaia's brain a vast data bank, it is one I can call on, but there is no need for me to remember consciously any particular item I have made use of. Once I have made use of a fact or memory, I can allow it to pass out of memory. For that matter, I can deliberately put it back, so to speak, in the place I got it from.'

'How many people on Gaia, Bliss? How many human beings?'

'About a billion. Do you want the exact figure as of now?'

Trevize smiled ruefully. 'I quite see you can call up the exact figure if you wish, but I'll take the approximation.'

'Actually,' said Bliss, 'the population is stable and oscillates about a particular number that is slightly in excess of a billion. I can tell you by how much the number exceeds or falls short of the mean by extending my consciousness and – well – feeling the boundaries. I can't explain it better than that to someone who has never shared the experience.'

'It seems to me, however, that a billion human minds – a number of them being those of children – are surely not enough to hold in memory all the data needed by a complex society.'

'But human beings are not the only living things on Gaia, Trev.'

'Do you mean that animals remember, too?'

'Non-human brains can't store memories with the same density human brains can, and much of the room in all brains, human and non-human alike, must be given over to personal memories which are scarcely useful except to the particular component of the planetary consciousness that harbours them. However, significant quantities of advanced data can be, and are, stored in animal brains, also in plant tissue, and in the mineral structure of the planet.'

'In the mineral structure? The rocks and mountain range, you mean?'

'And, for some kinds of data, the ocean and atmosphere. All that is Gaia, too.'

'But what can non-living systems hold?'

'A great deal. The intensity is low but the volume is so great that a large majority of Gaia's total memory is in its rocks. It takes a little longer to retrieve and replace rock memories so that it is the preferred place for storing dead data, so to speak – items that, in the normal course of events, would rarely be called upon.'

'What happens when someone dies whose brain stores data of considerable value?'

'The data is not lost. It is slowly crowded out as the brain disorganizes after death, but there is ample time to distribute the memories into other parts of Gaia. And as new brains appear in babies and become more organized with growth, they not only develop their personal memories and thoughts but are fed appropriate knowledge from other sources. What you would call education is entirely automatic with me/us/Gaia.'

Pelorat said, 'Frankly, Golan, it seems to me that this notion of a living world has a great deal to be said for it.'

Trevize gave his fellow-Foundationer a brief, sidelong glance. 'I'm sure of that, Janov, but I'm not impressed. The planet, however big and however diverse, represents one brain. One! Every new brain that arises is melted into the whole. Where's the opportunity for opposition, for disagreement? When you think of human history, you think of the occasional human being whose minority view may be condemned by society but who wins out in the end and changes the world. What chance is there on Gaia for the great rebels of history?'

'There is internal conflict,' said Bliss. 'Not every aspect of Gaia necessarily accepts the common view.'

'It must be limited,' said Trevize. 'You cannot have too much turmoil within a single organism, or it would not work properly. If progress and development are not stopped altogether, they must certainly be slowed. Can we take the chance of inflicting that on the entire Galaxy? On all of humanity?'

Bliss said, without open emotion, 'Are you now questioning your own decision? Are you changing your mind and are you now saying that Gaia is an undesirable future for humanity?'

Trevize tightened his lips and hesitated. Then, he said, slowly, I would like to, but – not yet. I made my decision on some basis – some unconscious basis – and until I find out what that basis was, I cannot truly decide whether I am to maintain or change my decision. Let us therefore return to the matter of Earth.'

'Where you feel you will learn the nature of the basis on which you made your decision. Is that it, Trevize?'

'That is the feeling I have. – Now Dom says Gaia does not know the location of Earth. And you agree with him, I believe.'

'Of course I agree with him. I am no less Gaia than he is.'

'And do you withhold knowledge from me? Consciously, I mean?'

'Of course not. Even if it were possible for Gaia to lie, it would not lie to *you*. Above all, we depend upon your conclusions, and we need them to be accurate, and that requires that they be based on reality.'

'In that case,' said Trevize, 'let's make use of your world-memory. Probe backwards and tell me how far you can remember.'

There was a small hesitation. Bliss looked blankly at Trevize, as though, for a moment, she was in a trance. Then she said, 'Fifteen thousand years.'

'Why did you hesitate?'

'It took time. Old memories – really old – are almost all in the mountain roots where it takes time to dig them out.'

'Fifteen thousand years ago, then? Is that when Gaia was settled?'

'No, to the best of our knowledge that took place some three thousand years before that.'

'Why are you uncertain? Don't you – or Gaia – remember?'

Bliss said, 'That was before Gaia had developed to the point where memory became a global phenomenon.'

'Yet before you could rely on your collective memory, Gaia must have kept records, Bliss. Records in the usual sense – recorded, written, filmed, and so on.'

'I imagine so, but they could scarcely endure all this time.'

'They could have been copied or, better yet, transferred into the global memory, once that was developed.'

Bliss frowned. There was another hesitation, longer this time. 'I find no sign of these earlier records you speak of.'

'Why is that?'

'I don't know, Trevize. I presume that they proved of no great importance. I imagine that by the time it was understood that the early nonmemory records were decaying, it was decided that they had grown archaic and were not needed.'

'You don't know that. You presume and you imagine, but you don't know that. Gaia doesn't know that.'

Bliss's eyes fell. 'It must be so.'

'Must be? I am not a part of Gaia and therefore I need not presume what Gaia presumes – which gives you an example of the importance of isolation. I, as an Isolate, presume something else.'

'What do you presume?'

'First, there is something I am sure of. A civilization in being is not likely to destroy its early records. Far from judging them to be archaic and unnecessary, they are likely to treat them with exaggerated reverence and would labour to preserve them. If Gaia's pre-global records were destroyed, Bliss, that destruction is not likely to have been voluntary.'

'How would you explain it, then?'

'In the library at Trantor, all references to Earth were removed by someone or some force other than that of the Trantorian Second Foundationers themselves. Isn't it possible, then, that on Gaia, too, all references to Earth were removed by something other than Gaia itself?'

'How do you know the early records involved Earth?'

'According to you, Gaia was founded at least eighteen thousand years ago. That brings us back to the period before the establishment of the Galactic Empire, to the period when the Galaxy was being settled and the prime source of Settlers was Earth. Pelorat will confirm that.'

Pelorat, caught a little by surprise by suddenly being called on, cleared his throat. 'So go the legends, my dear. I take those legends seriously and I think, as Golan Trevize does, that the human species was originally confined to a single planet and that planet was Earth. The earliest Settlers came from Earth.'

'If, then,' said Trevize, 'Gaia was founded in the early days of hyperspatial travel, then it is very likely to have been colonized by Earthmen, or possibly by natives of a not very old world that had not long before been colonized by Earthmen. For that reason, the records of Gaia's settlement and of the first few millennia thereafter must clearly have involved Earth and Earthmen and those records are gone. *Something* seems to be seeing to it that Earth is not mentioned anywhere in the records of the Galaxy. And if so, there must be some reason for it.'

Bliss said indignantly, 'This is conjecture, Trevize. You have no evidence for this.'

'But it is Gaia that insists that my special talent is that of coming to correct conclusions on the basis of insufficient evidence. If, then, I come to a firm conclusion, don't tell me I lack evidence.'

Bliss was silent.

Trevize went on, 'All the more reason then for finding Earth. I intend to leave as soon as the *Far Star* is ready. Do you two still want to come?'

'Yes,' said Bliss at once, and 'Yes,' said Pelorat.

2

Towards Comporellon

5

It was raining lightly. Trevize looked up at the sky, which was a solid greyish white.

He was wearing a rain hat that repelled the drops and sent them flying well away from his body in all directions. Pelorat, standing out of range of the flying drops, had no such protection.

Trevize said, 'I don't see the point of your letting yourself get wet, Janov.'

'The wet doesn't bother me, my dear chap,' said Pelorat, looking as solemn as he always did. 'It's a light and warm rain. There's no wind to speak of. And besides, to quote the old saying: In Anacreon, do as the Anacreonians do.' He indicated the few Gaians standing near the *Far Star*, watching quietly. They were well scattered, as though they were trees in a Gaian grove, and none wore rain hats.

'I suppose,' said Trevize, 'they don't mind being wet, because all the rest of Gaia is getting wet. The trees – the grass – the soil – all wet, and all equally part of Gaia, along with the Gaians.'

'I think it makes sense,' said Pelorat. 'The sun will come out soon enough and everything will dry quickly. The clothing won't wrinkle or shrink, there's no chilling effect, and, since there aren't any unnecessary pathogenic micro-organisms, no one will get colds, or flu, or pneumonia. Why worry about a bit of damp then?'

Trevize had no trouble in seeing the logic of that, but he hated to let go of his grievance. He said, 'Still, there is no need for it to rain as we are leaving. After all, the rain is voluntary. Gaia wouldn't rain if it didn't want to. It's almost as though it were showing its contempt for us.'

'Perhaps,' and Pelorat's lip twitched a bit, 'Gaia is weeping with sorrow at our leaving.'

Trevize said, 'That may be, but I'm not.'

'Actually,' Pelorat went on, 'I presume that the soil in this region needs a wetting down, and that need is more important than your desire to have the sun shine.'

Trevize smiled. 'I suspect you really like this world, don't you? Even aside from Bliss, I mean.'

'Yes, I do,' said Pelorat, a trace defensively. 'I've always led a quiet, orderly life, and think how I could manage here, with a whole world labouring to keep it quiet and orderly. – After all, Golan, when we build a house – or that ship – we try to create a perfect shelter. We equip it with everything we need; we arrange to have its temperature, air quality, illumination, and everything else of importance, controlled by us and manipulated in a way to make it perfectly accommodating to us. Gaia is just an extension of the desire for comfort and security extended to an entire planet. What's wrong with that?'

'What's wrong with that,' said Trevize, 'is that my house or my ship is engineered to suit *me*. I am not engineered to suit *it*. If I were part of Gaia, then no matter how ideally the planet was devised to suit me, I would be greatly disturbed over the fact that I was also being devised to suit it.'

Pelorat pursed his lips. 'One could argue that every society moulds its population to fit itself. Customs develop that make sense within the society, and that chain every individual firmly to its needs.'

'In the societies I know, one can revolt. There are eccentrics, even criminals.'

'Do you *want* eccentrics and criminals?'

'Why not? You and I are eccentrics. We're certainly not typical of the people living on Terminus. As for criminals, that's a matter of definition. And if criminals are the price we must pay for rebels, heretics and genius, I'm willing to pay it. I *demand* the price be paid.'

'Are criminals the only possible payment? Can't you have genius without criminals?'

'You can't have geniuses and saints without having people far outside the norm, and I don't see how you can have such things on only one side of the norm. There is bound to be a certain symmetry. – In any case, I want a better reason for my decision to make Gaia the model for the future of humanity than that it is a planetary version of a comfortable house.'

'Oh, my dear fellow. I wasn't trying to argue you into being satisfied with your decision. I was just making an observa –'

He broke off. Bliss was striding towards them, her dark hair wet and her robe clinging to her body and emphasizing the rather generous width of her hips. She was nodding to them as she came.

'I'm sorry I delayed you,' she said, panting a little. 'It took longer to check with Dom than I had anticipated.'

'Surely,' said Trevize, 'you know everything he knows.'

'Sometimes it's a matter of a difference in interpretation. We are not identical, after all, so we discuss. Look here,' she said, with a touch of asperity, 'you have two hands. They are each part of you, and they seem identical except for one being the mirror-image of the other. Yet you do not use them entirely alike, do you? There are some things you do with your right hand most of the time, and some with your left. Differences in interpretation, so to speak.'

'She's got you,' said Pelorat, with obvious satisfaction.

Trevize nodded. 'It's an effective analogy, if it were relevant, and I'm not at all sure it is. In any case, does this mean we can board the ship now? It *is* raining.'

'Yes, yes. Our people are all off it, and it's in perfect shape.' Then, with a sudden curious look at Trevize, 'You're keeping dry. The raindrops are missing you.'

'Yes, indeed,' said Trevize. 'I am avoiding wetness.'

'But doesn't it feel good to be wet now and then?'

'Absolutely. But at my choice, not the rain's.'

Bliss shrugged. 'Well, as you please. All our baggage is loaded so let's board.'

The three walked towards the *Far Star*. The rain was growing still lighter, but the grass was quite wet. Trevize found himself walking gingerly, but Bliss had kicked off her slippers, which she was now carrying in one hand, and was slogging through the grass barefoot.

'It feels delightful,' she said, in response to Trevize's downward glance.

'Good,' he said absently. Then, with a touch of irritation, 'Why are those other Gaians standing about, anyway?'

Bliss said, 'They're recording this event, which Gaia finds momentous. You are important to us, Trevize. Consider that if you should change your mind as a result of this trip and decide against us, we would never grow into Galaxia, or even remain as Gaia.'

'Then I represent life and death for Gaia; for the whole world.'

'We believe so.'

Trevize stopped suddenly, and took off his rain hat. Blue patches were appearing in the sky. He said, 'But you have my vote in your favour *now*. If you kill me, I'll never be able to change it.'

'Golan,' murmured Pelorat, shocked. 'That is a terrible thing to say.'

'Typical of an Isolate,' said Bliss calmly. 'You must understand, Trevize, that we are not interested in you as a person, or even in your vote, but in the truth, in the facts of the matter. You are only important as a conduit to the truth, and your vote as an indication of the truth. That is what we want from you, and if we kill you to avoid a change in your vote, we would merely be hiding the truth from ourselves.'

'If I tell you the truth is non-Gaia, will you all then cheerfully agree to die?'

'Not entirely cheerfully, perhaps, but it's what it would amount to in the end.'

Trevize shook his head. 'If anything ought to convince me that Gaia is a horror and *should* die, it might be that very statement you've just made.' Then he said, his eyes returning to the patiently watching (and, presumably, listening) Gaians, 'Why are they spread out like that? And why do you need so many? If one of them observes this event and stores it in his or her memory, isn't it available to all the rest of the planet? Can't it be stored in a million different places if you want it to be?'

Bliss said, 'They are observing this each from a different angle, and each is storing it in a slightly different brain. When all the observations are studied, it will be seen that what is taking place will be far better understood from all the observations together than from any one of them, taken singly.'

'The whole is greater than the sum of the parts, in other words.'

'Exactly. You have grasped the basic justification of Gaia's existence. You, as a human individual, are composed of perhaps 50 trillion cells, but you, as a multicellular individual, are far more important than those 50 trillion as the sum of their individual importances. Surely you would agree with that.'

'Yes,' said Trevize. 'I agree with that.'

He stepped into the ship, and turned briefly for one more look at Gaia. The brief rain had lent a new freshness to the atmosphere. He saw a green, lush, quiet, peaceful world; a garden of serenity set amid the turbulence of the weary Galaxy.

– And Trevize earnestly hoped he would never see it again.

6

When the airlock closed behind them, Trevize felt as though he had shut out not exactly a nightmare, but something so seriously abnormal that it had prevented him from breathing freely.

He was fully aware that an element of that abnormality was still with him in the person of Bliss. While she was there, Gaia was there – and yet he was also convinced that her presence was essential. It was the black box working again, and earnestly he hoped he would never begin believing in that black box too much.

He looked about the vessel and found it beautiful. It had been his only since Mayor Harla Branno of the Foundation had forced him into it and sent him out among the stars – a living lightning rod designed to draw the fire of those she considered enemies of the Foundation. That task was done but the ship was still his, and he had no plans to return it.

It had been his for merely a matter of a few months, but it seemed like home to him and he could only dimly remember what had once been his home in Terminus.

Terminus! The off-centre hub of the Foundation, destined, by Seldon's Plan, to form a second and greater Empire in the course of the next five centuries, except that he, Trevize, had now derailed it. By his own decision he was converting the Foundation to nothing, and was making possible instead a new way of society, a new scheme of life, a frightening revolution that would be greater than any since the development of multicellular life.

Now he was engaged in a journey designed to prove to himself (or to disprove) that what he had done was right.

He found himself lost in thought and motionless, so that he shook himself in self-irritation. He hastened to the pilot-room and found his computer still there.

It glistened; everything glistened. There had been a most careful cleaning. The contacts he closed, nearly at random, worked perfectly, and, it surely seemed, with greater ease than ever. The ventilating system was so noiseless that he had to put his hand over the vents to make sure he felt air currents.

The circle of light on the computer glowed invitingly. Trevize touched it and the light spread out to cover the desk top and the outline of a right and left hand appeared on it. He drew a deep breath and realized that he had stopped breathing for a while. The Gaians knew nothing about Foundation technology and they might easily have damaged the computer without meaning any malice. Thus far they had not – the hands were still there.

The crucial test came with the laying on of his own hands, however, and, for a moment, he hesitated. He would know, almost at once, if anything was wrong – but if something was, what could he do? For repairs, he would have to go back to Terminus, and if he did, he felt quite confident that Mayor Branno would not let him leave again: And if he did not –

He could feel his heart pounding, and there was clearly no point in deliberately lengthening the suspense.

He thrust his hands out, right, left, and placed them on the outlines upon the desk. At once, he had the illusion of another pair of hands holding his. His senses extended, and he could see Gaia in all directions, green and moist, the Gaians still watching. When he willed himself to look upwards, he saw a largely cloudy sky. Again, at his will, the clouds vanished and he looked at an unbroken blue sky with the orb of Gaia's sun filtered out.

Again he willed and the blue parted and he saw the stars.

He wiped them out, and willed and saw the Galaxy, like a fore-shortened pinwheel. He tested the computerized image, adjusting its orientation, altering the apparent progress of time, making it spin first in one direction, then the other. He located the sun of Sayshell, the nearest important star to Gaia; then the sun of Terminus; then of Trantor; one after the other. He travelled from star to star in the Galactic map that dwelt in the bowels of the computer.

Then he withdrew his hands and let the world of reality surround him again – and realized he had been standing all this time, half-bowing over the computer to make the hand contact. He felt stiff and had to stretch his back muscles before sitting down.

He stared at the computer with warm relief. It had worked perfectly. It had been, if anything, more responsive, and what he felt for it he could only describe as love. After all, while he held its hands (he resolutely refused to admit to himself that he thought of it as *her* hands) they were part of each other, and his will directed, controlled, experienced, and was part of a greater self. He and it must feel, in a small way (he suddenly, and disturbingly, thought) what Gaia did in a much larger way.

He shook his head. No! In the case of the computer and himself, it was he – Trevize – who was in entire control. The computer was a thing of total submission.

He rose and moved out to the compact galley and dining area. There was plenty of food of all kinds, with proper refrigeration and easy-heating facilities. He had already noted that the book-films in his room were in the proper order, and he was reasonably sure – no, completely sure – that Pelorat had his personal library in safe storage. He would otherwise surely have heard from him by now.

Pelorat! That reminded him. He stepped into Pelorat's room. 'Is there room for Bliss here, Janov?'

'Oh, yes, quite.'

'I can convert the common room into her bedroom.'

Bliss looked up, wide-eyed. 'I have no desire for a separate bedroom. I am quite content to stay here with Pel. I suppose, though, that I may use the other rooms when needed. The gym, for instance.'

'Certainly. Any room but mine.'

'Good. That's what I would have suggested be the arrangement, if I had had the making of it. Naturally, you will stay out of ours.'

'Naturally,' said Trevize, looking down and realizing that his shoes overlapped the threshold. He took a half-step backwards and said grimly, 'These are not honeymoon quarters, Bliss.'

'I should say, in view of its compactness, that it is exactly that, even though Gaia extended it to half again as wide as it was.'

Trevize tried not to smile. 'You'll have to be very friendly.'

'We are,' said Pelorat, clearly ill at ease at the topic of conversation, 'but really, old chap, you can leave it to us to make our own arrangements.'

'Actually, I can't,' said Trevize slowly. 'I still want to make it clear that this is not honeymoon accommodation. I have no objection to anything you do by mutual consent, but you must realize that you will have no privacy. I hope you understand that, Bliss.'

'There is a door,' said Bliss, 'and I imagine you will not disturb us when it is locked – short of a real emergency, that is.'

'Of course I won't. However, there is no soundproofing.'

'What you are trying to say, Trevize,' said Bliss, 'is that you will hear, quite clearly, any conversation we may have, and any sounds we may make in the course of sex.'

'Yes, that is what I am trying to say. With that in mind, I expect you may find you will have to limit your activities here. This may discommode you, and I'm sorry, but that's the situation as it is.'

Pelorat cleared his throat, and said gently, 'Actually, Golan, this is a problem I've already had to face. You realize that any sensation Bliss experiences, when together with me, is experienced by all of Gaia.'

'I have thought of that, Janov,' said Trevize, looking as though he were repressing a wince. 'I didn't intend to mention it – just in case the thought had not occurred to you.'

'But it did, I'm afraid,' said Pelorat.

Bliss said, 'Don't make too much of that, Trevize. At any given moment, there may be thousands of human beings on Gaia who are engaged in sex; millions who are eating, drinking, or engaged in other pleasure-giving activities. This gives rise to a general aura of delight that Gaia feels, every part of it. The lower animals, the plants, the minerals have their progressively milder pleasures that also contribute to a generalized joy of consciousness that Gaia feels in all its parts always, and that is unfelt in any other world.'

'We have our own particular joys,' said Trevize, 'which we can share after a fashion, if we wish; or keep private, if we wish.'

'If you could feel ours, you would know how poverty-stricken you Isolates are in that respect.'

'How can you know what we feel?'

'Without knowing how you feel, it is still reasonable to suppose that a world of common pleasures must be more intense than those available to a single isolated individual.'

'Perhaps, but even if my pleasures were poverty-stricken, I would keep my own joys and sorrows and be satisfied with them, thin as they are, and be *me* and not blood brother to the nearest rock.'

'Don't sneer,' said Bliss. 'You value every mineral crystal in your bones and teeth and would not have one of them damaged, though they have no more consciousness than the average rock crystal of the same size.'

'That's true enough,' said Trevize reluctantly, 'but we've managed to get off the subject. I don't care if all Gaia shares your joy, Bliss, but *I* don't want to share it. We're living here in close quarters and I do not wish to be forced to participate in your activities even indirectly.'

Pelorat said, 'This is an argument over nothing, my dear chap. I am no more anxious than you to have your privacy violated. Nor mine, for that matter. Bliss and I will be discreet; won't we, Bliss?'

'It will be as you wish, Pel.'

'After all,' said Pelorat, 'we are quite likely to be planet-bound for considerably longer periods than we will space-borne, and on planets, the opportunities for true privacy –'

'I don't care what you do on planets,' interrupted Trevize, 'but on this ship, I am master.'

'Exactly,' said Pelorat.

'Then, with that straightened out, it is time to take off.'

'But wait.' Pelorat reached out to tug at Trevize's sleeve. 'Take off for where? You don't know where Earth is, nor do I, nor does Bliss. Nor does your computer, for you told me long ago that it lacks any information on Earth. What do you intend doing, then? You can't simply drift through space at random, my dear chap.'

At that, Trevize smiled with what was almost joy. For the first time since he had fallen into the grip of Gaia, he felt master of his own fate.

'I assure you,' he said, 'that it is not my intention to drift, Janov. I know exactly where I am going.'

7

Pelorat walked quietly into the pilot-room after he had waited long moments while his small tap on the door had gone unanswered. He found Trevize looking with keen absorption at the starfield.

Pelorat said, 'Golan –' and waited.

Trevize looked up. 'Janov! Sit down. – Where's Bliss?'

'Sleeping. – We're out in space, I see.'

'You see correctly.' Trevize was not surprised at the other's mild surprise. In the new gravitic ships, there was simply no way of detecting takeoff. There were no inertial effects; no accelerational push; no noise; no vibration.

Possessing the capacity to insulate itself from outside gravitational fields to any degree up to total, the *Far Star* lifted from a planetary surface as though it were floating on some cosmic sea. And while it did so, the gravitational effect *within* the ship, paradoxically, remained normal.

While the ship was within the atmosphere, of course, there was no need to accelerate so that the whine and vibration of rapidly passing air would be absent. As the atmosphere was left behind, however, acceleration could take place, and at rapid rates, without affecting the passengers.

It was the ultimate in comfort and Trevize did not see how it could be improved upon until such time as human beings discovered a way of whisking through hyperspace without ships, and without concern about nearby gravitational fields that might be too intense. Right now, the *Far Star* would have to speed away from Gaia's for several days before the gravitational intensity was weak enough to attempt the Jump.

'Golan, my dear fellow,' said Pelorat. 'May I speak with you for a moment or two? You are not too busy?'

'Not at all busy. The computer handles everything once I instruct it properly. And sometimes it seems to guess what my instructions will be, and satisfies them almost before I can articulate them.' Trevize brushed the top of the desk lovingly.

Pelorat said, 'We've grown very friendly, Golan, in the short time we've known each other, although I must admit that it scarcely seems a short time to me. So much has happened. It's really peculiar when I stop to think of my moderately long life, that half of all the events I have experienced were squeezed into the last few months. Or so it would seem. I could almost suppose –'

Trevize held up a hand. 'Janov, you're spinning outwards from your original point, I'm sure. You began by saying we've grown very friendly in a very short time. Yes, we have, and we still are. For that matter, you've known Bliss an even shorter time and have grown even friendlier.'

'That's different, of course,' said Pelorat, clearing his throat in some embarrassment.

'Of course,' said Trevize, 'but what follows from our brief but enduring friendship?'

'If, my dear fellow, we still are friends, as you've just said, then I must pass on to Bliss, who, as you've also just said, is peculiarly dear to me.'

'I understand. And what of that?'

'I know, Golan, that you are not fond of Bliss, but for my sake, I wish –'

Trevize raised a hand. 'One moment, Janov. I am not overwhelmed by Bliss, but neither is she an object of hatred to me. Actually, I have no animosity towards her at all. She's an attractive young woman and, even if she weren't, then, for your sake, I would be prepared to find her so. It's *Gaia* I dislike.'

'But Bliss *is* Gaia.'

'I know, Janov. That's what complicates things so. As long as I think of Bliss as a person, there's no problem. If I think of her as Gaia, there is.'

'But you haven't given Gaia a chance, Golan. – Look, old chap, let me admit something. When Bliss and I are intimate, she sometimes lets me share her mind for a minute or so. Not for more than that because she says I'm too old to adapt to it. – Oh, don't grin, Golan, you would be too old for it, too. If an Isolate, such as you or I, were to remain part of Gaia for more than a minute or two, there might be brain damage and if it's as much as five or ten minutes, it would be irreversible. – If you could only experience it, Golan.'

'What? Irreversible brain damage? No, thanks.'

'Golan, you're deliberately misunderstanding me. I mean, just that small moment of union. You don't know what you're missing. It's indescribable. Bliss says there's a sense of joy. That's like saying there's a sense of joy when you finally drink a bit of water after you have all but died of thirst. I couldn't even begin to tell you what it's like. You share all the pleasures that a billion people separately experience. It isn't a steady joy; if it were you would quickly stop feeling it. It vibrates – twinkles – has a strange pulsing rhythm that doesn't let you go. It's more joy – no, not more – it's a *better* joy than you could ever experience separately. I could weep when she shuts the door on me –'

Trevize shook his head. 'You are amazingly eloquent, my good friend, but you sound very much as though you're describing pseudendorphin addiction, or that of some other drug that admits you to joy in the short term at the price of leaving you permanently in horror in the long term. Not for me! I am reluctant to sell my individuality for some brief feeling of joy.'

'I still have my individuality, Golan.'

'But for how long will you have it if you keep it up, Janov? You'll beg for more and more of your drug until, eventually, your brain will be damaged. Janov, you mustn't let Bliss do this to you. – Perhaps I had better speak to her about it.'

'No! Don't! You're not the soul of tact, you know, and I don't want her hurt. I assure you she takes better care of me in that respect than you can imagine. She's more concerned with the possibility of brain damage than I am. You can be sure of that.'

'Well, then, I'll speak to you. Janov, don't do this any more. You've lived for fifty-two years with your own kind of pleasure and joy, and your brain is adapted to withstanding that. Don't be snapped up by a new and unusual vice. There is a price for it; if not immediately, then eventually.'

'Yes, Golan,' said Pelorat in a low voice, looking down at the tips of his shoes. Then he said, 'Suppose you look at it this way. What if you were a one-celled creature –'

'I know what you're going to say, Janov. Forget it. Bliss and I have already referred to that analogy.'

'Yes, but think a moment. Suppose we imagine single-celled organisms with a human level of consciousness and with the power of thought and imagine them faced with the possibility of becoming a multicellular organism. Would not the single-celled organisms mourn their loss of individuality, and bitterly resent their forthcoming enforced regimentation into the personality of an overall organism? And would they not be wrong? Could an individual cell even imagine the power of the human brain?'

Trevize shook his head violently. 'No, Janov, it's a false analogy. Single-celled organisms *don't* have consciousness or any power of thought – or if they do it is so infinitesimal it might as well be considered zero. For such objects to combine and lose individuality is to lose something they have never really had. A human being, however, *is* and *does* have the power of thought. He has an actual consciousness and an actual independent intelligence to lose, so the analogy fails.'

There was silence between the two of them for a moment; an almost oppressive silence; and finally Pelorat, attempting to wrench the conversation in a new direction, said, 'Why do you stare at the windscreen?'

'Habit,' said Trevize, smiling wryly. 'The computer tells me that there are no Gaian ships following me and that there are no Sayshellian fleets coming to meet me. Still I look anxiously, comforted by my own failure to see such ships, when the computer's sensors are hundreds of times keener and more piercing than my eyes. What's more, the computer is capable of sensing some properties of space very delicately, properties that my senses can't perceive under any conditions. – Knowing all that, I still stare.'

Pelorat said, 'Golan, if we are indeed friends –'

'I promise you I will do nothing to grieve Bliss; at least, nothing I can help.'

'It's another matter now. You keep your destination from me, as though you don't trust me with it. Where are we going? Are you of the opinion you know where Earth is?'

Trevize looked up, eyebrows lifted. 'I'm sorry. I have been hugging the secret to my own bosom, haven't I?'

'Yes, but why?'

Trevize said, 'Why, indeed. I wonder, my friend, if it isn't a matter of Bliss.'

'Bliss? Is it that you don't want *her* to know? Really, old fellow, she is *completely* to be trusted.'

'It's not that. What's the use of not trusting her? I suspect she can tweak any secret out of my mind if she wishes to. I think I have a more childish reason than that. I have the feeling that you are paying attention only to her and that I no longer really exist.'

Pelorat looked horrified. 'But that's not true, Golan.'

'I know, but I'm trying to analyse my own feelings. You came to me just now with fears for our friendship, and thinking about it, I feel as though I've had the same fears. I haven't openly admitted it to myself, but I think I have felt cut out by Bliss. Perhaps I seek to "get even" by petulantly keeping things from you. Childish, I suppose.'

'Golan!'

'I said it was childish, didn't I? But where is the person who isn't childish now and then? However, we *are* friends. We've settled that and therefore I will play no further games. We're going to Comporellon.'

'Comporellon?' said Pelorat, for the moment not remembering.

'Surely you recall my friend, the traitor, Munn Li Compor. We three met on Sayshell.'

Pelorat's face assumed a visible expression of enlightenment. 'Of course I remember. Comporellon was the world of his ancestors.'

'*If* it was. I don't necessarily believe anything Compor said. But Comporellon is a known world, and Compor said that its inhabitants knew of Earth. Well, then, we'll go there and find out. It may lead to nothing but it's the only starting point we have.'

Pelorat cleared his throat and looked dubious. 'Oh, my dear fellow, are you sure?'

'There's nothing about which to be either sure or not sure. We have one starting point and, however feeble it might be, we have no choice but to follow it up.'

'Yes, but if we're doing it on the basis of what Compor told us, then perhaps we ought to consider *everything* he told us. I seem to remember that he told us, most emphatically, that Earth did not exist as a living planet – that its surface was radioactive and that it was utterly lifeless. And if that is so, then we are going to Comporellon for nothing.'

8

The three were lunching in the dining room, virtually filling it as they did so.

'This is very good,' said Pelorat, with considerable satisfaction. 'Is this part of our original Terminus supply?'

'No, not at all,' said Trevize. 'That's long gone. This is part of the supplies we bought on Sayshell, before we headed out towards Gaia. Unusual, isn't it. Some sort of seafood, but rather crunchy. As for this stuff – I was under the impression it was cabbage when I bought it, but it doesn't taste anything like it.'

Bliss listened but said nothing. She picked at the food on her own plate gingerly.

Pelorat said gently, 'You've got to eat, dear.'

'I know, Pel, and I'm eating.'

Trevize said, with a touch of impatience he couldn't quite suppress, 'We do have Gaian food, Bliss.'

'I know,' said Bliss, 'but I would rather conserve that. We don't know how long we will be out in space and eventually I must learn to eat Isolate food.'

'Is that so bad? Or must Gaia eat only Gaia.'

Bliss sighed. 'Actually, there's a saying of ours that goes "When Gaia eats Gaia, there is neither loss nor gain." It is no more than a transfer of consciousness up and down the scale. Whatever I eat on Gaia *is* Gaia and when much of it is metabolized and becomes me, it is *still* Gaia. In fact, by the fact that I eat, some of what I eat has a chance to participate in a higher intensity of consciousness, while, of course, other portions of it are turned into waste of one sort or another and therefore sink in the scale of consciousness.'

She took a firm bite of her food, chewed vigorously for a moment, swallowed, and said, 'It represents a vast circulation. Plants grow and are eaten by animals. Animals eat and are eaten. Any organism that dies is incorporated into the cells of moulds, decay bacteria and so on – still Gaia. In this vast circulation of consciousness, even inorganic matter participates, and everything in the circulation has its chance of periodically participating in a high intensity of consciousness.'

'All this,' said Trevize, 'can be said of any world. Every atom in me has a long history during which it may have been part of many living things, including human beings, and during which it may also have spent long periods as part of the sea, or in a lump of coal, or in a rock, or as a portion of the wind blowing upon us.'

'On Gaia, however,' said Bliss, 'all atoms are also continually part of a higher planetary consciousness of which you know nothing.'

'Well, what happens, then,' said Trevize, 'to these vegetables from Sayshell that you are eating. Do they become part of Gaia?'

'They do – rather slowly. And the wastes I excrete as slowly cease being part of Gaia. After all, what leaves me is altogether lacking in contact with Gaia. It lacks even the less-direct hyperspatial contact that I can maintain, thanks to my high level of conscious intensity. It is this hyperspatial contact that causes non-Gaian food to become part of Gaia – slowly – once I eat it.'

'What about the Gaian food in our stores? Will that slowly become non-Gaian? If so, you had better eat it while you can.'

'There is no need to be concerned about that,' said Bliss. 'Our Gaian stores have been treated in such a way that they will remain part of Gaia over a long interval.'

Pelorat said, suddenly, 'But what will happen when *we* eat the Gaian food. For that matter, what happened to us when we ate Gaian food on Gaia itself. Are we ourselves slowly turning into Gaia?'

Bliss shook her head and a peculiarly disturbed expression crossed her face. 'No, what you ate was lost to us. Or at least the portions that were metabolized into your tissues were lost to us. What you excreted stayed Gaia or very slowly became Gaia so that in the end the balance was maintained, but numerous atoms of Gaia became non-Gaia as a result of your visit to us.'

'Why was that?' asked Trevize curiously.

'Because you would not have been able to endure the conversion, even a very partial one. You were our guests, brought to our world under compulsion, in a manner of speaking, and we had to protect you from danger, even at the cost of the loss of tiny fragments of Gaia. It was a willing price we paid, but not a happy one.'

'We regret that,' said Trevize, 'but are you sure that non-Gaian food, or some kinds of non-Gaian food, might not, in their turn, harm *you*?'

'No,' said Bliss. 'What is edible for you would be edible to me. I merely have the additional problem of metabolizing such food into Gaia as well as into my own tissues. It represents a psychological barrier that rather spoils my enjoyment of the food and causes me to eat slowly, but I will overcome that with time.'

'What about infection?' said Pelorat, in high-pitched alarm. 'I can't understand why I didn't think of this earlier. Bliss! Any world you land on is likely to have micro-organisms against which you have no defence and you will die of some simple infectious disease. Trevize, we must turn back.'

'Don't be panicked, Pel dear,' said Bliss, smiling. 'Micro-organisms, too, are assimilated into Gaia when they are part of my food, or when they enter my body in any other way. If they seem to be in the process of doing harm, they will be assimilated the more quickly, and once they are Gaia, they will do me no harm.'

The meal drew to its end and Pelorat sipped at his spiced and heated mixture of fruit juices. 'Dear me,' he said, licking his lips, 'I think it is time to change the subject again. It does seem to me that my sole occupation on board ship is subject-changing. Why is that?'

Trevize said solemnly, 'Because Bliss and I cling to whatever subjects we discuss, even to the death. We depend upon you, Janov, to save our sanity. What subject do you want to change to, old friend?'

'I've gone through my reference material on Comporellon and the entire sector of which it is part is rich in legends of age. They set their settlement far back in time, in the first millennium of hyperspatial travel. Comporellon even speaks of a legendary founder named Benbally, though they don't say where he came from. They say that the original name of their planet was Benbally World.'

'And how much truth is there in that, in your opinion, Janov?'

'A kernel, perhaps, but who can guess what the kernel might be.'

'I never heard of anyone named Benbally in actual history. Have you?'

'No, I haven't, but you know that in the late Imperial era there was a deliberate suppression of pre-Imperial history. The Emperors, in the turbulent last centuries of the Empire, were anxious to reduce local patriotism, since they considered it, with ample justification, to be a disintegrating influence. In almost every sector of the Galaxy, therefore, true history, with complete records and accurate chronology, begins only with the days when Trantor's influence made itself felt and the sector in question had allied itself to the Empire or been annexed by it.'

'I shouldn't think that history would be that easy to eradicate,' said Trevize.

'In many ways, it isn't,' said Pelorat, 'but a determined and powerful government can weaken it greatly. If it is sufficiently weakened, early history comes to depend on scattered material and tends to degenerate into folk tales. Invariably such folk tales will fill with exaggeration and come to show the sector to be older and more powerful than, in all likelihood, it ever really was. And no matter how silly a particular legend is, or how impossible it might be on the very face of it, it becomes a matter of patriotism among the locals to believe it. I can show you tales from every corner of the Galaxy that speak of original colonization as having taken place from

Earth itself, though that is not always the name they give the parent planet.'

'What else do they call it?'

'Any of a number of names. They call it the Only, sometimes; and sometimes, the Oldest. Or they call it the Mooned World, which, according to some authorities is a reference to its giant satellite. Others claim it means "Lost World" and that "Mooned" is a version of "Marooned", a pre-Galactic word meaning "lost" or "abandoned".'

Trevize said gently, 'Janov, stop! You'll continue forever with your authorities and counter-authorities. These legends are everywhere, you say?'

'Oh, yes, my dear fellow. Quite. You have only to go through them to gain a feel for this human habit of beginning with some seed of truth and layering about it shell after shell of pretty falsehood – in the fashion of the oysters of Rhampora that build pearls about a piece of grit. I came across just exactly that metaphor once when –'

'Janov! Stop again! Tell me, is there anything about Comporellon's legends that is different from others?'

'Oh!' Pelorat gazed at Trevize blankly for a moment. 'Different? Well, they claim that Earth is relatively nearby and that's unusual. On most worlds that speak of Earth, under whatever name they choose, there is a tendency to be vague about its location – placing it indefinitely far away or in some never-never land.'

Trevize said, 'Yes, as some on Sayshell told us that Gaia was located in hyperspace.'

Bliss laughed.

Trevize cast her a quick glance. 'It's true. That's what we were told.'

'I don't disbelieve it. It's amusing, that's all. It is, of course, what we want them to believe. We only ask to be left alone right now, and where can we be safer and more secure than in hyperspace? If we're not there, we're as good as there, if people believe that to be our location.'

'Yes,' said Trevize drily, 'and in the same way there is something that causes people to believe that Earth doesn't exist, or that it is far away, or that it has a radioactive crust.'

'Except,' said Pelorat, 'that the Comporellians believe it to be relatively close to themselves.'

'But nevertheless give it a radioactive crust. One way or another every people with an Earth-legend consider Earth to be unapproachable.'

'That's more or less right,' said Pelorat.

Trevize said, 'Many on Sayshell believed Gaia to be nearby; some even identified its star correctly; and yet all considered it unapproachable. There may be some Comporellians who insist that Earth is radioactive and dead, but who can identify its star. We will then approach it, unapproachable though they may consider it. We did exactly that in the case of Gaia.'

Bliss said, 'Gaia was willing to receive you, Trevize. You were helpless in our grip but we had no thought of harming you. What if Earth, too, is powerful, but not benevolent. What then?'

'I must in any case try to reach it, and accept the consequences. However, that is *my* task. Once I locate Earth and head for it, it will not be too late for you to leave. I will put you off on the nearest Foundation world, or take you back to Gaia, if you insist, and then go on to Earth alone.'

'My dear chap,' said Pelorat, in obvious distress. 'Don't say such things. I wouldn't dream of abandoning you.'

'Or I of abandoning Pel,' said Bliss, as she reached out a hand to touch Pelorat's cheek.

'Very well, then. It won't be long before we're ready to take the Jump to Comporellon and thereafter, let us hope, it will be – on to Earth.'

Part II

Comporellon

3

At the Entry Station

9

Bliss, entering their chamber, said, 'Did Trevize tell you that we are going to take the Jump and go through hyperspace any moment now?'

Pelorat, who was bent over his viewing disc, looked up, and said, 'Actually, he just looked in and told me "within the half hour".'

'I don't like the thought of it, Pel. I've never liked the Jump. I get a funny inside-out feeling.'

Pelorat looked a bit surprised. 'I had not thought of you as a space-traveller, Bliss dear.'

'I'm not particularly, and I don't mean that this is so only in my aspect as a component. Gaia itself has no occasion for regular space travel. By my/our/Gaia's very nature, I/we/Gaia don't explore, trade or space junket. Still, there is the necessity of having someone at the entry stations –'

'As when we were fortunate enough to meet you.'

'Yes, Pel.' She smiled at him affectionately. 'Or even to visit Sayshell and other stellar regions, for various reasons – usually clandestine. But, clandestine or not, that always means the Jump and, of course, when any part of Gaia Jumps, all of Gaia feels it.'

'That's too bad,' said Pel.

'It could be worse. The large mass of Gaia is *not* undergoing the Jump, so the effect is greatly diluted. However, I seem to feel it much more than most of Gaia. As I keep trying to tell Trevize, though all of Gaia is Gaia, the individual components are not identical. We have our differences, and my makeup is, for some reason, particularly sensitive to the Jump.'

'Wait!' said Pelorat, suddenly remembering. 'Trevize explained that to me once. It's in ordinary ships that you have the worst of the sensation. In ordinary ships, one leaves the Galactic gravitational field on entering hyperspace, and comes back to it on returning to ordinary space. It's the leaving and returning that produces the sensation. But the *Far Star* is a gravitic ship. It is independent of the gravitational field, and does not truly leave it or return to it. For that reason, we won't feel a thing. I can assure you of that, dear, out of personal experience.'

'But that's delightful. I wish I had thought to discuss the matter earlier. I would have saved myself considerable apprehension.'

'That's an advantage in another way,' said Pelorat, feeling an expansion of spirit in his unusual role as explainer of matters astronautic. 'The ordinary ship has to recede from large masses such as stars for quite a long distance through ordinary space in order to make the Jump. Part of the reason is that the closer to a star, the more intense the gravitational field, and the more pronounced are the sensations of a Jump. Then, too, the more intense the gravitational field the more complicated the equations that must be solved in order to conduct the Jump safely and end at the point in ordinary space you wish to end at.

'In a gravitic ship, however, there is no Jump-sensation to speak of. In addition, this ship has a computer that is a great deal more advanced than ordinary computers and it can handle complex equations with unusual skill and speed. The result is that instead of having to move away from a star for a couple of weeks just to reach a safe and comfortable distance for a Jump, the *Far Star* need travel for only two or three days. This is especially so since we are not subject to a gravitational field and, therefore, to inertial effects – I admit I don't understand that, but that's what Trevize tells me – and can accelerate much more rapidly than an ordinary ship could.'

Bliss said, 'That's fine, and it's to Trev's credit that he can handle this unusual ship.'

Pelorat frowned slightly. 'Please, Bliss. Say "Trevize".'

'I do. I do. In his absence, however, I relax a little.'

'Don't. You don't want to encourage the habit even slightly, dear. He's so sensitive about it.'

'Not about that. He's sensitive about me. He doesn't like me.'

'That's not so,' said Pelorat earnestly. 'I talked to him about that. – Now, now, don't frown. I was extraordinarily tactful, dear child. He assured me he did not dislike you. He is suspicious of Gaia and unhappy over the fact that he has had to make it into the future of humanity. We have to make allowances for that. He'll get over it as he gradually comes to understand the advantages of Gaia.'

'I hope so, but it's not just Gaia. Whatever he may tell you, Pel – and remember that he's very fond of you and doesn't want to hurt your feelings – he dislikes me personally.'

'No, Bliss. He couldn't possibly.'

'Not everyone is forced to love me simply because you do, Pel. Let me explain. Trev – all right, Trevize – thinks I'm a robot.'

A look of astonishment suffused Pelorat's ordinarily stolid features. He said, 'Surely he can't think you're an artificial human being.'

'Why is that so surprising? Gaia was settled with the help of robots. That's a known fact.'

'Robots might help, as machines might, but it was *people* who settled Gaia; people from Earth. That's what Trevize thinks. I know he does.'

'There is nothing in Gaia's memory about Earth as I told you and Trevize. However, in our oldest memories there are still some robots, even after three thousand years, working at the task of completing the modification of Gaia into a habitable world. We were at that time also forming Gaia as a planetary consciousness – that took a long time, Pel dear, and that's another reason why our early memories are dim, and perhaps it wasn't a matter of Earth wiping them out, as Trevize thinks –'

'Yes, Bliss,' said Pelorat anxiously, 'but what of the robots?'

'Well, as Gaia formed, the robots left. We did not want a Gaia that included robots, for we were, and are, convinced that a robotic component is, in the long run, harmful to human society, whether Isolate in nature or Planetary. I don't know how we came to that conclusion but it is possible that it is based on events dating back to a particularly early time in Galactic history, so that Gaia's memory does not extend back to it.'

'If the robots left –'

'Yes, but what if some remained behind. What if I am one of them – fifteen thousand years old perhaps. Trevize suspects that.'

Pelorat shook his head slowly, 'But you're not.'

'Are you sure you believe that?'

'Of course I do. You're *not* a robot.'

'How do you know?'

'Bliss, I *know*. There's nothing artificial about you. If I don't know *that*, no one does.'

'Isn't it possible I may be so cleverly artificial that in every respect, from largest to smallest, I am indistinguishable from the natural. If I were, how could you tell the difference between me and a true human being.'

Pelorat said, 'I don't think it's possible for you to be so cleverly artificial.'

'What if it *were* possible, despite what you think.'

'I just don't believe it.'

'Then let's just consider it is a hypothetical case. If I were an indistinguishable robot, how would you feel about it?'

'Well, I – I –'

'To be specific. How would you feel about making love to a robot?'

Pelorat snapped the thumb and mid-finger of his right hand, suddenly. 'You know, there are legends of women falling in love with artificial men, and vice versa. I always thought there was an allegorical significance to that and never imagined the tales could represent literal truth. – Of course, Golan and I never even heard the word "robot" till we landed on Sayshell, but, now that I think of it, those artificial men and women must have been robots. Apparently, such robots did exist in early historic times. That means the legends should be reconsidered –'

He fell into silent thought, and, after Bliss had waited a moment, she suddenly clapped her hands sharply. Pelorat jumped.

'Pel dear,' said Bliss. 'You're using your mythography to escape the question. The question is: how would you feel about making love to a robot?'

He stared at her uneasily. 'A truly undistinguishable one? One that you couldn't tell from a human being?'

'Yes.'

'It seems to me, then, that a robot that can in no way be distinguished from a human being *is* a human being. If you were such a robot, you would be nothing but a human being to me.'

'That's what I wanted to hear you say, Pel.'

Pelorat waited, then said, 'Well, then, now that you've heard me say it, dear, aren't you going to tell me that you are a natural human being and that I don't have to wrestle with hypothetical situations?'

'No. I will do no such thing. You've defined a natural human being as an object that has all the properties of a natural human being. If you are satisfied that I have all those properties, then that ends the discussion. We've got the operational definition and need no other. After all, how do I know that *you're* not just a robot who happens to be indistinguishable from a human being.'

'Because I tell you that I am not.'

'Ah, but if you were a robot that was indistinguishable from a human being, you might be designed to tell me you were a natural human being, and you might even be programmed to believe it yourself. The operational definition is all we have, and all we *can* have.'

She put her arms about Pelorat's neck and kissed him. The kiss grew more passionate, and prolonged itself until Pelorat managed to say, in somewhat muffled fashion, 'But we promised Trevize not to embarrass him by converting this trip into a honeymooners' haven.'

Bliss said coaxingly, 'Let's be carried away and not leave ourselves any time to think of promises.'

Pelorat, troubled, said, 'But I can't do that, dear. I know it must irritate you, Bliss, but I am constantly thinking and I am constitutionally averse to letting myself be carried away by emotion. It's a lifelong habit, and probably very annoying to others. I've never lived with a woman who didn't seem to object to it sooner or later. My first wife – but I suppose it would be inappropriate to discuss that –'

'Rather inappropriate, yes, but not fatally so. You're not my first lover either.'

'Oh!' said Pelorat, rather at a loss, and then, aware of Bliss's small smile, he said, 'I mean, of course not. I wouldn't expect myself to have been – Anyway, my first wife didn't like it.'

'But I do. I find your endless plunging into thought attractive.'

'I can't believe *that*, but I do have another thought. Robot or human, that doesn't matter. We agree on that. However, I am an Isolate and you know it. I am not part of Gaia, and when we are intimate, you're sharing emotions outside Gaia even when you let me participate in Gaia for a short period, and it may not be the same intensity of emotion then that you would experience if it were Gaia loving Gaia.'

Bliss said, 'Loving you, Pel, has its own delight. I look no further than that.'

'But it's not just a matter of you loving me. You aren't merely you. What if Gaia considers it a perversion.'

'If it did, I would know, for I am Gaia. And since I have delight in you, Gaia does. When we make love, all of Gaia shares the sensation to some degree or other. When I say I love you, that means Gaia loves you, although it is only the part that I am that is assigned the immediate role. – You seem confused.'

'Being an Isolate, Bliss, I don't quite grasp it.'

'One can always form an analogy with the body of an Isolate. When you whistle a tune, your entire body, *you* as an organism, wishes to whistle the tune, but the immediate task of doing so is assigned to your lips, tongue, and lungs. Your right big toe does nothing.'

'It might tap to the tune.'

'But that is not necessary to the act of whistling. The tapping of the big toe is not the action itself but is a response to the action, and, to be sure, all parts of Gaia might well respond in some small way or other to my emotion, as I respond to theirs.'

Pelorat said, 'I suppose there's no use feeling embarrassed about this.'

'None at all.'

'But it does give me a queer sense of responsibility. When I try to make you happy, I find that I must be trying to make every last organism on Gaia happy.'

'Every last atom – but you do. You add to the sense of communal joy that I let you share briefly. I suppose your contribution is too small to be easily measurable, but it is there, and knowing it is there should increase your joy.'

Pelorat said, 'I wish I could be sure that Golan is sufficiently busy with his manœuvring through hyperspace to remain in the pilot-room for quite a while.'

'You wish to honeymoon, do you?'

'I do.'

'Then get a sheet of paper, write "Honeymoon Haven" on it, affix it to the outside of the door, and if he wants to enter, that's his problem.'

Pelorat did so, and it was during the pleasurable proceedings that followed that the *Far Star* made the Jump. Neither Pelorat nor Bliss detected the action, nor would they have, had they been paying attention.

10

It had been only a matter of a few months since Pelorat had met Trevize and had left Terminus for the first time. Until then, for the more than half-century (Galactic Standard) of his life, he had been utterly planet-bound.

In his own mind, he had in those months become an old space dog. He had seen three planets from space: Terminus itself, Sayshell and Gaia. And on the viewscreen, he now saw a fourth, albeit through a computer-controlled telescopic device. The fourth was Comporellon.

And again, for the fourth time, he was vaguely disappointed. Somehow, he continued to feel that looking down upon a habitable world from space meant seeing an outline of its continents against a surrounding sea; or, if it were a dry world, the outline of its lakes against a surrounding body of land.

It was never so.

If a world was habitable, it had an atmosphere as well as a hydrosphere. And if it had both air and water, it had clouds; and if it had clouds, it had an obscured view. Once again, then, Pelorat found himself looking down on white swirls with an occasional glimpse of pale blue or rusty brown.

He wondered gloomily if anyone could identify a world if a view of it from, say, 300,000 kilometres, were cast upon a screen. How does one tell one cloud swirl from another?

Bliss looked at Pelorat with some concern. 'What is it, Pel? You seem to be unhappy.'

'I find that all planets look alike from space.'

Trevize said, 'What of that, Janov? So does every shoreline on Terminus, when it is on the horizon, unless you know what you're looking for – a particular mountain peak, or a particular offshore islet of characteristic shape.'

'I dare say,' said Pelorat, with clear dissatisfaction, 'but what do you look for in a mass of shifting clouds? And even if you try, before you can decide, you're likely to be moving into the dark side.'

'Look a little more carefully, Janov. If you follow the shape of the clouds, you see that they tend to fall into a pattern that circles the planet and that moves about a centre. That centre is more or less at one of the poles.'

'Which one?' asked Bliss with interest.

'Since, relative to ourselves, the planet is rotating in clockwise fashion, we are looking down, by definition, upon the south pole. Since the centre seems to be about fifteen degrees from the termi- nator – the planet's line of shadow – and the planetary axis is tilted twenty-one degrees to the perpendicular of its plane of revolution, we're either in mid-spring or mid-summer depending on whether the pole is moving away from the terminator or towards it. The computer can calculate its orbit and tell me in short order if I were to ask it. The capital is on the northern side of the equator so it is either in mid-fall or mid-winter.'

Pelorat frowned. 'You can tell all that?' He looked at the cloud layer as though he thought it would, or should, speak to him now, but, of course, it didn't.

'Not only that,' said Trevize, 'but if you'll look at the polar regions, you'll see that there are no breaks in the cloud layer as there are away from the poles. Actually, there are breaks, but through the breaks you see ice, so it's a matter of white on white.'

'Ah,' said Pelorat. 'I suppose you expect that at the poles.'

'Of habitable planets, certainly. Lifeless planets might be airless or waterless, or might have certain stigmata showing that the clouds are not water clouds, or that the ice is not water ice. This planet lacks those stigmata, so we know we are looking at water clouds and water ice.

'The next thing we notice is the size of the area of unbroken white on the day side of the terminator, and to the experienced eye it is at once seen as larger than average. Furthermore, you can detect a certain orange glint, a quite faint one, to the reflected light, and that means Comporellon's sun is rather cooler than Terminus's sun. Although Comporellon is closer to its sun than Terminus is to hers, it is not sufficiently closer to make up for its star's lower temperature. Therefore, Comporellon is a cold world as habitable worlds go.'

'You read it like a film, old chap,' said Pelorat admiringly.

'Don't be too impressed,' said Trevize, smiling affectionately. 'The computer has given me the applicable statistics of the world, including its slightly low average temperature. It is easy to deduce something you already know. In fact, Comporellon is at the edge of an ice age and would be having one, if the configuration of its continents were more suitable to such a condition.'

Bliss bit at her lower lip. 'I don't like a cold world.'

'We've got warm clothing,' said Trevize.

'That doesn't matter. Human beings aren't adapted to cold weather, really. We don't have thick coats of hair or feathers, or a subcutaneous layer of blubber. For a world to have cold weather seems to indicate a certain indifference to the welfare of its own parts.'

Trevize said, 'Is Gaia a uniformly mild world?'

'Most of it, yes. There are some cold areas for cold-adapted plants and animals, and some hot areas for heat-adapted plants and animals, but most parts are uniformly mild, never getting uncomfortably hot or uncomfortably cold, for those between, including human beings, of course.'

'Human beings, of course. All parts of Gaia are alive and equal in that respect, but some, like human beings, are obviously more equal than others.'

'Don't be foolishly sarcastic,' said Bliss, with a trace of waspishness. 'The level and intensity of consciousness and awareness are important. A human being is a more useful portion of Gaia than a rock of the same weight would be, and the properties and functions of Gaia as a whole are necessarily weighted in the direction of the human being – not as much so as on your Isolate worlds, however. What's more, there are times when it is weighted in other directions, when that is needed for Gaia as a whole. It might even, at long intervals, be weighted in the direction of the rocky interior. That, too, demands attention or, in the lack of that attention, all parts of Gaia might suffer. We wouldn't want an unnecessary volcanic eruption, would we?'

'No,' said Trevize. 'Not an unnecessary one.'

'You're not impressed, are you?'

'Look,' said Trevize. 'We have worlds that are colder than average and worlds that are warmer; worlds that are tropical forests to a large extent, and worlds that are vast savannahs. No two worlds are alike, and every one of them is home to those who are used to it. I am used to the relative mildness of Terminus – we've tamed it to an almost Gaian moderation, actually – but I like to get away, at least temporarily, to something different. What we have, Bliss, that Gaia doesn't have, is variation. If Gaia expands into Galaxia, will every world in the Galaxy be forced into mildness? The sameness would be unbearable.'

Bliss said, 'If that is so, and if variety seems desirable, variety will be maintained.'

'As a gift from the central committee, so to speak?' said Trevize drily. 'And as little of it as they can bear to part with? I'd rather leave it to nature.'

'But you *haven't* left it to nature. Every habitable world in the Galaxy has been modified. Every single one was found in a state of nature that was uncomfortable for humanity, and every single one was modified until it was as mild as could be managed. If this world here is cold, I am certain that is because its inhabitants couldn't warm it any further without unacceptable expense. And even so, the portions they actually inhabit we can be sure are artificially warmed into mildness. So don't be so loftily virtuous about leaving it to nature.'

Trevize said, 'You speak for Gaia, I suppose.'

'I always speak for Gaia. I *am* Gaia.'

'Then if Gaia is so certain of its own superiority, why did you require *my* decision? Why have you not gone ahead without me?'

Bliss paused, as though to collect her thoughts. She said, 'Because it is not wise to trust one's self overmuch. We naturally see our virtues with clearer eyes than we see our defects. We are anxious to do what is right; not necessarily what *seems* right to us, but what *is* right, objectively, if such a thing as objective right exists. You seem to be the nearest approach to objective right that we can find, so we are guided by you.'

'So objectively right,' said Trevize sadly, 'that I don't even understand my own decision and I seek its justification.'

'You'll find it,' said Bliss.

'I hope so,' said Trevize.

'Actually, old chap,' said Pelorat, 'it seems to me that this recent
exchange was won rather handily by Bliss. Why don't you recognize
the fact that her arguments justify your decision that Gaia is the
wave of the future for humanity?'

'Because,' said Trevize harshly, 'I did not know those arguments
at the time I made my decision. I knew none of these details about
Gaia. Something else influenced me, at least unconsciously, something that doesn't depend upon Gaian detail, but must be more
fundamental. It is that which I must find out.'

Pelorat held up a placating hand. 'Don't be angry, Golan.'

'I'm not angry. I'm just under rather unbearable tension. I don't
want to be the focus of the Galaxy.'

Bliss said, 'I don't blame you for that, Trevize, and I'm truly sorry
that your own makeup has somehow forced you into the post. –
When will we be landing on Comporellon?'

'In three days,' said Trevize, 'and only after we stop at one of the
entry stations in orbit about it.'

Pelorat said, 'There shouldn't be any problem with that, should
there?'

Trevize shrugged. 'It depends on the number of ships approaching
the world, the number of entry stations that exist, and, most of all,
on the particular rules for permitting and refusing admittance. Such
rules change from time to time.'

Pelorat said, indignantly, 'What do you mean *refusing* admittance.
How can they refuse admittance to citizens of the Foundation? Isn't
Comporellon part of the Foundation dominion?'

'Well, yes – and no. There's a delicate matter of legalism about
the point and I'm not sure how Comporellon interprets it. I suppose
there's a chance we'll be refused admission, but I don't think it's a
large chance.'

'And if we are refused, what do we do?'

'I'm not sure,' said Trevize. 'Let's wait and see what happens before we wear ourselves out making contingency plans.'

11

They were close enough to Comporellon now for it to appear as a substantial globe without telescopic enlargement. When such enlargement was added, however, the entry stations themselves could be seen. They were further out than most of the orbiting structures about the planet and they were well lit.

Approaching as the *Far Star* was from the direction of the planet's southern pole, half its globe was sunlit constantly. The entry stations on its night side were naturally more clearly seen as sparks of light. They were evenly spaced in an arc about the planet. Six of them were visible (plus six on the day side undoubtedly) and all were circling the planet at even and identical speeds.

Pelorat, a little awed at the sight, said, 'There are other lights closer to the planet. What are they?'

Trevize said, 'I don't know the planet in detail so I can't tell you. Some might be orbiting factories or laboratories or observatories, or even populated townships. Some planets prefer to keep all orbiting objects outwardly dark, except for the entry stations. Terminus does, for instance. Comporellon conducts itself on a more liberal principle, obviously.'

'Which entry station do we go to, Golan?'

'It depends on them. I've sent in my request to land on Comporellon and we'll eventually get our directions as to which entry station to go to, and when. Much depends on how many incoming ships are trying to make entry at present. If there are a dozen ships lined up at each station, we will have no choice but to be patient.'

Bliss said, 'I've only been at hyperspatial distances from Gaia twice before, and those were both when I was at or near Sayshell. I've never been at anything like *this* distance.'

Trevize looked at her sharply. 'Does it matter? You're still Gaia, aren't you?'

For a moment, Bliss looked irritated, but then dissolved into what was almost an embarrassed titter. 'I must admit you've caught me this time, Trevize. There is a double meaning in the word "Gaia". It can be used to refer to the physical planet as a solid globular object in space. It can also be used to refer to the living object that includes that globe. Properly speaking, we should use two different words for these two different concepts, but Gaians always know from the context what is being referred to. I admit that an Isolate might be puzzled at times.'

'Well, then,' said Trevize, 'admitting that you are many thousands of parsecs from Gaia as globe, are you still part of Gaia as organism?'

'Referring to the organism, I am still Gaia.'

'No attenuation?'

'Not in essence. I'm sure I've already told you there is some added complexity in remaining Gaia across hyperspace, but I remain Gaia.'

Trevize said, 'Does it occur to you that Gaia may be viewed as a Galactic kraken – the tentacled monster of the legends – with its tentacles reaching everywhere. You have but to put a few Gaians on each of the populated worlds and you will virtually have Galaxia right there. In fact, you have probably done exactly that. Where are your Gaians located? I presume that one or more are on Terminus and one or more are on Trantor. How much further does this go?'

Bliss looked distinctly uncomfortable. 'I have said I won't lie to you, Trevize, but that doesn't mean I feel compelled to give you the whole truth. There are some things you have no need to know, and the position and identity of individual bits of Gaia are among them.'

'Do I need to know the reason for the existence of those tentacles, Bliss, even if I don't know where they are?'

'It is the opinion of Gaia that you do not.'

'I presume, though, that I may guess. You believe you serve as the guardians of the Galaxy.'

'We are anxious to have a stable and secure Galaxy; a peaceful and prosperous one. The Seldon Plan, as originally worked out by Hari Seldon, at least, is designed to develop a Second Galactic Empire, one that is more stable and more workable than the First was. The Plan, which has been continually modified and improved by the Second Foundation, has appeared to be working well so far.'

'But Gaia doesn't want a Second Galactic Empire in the classic sense, does it? You want Galaxia – a living Galaxy.'

'Since you permit it, we hope, in time, to have Galaxia. If you had not permitted it, we would have striven for Seldon's Second Empire and made it as secure as we could.'

'But what is wrong with –'

His ear caught the soft, burring signal. Trevize said, 'The computer is signalling me. I suppose it is receiving directions concerning the entry station. I'll be back.'

He stepped into the pilot-room and placed his hands on those marked out on the desk top and found that there *were* directions for the specific entry station he was to approach – its co-ordinates with reference to the line from Comporellon's centre to its north pole – the prescribed route of approach.

Trevize signalled his acceptance, and then sat back for a moment.

The Seldon Plan! He had not thought of it for quite a time. The First Galactic Empire had crumbled and for five hundred years the Foundation had grown, first in competition with that Empire, and then upon its ruins – all in accordance with the Plan.

There had been the interruption of the Mule, which, for a time, had threatened to shiver the Plan into fragments, but the Foundation had pulled through – probably with the help of the ever-hidden Second Foundation – possibly with the help of the even better-hidden Gaia.

Now the plan was threatened by something more serious than the Mule had ever been. It was to be diverted from a renewal of Empire to something utterly different from anything in history – Galaxia. *And he himself had agreed to that.*

But why? Was there a flaw in the Plan? A basic flaw?

For one flashing moment, it seemed to Trevize that this flaw did indeed exist and that he knew what it was, that he had known what it was when he made his decision – but the knowledge . . . if that were what it was . . . vanished as fast as it came, and it left him with nothing.

Perhaps it was all only an illusion; both when he had made his decision, and now. After all, he knew nothing about the Plan beyond the basic assumptions that validated psychohistory. Beyond that, he knew no detail, and certainly not a single scrap of its mathematics.

He closed his eyes and thought –

There was nothing.

Might it be the added power he received from the computer? He placed his hands on the desk top and felt the warmth of the computer's hands embracing them. He closed his eyes and once more he thought –

There was still nothing.

12

The Comporellian who boarded the ship wore a holographic identity card. It displayed his chubby, lightly bearded face with remarkable fidelity, and underneath it was his name, A. Kendray.

He was rather short, and his body was as softly rounded as his face was. He had a fresh and easy-going look and manner, and he stared about the ship with clear amazement.

He said, 'How did you get down this fast? We weren't expecting you for two hours.'

'It's a new-model ship,' said Trevize, with non-committal politeness.

Kendray was not quite the young innocent he looked, however. He stepped into the pilot-room and said at once, 'Gravitic?'

Trevize saw no point in denying anything that was apparently that obvious. He said tonelessly, 'Yes.'

'Very interesting. You hear of them, but you never see them somehow. Motors in the hull?'

'That's so.'

Kendray looked at the computer. 'Computer circuits, likewise?'

'That's so. Anyway, I'm told so. I've never looked.'

'Oh, well. What I need is the ship's documentation; engine number, place of manufacture, identification code, the whole patty-cake. It's all in the computer, I'm sure, and it can probably turn out the formal card I need in half a second.'

It took very little more than that. Kendray looked about again. 'You three all the people on board.'

Trevize said, 'That's right.'

'Any live animals? Plants? State of health?'

'No. No. And good,' said Trevize, crisply.

'Um!' said Kendray, making notes. 'Could you put your hand in here? Just routine. – Right hand, please.'

Trevize looked at the device without favour. It was being used more and more commonly, and was growing quickly more elaborate. You could almost tell the backwardness of a world at a glance by the backwardness of its micro-detector. There were now few worlds, however backward, that didn't have one at all. The start had come with the final breakup of the Empire, as each fragment of the whole grew increasingly anxious to protect itself from the diseases and alien micro-organisms of all the others.

'What is that?' asked Bliss, in a low and interested voice, craning her head to see it first on one side, then the other.

Pelorat said, 'A micro-detector, I believe they call it.'

Trevize added, 'It's nothing mysterious. It's a device that automatically checks a portion of your body, inside and out, for any micro-organism capable of transmitting disease.'

'This will classify the micro-organisms, too,' said Kendray, with rather more than a hint of pride. 'It's been worked out right here on Comporellon. – And if you don't mind, I still want your right hand.'

Trevize inserted his right hand, and watched as a series of small red markings danced along a set of horizontal lines. Kendray touched a contact and a facsimile in colour appeared at once. 'If you'll sign that, sir,' he said.

Trevize did so. 'How badly off am I?' he asked. 'I'm not in any great danger, am I?'

Kendray said, 'I'm not a physician, so I can't say in detail, but it shows none of the marks that would require you to be turned away or to be put in quarantine. That's all I'm interested in.'

'What a lucky break for me,' said Trevize drily, shaking his hand to rid himself of the slight tingle he felt.

'You, sir,' said Kendray.

Pelorat inserted his hand with a certain hesitancy, then signed the facsimile.

'And you, ma'am?'

A few moments later, Kendray was staring at the result, saying, 'I never saw anything like this before.' He looked up at Bliss with an expression of awe. 'You're negative. Altogether.'

Bliss smiled engagingly. 'How nice.'

'Yes, ma'am. I envy you.' He looked back at the first facsimile, and said, 'Your identification, Mr Trevize.'

Trevize presented it. Kendray, glancing at it, again looked up in surprise. 'Councilman of the Terminus Legislature?'

'That's right.'

'High official of the Foundation?'

Trevize said coolly, 'Exactly right. So let's get through with this quickly, shall we?'

'You're captain of the ship?'

'Yes, I am.'

'Purpose of visit?'

'Foundation security, and that's all the answer I'm going to give you. Do you understand that?'

'Yes, sir. How long do you intend to stay?'

'I don't know. Perhaps a week.'

'Very well, sir. And this other gentleman?'

'He is Dr Janov Pelorat,' said Trevize. 'You have his signature there and I vouch for him. He is a scholar of Terminus and he is my assistant in this business of my visit.'

'I understand, sir, but I must see his identification. Rules are rules, I'm afraid. I hope *you* understand, sir.'

Pelorat presented his papers.

Kendray nodded. 'And you, miss?'

Trevize said, quietly, 'No need to bother the lady. I vouch for her, too.'

'Yes, sir. But I need the identification.'

Bliss said, 'I'm afraid I don't have any papers, sir.'

Kendray frowned. 'I beg your pardon.'

Trevize said, 'The young lady didn't bring any with her. An oversight. It's perfectly all right. I'll take full responsibility.'

Kendray said, 'I wish I could let you do that, but I'm not allowed. The responsibility is mine. Under the circumstances, it's not terribly important. There should be no difficulty getting duplicates. The young woman, I presume, is from Terminus.'

'No, she's not.'

'From somewhere in Foundation territory, then?'

'As a matter of fact, she isn't.'

Kendray looked at Bliss keenly, then at Trevize. 'That's a complication, Councilman. It may take additional time to obtain a duplicate from some non-Foundation world. Since you're not a Foundation citizen, Miss Bliss, I must have the name of your world of birth and of the world of which you're a citizen. You will then have to wait for duplicate papers to arrive.'

Trevize said, 'See here, Mr Kendray. I see no reason why there need be any delay whatever. I am a high official of the Foundation government and I am here on a mission of great importance. I must not be delayed by a matter of trivial paperwork.'

'The choice isn't mine, Councilman. If it were up to me, I'd let you down to Comporellon right now, but I have a thick book of rules that guides my every action. I've got to go by the book or I get it thrown at me. – Of course, I presume there must be some

Comporellian government figure who's waiting for you. If you'll tell me who it is, I will contact him, and if he orders me to let you through, then that's it.'

Trevize hesitated a moment. 'That would not be politic, Mr Kendray. May I speak with your immediate superior?'

'You certainly may, but you can't just see him off-hand –'

'I'm sure he will come at once when he understands he's speaking to a Foundation official –'

'Actually,' said Kendray, 'just between us, that would make matters worse. We're not part of the Foundation metropolitan territory, you know. We come under the heading of an Associated Power, and we take it seriously. The people are anxious not to appear to be Foundation puppets – I'm using the popular expression only, you understand – and they bend backwards to demonstrate independence. My superior would expect to get extra points if he *resists* doing a special favour for a Foundation official.'

Trevize's expression darkened. 'And you, too?'

Kendray shook his head. 'I'm below politics, sir. No one gives me extra points for anything. I'm just lucky if they pay my salary. And though I don't get extra points, I *can* get demerits, and quite easily, too. I wish that were not so.'

'Considering my position, you know, I can take care of you.'

'No, sir. I'm sorry if that sounds impertinent, but I don't think you can. – And, sir, it's embarrassing to say this, but please don't offer me anything valuable. They make examples of officials who accept such things and they're pretty good at digging them out, these days.'

'I wasn't thinking of bribing you. I'm only thinking of what the Mayor of Terminus can do to you if you interfere with my mission.'

'Councilman, I'll be perfectly safe as long as I can hide behind the rulebook. If the members of the Comporellian Presidium get some sort of Foundation discipline, that is their concern, and not mine. – But if it will help, sir, I can let you and Dr Pelorat through on your ship. If you'll leave Miss Bliss behind at the entry station, we'll hold her for a time and send her down to the surface as soon as her duplicate papers come through. If her papers should not be obtainable, for any reason, we will send her back to her world on commercial transportation. I'm afraid, though, that someone will have to pay her fare, in that case.'

Trevize caught Pelorat's expression at that, and said, 'Mr Kendray, may I speak to you privately in the pilot-room?'

'Very well, but I can't remain on board very much longer, or I'll be questioned.'

'This won't take long,' said Trevize.

In the pilot-room, Trevize made a show of closing the door tightly, then said, in a low voice, 'I've been many places, Mr Kendray, but I've never been any place where there has been such harsh emphasis on the minutiae of the rules of immigration, particularly for Foundation people and Foundation *officials*.'

'But the young woman is not from the Foundation.'

'Even so.'

Kendray said, 'These things go in rhythms. We've had some scandals and, right now, things are tough. If you'll come back next year, you might not have any trouble at all, but right now, I can do nothing.'

'Try, Mr Kendray,' said Trevize, his voice growing mellow. 'I'm going to throw myself on your mercy and appeal to you, man to man. Pelorat and I have been on this mission for quite some while. He and I. Just he and I. We're good friends, but there's something lonely about it, if you get me. Some time ago, Pelorat found this little lady. I don't have to tell you what happened, but we decided to bring her along. It keeps us healthy to make use of her now and then.

'Now the thing is Pelorat's got a relationship back on Terminus. I'm clear, you understand, but Pelorat is an older man and he's got to the age when they get a little – desperate. They need their youth back, or something. He can't give her up. At the same time, if she's even mentioned, officially, there's going to be misery galore on Terminus for old Pelorat when he gets back.

'There's no harm being done, you understand. Miss Bliss, as she calls herself – a good name considering her profession – is not exactly a bright kid; that's not what we want her for. Do you have to mention her at all? Can't you just list me and Pelorat on the ship? Only we were originally listed when we left Terminus. There need be no official notice of the woman. After all, she's absolutely free of disease. You noted that yourself.'

Kendray made a face. 'I don't really want to inconvenience you. I understand the situation and, believe me, I sympathize. Listen, if you think holding down a shift on this station for months at a time is any fun, think again. And it isn't co-educational, either; not on Comporellon.' He shook his head. 'And I have a wife, too, so I understand. – But, look, even if I let you through, as soon as they find out that the – uh – lady is without papers, she's in prison, you and Mr Pelorat are in the kind of trouble that will get back to Terminus. And I myself will surely be out of a job.'

'Mr Kendray,' said Trevize, 'trust me in this. Once I'm on Comporellon, I'll be safe. I can talk about my mission to some of the right people and, when that's done, there'll be no further trouble. I'll take full responsibility for what has happened here, if it ever comes up – which I doubt. What's more, I will recommend your promotion, and you will get it, because I'll see to it that Terminus leans all over anyone who hesitates. – And we can give Pelorat a break.'

Kendray hesitated, then said, 'All right. I'll let you through – but take a word of warning. I start from this minute figuring out a way to save my butt if the matter comes up. I don't intend to do one thing to save yours. What's more I know how these things work on Comporellon and you don't, and Comporellon isn't an easy world for people who step out of line.'

'Thank you, Mr Kendray,' said Trevize. 'There'll be no trouble. I assure you of that.'

4

On Comporellon

13

They were through. The entry station had shrunk to a rapidly dimming star behind them, and in a couple of hours they would be crossing the cloud layer.

A gravitic ship did not have to brake its path by a long route of slow spiral contraction, but neither could it swoop downwards too rapidly. Freedom from gravity did not mean freedom from air resistance. The ship could descend in a straight line, but it was still a matter for caution; it could not be too fast.

'Where are we going to go?' asked Pelorat, looking confused. 'I can't tell one place in the clouds from another, old fellow.'

'No more can I,' said Trevize, 'but we have an official holographic map of Comporellon, which gives the shape of the land masses and an exaggerated relief for both land heights and ocean depths – and political subdivisions, too. The map is in the computer and that will do the work. It will match the planetary land-sea design to the map, thus orientating the ship properly and it will then take us to the capital by a cycloidic pathway.'

Pelorat said, 'If we go to the capital, we plunge immediately into the political vortex. If the world is anti-Foundation, as the fellow at the entry station implied, we'll be asking for trouble.'

'On the other hand, it's bound to be the intellectual centre of the planet, and if we want information, that's where we'll find it, if anywhere. As for being anti-Foundation, I doubt that they will be able to display that too openly. The Mayor may have no great liking for me, but neither can she afford to have a Councilman mistreated. She would not care to allow the precedent to be established.'

Bliss had emerged from the toilet, her hands still damp from scrubbing. She adjusted her underclothes with no sign of concern and said, 'By the way, I trust the excreta is thoroughly recycled.'

'No choice,' said Trevize. 'How long do you suppose our water supply would last without recycling of excreta? On what do you think those choicely flavoured yeast cakes that we eat to lend spice to our frozen staples, grow? – I hope that doesn't spoil your appetite, my efficient Bliss.'

'Why should it? Where do you suppose food and water come from on Gaia, or on this planet, or on Terminus?'

'On Gaia,' said Trevize, 'the excreta is, of course, as alive as you are.'

'Not alive. Conscious. There is a difference. The level of consciousness is, naturally, very low.'

Trevize sniffed in a disparaging way, but didn't try to answer. He said, 'I'm going into the pilot-room to keep the computer company. Not that it needs me.'

Pelorat said, 'May we come in and help you keep it company? I can't quite get used to the fact that it can get us down all by itself, that it can sense other ships, or storms, or – whatever?'

Trevize smiled broadly. 'Get used to it, please. The ship is far safer under the computer's control than it ever would be under mine. – But certainly, come on. It will do you good to watch what happens.'

They were over the sunlit side of the planet now for, as Trevize explained, the map in the computer could be more easily matched to reality in the sunlight than in the dark.

'That's obvious,' said Pelorat.

'Not at all obvious. The computer will judge just as rapidly by the infrared light which the surface radiates even in the dark. However, the longer waves of infrared don't allow the computer quite the resolution that visible light would. That is, the computer doesn't see quite as finely and sharply by infrared, and where necessity doesn't drive, I like to make things as easy as possible for the computer.'

'What if the capital is on the dark side?'

'The chance is fifty-fifty,' said Trevize, 'but if it is, once the map is matched by daylight, we can skim down to the capital quite unerringly even if it is in the dark. And long before we come anywhere near the capital, we'll be intersecting microwave beams and will be receiving messages directing us to the most convenient spaceport. – There's nothing to worry about.'

'Are you sure?' said Bliss. 'You're bringing me down without papers and without any native world that these people here will recognize – and I'm bound and determined not to mention Gaia to them in any case. So what do we do, if I'm asked for my papers once we're on the surface?'

Trevize said, 'That's not likely to happen. Everyone will assume that was taken care of at the entry station.'

'But if they ask?'

'Then, when that time comes, we'll face the problem. Meanwhile, let's not manufacture problems out of air.'

'By the time we face the problems that may arise, it might well be too late to solve them.'

'I'll rely on my ingenuity to keep it from being too late.'

'Talking about ingenuity, how did you get us through the entry station?'

Trevize looked at Bliss, and let his lips slowly expand into a smile that made him seem like an impish teenager. 'Just brains.'

Pelorat said, 'What did you do, old man?'

Trevize said, 'It was a matter of appealing to him in the correct manner. I'd tried threats and subtle bribes. I had appealed to his logic and his loyalty to the Foundation. Nothing worked, so I fell back on the last resort. I said that you were cheating on your wife, Pelorat.'

'My *wife*? But my dear fellow, I don't have a wife at the moment.'

'I know that, but *he* didn't.'

Bliss said, 'By "wife", I presume you mean a woman who is a particular man's regular companion.'

Trevize said, 'A little more than that, Bliss. A *legal* companion, one with enforceable rights in consequence of that companionship.'

Pelorat said nervously, 'Bliss, I do *not* have a wife. I have had one now and then in the past, but I haven't had one for quite a while. If you would care to undergo the legal ritual –'

'Oh, Pel,' said Bliss, making a sweeping-away movement with her right hand, 'what would I care about that? I have innumerable companions that are as close to me as your arm is close companion to your other arm. It is only Isolates who feel so alienated that they have to use artificial conventions to enforce a feeble substitute for true companionship.'

'But I *am* an Isolate, Bliss dear.'

'You will be less Isolate in time, Pel. Never truly Gaia, perhaps, but less Isolate, and you will have a flood of companions.'

'I only want you, Bliss,' said Pel.

'That's because you know nothing about it. You'll learn.'

Trevize was concentrating on the viewscreen during that exchange with a look of strained tolerance on his face. The cloud cover had come up close and, for a moment, all was grey fog.

Microwave vision, he thought, and the computer switched at once to the detection of radar echoes. The clouds disappeared and the surface of Comporellon appeared in false colour, the boundaries between sectors of different constitution a little fuzzy and wavering.

'Is that the way it's going to look from now on?' asked Bliss, with some astonishment.

'Only till we drift below the clouds. Then it's back to sunlight.' Even as he spoke, the sunshine and normal visibility returned.

'I see,' said Bliss. Then, turning to him, 'But what I don't see is why it should matter to that official at the entry station whether Pel was deceiving his wife or not?'

'If that fellow, Kendray, had held you back, the news, I said, might reach Terminus and, therefore, Pelorat's wife. Pelorat would then be in trouble. I didn't specify the sort of trouble he would be in, but I tried to sound as though it would be bad. – There is a kind of freemasonry among males,' Trevize was grinning, now, 'and one male doesn't betray another fellow male. He would even help, if requested. The reasoning, I suppose, is that it might be the helper's turn next to be helped. I presume,' he added, turning a bit graver, 'that there is a similar freemasonry among women, but, not being a woman, I have never had an opportunity to observe it closely.'

Bliss's face resembled a pretty thundercloud. 'Is this a joke?' she demanded.

'No, I'm serious,' said Trevize. 'I don't say that that Kendray fellow let us through only to help Janov avoid angering his wife. The masculine freemasonry may simply have added the last push to my other arguments.'

'But that is horrible. It is its rules that hold society together and bind it into a whole. Is it such a light thing to disregard the rules for trivial reasons?'

'Well,' said Trevize, in instant defensiveness, 'some of the rules are themselves trivial. Few worlds are very particular about passage in and out of their space in times of peace and commercial prosperity, such as we have now, thanks to the Foundation. Comporellon, for some reason, is out of step – probably because of an obscure matter of internal politics. Why should we suffer over that?'

'That is beside the point. If we only obey those rules that we think are just and reasonable, then no rule will stand, for there is no rule that *some* will not think is unjust and unreasonable. And if we wish to push our own individual advantage, as we see it, then we will always find reason to believe that some hampering rule is unjust and unreasonable. What starts, then, as a shrewd trick ends in anarchy and disaster, even for the shrewd trickster, since he, too, will not survive the collapse of society.'

Trevize said, 'Society will not collapse that easily. You speak as Gaia, and Gaia cannot possibly understand the association of free individuals. Rules, established with reason and justice, can easily outlive their usefulness as circumstances change, yet can remain in force through inertia. It is then not only right, but useful, to break those rules as a way of advertising the fact that they have become useless – or even actually harmful.'

'Then every thief and murderer can argue he is serving humanity.'

'You go to extremes. In the superorganism of Gaia, there is automatic consensus on the rules of society and it occurs to no one to break them. One might as well say that Gaia vegetates and fossilizes. There is admittedly an element of disorder in free association, but that is the price one must pay for the ability to induce novelty and change. – On the whole, it's a reasonable price.'

Bliss's voice rose a notch. 'You are quite wrong if you think Gaia vegetates and fossilizes. Our deeds, our ways, our views are under constant self-examination. They do not persist, out of inertia, beyond reason. Gaia learns by experience and thought; and therefore changes when that is necessary.'

'Even if what you say is so, the self-examination and learning must be slow, because nothing but Gaia exists on Gaia. Here, in freedom, even when almost everyone agrees, there are bound to be a few who disagree and, in some cases, those few may be right, and if they are clever enough, enthusiastic enough, *right* enough, they will win out in the end and be heroes in future ages – like Hari Seldon, who perfected psychohistory, pitted his own thoughts against the entire Galactic Empire, and won.'

'He has won only so far, Trevize. The Second Empire he planned for will not come to pass. There will be Galaxia instead.'

'Will there?' said Trevize, grimly.

'It was *your* decision, and, however much you argue with me in favour of Isolates and of their freedom to be foolish and criminal, there is something in the hidden recesses of your mind that forced you to agree with me/us/Gaia when you made your choice.'

'What is present in the hidden recesses of my mind,' said Trevize, more grimly still, 'is what I seek. – There, to begin with,' he added, pointing to the viewscreen where a great city spread out to the horizon, a cluster of low structures climbing to occasional heights, surrounded by fields that were brown under a light frost.

Pelorat shook his head. 'Too bad. I meant to watch the approach, but I got caught up in listening to the argument.'

Trevize said, 'Never mind, Janov. You can watch when we leave. I'll promise to keep my mouth shut then, if you can persuade Bliss to control her own.'

And the *Far Star* descended a microwave beam to a landing at the spaceport.

14

Kendray looked grave when he returned to the entry station and watched the *Far Star* pass through. He was still clearly depressed at the close of his shift.

He was sitting down to his closing meal of the day when one of his mates, a gangling fellow with wide-set eyes, thin light hair, and eyebrows so blond they seemed absent, sat down next to him.

'What's wrong, Ken?' said the other.

Kendray's lips twisted. He said, 'That was a gravitic ship that just passed through, Gatis.'

'The odd-looking one with zero radioactivity?'

'That's why it wasn't radioactive. No fuel. Gravitic.'

Gatis nodded his head. 'What we were told to watch for, right?'

'Right.'

'And you got it. Leave it to you to be the lucky one.'

'Not so lucky. A woman without identification was on it – and I didn't report her.'

'*What?* Look, don't tell *me*. I don't want to know about it. Not another word. You may be a pal, but I'm not going to make myself an accomplice after the fact.'

'I'm not worried about that. Not very much. I *had* to send the ship down. They want that gravitic – or any gravitic. You know that.'

'Sure, but you could at least have reported the woman.'

'Didn't like to. She's not married. She was just picked up for – for use.'

'How many men on board?'

'Two.'

'And they just picked her up for – for that. They must be from Terminus.'

'That's right.'

'They don't care what they do on Terminus.'

'That's right.'

'Disgusting. And they get away with it.'

'One of them was married, and he didn't want his wife to know. If I reported her, his wife would find out.'

'Wouldn't she be back on Terminus?'

'Of course, but she'd find out anyway.'

'Serve the fellow right if his wife did find out.'

'I agree – but *I* can't be the one to be responsible for it.'

'They'll hammer you for not reporting it. Not wanting to make trouble for a guy is no excuse.'

'Would *you* have reported him?'

'I'd have had to, I suppose.'

'No, you wouldn't. The government wants that ship. If I had insisted on putting the woman on report, the men on the ship would have changed their minds about landing and would have pulled away to some other planet. The government wouldn't have wanted that.'

'But will they believe you?'

'I think so. – A very cute-looking woman, too. Imagine a woman like that being willing to come along with two men, and married men with the nerve to take advantage. – You know, it's tempting.'

'I don't think you'd want the missus to know you said that – or even thought that.'

Kendray said defiantly, 'Who's going to tell her? You?'

'Come on. You know better than that.' Gatis' look of indignation faded quickly, and he said, 'It's not going to do those guys any good, you know, you letting them through.'

'I know.'

'The people down surface-way will find out soon enough, and even if *you* get away with it, *they* won't.'

'I know,' said Kendray, 'but I'm sorry for them. Whatever trouble the woman will make for them will be as nothing to what the ship will make for them. The captain made a few remarks –'

Kendray paused, and Gatis said eagerly, 'Like what?'

'Never mind,' said Kendray. 'If it comes out, it's my butt.'

'I'm not going to repeat it.'

'Neither am I. But I'm sorry for those two men from Terminus.'

15

To anyone who has been in space and experienced its changelessness, the real excitement of space flight comes when it is time to land on a new planet. The ground speeds backwards under you as you catch glimpses of land and water, of geometrical areas and lines that might represent fields and roads. You become aware of the green of growing things, the grey of concrete, the brown of bare ground, the white of snow. Most of all, there is the excitement of populated conglomerates; cities which, on each world, have their own characteristic geometry and architectural variants.

In an ordinary ship, there would have been the excitement of touching down and skimming across a runway. For the *Far Star*, it was different. It floated through the air, was slowed by skilfully balancing air resistance and gravity, and finally made to come to rest above the spaceport. The wind was gusty and that introduced an added complication. The *Far Star*, when adjusted to low response to gravitational pull, was not only abnormally low in weight, but in mass as well. If its mass were too close to zero, the wind would blow it away rapidly. Hence, gravitational response had to be raised and jet-thrusts had to be delicately used not only against the planet's pull but against the wind's push, and in a manner that matched the shift in wind intensity closely. Without an adequate computer, it could not possibly have been done properly.

Downward and downward, with small unavoidable shifts in this direction and that, drifted the ship until it finally sank into the outlined area that marked its assigned position in the port.

The sky was a pale blue, intermingled with flat white, when the *Far Star* landed. The wind remained gusty even at ground level and though it was now no longer a navigational peril, it produced a chill that Trevize winced at. He realized at once that their clothing supply was totally unsuited to Comporellian weather.

Pelorat, on the other hand, looked about with appreciation and drew his breath deeply through his nose with relish, liking the bite of the cold, at least for the moment. He even deliberately unseamed his coat in order to feel the wind against his chest. In a little while, he knew, he would seam up again and adjust his scarf, but for now he wanted to *feel* the existence of an atmosphere. One never did aboard ship.

Bliss drew her coat closely about herself, and, with gloved hands, dragged her hat down to cover her ears. Her face was crumpled in misery and she seemed close to tears.

She muttered, 'This world is evil. It hates and mistreats us.'

'Not at all, Bliss dear,' said Pelorat earnestly. 'I'm sure the inhabitants like this world, and that it – uh – likes them, if you want to put it that way. We'll be indoors soon enough, and it will be warm there.'

Almost as an afterthought, he flipped one side of his coat outwards and curved it about her, while she snuggled against his shirtfront.

Trevize did his best to ignore the temperature. He obtained a magnetized card from the port authority, checking it on his pocket computer to make sure that it gave the necessary details – his aisle and lot number, the name and engine number of his ship, and so on. He checked once more to make sure that the ship was tightly secured, and then took out the maximum insurance allowed against the chance of misadventure (useless, actually, since the *Far Star* should be invulnerable at the likely Comporellian level of technology, and was entirely irreplaceable at whatever price, if it were not).

Trevize found the taxi-station where it ought to be. (A number of the facilities at spaceports were standardized in position, appearance, and manner of use. They had to be, in view of the multiworld nature of the clientele.)

He signalled for a taxi, punching out the destination merely as 'City'.

A taxi glided up to them on diamagnetic skis, drifting slightly under the impulse of the wind, and trembling under the vibration of its not-quite-silent engine. It was a dark grey in colour and bore its white taxi-insignia on the back doors. The taxi-driver was wearing a dark coat and a white, furred hat.

Pelorat, becoming aware, said softly, 'The planetary decor seems to be black and white.'

Trevize said, 'It may be more lively in the city proper.'

The driver spoke into a small microphone, perhaps in order to avoid opening the window. 'Going to the city, folks?'

There was a gentle singsong to his Galactic dialect that was rather attractive, and he was not hard to understand – always a relief on a new world.

Trevize said, 'That's right,' and the rear door slid open.

Bliss entered, followed by Pelorat, and then by Trevize. The door closed and warm air welled upwards.

Bliss rubbed her hands and breathed a long sigh of relief.

The taxi pulled out slowly, and the driver said, 'That ship you came in is gravitic, isn't it?'

Trevize said drily, 'Considering the way it came down, would you doubt it?'

The driver said, 'Is it from Terminus, then?'

Trevize said, 'Do you know any other world that could build one?'

The driver seemed to digest that as the taxi took on speed. He then said, 'Do you always answer a question with a question?'

Trevize couldn't resist. 'Why not?'

'In that case, how would you answer me if I asked if your name were Golan Trevize?'

'I would answer: What makes you ask?'

The taxi came to a halt at the outskirts of the spaceport and the driver said, 'Curiosity! I ask again: Are you Golan Trevize?'

Trevize's voice became stiff and hostile, 'What business is that of yours?'

'My friend,' said the driver. 'We're not moving till you answer the question. And if you don't answer in a clear yes or no in about two seconds, I'm turning the heat off in the passenger compartment and we'll keep on waiting. Are you Golan Trevize, Councilman of Terminus? If your answer is in the negative you will have to show me your identification papers.'

Trevize said, 'Yes, I am Golan Trevize, and as a Councilman of the Foundation, I expect to be treated with all the courtesy due my rank. Your failure to do so will have you in hot water, fellow. Now what?'

'Now we can proceed a little more lightheartedly.' The taxi began to move again. 'I choose my passengers carefully, and I had expected to pick up two men only. The woman was a surprise and I might have made a mistake. As it is, if I have you, then I can leave it to you to explain the woman when you reach your destination.'

'You don't know my destination.'

'As it happens, I do. You're going to the Department of Transportation.'

'That's not where I want to go.'

'That matters not one little bit, Councilman. If I were a taxi-driver, I'd take you where you want to go. Since I'm not, I take you where *I* want you to go.'

'Pardon me,' said Pelorat, leaning forward, 'you certainly seem to be a taxi-driver. You're driving a taxi.'

'Anyone might drive a taxi. Not everyone has a licence to do so. And not every car that looks like a taxi is a taxi.'

Trevize said, 'Let's stop playing games. Who are you and what are you doing? Remember that you'll have to account for this to the Foundation.'

'Not I,' said the driver. 'My superiors, perhaps. I'm an agent of the Comporellian Security Force. I am under orders to treat you with all respect due to your rank, but you must go where I take you. And be very careful how you react, for this vehicle is armed, and I am under orders to defend myself against attack.'

16

The vehicle, having reached cruising speed, moved with absolute, smooth quiet, and Trevize sat there in quietness as if frozen. He was aware, without actually looking, of Pelorat glancing at him now and then with a look of uncertainty on his face, a 'What do we do now? Please tell me' look.

Bliss, a quick glance told him, sat calmly, apparently unconcerned. Of course, she was a whole world in herself. All of Gaia, though it might be at Galactic distances, was wrapped up in her skin. She had resources that could be called on in a true emergency.

But, then, what had happened?

Clearly, the official at the entry station, following routine, had sent down his report – omitting Bliss – and it had attracted the interest of the security people and, of all things, the Department of Transportation. Why?

It was peacetime and he knew of no specific tensions between Comporellon and the Foundation. He himself was an important Foundation official –

Wait, he had told the official at the entry station – Kendray, his name had been – that he was on important business with the Comporellian government. He had stressed that in his attempt to get through. Kendray must have reported that as well and *that* would rouse all sorts of interest.

He hadn't anticipated that, and he certainly should have.

What, then, about his supposed gift of rightness? Was he beginning to believe that he was the black box that Gaia thought he was – or said it thought he was. Was he being led into a quagmire by the growth of an overconfidence built on superstition?

How could he for one moment be trapped in that folly? Had he never in his life been wrong? Did he know what the weather would be tomorrow? Did he win large amounts in games of chance? The answers were no, no, and no.

Well, then, was it only in the large, inchoate things that he was always right? How could he tell?

Forget that! – After all, the mere fact that he had stated he had important state business – no, it was 'Foundation security' that he had said –

Well, then, the mere fact that he was there on a matter of Foundation security, coming, as he had, secretly and unheralded, would surely attract their attention. – Yes, but until they knew what it was all about they would surely act with the utmost circumspection. They would be ceremonious and treat him as a high dignitary. They would *not* kidnap him and make use of threats.

Yet that was exactly what they had done. Why?

What made them feel strong enough and powerful enough to treat a Councilman of Terminus in such a fashion?

Could it be Earth? Was the same force that hid the world of origin so effectively, even against the great mentalists of the Second Foundation, now working to circumvent his search for Earth in the very first stage of that search. Was Earth omniscient? Omnipotent.

Trevize shook his head. That way lay paranoia. Was he going to blame Earth for everything? Was every quirk of behaviour, every bend in the road, every twist of circumstance, to be the result of the secret machinations of Earth? As soon as he began to think in that fashion, he was defeated.

At that point, he felt the vehicle decelerating and was brought back to reality at a stroke.

It occurred to him that he had never, even for one moment,

looked at the city through which they had been passing. He looked about now, a touch wildly. The buildings were low, but it was a cold planet – most of the structures were probably underground.

He saw no trace of colour and that seemed against human nature.

Occasionally, he could see a person pass, well bundled. But, then, the people, like the buildings themselves, were probably mostly underground.

The taxi had stopped before a low, broad building, set in a depression, the bottom of which Trevize could not see. Some moments passed and it continued to remain there, the driver himself motionless as well. His tall, white hat nearly touched the roof of the vehicle.

Trevize wondered fleetingly how the driver managed to step in and out of the vehicle without knocking his hat off, then said, with the controlled anger one would expect in a haughty and mistreated official, 'Well, driver, what now?'

The Comporellian version of the glittering field-partition that separated the driver from the passengers was not at all primitive. Sound waves could pass through – though Trevize was quite certain that material objects, at reasonable energies, could not.

The driver said, 'Someone will be up to get you. Just sit back and take it easy.'

Even as he said this, three heads appeared in a low, smooth ascent from the depression in which the building rested. After that, there came the rest of the bodies. Clearly, the newcomers were moving up the equivalent of an escalator, but Trevize could not see the details of the device from where he sat.

As the three approached, the passenger door of the taxi opened and a flood of cold air swept inward.

Trevize stepped out, seaming his coat to the neck. The other two followed him – Bliss with considerable reluctance.

The three Comporellians were shapeless, wearing garments that ballooned outwards and were probably electrically heated. Trevize felt scorn at that. There was little use for such things on Terminus, and the one time he had borrowed a heat-coat during winter on the nearby planet of Anacreon, he discovered it had a tendency to grow warmer at a slow rate so that by the time he realized he was too warm he was perspiring uncomfortably.

As the Comporellians approached, Trevize noted with a distinct sense of indignation that they were armed. Nor did they try to conceal the fact. Quite the contrary. Each had a blaster in a holster attached to the outer garment.

One of the Comporellians, having stepped up to confront Trevize, said gruffly, 'Your pardon, Councilman,' and then pulled his coat open with a rough movement. He had inserted questing hands which moved quickly up and down Trevize's sides, back, chest, and thighs. The coat was shaken and felt. Trevize was too overcome by confused astonishment to realize he had been rapidly and efficiently searched till it was over.

Pelorat, his chin drawn down and his mouth in a twisted grimace, was undergoing a similar indignity at the hands of a second Comporellian.

The third was approaching Bliss, who did not wait to be touched. She, at least, knew what to expect, somehow, for she whipped off her coat and, for a moment, stood there in her light clothing exposed to the whistle of the wind.

She said, freezingly enough to match the temperature, 'You can see I'm not armed.'

And indeed anyone could. The Comporellian shook the coat, as though by its weight he could tell if it contained a weapon – perhaps he could – and retreated.

Bliss put on her coat again, huddling into it, and for a moment Trevize admired her gesture. He knew how she felt about the cold, but she had not allowed a tremor or shiver to escape her as she had stood there in thin blouse and slacks. (Then he wondered if, in the emergency, she might not have drawn warmth from the rest of Gaia.)

One of the Comporellians gestured, and the three Outworlders followed him. The other two Comporellians fell behind. The one or two pedestrians who were on the street did not bother to watch what was happening. Either they were too accustomed to the sight or, more likely, had their minds occupied with getting to some indoor destination as soon as possible.

Trevize saw now that it was a moving ramp up which the Comporellians had ascended. They were descending now, all six of them, and passed through a lock arrangement almost as complicated as that on a spaceship – to keep heat inside, no doubt, rather than air.

And then, at once, they were inside a huge building.

5
Struggle for the Ship

17

Trevize's first impression was that he was on the set of a hyperdrama – specifically, that of a historical romance of Imperial days. There was a particular set, with few variations (perhaps only one existed and was used by every hyperdrama producer, for all he knew), that represented the great world-girdling planet-city of Trantor in its prime.

There were the large spaces, the busy scurry of pedestrians, the small vehicles speeding along the lanes reserved for them.

Trevize looked up, almost expecting to see air-taxis climbing into dim vaulted recesses, but that at least was absent. In fact, as his initial astonishment subsided, it was clear that the building was far smaller than one would expect on Trantor. It was *only* a building and not part of a complex that stretched unbroken for thousands of miles in every direction.

The colours were different, too. On the hyperdramas, Trantor was always depicted as impossibly garish in colouring and the clothing was, if taken literally, thoroughly impractical and unserviceable. However, all those colours and frills were meant to serve a symbolic purpose for they indicated the decadence (a view that was obligatory, these days) of the Empire, and of Trantor particularly.

If that were so, however, Comporellon was the very reverse of decadent, for the colour-scheme that Pelorat had remarked upon at the spaceport was here borne out.

The walls were in shades of grey, the ceilings white, the clothing of the population in black, grey and white. Occasionally, there was an all-black costume; even more occasionally, an all-grey; never an all-white that Trevize could see. The pattern was always different, however, as though people, deprived of colour, still managed, irrepressibly, to find ways of asserting individuality.

Faces tended to be expressionless or, if not that, then grim. Women wore their hair short; men longer, but pulled backwards into short queues. No one looked at anyone else as he or she passed. Everyone seemed to breathe a purposefulness, as though there was definite business on each mind and room for nothing else. Men and women dressed alike, with only length of hair and the slight bulge of breast and width of hip marking the difference.

The three were guided into an elevator that went down five levels. There they emerged and were moved on to a door on which there appeared in small and unobtrusive lettering, white on grey, 'Mitza Lizalor, MinTrans'.

The Comporellian in the lead touched the lettering, which, after a moment, glowed in response. The door opened and they walked in.

It was a large room and rather empty, the bareness of content serving, perhaps, as a kind of conscious consumption of space designed to show the power of the occupant.

Two guards stood against the far wall, faces expressionless and eyes firmly fixed on those entering. A large desk filled the centre of the room, set perhaps just a little back of centre. Behind the desk was, presumably, Mitza Lizalor, large of body, smooth of face, dark of eyes. Two strong and capable hands with long, square-ended fingers, rested on the desk.

The MinTrans (Minister of Transportation, Trevize assumed) had the lapels of the outer garment a broad and dazzling white against the dark grey of the rest of the costume. The double bar of white extended diagonally below the lapels, across the garment itself and crossing at the centre of the chest. Trevize could see that although the garment was cut in such a fashion as to obscure the swelling of women's breasts on either side, the white X called attention to them.

The Minister was undoubtedly a woman. Even if her breasts were ignored, her short hair showed it, and though there was no makeup on her face, her features showed it, too.

Her voice, too, was indisputably feminine, a rich contralto.

She said, 'Good afternoon. It is not often that we are honoured by a visit of men from Terminus. – And of an unreported woman as well.' Her eyes passed from one to another, then settled on Trevize, who was standing stiffly and frowningly erect. 'And one of the men a member of the Council, too.'

'A Councilman of the Foundation,' said Trevize, trying to make his voice ring. 'Councilman Golan Trevize on a mission from the Foundation.'

'On a mission?' The Minister's eyebrows rose.

'On a mission,' repeated Trevize. 'Why, then, are we being treated as felons? Why have we been taken into custody by armed guards and brought here as prisoners? The Council of the Foundation, I hope you understand, will not be pleased to hear of this.'

'And in any case,' said Bliss, her voice seeming a touch shrill in comparison with that of the older woman, 'are we to remain standing indefinitely?'

The Minister gazed coolly at Bliss for a long moment, then raised an arm and said, 'Three chairs! Now!'

A door opened and three men, dressed in the usual sombre Comporellian fashion, brought in three chairs at a semitrot. The three people standing before the desk sat down.

'There,' said the Minister, with a wintry smile, 'are we comfortable?'

Trevize thought not. The chairs were uncushioned, cold to the touch, flat of surface and back, making no compromise with the shape of the body. He said, 'Why are we here?'

The Minister consulted papers lying on her desk. 'I will explain as soon as I am certain of my facts. Your ship is the *Far Star* out of Terminus. Is that correct, Councilman?'

'It is.'

The Minister looked up. 'I used your title, Councilman. Will you, as a courtesy, use mine?'

'Would Madam Minister be sufficient? Or is there an honorific?'

'No honorific, sir, and you need not double your words. "Minister" is sufficient, or "Madam" if you weary of repetition.'

'Then my answer to your question is: It is, Minister.'

'The Captain of the ship is Golan Trevize, citizen of the Foundation and member of the Council on Terminus – a freshman Councilman, actually. And you are Trevize. Am I correct in all this, Councilman?'

'You are, Minister. And since I am a citizen of the Foundation –'

'I am not yet done, Councilman. Save your objections till I am. Accompanying you is Janov Pelorat, scholar, historian, and citizen of the Foundation. And that is you, is it not, Dr Pelorat?'

Pelorat could not suppress a slight start as the Minister turned her keen glance on him. He said, 'Yes, it is, my d–' He paused, and began again, 'Yes, it is, Minister.'

The Minister clasped her hands stiffly. 'There is no mention in the report that has been forwarded to me of a woman. Is this woman a member of the ship's complement?'

'She is, Minister,' said Trevize.

'Then I address myself to the woman. Your name?'

'I am known as Bliss,' said Bliss, sitting erectly and speaking with calm clarity, 'though my full name is longer, Madam. Do you wish it all?'

'I will be content with Bliss for the moment. Are you a citizen of the Foundation, Bliss?'

'I am not, Madam.'

'Of what world are you a citizen, Bliss?'

'I have no documents attesting to citizenship with respect to any world, Madam.'

'No papers, Bliss?' She made a small mark on the papers before her. 'That fact is noted. What is it you are doing on board the ship?'

'I am a passenger, Madam.'

'Did either Councilman Trevize or Dr Pelorat ask to see your papers before you boarded, Bliss?'

'No, Madam.'

'Did you inform them that you were without papers, Bliss?'

'No, Madam.'

'What is your function on board ship, Bliss? Does your name suit your function?'

Bliss said, proudly, 'I am a passenger and have no other function.'

Trevize broke in, 'Why are you badgering this woman, Minister? What law has she broken?'

Minister Lizalor's eyes shifted from Bliss to Trevize. She said, 'You are an Outworlder, Councilman, and do not know our laws. Nevertheless, you are subject to them if you choose to visit our world. You do not bring your laws with you; that is a general rule of Galactic law, I believe.'

'Granted, Minister, but that doesn't tell me which of your laws she has broken.'

'It is a general rule in the Galaxy, Councilman, that a visitor from a world outside the dominions of the world she is visiting have her identification papers with her. Many worlds are lax in this respect, valuing tourism, or indifferent to the rule of order. We of Comporellon are not. We are a world of law and rigid in its application. She is a worldless person, and as such, breaks our law.'

Trevize said, 'She had no choice in the matter. I was piloting the ship, and I brought it down to Comporellon. She had to accompany us, Minister, or do you suggest she should have asked to be jettisoned in space.'

'This merely means that you, too, have broken our law, Councilman.'

'No, that is not so, Minister. I am not an Outworlder. I am a citizen of the Foundation, and Comporellon and the worlds subject to it are an Associated Power of the Foundation. As a citizen of the Foundation, I can travel freely here.'

'Certainly, Councilman, as long as you have documentation to prove that you are indeed a citizen of the Foundation.'

'Which I do, Minister.'

'Yet even as a citizen of the Foundation, you do not have the right to break our law by bringing a worldless person with you.'

Trevize hesitated. Clearly, the border guard, Kendray, had not kept faith with him, so there was no point in protecting him. He said, 'We were not stopped at the immigration station and I considered that implicit permission to bring this woman with me, Minister.'

'It is true you were not stopped, Councilman. It is true the woman was not reported by the immigration authorities and was passed through. I can suspect, however, that the officials at the entry station decided – and quite correctly – that it was more important to get your ship to the surface than to worry about a worldless person. What they did was, strictly speaking, an infraction of the rules, and the matter will have to be dealt with in the proper fashion, but I have no doubt that the decision will be that the infraction was justified. We are a world of rigid law, Councilman, but we are not rigid beyond the dictates of reason.'

Trevize said at once, 'Then I call upon reason to bend your rigour now, Minister. If, indeed, you received no information from the immigration station to the effect that a worldless person was on board ship, then you had no knowledge that we were breaking any law at the time we landed. Yet it is quite apparent that you were prepared to take us into custody the moment we landed, and you did, in fact, do so. Why did you do so, when you had no reason to think any law was being broken?'

The Minister smiled. 'I understand your confusion, Councilman. Please let me assure you that whatever knowledge we had gained – or had not gained – as to the worldless condition of your passenger had nothing to do with your being taken into custody. We are acting on behalf of the Foundation, of which, as you point out, we are an Associated Power.'

Trevize stared at her. 'But that's impossible, Minister. It's even worse. It's ridiculous.'

The Minister's chuckle was like the smooth flow of honey. She said, 'I am interested in the way you consider it worse to be ridiculous than impossible, Councilman. I agree with you there. Unfortunately for you, however, it is neither. Why should it be?'

'Because I am an official of the Foundation government, on a mission for them, and it is absolutely inconceivable that they would wish to arrest me, or that they would even have the power to do so, since I have legislative immunity.'

'Ah, you omit my title, but you are deeply moved and that is perhaps forgivable. Still, I am not asked to arrest you directly. I do so only that I may carry out what I *am* asked to do, Councilman.'

'Which is, Minister?' said Trevize, trying to keep his emotion under control in the face of this formidable woman.

'Which is to commandeer your ship, Councilman, and return it to the Foundation.'

'What?'

'Again you omit my title, Councilman. That is very slipshod of you and no way to press your own case. The ship is not yours, I presume. Was it designed by you, or built by you, or paid for by you?'

'Of course not, Minister. It was assigned to me by the Foundation government.'

'Then, presumably, the Foundation government has the right to cancel that assignment, Councilman. It is a valuable ship, I imagine.'

Trevize did not answer.

The Minister said, 'It is a gravitic ship, Councilman. There cannot be many and even the Foundation must have but a very few. They must regret having assigned one of those very few to you. Perhaps you can persuade them to assign you another and less valuable ship that will nevertheless amply suffice for your mission. – But we must have the ship in which you have arrived.'

'No, Minister, I cannot give up the ship. I cannot believe the Foundation asks it of you.'

The Minister smiled. 'Not of me solely, Councilman. Not of Comporellon, specifically. We have reason to believe that the request was sent out to every one of the many worlds and regions under Foundation jurisdiction or association. From this, I deduce that the Foundation does not know your itinerary and is seeking you with a certain angry vigour. From which I further deduce that you have no mission to deal with Comporellon on behalf of the Foundation – since in that case they would know where you were and deal with us specifically. In short, Councilman, you have been lying to me.'

Trevize said, with a certain difficulty, 'I would like to see a copy of the request you have received from the Foundation government, Minister. I am entitled, I think, to that.'

'Certainly, if all this comes to legal action. We take our legal forms very seriously, Councilman, and your rights will be fully protected, I assure you. It would be better and easier, however, if we come to an agreement here without the publicity and delay of legal action. We would prefer that, and, I am certain, so would the Foundation which cannot wish the Galaxy at large to know of a runaway Legislator. That would put the Foundation in a ridiculous light, and, by your estimate and mine, that would be worse than impossible.'

Trevize was again silent.

The Minister waited a moment, then went on, as imperturbable as ever. 'Come, Councilman, either way, by informal agreement or by legal action, we intend to have the ship. The penalty for bringing in a worldless passenger will depend on which route we take. Demand the law and she will represent an additional point against you and you will all suffer the full punishment for the crime, and that will not be light, I assure you. Come to an agreement, and your passenger can be sent away by commercial flight to any destination she wishes, and, for that matter, you two can accompany her, if you wish. Or, if the Foundation is willing, we can supply you with one of our own ships, a perfectly adequate one, provided, of course, that the Foundation will replace it with an equivalent ship of their own. Or, if, for any reason, you do not wish to return to Foundation-controlled territory, we might be willing to offer you refuge here and, perhaps, eventual Comporellian citizenship. You see you have many possibilities of gain if you come to a friendly arrangement, but none at all if you insist on your legal rights.'

Trevize said, 'Minister, you are too eager. You promise what you cannot do. You cannot offer me refuge in the face of a Foundation request that I be delivered to them.'

The Minister said, 'Councilman, I never promise what I cannot do. The Foundation's request is only for the ship. They make no request concerning you as an individual, or for anyone else on the ship. Their sole request is for the vessel.'

Trevize glanced quickly at Bliss, and said, 'May I have your permission, Minister, to consult with Dr Pelorat and Miss Bliss for a short while?'

'Certainly, Councilman. You may have fifteen minutes.'

'Privately, Minister.'

'You will be led to a room and, after fifteen minutes, you will be led back, Councilman. You will not be interfered with while you are there nor will we attempt to monitor your conversation. You have my word on that and I keep my word. However, you will be adequately guarded so do not be so foolish as to think of escaping.'

'We understand, Minister.'

'And when you come back, we will expect your free agreement to give up the ship. Otherwise, the law will take its course, and it will be much the worse for all of you, Councilman. Is that understood?'

'That is understood, Minister,' said Trevize, keeping his rage under tight control, since its expression would do him no good at all.

18

It was a small room, but it was well-lit, it contained a couch and two chairs, and one could hear the soft sound of a ventilating fan. On the whole, it was clearly more comfortable than the Minister's large and sterile office.

A guard had led them there, grave and tall, his hand hovering near the butt of his blaster. He remained outside the door as they entered and said, in a heavy voice, 'You have fifteen minutes.'

He had no sooner said that than the door slid shut, with a thud.

Trevize said, 'I can only hope that we can't be overheard.'

Pelorat said, 'She did give us her word, Golan.'

'You judge others by yourself, Janov. Her so-called "word" will not suffice. She will break it without hesitation if she wants to.'

'It doesn't matter,' said Bliss. 'I can shield this place.'

'You have a shielding device?' asked Pelorat.

Bliss smiled, with a sudden flash of white teeth. 'Gaia's mind is a shielding device, Pel. It's an enormous mind.'

'We are here,' said Trevize, angrily, 'because of the limitations of that enormous mind.'

'What do you mean?' said Bliss.

'When the triple confrontation broke up, you withdrew me from the minds of both the Mayor and that Second Foundationer, Gendibal. Neither was to think of me again, except distantly and indifferently. I was to be left to myself.'

'We had to do that,' said Bliss. 'You are our most important resource.'

'Yes. Golan Trevize, the ever-right. But you did not withdraw my ship from their minds, did you? Mayor Branno did not ask for me; she has no interest in me, but she *did* ask for the ship. She has not forgotten the ship.'

Bliss frowned.

Trevize said, 'Think about it. Gaia casually assumed that I included my ship; that we were a unit. If Branno didn't think of me, she wouldn't think of the ship. The trouble is that Gaia doesn't understand individuality. It thought of the ship and me as a single organism, and it was wrong to think that.'

Bliss said, softly, 'That is possible.'

'Well, then,' said Trevize, flatly, 'it's up to you to rectify that mistake. I must have my gravitic ship and my computer. Nothing else will do. Therefore, Bliss, make sure that I keep the ship. You can control minds.'

'Yes, Trevize, but we do not exercise that control lightly. We did it in connection with the triple confrontation, but do you know how long that confrontation was planned? Calculated? Weighed? It took – literally – many years. I cannot simply walk up to a woman and adjust the mind to suit someone's convenience.'

'Is this a time –'

Bliss went on forcefully. 'If I began to follow such a course of action where do we stop? I might have influenced the agent's mind at the entry station and we would have passed through at once. I might have influenced the agent's mind in the vehicle, and he would have let us go.'

'Well, since you mention it, why didn't you do these things?'

'Because we don't know where it would lead. We don't know the side-effects, which may well turn out to make the situation worse. If I adjust the Minister's mind now, that will affect her dealings with others with whom she will come in contact and, since she is a high official in her government, it may affect interstellar relations. Until such time as the matter is thoroughly worked out, we dare not touch her mind.'

'Then why are you with us.'

'Because the time may come when your life is threatened. I must protect your life at all costs, even at the cost of my Pel or of myself. Your life was not threatened at the entry station. It is not threatened now. You must work this out for yourself, and do so at least until Gaia can estimate the consequences of some sort of action and take it.'

Trevize fell into a period of thought. Then he said, 'In that case, I have to try something. It may not work.'

The door moved open, thwacking into its socket as noisily as it had closed.

The guard said, 'Come out.'

As they emerged, Pelorat whispered, 'What are you going to do, Golan?'

Trevize shook his head and whispered, 'I'm not entirely sure. I will have to improvise.'

19

Minister Lizalor was still at her desk when they returned to her office. Her face broke into a grim smile as they walked in.

She said, 'I trust, Councilman Trevize, that you have returned to tell me that you are giving up this Foundation ship you have.'

'I have come, Minister,' said Trevize calmly, 'to discuss terms.'

'There are no terms to discuss, Councilman. A trial, if you insist on one, can be arranged very quickly and would be carried through even more quickly. I guarantee your conviction even in a perfectly fair trial since your guilt in bringing in a worldless person is obvious and indisputable. After that, we will be legally justified in seizing the ship and you three would suffer heavy penalties. Don't force those penalties on yourself just to delay us for a day.'

'Nevertheless, there are terms to discuss, Minister, because no matter how quickly you convict us, you cannot seize the ship without my consent. Any attempt you make to force your way into the ship without me will destroy it, and the spaceport with it, and every human being in the spaceport. This will surely infuriate the Foundation, something you dare not do. Threatening us or mistreating us in order to force me to open the ship, is surely against your law, and if you break your own law in desperation and subject us to torture or even to a period of cruel and unusual imprisonment, the Foundation will find out about it and they will be even more furious. However much they want the ship they cannot allow a precedent that would permit the mistreatment of Foundation citizens. – Shall we talk terms?'

'This is all nonsense,' said the Minister, scowling. 'If necessary, we will call in the Foundation itself. They will know how to open their own ship, or *they* will force you to open it.'

Trevize said, 'You do not use my title, Minister, but you are emotionally moved, so that is perhaps forgivable. You know that the very last thing you will do is call in the Foundation, since you have no intention of delivering the ship to them.'

The smile faded from the Minister's face. 'What nonsense is this, Councilman?'

'The kind of nonsense, Minister, that others, perhaps, ought not to hear. Let my friend and the young woman go to some comfortable hotel room and obtain the rest they need so badly and let your guards leave, too. They can remain just outside and you can have them leave you a blaster. You are not a small woman and, with a blaster, you have nothing to fear from me. I am unarmed.'

The Minister leaned towards him across the desk. 'I have nothing to fear from you in any case.'

Without looking behind her, she beckoned to one of the guards, who approached at once and came to a halt at her side with a stamp of his feet. She said, 'Guard, take that one and that one to Suite 5. They are to stay there and to be made comfortable and to be well guarded. You will be held responsible for any mistreatment they may receive, as well as for any breach of security.'

She stood up, and not all of Trevize's determination to maintain an absolute composure sufficed to keep him from flinching a little.

She was tall; as tall, at least, as Trevize's 1.85 metres, perhaps a centimetre or so taller. She had a narrow waistline, with the two white strips across her chest continuing into an encirclement of her waist, making it look even narrower. There was a massive grace about her and Trevize thought ruefully that her statement that she had nothing to fear from him might well be correct. In a rough-and-tumble, he thought, she would have no trouble pinning his shoulders to the mat.

She said, 'Come with me, Councilman. If you are going to talk nonsense, then, for your own sake, the fewer who hear you, the better.'

She led the way in a brisk stride, and Trevize followed, feeling shrunken in her massive shadow, a feeling he had never before had with a woman.

They entered an elevator and, as the door closed behind them, she said, 'We are alone now and if you are under the illusion, Councilman, that you can use force with me in order to accomplish some imagined purpose, please forget that.' The sing-song in her voice grew more pronounced as she said, with clear amusement, 'You look like a reasonably strong specimen, but I assure you I will have no trouble in breaking your arm – or your back, if I must. I am armed, but I will not have to use any weapon.'

Trevize scratched at his cheek as his eyes drifted first down, then up her body. 'Minister, I can hold my own in a wrestling match with any man my weight, but I have already decided to forfeit a bout with you. I know when I am outclassed.'

'Good,' said the Minister, and looked pleased.

Trevize said, 'Where are we going, Minister?'

'Down! Quite far down. Don't be upset, however. In the hyper-dramas, this would be a preliminary to taking you to a dungeon, I suppose, but we have no dungeons on Comporellon – only reasonable prisons. We are going to my private apartment; not as romantic as a dungeon in the bad old Imperial days, but much more comfortable.'

Trevize estimated that they were at least 50 metres below the surface of the planet, when the elevator door slid to one side and they stepped out.

20

Trevize looked about the apartment with clear surprise.

The Minister said primly, 'Do you disapprove of my living quarters, Councilman?'

'No, I have no reason to, Minister. I am merely surprised. I find it unexpected. The impression I had of your world from what little I saw and heard since arriving was that it was an – abstemious one, eschewing useless luxury.'

'So it is, Councilman. Our resources are limited, and our life must be as harsh as our climate.'

'But this, Minister,' and Trevize held out both hands as though to embrace the room where, for the first time on this world, he saw colour, where the couches were well-cushioned, where the light from the illuminated walls was soft, and where the floor was force-carpeted so that steps were springy and silent. 'This is surely luxury.'

'We eschew, as you say, Councilman, useless luxury; ostentatious luxury; wastefully excessive luxury. This, however, is private luxury which has its use. I work hard and bear much responsibility. I need a place where I can forget, for a while, the difficulties of my post.'

Trevize said, 'And do all Comporellians live like this when the eyes of others are averted, Minister?'

'It depends on the degree of work and responsibility. Few can afford to, or deserve to, or, thanks to our code of ethics, want to.'

'But you, Minister, can afford to, deserve to – and want to?'

The Minister said, 'Rank has its privileges as well as its duties. And now sit down, Councilman, and tell me of this madness of yours.' She sat down on the couch, which gave slowly under her solid weight, and pointed to an equally soft chair in which Trevize would be facing her at not too great a distance.

Trevize sat down. 'Madness, Minister?'

The Minister relaxed visibly, leaning her right elbow on a pillow. 'In private conversation, we need not observe the rules of formal discourse too punctiliously. You may call me Lizalor. I will call you Trevize. – Tell me what is on your mind, Trevize, and let us inspect it.'

Trevize crossed his legs and sat back in his chair. 'See here, Lizalor, you gave me the choice of either agreeing to give up the ship voluntarily, or of being subjected to a formal trial. In both cases, you would end up with the ship. – Yet you have been going out of your way to persuade me to adopt the former alternative. You are willing to offer me another ship to replace mine, so that my friends and I might go anywhere we chose. We might even stay here on Comporellon and qualify for citizenship, if we chose. In smaller things, you were willing to allow me fifteen minutes to consult with my friends. You were even willing to bring me here to your private quarters, while my friends are now, presumably, in comfortable quarters. In short, you are bribing me, Lizalor, rather desperately, to grant you the ship without the necessity of a trial.'

'Come, Trevize, are you in no mood to give me credit for humane impulses?'

'None.'

'Or the thought that voluntary surrender would be quicker and more convenient than a trial would be?'

'No! I would offer a different suggestion.'

'Which is?'

'A trial has one thing in its strong disfavour; it is a public affair. You have several times referred to this world's rigorous legal system, and I suspect it would be difficult to arrange a trial without its being fully recorded. If that were so, the Foundation would know of it and you would have to hand over the ship to it once the trial was over.'

'Of course,' said Lizalor, without expression. 'It is the Foundation that owns the ship.'

'But,' said Trevize, 'a private agreement with me would not have to be placed on formal record. You could have the ship and, since the Foundation would not know of the matter – they don't even know that we are on this world – Comporellon could keep the ship. That, I am sure, is what you intend to do.'

'Why should we do that?' She was still without expression. 'Are we not part of the Foundation Confederation?'

'Not quite. Your status is that of an Associated Power. In any Galactic map on which the member worlds of the Federation are shown in red, Comporellon and its dependent worlds would show up as a patch of pale pink.'

'Even so, as an Associated Power, we would surely co-operate with the Foundation.'

'Would you? Might not Comporellon be dreaming of total independence; even leadership? You are an old world. Almost all worlds claim to be older than they are, but Comporellon *is* an old world.'

Minister Lizalor allowed a cold smile to cross her face. 'The oldest, if some of our enthusiasts are to be believed.'

'Might there not have been a time when Comporellon was indeed the leading world of a relatively small group of worlds? Might you not still dream of recovering that lost position of power?'

'Do you think we dream of so impossible a goal. I called it madness before I knew your thoughts, and it is certainly madness now that I do.'

'Dreams may be impossible, yet still be dreamed. Terminus, located at the very edge of the Galaxy and with a five-century history that is briefer than that of any other world virtually rules the Galaxy. And shall Comporellon not? Eh?' Trevize was smiling.

Lizalor remained grave. 'Terminus reached that position, we are given to understand, by the working out of Hari Seldon's plan.'

'That is the psychological buttress of its superiority and it will hold only as long, perhaps, as people believe it. It may be that the Comporellian government does not believe it. Even so, Terminus also enjoys a technological buttress. Terminus's hegemony over the Galaxy undoubtedly rests on its advanced technology – of which the gravitic ship you are so anxious to have is an example. No other world but Terminus disposes of gravitic ships. If Comporellon could have one, and could learn its workings in detail, it would be bound to have taken a giant technological step forward. I don't think it would be sufficient to help you overcome Terminus's lead, but your government might think so.'

Lizalor said, 'You can't be serious in this. Any government that kept the ship in the face of the Foundation's desire to have it would surely experience the Foundation's wrath, and history shows that the Foundation can be quite uncomfortably wrathful.'

Trevize said, 'The Foundation's wrath would only be exerted if the Foundation knew there was something to be wrathful about.'

'In that case, Trevize – if we assume your analysis of the situation is something other than mad – would it not be to your benefit to give us the ship and drive a hard bargain? We would pay well for the chance of having it quietly, according to your line of argument.'

'Could you then rely on my not reporting the matter to the Foundation?'

'Certainly. Since you would have to report your own part in it.'

'I could report having acted under duress.'

'Yes. Unless your good sense told you that your Mayor would never believe that. – Come, make a deal.'

Trevize shook his head. 'I will not, Madam Lizalor. The ship is mine and it must stay mine. As I have told you, it will blow up with extraordinary power if you attempt to force an entry. I assure you I am telling you the truth. Don't rely on its being a bluff.'

'*You* could open it, and reinstruct the computer.'

'Undoubtedly, but I won't do that.'

Lizalor drew a heavy sigh. 'You know we could make you change your mind – if not by what we could do to you, then by what we could do to your friend, Dr Pelorat, or to the young woman.'

'Torture, Minister? Is that your law?'

'No, Councilman. But we might not have to do anything so crude. There is always the Psychic Probe.'

For the first time since entering the Minister's apartment, Trevize felt an inner chill.

'You can't do that either. The use of the Psychic Probe for anything but medical purposes is outlawed throughout the Galaxy.'

'But if we are driven to desperation –'

'I am willing to chance that,' said Trevize, 'for it would do you no good. My determination to retain my ship is so deep that the Psychic Probe would destroy my mind before it twisted it into giving it to you.' (*That* was a bluff, he thought, and the chill inside him deepened.) 'And even if you were so skilful as to persuade me without destroying my mind and if I were to open the ship and disarm it and hand it over to you, it would still do you no good. The ship's computer is even more advanced than the ship is, and it is designed somehow – I don't know how – to work at its full potential only with me. It is what I might call a one-person computer.'

'Suppose, then, you retained the ship, and remained its pilot. Would you consider piloting it for us – as an honoured Comporellian citizen? A large salary. Considerable luxury. Your friends, too.'

'No.'

'What is it you suggest? That we simply let you and your friends launch your ship and go off into the Galaxy? I warn you that before we allow you to do this, we might simply inform the Foundation that you are here with your ship, and leave all to them.'

'And lose the ship yourself?'

'If we must lose it, perhaps we would rather lose it to the Foundation than to an impudent Outworlder.'

'Then let me suggest a compromise of my own.'

'A compromise? Well, I will listen. Proceed.'

Trevize said carefully, 'I am on an important mission. It began with Foundation support. That support seems to have been suspended, but the mission remains important. Let me have Comporellian support instead and if I complete the mission successfully, Comporellon will benefit.'

Lizalor wore a dubious expression. 'And you will not return the ship to the Foundation?'

'I have never planned to do that. The Foundation would not be searching for the ship so desperately if *they* thought there was any intention of my casually returning it to them.'

'That is not quite the same thing as saying that you will give the ship to us.'

'Once I have completed the mission, the ship may be of no further use to me. In that case, I would not object to Comporellon having it.'

The two looked at each other in silence for a few moments.

Lizalor said, 'You use the conditional. The ship "may be". That is of no value to us.'

'I could make wild promises, but of what value would that be to you? The fact that my promises are cautious and limited should show you that they are at least sincere.'

'Clever,' said Lizalor, nodding. 'I like that. Well, what is your mission and how might it benefit Comporellon?'

Trevize said, 'No, no, it is your turn. Will you support me if I show you that the mission is of importance to Comporellon?'

Minister Lizalor rose from the couch, a tall, overpowering presence. 'I am hungry, Councilman Trevize, and I will get no further on an empty stomach. I will offer you something to eat and drink – in moderation. After that, we will finish the matter.'

And it seemed to Trevize that there was a rather carnivorous look of anticipation about her at that moment, so that he tightened his lips with just a bit of unease.

21

The meal might have been a nourishing one, but it was not one to delight the palate. The main course consisted of boiled beef in a mustardy sauce, resting on a foundation of a leafy vegetable Trevize did not recognize. Nor did he like it for it had a bitter-salty taste he did not enjoy. He found out later it was a form of seaweed.

There was, afterwards, a piece of fruit that tasted something like an apple tainted by peach (not bad, actually) and a hot, dark beverage that was bitter enough for Trevize to leave half behind and ask if he might have some cold water instead. The portions were all small, but, under the circumstances, Trevize did not mind.

The meal had been private, with no servants in view. The Minister had herself heated and served the food, and herself cleared away the dishes and cutlery.

'I hope you found the meal pleasant,' said Lizalor, as they left the dining room.

'Quite pleasant,' said Trevize, without enthusiasm.

The Minister again took her seat on the couch. 'Let us return then,' she said, 'to our earlier discussion. You had mentioned that Comporellon might resent the Foundation's lead in technology and its overlordship of the Galaxy. In a way that's true, but that aspect of the situation would interest only those who are interested in interstellar politics, and they are comparatively few. What is much more to the point is that the average Comporellian is horrified at the immorality of the Foundation. There is immorality in most worlds, but it seems most marked in Terminus. I would say that any anti-Terminus animus that exists on this world is rooted in that, rather than in more abstract matters.'

'Immorality?' said Trevize, puzzled. 'Whatever the faults of the Foundation you have to admit it runs its part of the Galaxy with reasonable efficiency and fiscal honesty. Civil rights are, by and large, respected and –'

'Councilman Trevize, I speak of *sexual* morality.'

'In that case, I certainly don't understand you. We are a thoroughly moral society, sexually speaking. Women are well-represented in every facet of social life. Our Mayor is a woman and nearly half the council consists of –'

The Minister allowed a look of exasperation to fleet across her face. 'Councilman, are you mocking me? Surely you know what sexual morality means. Is, or is not, marriage a sacrament upon Terminus?'

'What do you mean by sacrament?'

'Is there a formal marriage ceremony binding a couple together?'

'Certainly, if people wish it. Such a ceremony simplifies tax problems and inheritance.'

'But divorce can take place.'

'Of course. It would certainly be sexually immoral to keep people tied to each other, when –'

'Are there no religious restrictions?'

'Religious? There are people who make a philosophy out of ancient cults, but what has that to do with marriage?'

'Councilman, here on Comporellon, every aspect of sex is strongly controlled. It may not take place out of marriage. Its expression is limited even within marriage. We are sadly shocked at those worlds, at Terminus, particularly, where sex seems to be considered a mere social pleasure of no great importance to be indulged in when, how, and with whom one pleases without regard to the values of religion.'

Trevize shrugged. 'I'm sorry, but I can't undertake to reform the Galaxy, or even Terminus – and what has this to do with the matter of my ship?'

'I'm talking about public opinion in the matter of your ship and how it limits my ability to compromise the matter. The people of Comporellon would be horrified if they found you had taken a young and attractive woman on board to serve the lustful urges of you and your companion. It is out of consideration for the safety of the three of you that I have been urging you to accept peaceful surrender in place of a public trial.'

Trevize said, 'I see you have used the meal to think of a new type of persuasion by threat. Am I now to fear a lynch mob?'

'I merely point out dangers. Will you be able to deny that the woman you have taken on board ship is anything other than a sexual convenience?'

'Of course I can deny it. Bliss is the companion of my friend, Dr Pelorat. He has no other competing companion. You may not define their state as marriage, but I believe that in Pelorat's mind, and in the woman's, too, there is a marriage between them.'

'Are you telling me you are not involved yourself?'

'Certainly not,' said Trevize. 'What do you take me for?'

'I cannot tell. I do not know your notions of morality.'

'Then let me explain that my notions of morality tell me that I don't trifle with my friend's possessions – or his companionships.'

'You are not even tempted?'

'I can't control the fact of temptation, but there's no chance of my giving in to it.'

'No chance at all? Perhaps you are not interested in women.'

'Don't you believe that. I am interested.'

'How long has it been since you have had sex with a woman?'

'Months. Not at all since I left Terminus.'

'Surely you don't enjoy that.'

'I certainly don't,' said Trevize, with strong feeling, 'but the situation is such that I have no choice.'

'Surely your friend, Pelorat, noting your suffering, would be willing to share his woman.'

'I show him no evidence of suffering, but if I had, he would not be willing to share Bliss. Nor, I think, would the woman consent. She is not attracted to me.'

'Do you say that because you have tested the matter?'

'I have not tested it. I make the judgement without feeling the need to test it. In any case, I don't particularly like her.'

'Astonishing! She is what a man would consider attractive.'

'Physically, she *is* attractive. Nevertheless, she does not appeal to me. For one thing, she is too young, too child-like in some ways.'

'Do you prefer women of maturity, then?'

Trevize paused. Was there a trap here? He said cautiously, 'I am old enough to value some women of maturity. And what has this to do with my ship?'

Lizalor said, 'For a moment, forget your ship. – I am forty-six years old, and I am not married. I have somehow been too busy to marry.'

'In that case, by the rules of your society, you must have remained continent all your life. Is that why you asked how long it had been since I have had sex? Are you asking my advice in the matter? – If so, I say it is not food and drink. It is uncomfortable to do without sex, but not impossible.'

The Minister smiled and there was again that carnivorous look in her eyes. 'Don't mistake me, Trevize. Rank has its privileges and it is possible to be discreet. I am not altogether an abstainer. Nevertheless, Comporellian men are unsatisfying. I accept the fact that morality is an absolute good, but it does tend to burden the men of this world with guilt, so that they become unadventurous, unenterprising, slow to begin, quick to conclude, and, in general, unskilled.'

Trevize said, very cautiously, 'There is nothing I can do about that, either.'

'Are you implying that the fault may be mine? That I am uninspiring?'

Trevize raised a hand. 'I don't say that at all.'

'In that case, how would *you* react, given the opportunity? You, a man from an immoral world, who must have had a vast variety of sexual experiences of all kinds, who is under the pressure of several months of enforced abstinence even though in the constant presence of a young and charming woman. How would *you* react in the presence of a woman such as myself, who is the mature type you profess to like?'

Trevize said, 'I would behave with the respect and decency appropriate to your rank and importance.'

'Don't be a fool!' said the Minister. Her hand went to the right side of her waist. The strip of white that encircled it came loose and unwound from her chest and neck. The bodice of her black gown hung noticeably looser.

Trevize sat frozen. Had this been in her mind since – when? Or was it a bribe to accomplish what threats had not?

The bodice flipped down, along with its sturdy reinforcement at the breasts. The Minister sat there, with a look of proud disdain on her face, and bare from the waist up. Her breasts were a smaller version of the woman herself – massive, firm, and overpoweringly impressive.

'Well?' she said.

Trevize said, in all honesty, 'Magnificent!'

'And what will you do about it?'

'What does morality dictate on Comporellon, Madame Lizalor?'

'What is that to a man of Terminus? What does *your* morality dictate? – And begin. My chest is cold and wishes warmth.'

Trevize stood up and began to disrobe.

6

The Nature of Earth

22

Trevize felt almost drugged, and wondered how much time had elapsed.

Beside him lay Mitza Lizalor, Minister of Transportation. She was on her stomach, head to one side, mouth open, snoring distinctly. Trevize was relieved that she was asleep. Once she woke up, he hoped she would be quite aware that she had been asleep.

Trevize longed to sleep himself, but he felt it important that he not do so. She must not wake to find him asleep. She must realize that while she had been ground down to unconsciousness, he had endured. She would expect such endurance from a Foundation-reared immoralist and, at this point, it was better she not be disappointed.

In a way; he had done well. He had guessed, correctly, that Lizalor, given her physical size and strength, her political power, her contempt for the Comporellian men she had encountered, her mingled horror and fascination with tales (what had she heard? Trevize wondered) of the sexual feats of the decadents of Terminus, would want to be dominated. She might even expect to be, without being able to express her desire and expectation.

He had acted on that belief and, to his good fortune, found he was correct. (Trevize, the ever-right, he mocked himself.) It pleased the woman and it enabled Trevize to steer activities in a direction that would tend to wear her out while leaving himself relatively untouched.

It had not been easy. She had a marvellous body (forty-six, she had said, but it would not have shamed a twenty-five-year-old athlete) and enormous stamina – a stamina exceeded only by the careless zest with which she had spent it.

Indeed, if she could be tamed and taught moderation; if practice (but could he himself survive the practice?) brought her to a better sense of her own capacities, and, even more important, *his*, it might be pleasant to –

The snoring stopped suddenly and she stirred. He placed his hand on the shoulder nearest him and stroked it lightly – and her eyes opened. Trevize was leaning on his elbow, and did his best to look unworn and full of life.

'I'm glad you were sleeping, dear,' he said. 'You needed your rest.'

She smiled at him sleepily and, for one queasy moment, Trevize thought she might suggest renewed activity, but she merely heaved herself about till she was resting on her back. She said, in a soft and satisfied voice, 'I had you judged correctly from the start. You are a king of sexuality.'

Trevize tried to look modest. 'I must be more moderate.'

'Nonsense. You were just right. I was afraid that you had been kept active and drained by that young woman, but you assured me you had not. That *is* true, isn't it?'

'Have I acted like someone who was half-sated to begin with?'

'No, you did not,' and her laughter boomed.

'Are you still thinking of Psychic Probes?'

She laughed again. 'Are you mad? Would I want to lose you *now*?'

'Yet it would be better if you lost me temporarily –'

'What!' She frowned.

'If I were to stay here permanently, my – my dear, how long would it be before eyes would begin to watch, and mouths would begin to whisper. If I went off on my mission, however, I would naturally return periodically to report, and it would then be only natural that we should be closeted together for a while – and my mission *is* important.'

She thought about that, scratching idly at her right hip. Then she said, 'I suppose you're right. I hate the thought but – I suppose you're right.'

'And you need not think I would not come back,' said Trevize. 'I am not so witless as to forget what I would have waiting for me here.'

She smiled at him, touched his cheek gently, and said, looking into his eyes. 'Did you find it pleasant, love?'

'Much more than pleasant, dear.'

'Yet you are a Foundationer. A man in the prime of youth from Terminus itself. You must be accustomed to all sorts of women with all sorts of skills –'

'I have encountered nothing – *nothing* – in the least like you,' said Trevize, with a forcefulness that came easily to someone who was but telling the truth, after all.

Lizalor said, complacently, 'Well, if you say so. Still, old habits die hard, you know, and I don't think I could bring myself to trust a man's word without some sort of surety. You and your friend, Pelorat, might conceivably go on this mission of yours once I hear about it and approve, but I will keep the young woman here. She will be well treated, never fear, but I presume your Dr Pelorat will want her, and he will see to it that there are frequent returns to

Comporellon, even if your enthusiasm for this mission might tempt you to stay away too long.'

'But Lizalor, that's impossible.'

'Indeed?' Suspicion at once seeped into her eyes. 'Why impossible? For what purpose would you need the woman?'

'Not for sex. I told you that, and I told you truthfully. She is Pelorat's and I have no interest in her. Besides, I'm sure she'd break in two if she attempted what you so triumphantly carried through.'

Lizalor almost smiled, but repressed it and said severely, 'What is it to you, then, if she remains in Comporellon?'

'Because she is of essential importance to our mission. That is why we must have her.'

'Well, then, what is your mission? It is time you told me.'

Trevize hesitated very briefly. It would have to be the truth. He could think of no lie as effective.

'Listen to me,' he said. 'Comporellon may be an old world, even among the oldest, but it can't be *the* oldest. Human life did not originate here. The earliest human beings reached here from some other world, and perhaps human life didn't originate there either, but came from still another and still older world. Eventually, though, those probings back into time must stop, and we must reach the first world, the world of human origins. I am seeking Earth.'

The change that suddenly came over Mitza Lizalor staggered him.

Her eyes had widened, her breathing took on a sudden urgency, and every muscle seemed to stiffen as she lay there in bed. Her arms shot upward rigidly, and the first two fingers of both hands crossed.

'You named it,' she whispered, hoarsely.

23

She didn't say anything after that; she didn't look at him. Her arms slowly came down, her legs swung over the side of the bed, and she sat up, back to him. Trevize lay where he was, frozen.

He could hear, in memory, the words of Munn Li Compor, as they stood there in the empty tourist centre at Sayshell. He could hear him saying of his own ancestral planet – the one that Trevize was on now – 'They're superstitious about it. Every time they mention the word, they lift up both hands with first and second fingers crossed to ward off misfortune.'

How useless to remember after the fact.

'What should I have said, Mitza?' he muttered.

She shook her head slightly, stood up, stalked towards and then through a door. It closed behind her and, after a moment, there was the sound of water running.

He had no recourse but to wait, bare, undignified, wondering whether to join her in the shower, and then quite certain he had better not. And because, in a way, he felt the shower denied him, he at once experienced a growing need for one.

She emerged at last and silently began to select clothing.

He said, 'Do you mind if I –'

She said nothing, and he took silence for consent. He tried to stride into the room in a strong and masculine way but he felt uncommonly as he had in those days when his mother, offended by some misbehaviour on his part, offered him no punishment but silence, causing him to shrivel in discomfort.

He looked about inside the smoothly-walled cubicle that was bare – completely bare. He looked more minutely. – There was nothing.

He opened the door again, thrust his head out and said, 'Listen, how are you supposed to start the shower?'

She put down the deodorant (at least, Trevize guessed that was its function), strode to the shower-room and, still without looking at him, pointed. Trevize followed the finger and noted a spot on the wall that was round and faintly pink, barely coloured, as though the designer resented having to spoil the starkness of the white, for no reason more important than to give a hint of function.

Trevize shrugged lightly, leaned towards the wall, and touched the spot. Presumably that was what one had to do, for in a moment a deluge of fine-sprayed water struck him from every direction. Gasping, he touched the spot again and it stopped.

He opened the door, knowing he looked several degrees more undignified still as he shivered hard enough to make it difficult to articulate words. He croaked, 'How do you get *hot* water?'

Now she looked at him and, apparently, his appearance overcame her anger (or fear, or whatever emotion was victimizing her) for she snickered and then, without warning, boomed her laughter at him.

'What hot water?' she said. 'Do you think we're going to waste the energy to heat water for washing? That's good mild water you had, water with the chill taken off. What more do you want? You sludge-soft Terminians! – Get back in there and wash!'

Trevize hesitated, but not for long, since it was clear he had no choice in the matter.

With remarkable reluctance he touched the pink spot again and this time steeled his body for the icy spray. *Mild* water? He found suds forming on his body and he rubbed hastily, here, there, everywhere, judging it to be the wash cycle and suspecting it would not last long.

Then came the rinse cycle. Ah, warm – Well, perhaps not warm, but not quite as cold, and definitely feeling warm to his thoroughly chilled body. Then, even as he was considering touching the contact spot again to stop the water, and was wondering how Lizalor had come out dry when there was absolutely no towel or towel-substitute in the place – the water stopped. It was followed by a blast of air that would have certainly bowled him over if it had not come from various directions equally.

It was hot; almost too hot. It took far less energy, Trevize knew, to heat air than to heat water. The hot air steamed the water off him and, in a few minutes, he was able to step out as dry as though he had never encountered water in his life.

Lizalor seemed to have recovered completely. 'Do you feel well?'

'Pretty well,' said Trevize. Actually, he felt astonishingly comfortable. 'All I had to do was prepare myself for the temperature. You didn't tell me –'

'Sludge-soft,' said Lizalor, with mild contempt.

He borrowed her deodorant, then began to dress, conscious of the fact that she had fresh underwear and he did not. He said, 'What should I have called – that world.'

She said, 'We refer to it as the Oldest.'

He said, 'How was I to know the name I used was forbidden? Did you tell me?'

'Did you ask?'

'How was I to know to ask?'

'You know now.'

'I'm bound to forget.'

'You had better not.'

'What's the difference?' Trevize felt his temper rising. 'It's just a word, a sound.'

Lizalor said darkly, 'There are words one doesn't say. Do you say every word you know under all circumstances?'

'Some words are vulgar, some are inappropriate, some under particular circumstances would be hurtful. Which is – that word I used?'

Lizalor said, 'It's a sad word, a solemn word. It represents a world that was ancestor to us all and that now doesn't exist. It's tragic, and we feel it because it was near to us. We prefer not to speak of it or, if we must, not to use its name.'

'And the crossing of fingers at me? How does that relieve the hurt and sadness?'

Lizalor's face flushed. 'That was an automatic reaction, and I don't thank you for forcing it on me. There are people who believe that the word, even the thought, brings on misfortune – and that is how they ward it off.'

'Do you, too, believe crossing fingers wards off misfortune?'

'No. – Well, yes, in a way. It makes me uneasy if I don't do it.' She didn't look at him. Then, as though eager to shift the subject, she said quickly, 'And how is that black-haired woman of yours of the essence with respect to your mission to reach – that world you mentioned.'

'Say "the Oldest". Or would you rather not even say that?'

'I would rather not discuss it at all, but I asked you a question.'

'I believe that her people reached their present world as emigrants from the Oldest.'

'As we did,' said Lizalor proudly.

'But her people have traditions of some sort which she says are the key to understanding the Oldest, but only if we reach it and can study its records.'

'She is lying.'

'Perhaps, but we must check it out.'

'If you have this woman with her problematical knowledge, and if you want to reach the Oldest with her, why did you come to Comporellon?'

'To find the location of the Oldest. I had a friend once, who, like myself, was a Foundationer. He, however, was descended from Comporellian ancestors and he assured me that much of the history of the Oldest was well known on Comporellon.'

'Did he indeed? And did *he* tell you any of its history?'

'Yes,' said Trevize, reaching for the truth again. 'He said that the Oldest was a dead world, entirely radioactive. He did not know why, but he thought that it might be the result of nuclear explosions. In a war, perhaps.'

'No!' said Lizalor explosively.

'No, there was no war? Or no, the Oldest is not radioactive?'

'It is radioactive, but there was no war.'

'Then how did it become radioactive? It could not have been radioactive to begin with since human life began on the Oldest. There would have been no life on it ever.'

Lizalor seemed to hesitate. She stood erect, and was breathing deeply, almost gasping. She said, 'It was a punishment. It was a world that used robots. Do you know what robots are?'

'Yes.'

'They had robots and for that they were punished. Every world that has had robots has been punished and no longer exists.'

'Who punished them, Lizalor?'

'He Who Punishes. The forces of history. I don't know.' She looked away from him, uncomfortable, then said, in a lower voice, 'Ask others.'

'I would like to, but whom do I ask? Are there those on Comporellon who have studied primeval history?'

'There are. They are not popular with us – with the average Comporellian – but the Foundation, *your* Foundation, insists on intellectual freedom, as they call it.'

'Not a bad insistence, in my opinion,' said Trevize.

'All is bad that is imposed from without,' said Lizalor.

Trevize shrugged. There was no purpose in arguing the matter. He said, 'My friend, Dr Pelorat, is himself a primeval historian of a sort. He would, I am sure, like to meet his Comporellian colleagues. Can you arrange that, Lizalor?'

She nodded. 'There is a historian named Vasil Deniador, who is based at the University here in the city. He does not teach class, but he may be able to tell you what you want to know.'

'Why doesn't he teach class?'

'It's not that he is forbidden; it's just that students do not elect his course.'

'I presume,' said Trevize, trying not to say it sardonically, 'that the students are encouraged not to elect it.'

'Why should they want to? He is a Sceptic. We have them, you know. There are always individuals who pit their minds against the general modes of thought and who are arrogant enough to feel that they alone are right and that the many are wrong.'

'Might it not be that that could actually be so in some cases.'

'Never!' snapped Lizalor, with a firmness of belief that made it quite clear that no further discussion in that direction would be of any use. 'And for all his scepticism, he will be forced to tell you exactly what any Comporellian would tell you.'

'And that is?'

'That if you search for the Oldest, you will not find it.'

24

In the private quarters assigned them, Pelorat listened to Trevize thoughtfully, his long solemn face expressionless, then said, 'Vasil Deniador? I do not recall having heard of him, but it may be that back on the ship I will find papers by him in my library.'

'Are you sure you haven't heard of him? Think!' said Trevize.

'I don't recall, at the moment, having heard of him,' said Pelorat cautiously, 'but after all, my dear chap, there must be hundreds of estimable scholars I haven't heard of; or have, but can't remember.'

'Still, he can't be first-class, or you would have heard of him.'

'The study of Earth –'

'Practise saying "the Oldest", Janov. It would complicate matters otherwise.'

'The study of the Oldest,' said Pelorat, 'is not a well-rewarded niche in the corridors of learning, so that first-class scholars, even in the field of primeval history, would not tend to find their way there. Or, if we put it the other way round, those who are already there do not make enough of a name for themselves in an uninterested world to be considered first-class, even if they were. – I am not first-class in anyone's estimation, I am sure.'

Bliss said tenderly, 'In mine, Pel.'

'Yes, certainly in yours, my dear,' said Pelorat, smiling slightly, 'but you are not judging me in my capacity as scholar.'

It was almost night now, going by the clock, and Trevize felt himself grow slightly impatient, as he always did when Bliss and Pelorat traded endearments.

He said, 'I'll try to arrange our seeing this Deniador tomorrow, but if he knows as little about the matter as the Minister does, we're not going to be much better off than we are now.'

Pelorat said, 'He may be able to lead us to someone more useful.'

'I doubt it. This world's attitude towards Earth – but I had better practise speaking of it elliptically, too. This world's attitude towards the Oldest is a foolish and superstitious one.' He turned away. 'But it's been a rough day and we ought to think of an evening meal – if we can face their uninspired cookery – and then begin thinking of getting some sleep. Have you two learned how to use the shower?'

'My dear fellow,' said Pelorat, 'we have been very kindly treated. We've received all sorts of instructions, most of which we didn't need.'

Bliss said, 'Listen, Trevize. What about the ship?'

'What about it?'

'Is the Comporellian government confiscating it?'

'No. I don't think they will.'

'Ah. Very pleasant. Why aren't they?'

'Because I persuaded the Minister to change her mind.'

Pelorat said, 'Astonishing. She didn't seem a particularly persuadable individual to me.'

Bliss said, 'I don't know. It was clear from the texture of her mind that she was attracted to Trevize.'

Trevize looked at Bliss with sudden exasperation. 'Did you do that, Bliss?'

'What do you mean, Trevize.'

'I mean tamper with her –'

'I didn't tamper. However, when I noted that she was attracted to you, I couldn't resist just snapping an inhibition or two. It was a very small thing to do. Those inhibitions might have snapped anyway, and it seemed to be important to make certain that she was filled with goodwill towards you.'

'Goodwill? It was more than that! She softened, yes, but post-coitally.'

Pelorat said, 'Surely you don't mean, old man –'

'Why not?' said Trevize testily. 'She may be past her first youth, but she knew the art well. She was no beginner, I assure you. Nor will I play the gentleman and lie on her behalf. It was her idea – thanks to Bliss's fiddling with her inhibitions – and I was not in a position to refuse, even if that thought had occurred to me, which it didn't. – Come, Janov, don't stand there looking puritanical. It's been months since I've had an opportunity. You've –' and he waved his hand vaguely in Bliss's direction.

'Believe me, Golan,' said Pelorat, embarrassed, 'if you are interpreting my expression as puritanical, you mistake me. I have no objection.'

Bliss said, 'But *she* is puritanical. I meant to make her warm towards you; I did *not* count on a sexual paroxysm.'

Trevize said, 'But that is exactly what you brought on, my little interfering Bliss. It may be necessary for the Minister to play the puritan in public, but if so, that seems merely to stoke the fires.'

'And so, provided you scratch the itch, she will betray the Foundation –'

'She would have done that in any case,' said Trevize. 'She wanted the ship –' He broke off, and said in a whisper. 'Are we being overheard?'

Bliss said, 'No!'

'Are you sure?'

'It is certain. It is impossible to impinge upon the mind of Gaia in any unauthorized fashion without Gaia being aware of it.'

'In that case, Comporellon wants the ship for itself – a valuable addition to its fleet.'

'Surely, the Foundation would not allow that.'

'Comporellon does not intend to have the Foundation know.'

Bliss sighed. 'There are your Isolates. The Minister intends to betray the Foundation on behalf of Comporellon and, in return for sex, will promptly betray Comporellon, too. – And as for Trevize, he will gladly sell his body's services as a way of inducing the betrayal. What anarchy there is in this Galaxy of yours. What *chaos*.'

Trevize said coldly, 'You are wrong, young woman –'

'In what I have just said, I am not a young woman, I am Gaia. I am all of Gaia.'

'Then you are wrong, *Gaia*. I did not sell my body's services. I gave them gladly. I enjoyed it and did no one harm. As for the consequences, they turned out well from my standpoint and I accept that. And if Comporellon wants the ship for its own purposes, who is to say who is right in this matter? It is a Foundation ship, but it was given me to search for Earth. It is mine then until I complete the search and I feel that the Foundation has no right to go back on its agreement. As for Comporellon, it does not enjoy Foundation domination, so it dreams of independence. In its own eyes, it is correct to do so and to deceive the Foundation, for that is not an act of treason to them but an act of patriotism. Who knows?'

'Exactly. Who knows? In a Galaxy of anarchy, how is it possible to sort out reasonable actions from unreasonable ones? How decide between right and wrong, good and evil, justice and crime, useful and useless? And how do you explain the Minister's betrayal of her own government, when she lets you keep the ship. Does she long for personal independence from an oppressive world? Is she a traitor or a personal one-woman self-patriot?'

'To be truthful,' said Trevize, 'I don't know that she was willing to let me have my ship simply because she was grateful to me for the pleasure I gave her. I believe she made that decision only when I told her I was searching for the Oldest. It is a world of ill-omen to her and we and the ship that carries us, by searching for it have become ill-omened, too. It is my feeling that she feels she incurred the ill-omen for herself and her world by attempting to take the ship, which she may, by now, be viewing with horror. Perhaps she feels that by allowing us and our ship to leave and go about our business, she is averting the misfortune from Comporellon and is, in that way, performing a patriotic act.'

'If that were so, which I doubt, Trevize, superstition is the spring of the action. Do you admire that?'

'I neither admire nor condemn. Superstition always directs action in the absence of knowledge. The Foundation believes in the Seldon Plan, though no one in our realm can understand it, interpret its details, or use it to predict. We follow blindly out of ignorance and faith, and isn't that superstition?'

'Yes, it might be.'

'And Gaia, too. You believe I have given the correct decision in judging that Gaia should absorb the Galaxy into one large organism, but you do not know why I should be right, or how safe it would be for you to follow that decision. You are willing to go along only out of ignorance and faith, and are even annoyed with me for trying to find evidence that will remove the ignorance and make mere faith unnecessary. Isn't that superstition?'

'I think he has you there, Bliss,' said Pelorat.

Bliss said, 'Not so. He will either find nothing at all in this search, or he will find something that confirms his decision.'

Trevize said, 'And to back up that belief, you have only ignorance and faith. In other words, superstition!'

25

Vasil Deniador was a small man, little of feature, with a way of looking up by raising his eyes without raising his head. This, combined with the brief smiles that periodically lit his face, gave him the appearance of laughing silently at the world.

His office was long and narrow, filled with tapes that seemed to be in wild disorder, not because there was any definite evidence for that, but because they were not evenly placed in their recesses so that they gave the shelves a snaggle-toothed appearance. The three seats he indicated for his visitors were not matched and showed signs of having been recently, and imperfectly, dusted.

He said, 'Janov Pelorat, Golan Trevize, and Bliss. – I do not have your second name, madam.'

'Bliss,' she said, 'is all I am usually called,' and sat down.

'It is enough after all,' said Deniador, twinkling at her. 'You are attractive enough to be forgiven if you had no name at all.'

All were sitting now. Deniador said, 'I have heard of you, Dr Pelorat, though we have never corresponded. You are a Foundationer, are you not? From Terminus?'

'Yes, Dr Deniador.'

'And you, Councilman Trevize. I seem to have heard that recently you were expelled from the Council and exiled. I don't think I have ever understood why.'

'Not expelled, sir, I am still a member of the Council although I don't know when I will take up my duties again. Nor exiled, quite. I was assigned a mission, concerning which we wish to consult you.'

'Happy to try to help,' said Deniador. 'And the blissful lady? Is she from Terminus, too.'

Trevize interposed quickly. 'She is from elsewhere, Doctor.'

'Ah, a strange world, this Elsewhere. A most unusual collection of human beings are native to it. – But since two of you are from the Foundation's capital at Terminus, and the third is an attractive young woman, and Mitza Lizalor is not known for her affection for either category, how is it that she recommends you to my care so warmly?'

'I think,' said Trevize, 'to get rid of us. The sooner you help us, you see, the sooner we will leave Comporellon.'

Deniador eyed Trevize with interest (again the twinkling smile) and said, 'Of course, a vigorous young man such as yourself might attract her whatever his origin. She plays the role of cold vestal well, but not perfectly.'

'I know nothing about that,' said Trevize stiffly.

'And you had better not. In public, at least. But I am a Sceptic and I am professionally unattuned to believing in surfaces. So come, Councilman, what is your mission? Let me find out if I can help you.'

Trevize said, 'In this, Dr Pelorat is our spokesman.'

'I have no objection to that,' said Deniador. 'Dr Pelorat?'

Pelorat said, 'To put it at the simplest, dear doctor, I have all my mature life attempted to penetrate to the basic core of knowledge concerning the world on which the human species originated, and I was sent out along with my good friend, Golan Trevize – although, to be sure, I did not know him at the time – to find, if we could, the – uh – Oldest, I believe you call it.'

'The Oldest?' said Deniador. 'I take it you mean Earth.'

Pelorat's jaw dropped. Then he said, with a slight stutter, 'I was under the impression – that is, I was given to understand – that one did not –'

He looked at Trevize, rather helplessly.

Trevize said, 'Minister Lizalor told me that that word was not used on Comporellon.'

'You mean she did this?' Deniador's mouth turned downwards, his nose screwed up, and he thrust his arms vigorously forward, crossing the first two fingers on each hand.

'Yes,' said Trevize. 'That's what I mean.'

Deniador relaxed and laughed. 'Nonsense, gentlemen. We do it as a matter of habit, and in the backwoods they may be serious about it but, on the whole, it doesn't matter. I don't know any Comporellian who wouldn't say "Earth" when annoyed or startled. It's the most common vulgarism we have.'

'Vulgarism?' said Pelorat faintly.

'Or expletive, if you prefer.'

'Nevertheless,' said Trevize, 'the Minister seemed quite upset when I used the word.'

'Oh well, she's a mountain woman.'

'What does that mean, sir?'

'What it says. Mitza Lizalor is from the Central Mountain Range. The children out there are brought up in what is called the good old-fashioned way, which means that no matter how well educated they become you can never knock those crossed fingers out of them.'

'Then the word Earth doesn't bother you at all, does it, doctor?' said Bliss.

'Not at all, dear lady. I am a Sceptic.'

Trevize said, 'I know what the word Sceptic means in Galactic, but how do you use the word?'

'Exactly as you do, Councilman. I accept only what I am forced to accept by reasonably reliable evidence, and keep that acceptance tentative pending the arrival of further evidence. That doesn't make us popular.'

'Why not?' said Trevize.

'We wouldn't be popular anywhere. Where is the world whose people don't prefer a comfortable, warm, and well-worn belief, however illogical, to the chilly winds of uncertainty? – Consider how you believe in the Seldon Plan without evidence.'

'Yes,' said Trevize, studying his finger ends. 'I put that forward yesterday as an example, too.'

Pelorat said, 'May I return to the subject, old fellow? What is known about Earth that a Sceptic would accept?'

Deniador said, 'Very little. We can assume that there is a single planet on which the human species developed, because it is unlikely in the extreme that the same species, so nearly identical as to be interfertile, would develop on a number of worlds, or even on just two, independently. We can choose to call this world of origin, Earth. The belief is general, here, that Earth exists in this corner of the Galaxy, for the worlds here are unusually old and it is likely that the first worlds to be settled were close to Earth rather than far from it.'

'And has the Earth any unique characteristics aside from being the planet of origin?' asked Pelorat eagerly.

'Do you have something in mind?' said Deniador, with his quick smile.

'I'm thinking of its satellite, which some call the Moon. That would be unusual, wouldn't it?'

'That's a leading question, Dr Pelorat. You may be putting thoughts into my mind.'

'I do not say what it is that would make the Moon unusual.'

'Its size, of course. Am I right? – Yes, I see I am. All the legends of Earth speak of its vast array of living species and of its vast satellite – one that is some 3,000 to 3,500 kilometres in diameter. The vast array of life is easy to accept since it would naturally have come about through biological evolution, if what we know of the process is accurate. A giant satellite is more difficult to accept. No other inhabited world in the Galaxy has such a satellite. Large satellites are invariably associated with the uninhabited and uninhabitable gas-giants. As a Sceptic, then, I prefer not to accept the existence of the Moon.'

Pelorat said, 'If Earth is unique in its possession of millions of species, might it not also be unique in its possession of a giant satellite? One uniqueness might imply the other.'

Deniador smiled. 'I don't see how the presence of millions of species on Earth could create a giant satellite out of nothing.'

'But the other way around – Perhaps a giant satellite could help create the millions of species.'

'I don't see how that could be either.'

Trevize said, 'What about the story of Earth's radioactivity?'

'That is universally told; universally believed.'

'But,' said Trevize, 'Earth could not have been so radioactive as to preclude life in the billions of years when it supported life. How did it become radioactive? A nuclear war?'

'That is the most common opinion, Councilman Trevize.'

'From the manner in which you say that, I gather you don't believe it.'

'There is no evidence that such a war took place. Common belief, even universal belief, is not, in itself, evidence.'

'What else might have happened?'

'There is no evidence that anything happened. The radioactivity might be as purely invented a legend as the large satellite.'

Pelorat said, 'What is the generally accepted story of Earth's history? I have, during my professional career, collected a large number of origin-legends, many of them involving a world called Earth, or some name very much like that. I have none from Comporellon, nothing beyond the vague mention of a Benhally who might have come from nowhere for all that Comporellian legends say.'

'That's not surprising. We don't usually export our legends and I'm astonished you have found references to Benhally. Superstition, again.'

'But you are not superstitious and you would not hesitate to talk about it, would you?'

'That's correct,' said the small historian, casting his eyes upwards at Pelorat. 'It would certainly add greatly, perhaps even dangerously, to my unpopularity if I did, but you three are leaving Comporellon soon and I take it you will never quote me as a source.'

'You have our word of honour,' said Pelorat quickly.

'Then here is a summary of what is supposed to have happened, shorn of any supernaturalism or moralizing. Earth existed as the sole world of human beings for an immeasurable period and then, about twenty to twenty-five thousand years ago, the human species developed interstellar travel by way of the hyperspatial Jump and colonized a group of planets.

'The Settlers on these planets made use of robots, which had first been devised on Earth before the days of hyperspatial travel and – do you know what robots are, by the way?'

'Yes,' said Trevize. 'We have been asked that more than once. We know what robots are.'

'The Settlers, with a thoroughly roboticized society, developed a high technology and unusual longevity and despised their ancestral world. According to more dramatic versions of their story, they dominated and oppressed the ancestral world.

'Eventually, then, Earth sent out a new group of Settlers, among whom robots were forbidden. Of the new worlds, Comporellon was among the first. Our own patriots insist it was *the* first, but there is no evidence of that that a Sceptic can accept. The first group of Settlers died out, and –'

Trevize said, 'Why did the first set die out, Dr Deniador?'

'Why? Usually they are imagined by our romantics as having been punished for their crimes by He Who Punishes, though no one bothers to say why He waited so long. But one doesn't have to resort to fairy tales. It is easy to argue that a society that depends totally on robots becomes soft and decadent, dwindling and dying out of sheer boredom or, more subtly, by losing the will to live.

'The second wave of settlers, without robots, lived on and took over the entire Galaxy, but Earth grew radioactive and slowly dropped out of sight. The reason usually given for this is that there were robots on Earth, too, since the first wave had encouraged that.'

Bliss, who had listened to the account with some visible impatience, said, 'Well, Dr Deniador, radioactivity or not, and however many waves of Settlers there might have been, the crucial question is a simple one. Exactly where *is* Earth? What are its co-ordinates?'

Deniador said, 'The answer to that question is: I don't know. – But come, it is time for lunch. I can have one brought in, and we can discuss Earth over it for as long as you want.'

'You don't *know*?' said Trevize, the sound of his voice rising in pitch and intensity.

'Actually, as far as I know, no one knows.'

'But that is impossible.'

'Councilman,' said Deniador, with a soft sigh, 'if you wish to call the truth impossible, that is your privilege, but it will get you nowhere.'

7

Leaving Comporellon

26

Luncheon consisted of a heap of soft, crusty balls that came in different shades and that contained a variety of fillings.

Deniador picked up a small object which unfolded into a pair of thin, transparent gloves, and put them on. His guests followed suit.

Bliss said, 'What is inside these objects, please?'

Deniador said, 'The pink ones are filled with spicy chopped fish, a great Comporellian delicacy. These yellow ones contain a cheese filling that is very mild. The green ones contain a vegetable mixture. Do eat them while they are quite warm. Later we will have hot almond pie and the usual beverages. I might recommend the hot cider. In a cold climate, we have a tendency to heat our foods, even desserts.'

'You do yourself well,' said Pelorat.

'Not really,' said Deniador. 'I'm being hospitable to guests. For myself, I get along on very little. I don't have much body mass to support, as you have probably noticed.'

Trevize bit into one of the pink ones and found it very fishy indeed, with an overlay of spices that was pleasant to the taste but which, he thought, along with the fish itself, would remain with him for the rest of the day and, perhaps, into the night.

When he withdrew the object with the bite taken out of it, he found that the crust had closed in over the contents. There was no squirt, no leakage, and, for a moment, he wondered at the purpose of the gloves. There seemed no chance of getting his hands moist and sticky if he didn't use them, so he decided it was a matter of hygiene. The gloves substituted for a washing of the hands if that were inconvenient and custom, probably, now dictated their use even if the hands were washed. (Lizalor hadn't used gloves when he had eaten with her the day before. – Perhaps that was because she was a mountain woman.)

He said, 'Would it be unmannerly to talk business over lunch?'

'By Comporellian standards, Councilman, it would be, but you are my guests, and we will go by your standards. If you wish to speak seriously, and do not think – or care – that that might diminish your pleasure in the food, please do so, and I will join you.'

Trevize said, 'Thank you. Minister Lizalor implied – no, she stated bluntly – that Sceptics were unpopular on this world. Is that so?'

Deniador's good humour seemed to intensify. 'Certainly. How

hurt we'd be if we weren't. Comporellon, you see, is a frustrated world. Without any knowledge of the details, there is the general mythic belief that once, many millennia ago, when the inhabited Galaxy was small, Comporellon was the leading world. We never forget that, and the fact that in known history we have *not* been leaders irks us, fills us . . . the population in general, that is . . . with a feeling of injustice.

'Yet what can we do? The government was forced to be a loyal vassal of the Emperor once, and is a loyal Associate of the Foundation now. And the more we are made aware of our subordinate position, the stronger the belief in the great, mysterious days of the past becomes.

'What, then, can Comporellon do? They could never defy the Empire in older times and they can't openly defy the Foundation now. They take refuge, therefore, in attacking and hating us, since we don't believe the legends and laugh at the superstitions.

'Nevertheless, we are safe from the grosser effects of persecution. We control the technology, and we fill the faculties of the Universities. Some of us, who are particularly outspoken, have difficulty in teaching classes openly. I have that difficulty, for instance, though I have my students and hold meetings quietly off-campus. Nevertheless, if we were really driven out of public life, the technology would fail and the Universities would lose accreditation with the Galaxy generally. Presumably, such is the folly of human beings, the prospects of intellectual suicide might not stop them from indulging their hatred, but the Foundation supports us. Therefore, we are constantly scolded and sneered at and denounced – and never touched.'

Trevize said, 'Is it popular opposition that keeps you from telling us where Earth is? Do you fear that, despite everything, the anti-Sceptic feeling might turn ugly if you go too far?'

Deniador shook his head. 'No. Earth's location is unknown. I am not hiding anything from you out of fear – or for any other reason.'

'But look,' said Trevize urgently. 'There's a limited number of planets in this sector of the Galaxy that possess the physical characteristics associated with habitability, and almost all of them must be not only inhabitable, but inhabited, and therefore well known to you. How difficult would it be to explore the sector for a planet that would be habitable were it not for the fact that it was radioactive? Besides that, you would look for such a planet with a large satellite in attendance. Between radioactivity and a large satellite, Earth would be absolutely unmistakable and could not be missed even with only a casual search. It might take some time but that would be the only difficulty.'

Deniador said, 'The Sceptic's view is, of course, that Earth's radioactivity and its large satellite are both simply legends. If we look for them, we look for sparrow-milk and rabbit-feathers.'

'Perhaps, but that shouldn't stop Comporellon from at least taking on the search. If they find a radioactive world of the proper size for habitability, with a large satellite, what an appearance of credibility it would lend to Comporellian legendry in general.'

Deniador laughed. 'It may be that Comporellon doesn't search for that very reason. If we fail, or if we find an Earth obviously different from the legends, the reverse would take place. Comporellian legendry in general would be blasted and made into a laughing stock. Comporellon wouldn't risk that.'

Trevize paused, then went on, very earnestly, 'Besides, even if we discount those two uniquities – if there is such a word in Galactic – of radioactivity and a large satellite, there is a third that, by definition, *must* exist, without any reference to legends. Earth must have upon it either a flourishing life of incredible diversity, or the remnants of one, or, at the very least, the fossil record of such a one.'

Deniador said, 'Councilman, while Comporellon has sent out no organized search party for Earth, we *do* have occasion to travel through space, and we occasionally have reports from ships that have strayed from their intended routes for one reason or another. Jumps are not always perfect, as perhaps you know. Nevertheless, there have been no reports of any planets with properties resembling those of the legendary Earth, or any planet that is bursting with life.

Nor is any ship likely to land on what seems an uninhabited planet in order that the crew might go fossil-hunting. If, then, in thousands of years nothing of the sort has been reported, I am perfectly willing to believe that locating Earth is impossible, because Earth is not there to be located.'

Trevize said, in frustration, 'But Earth must be *somewhere*. Somewhere there is a planet on which humanity and all the familiar forms of life associated with humanity evolved. If Earth is not in this section of the Galaxy, it must be elsewhere.'

'Perhaps,' said Deniador cold-bloodedly, 'but in all this time, it hasn't turned up anywhere.'

'People haven't really looked for it.'

'Well, apparently you are. I wish you luck, but I would never bet on your success.'

Trevize said, 'Have there been attempts to determine the possible position of Earth by indirect means, by some means other than a direct search?'

'Yes,' said two voices at once. Deniador, who was the owner of one of the voices, said to Pelorat, 'Are you thinking of Yariff's project?'

'I am,' said Pelorat.

'Then would you explain it to the Councilman. I think he would more readily believe you than me.'

Pelorat said, 'You see, Golan, in the last days of the Empire, there was a time when the Search for Origins, as they called it, was a popular pastime, perhaps to get away from the unpleasantness of the surrounding reality. The Empire was in a process of disintegration at that time, you know.

'It occurred to a Livian historian, Humbal Yariff, that whatever the planet of origin, it would have settled worlds near itself sooner than it would settle planets further away. In general, the further a world from the point of origin the later it would have been settled.

'Suppose, then, one recorded the date of settlement of all habitable planets in the Galaxy, and made networks of all that were a given number of millennia old. There could be a network drawn through all planets ten thousand years old; another through those twelve thousand years old, still another through those fifteen thousand years old. Each network would, in theory, be roughly spherical and they should be roughly concentric. The older networks would form spheres smaller in radius than the younger ones, and if one worked out all the centres they should fall within a comparatively small volume of space that would include the planet of origin – Earth.'

Pelorat's face was very earnest as he kept drawing spherical surfaces with his cupped hands. 'Do you see my point, Golan?'

Trevize nodded. 'Yes. But I take it that it didn't work.'

'Theoretically, it should have, old fellow. One trouble was that times of origin were totally inaccurate. Every world exaggerated its own age to one degree or another and there was no easy way of determining age independently of legend.'

Bliss said, 'Carbon-14 decay in ancient timber.'

'Certainly, dear,' said Pelorat, 'but you would have had to get co-operation from the worlds in question, and that was never given. No world wanted its own exaggerated claim of age to be destroyed and the Empire was then in no position to override local objections in a matter so unimportant. It had other things on its mind.

'All that Yariff could do was to make use of worlds that were only two thousand years old at most, and whose founding had been meticulously recorded under reliable circumstances. There were few of those, and while they were distributed in roughly spherical symmetry, the centre was relatively close to Trantor, the Imperial capital, because that was where the colonizing expeditions had originated for those relatively few worlds.

'That, of course, was another problem. Earth was not the only point of origin of settlement for other worlds. As time went on, the older worlds sent out settlement expeditions of their own, and at the time of the height of Empire, Trantor was a rather copious source of those. Yariff was, unfairly, laughed at and ridiculed and his professional reputation was destroyed.'

Trevize said, 'I get the story, Janov. – Dr Deniador, is there then nothing at all you could give me that represents the faintest possibility of hope? Is there any other world where it is conceivable there may be some information concerning Earth?'

Deniador sank into doubtful thought for a while. 'We-e-ell,' he said at last, drawing out the word hesitantly, 'as a Sceptic I must tell you that I'm not sure that Earth exists, or has ever existed. However –' He fell silent again.

Finally, Bliss said, 'I think you've thought of something that might be important, doctor.'

'Important? I doubt it,' said Deniador faintly. 'Perhaps amusing, however. Earth is not the only planet whose position is a mystery. There are the worlds of the first group of Settlers; the Spacers, as they are called in our legends. Some call the planets they inhabited the "Spacer worlds"; others call them the "Forbidden Worlds". The latter name is now the usual one.

'In their pride and prime, the legend goes, the Spacers had lifetimes stretching out for centuries, and refused to allow our own short-lived ancestors to land on their worlds. After we had defeated them, the situation was reversed. We scorned to deal with them and left them to themselves, forbidding our own ships and Traders to deal with them. Hence those planets became the Forbidden Worlds. We were certain, so the legend states, that He Who Punishes would destroy them without our intervention, and, apparently, He did. At least, no Spacer has appeared in the Galaxy to our knowledge in many millennia.'

'Do you think that the Spacers would know about Earth?' said Trevize.

'Conceivably, since their worlds were older than any of ours. That is, if any Spacers exist, which is extremely unlikely.'

'Even if they don't exist, their worlds do and may contain records.'

'If you can find the worlds.'

Trevize looked exasperated. 'Do you mean to say that the key to Earth, the location of which is unknown, may be found on Spacer worlds, the location of which is also unknown?'

Deniador shrugged. 'We have had no dealings with them for twenty thousand years. No thought of them. They, too, like Earth, have receded into the mists.'

'How many worlds did the Spacers live on?'

'The legends speak of fifty such worlds – a suspiciously round number. There were probably far fewer.'

'And you don't know the location of a single one of the fifty?'

'Well, now, I wonder –'

'What do you wonder?'

Deniador said, 'Since primeval history is my hobby, as it is Dr Pelorat's, I have occasionally explored old documents in search of anything that might refer to early time; something more than legends. Last year, I came upon the records of an old ship, records that were almost indecipherable. It dated back to the very old days when our world was not yet known as Comporellon. The name "Baleyworld" was used, which, it seems to me, may be an even earlier term of the "Benbally world" of our legends.'

Pelorat said, excitedly, 'Have you published?'

'No,' said Deniador. 'I do not wish to dive until I am sure there is water in the swimming pool, as the old saying has it. You see, the record says that the captain of the ship had visited a Spacer world and taken off with him a Spacer woman.'

Bliss said, 'But you said that the Spacers did not allow visitors.'

'Exactly, and that is the reason I don't publish the material. It sounds incredible. There are vague tales that could be interpreted as referring to the Spacers and to their conflict with the Settlers – our own ancestors. – Such tales exist not only on Comporellon but on many worlds in many variations, but all are in absolute accord in one respect. The two groups, Spacers and Settlers, did not mingle. There was no social contact, let alone sexual contact, and yet apparently the Settler captain and the Spacer woman were held together by bonds of love. This is so incredible that I see no chance of the story being accepted as anything but, at best, a piece of romantic historical fiction.'

Trevize looked disappointed. 'Is that all?'

'No, Councilman, there is one more matter. I came across some figures in what was left of the log of the ship that might – or might not – represent spatial co-ordinates. If they were – and I repeat, since my Sceptic's honour compels me to, that they might not be – then internal evidence made me conclude they were the spatial co-ordinates of three of the Spacer worlds. One of them might be the Spacer world where the captain landed and from which he withdrew his Spacer love.'

Trevize said, 'Might it not be that even if the tale is fiction, the co-ordinates are real?'

'It might be,' said Deniador. 'I will give you the figures, and you are free to use them, but you might get nowhere. – And yet I have an amusing notion.' His quick smile made its appearance.

'What is that?' said Trevize.

'What if one of those sets of co-ordinates represented Earth.'

27

Comporellon's sun, distinctly orange, was larger in appearance than the sun of Terminus, but it was low in the sky and gave out little heat. The wind, fortunately light, touched Trevize's cheek with icy fingers.

He shivered inside the electrified coat he had been given by Mitza Lizalor, who now stood next to him. He said, 'It must warm up some time, Mitza.'

She glanced up at the sun briefly, and stood there in the emptiness of the spaceport, showing no signs of discomfort – tall, large, wearing a lighter coat than Trevize had on, and if not impervious to the cold, at least scornful of it.

She said, 'We have a beautiful summer. It is not a long one but our food crops are adapted to it. The strains are carefully chosen so that they grow quickly in the sun and do not frostbite easily. Our domestic animals are well-furred, and Comporellian wool is the best in the Galaxy by general admission. Then, too, we have farm settlements in orbit about Comporellon that grow tropical fruit. We actually export canned pineapples of superior flavour. Most people who know us as a cold world, don't know that.'

Trevize said, 'I thank you for coming to see us off, Mitza, and for being willing to co-operate with us on this mission of ours. For my own peace of mind, however, I must ask whether you will find yourself in serious trouble over this.'

'No!' She shook her head proudly. 'No trouble. In the first place, I will not be questioned. I am in control of transportation, which means I alone set the rules for this spaceport and others, for the entry stations, for the ships that come and go. The Prime Minister depends on me for all that and is only too delighted to remain ignorant of its details. – And even if I were questioned, I have but to tell the truth. The government would applaud me for not turning the ship over to the Foundation. So would the people if it were safe to let them know. And the Foundation itself would not know of it.'

Trevize said, 'The government might be willing to keep the ship from the Foundation, but would they be willing to approve your letting us take it away?'

Lizalor smiled. 'You are a decent human being, Trevize. You have fought tenaciously to keep your ship and now that you have it you take the trouble to concern yourself with our welfare.' She reached towards him tentatively as though tempted to give some sign of affection and then, with obvious difficulty, controlled the impulse.

She said, with a renewed brusqueness, 'Even if they question my decision, I have but to tell them that you have been, and still are, searching for the Oldest, and they will say I did well to get rid of you as quickly as I did, ship and all. And they will perform the rites of atonement that you were ever allowed to land in the first place, though there was no way we might have guessed what you were doing.'

'Do you truly fear misfortune to yourself and the world because of my presence?'

'Indeed,' said Lizalor stolidly. Then she said, more softly, 'You have brought misfortune to me, already, for now that I have known you, Comporellian men will seem more sapless still. I will be left with an unappeasable longing. He Who Punishes has already seen to that.'

Trevize hesitated, then said, 'I do not wish you to change your mind on this matter, but I do not wish you to suffer needless apprehension, either. You must know that this matter of my bringing misfortune on you is simply superstition.'

'The Sceptic told you that, I presume.'

'I know it without his telling me.'

Lizalor brushed her face, for a thin rime was gathering on her prominent eyebrows and said, 'I know there are some who think it superstition. That the Oldest brings misfortune is, however, a fact. It has been demonstrated many times and all the clever Sceptical arguments can't legislate the truth out of existence.'

She thrust out her hand suddenly, 'Goodbye, Golan. Get on the ship and join your companions before your soft Terminian body freezes in our cold, but kindly wind.'

'Goodbye, Mitza, and I hope to see you when I return.'

'Yes, you have promised to return and I have tried to believe that you would. I have even told myself that I would come out and meet you at your ship in space so that misfortune would fall only on me and not upon my world – but you will not return.'

'Not so! I will! I would not give you up that easily, having had pleasure of you.' And at that moment, Trevize was firmly convinced that he meant it.

'I do not doubt your romantic impulses, my sweet Foundationer, but those who venture outwards on a search for the Oldest will never come back – anywhere. I know that in my heart.'

Trevize tried to keep his teeth from chattering. It was from cold and he didn't want her to think it was from fear. He said, 'That, too, is superstition.'

'And yet,' she said, 'that, too, is true.'

28

It was good to be back in the pilot-room of the *Far Star*. It might be cramped for room. It might be a bubble of imprisonment in infinite space. Nevertheless, it was familiar, friendly, and warm.

Bliss said, 'I'm glad you finally came aboard. I was wondering how long you would remain with the Minister.'

'Not long,' said Trevize. 'It was cold.'

'It seemed to me,' said Bliss, 'that you were considering remaining with her and postponing the search for Earth. I do not like to probe your mind even lightly, but I was concerned for you and that temptation under which you laboured seemed to leap out at me.'

Trevize said, 'You're quite right. Momentarily at least, I felt the temptation. The Minister is a remarkable woman and I've never met anyone quite like her. – Did you strengthen my resistance, Bliss?'

She said, 'I've told you many times I must not and will not tamper with your mind in any way, Trevize. You beat down the temptation, I imagine, through your strong sense of duty.'

'No, I rather think not.' He smiled wryly. 'Nothing so dramatic and noble. My resistance was strengthened, for one thing, by the fact that it *was* cold, and for another, by the sad thought that it wouldn't take many sessions with her to kill me. I could never keep up the pace.'

Pelorat said, 'Well, anyway, you are safely aboard. What are we going to do next?'

'In the immediate future, we are going to move outwards through the planetary system at a brisk pace until we are far enough from Comporellon's sun to make a Jump.'

'Do you think we will be stopped or followed?'

'No, I really think that the Minister is anxious only that we go away as rapidly as possible and stay away, in order that the vengeance of He Who Punishes not fall upon the planet. In fact –'

'Yes?'

'She believes the vengeance will surely fall on us. She is under the firm conviction that we will never return. This, I hasten to add, is not an estimate of my probable level of infidelity, which she has had no occasion to measure. She meant that Earth is so terrible a bearer of misfortune that anyone who seeks it must die in the process.'

Bliss said, 'How many have left Comporellon in search of Earth that she can make such a statement?'

'I doubt that any Comporellian has ever left on such a search. I told her that her fears were mere superstition.'

'Are you sure you believe that, or have you let her shake you?'

'I know her fears are the purest superstition in the form she expresses them, but they may be well founded just the same.'

'You mean, radioactivity will kill us if we try to land on it?'

'I don't believe that Earth is radioactive. What I do believe is that Earth protects itself. Remember that all reference to Earth in the library on Trantor has been removed. Remember that Gaia's marvellous memory in which all the planet takes part down to the rock strata of the surface and the molten metal at the core, stops short of penetrating far enough back to tell us anything of Earth.

'Clearly, if Earth is powerful enough to do that, it might also be capable of adjusting minds in order to force belief in its radioactivity, and thus preventing any search for it. Perhaps because Comporellon is so close that it represents a particular danger to Earth, there is the further reinforcement of a curious blankness. Deniador, who is a Sceptic and a scientist, is utterly convinced that there is no use searching for Earth. He says it cannot be found. – And that is why the Minister's superstition may be well founded. If Earth is so intent on concealing itself, might it not kill us, or distort us, rather than allow us to find it?'

Bliss frowned and said, 'Gaia –'

Trevize said, quickly, 'Don't say Gaia will protect us. Since Earth was able to remove Gaia's earliest memories, it is clear that in any conflict between the two Earth will win.'

Bliss said, coldly, 'How do you know that the memories were removed. It might be that it simply took time for Gaia to develop a planetary memory and that we can now probe backwards only to the time of the completion of that development. And if the memory *was* removed, how can you be sure that it was Earth that did it?'

Trevize said, 'I don't know. I merely advance my speculations.'

Pelorat put in, rather timidly, 'If Earth is so powerful, and so intent on preserving its privacy, so to speak, of what use is our search? You seem to think Earth won't allow us to succeed and will kill us if that will be what it takes to keep us from succeeding. In that case, is there any sense in not abandoning this whole thing?'

'It might seem we ought to give up, I admit, but I have this powerful conviction that Earth exists, and I must and will find it. And Gaia tells me that when I have powerful convictions of this sort, I am always right.'

'But how can we survive the discovery, old chap?'

'It may be,' said Trevize, with an effort at lightness, 'that Earth, too, will recognize the value of my extraordinary rightness and will leave me to myself. *But* – and this is what I am finally getting at – I cannot be certain that you two will survive and that is of concern to me. It always has been, but it is increasing now and it seems to me that I ought to take you two back to Gaia and then proceed on my own. It is I, not you, who first decided I must search for Earth; it is I, not you, who see value in it; it is I, not you, who am driven. Let it be I, then, not you, who takes the risk. Let me go on alone. – Janov?'

Pelorat's long face seemed to grow longer as he buried his chin in his neck. 'I won't deny I feel nervous, Golan, but I'd be ashamed to abandon you. I would disown myself if I did so.'

'Bliss?'

'Gaia will not abandon you, Trevize, whatever you do. If Earth should prove dangerous, Gaia will protect you as far as it can. And in any case, in my role as Bliss, I will not abandon Pel, and if he clings to you, then I certainly cling to him.'

Trevize said grimly, 'Very well, then. I've given you your chance. We go on together.'

'Together,' said Bliss.

Pelorat smiled slightly, and gripped Trevize's shoulder. 'Together. Always.'

29

Bliss said, 'Look at that, Pel.'

She had been making use of the ship's telescope by hand, almost aimlessly, as a change from Pelorat's library of Earth-legendry.

Pelorat approached, placed an arm about her shoulders and looked at the viewscreen. One of the gas giants of the Comporellian planetary system was in sight, magnified till it seemed the large body it really was.

In colour it was a soft orange streaked with paler stripes. Viewed from the planetary plane, and more distant from the sun than the ship itself was, it was almost a complete circle of light.

'Beautiful,' said Pelorat.

'The central streak extends beyond the planet, Pel.'

Pelorat furrowed his brow and said, 'You know, Bliss, I believe it does.'

'Do you suppose it's an optical illusion?'

Pelorat said, 'I'm not sure, Bliss. I'm as much a space-novice as you are. – Golan!'

Trevize answered the call with a rather feeble 'What is it?' and entered the pilot-room, looking a bit rumpled, as though he had just been napping on his bed with his clothes on – which was exactly what he had been doing.

He said, in a rather peevish way, 'Please! Don't be handling the instruments.'

'It's just the telescope,' said Pelorat. 'Look at that.'

Trevize did. 'It's a gas giant, the one they call Gallia according to the information I was given.'

'How can you tell it's that one, just looking?'

'For one thing,' said Trevize, 'at our distance from the Sun, and because of the planetary sizes and orbital positions, which I've been studying in plotting our course, that's the only one you could magnify to that extent at this time. For another thing, there's the ring.'

'Ring?' said Bliss, mystified.

'All you can see is a thin, pale marking, because we're viewing it almost edge-on. We can zoom up out of the planetary plane and give you a better view. Would you like that?'

Pelorat said, 'I don't want to make you have to recalculate positions and courses, Golan.'

'Oh well, the computer will do it for me with little trouble.' He sat down at the computer as he spoke and placed his hands on the markings that received them. The computer, finely attuned to his mind, did the rest.

The *Far Star*, free of fuel problems or of inertial sensations, accelerated rapidly, and once again Trevize felt a surge of love for a computer-and-ship that responded in such a way to him – as though it was his thought that powered and directed it, as though it were a powerful and obedient extension of his will.

It was no wonder the Foundation wanted it back; no wonder Comporellon had wanted it for itself. The only surprise was that the force of superstition had been strong enough to cause Comporellon to be willing to give it up.

Properly armed, it could outrun or outfight any ship in the Galaxy, or any combination of ships – provided only that it did not encounter another ship like itself.

Of course, it was not properly armed. Mayor Branno, in assigning him the ship, had at least been cautious enough to leave it unarmed.

Pelorat and Bliss watched intently as the planet, Gallia, slowly, slowly, tipped towards them. The upper pole (which ever it was) became visible, with turbulence in a large circular region around it, while the lower pole retired behind the bulge of the sphere.

At the upper end, the dark side of the planet invaded the sphere of orange light, and the beautiful circle became increasingly lopsided.

What seemed more exciting was that the central pale streak was no longer straight but had come to be curved, as were the other streaks to the north and south, but more noticeably so.

Now the central streak extended beyond the edges of the planet very distinctly and did so in a narrow loop on either side. There was no question of illusion; its nature was apparent. It was a ring of matter, looping about the planet, and hidden on the far side.

'That's enough to give you the idea, I think,' said Trevize. 'If we were to move over the planet, you would see the ring in its circular form, concentric about the planet, touching it nowhere. You'll probably see that it's not one ring either but several concentric rings.'

'I wouldn't have thought it possible,' said Pelorat, blankly. 'What keeps it in space?'

'The same thing that keeps a satellite in space,' said Trevize. 'The rings consist of tiny particles, every one of which is orbiting the planet. The rings are so close to the planet that tidal effects prevent them from coalescing into a single body.'

Pelorat shook his head. 'It's horrifying when I think of it, old man. How is it possible that I can have spent my whole life as a scholar and yet know so little about astronomy?'

'And I know nothing at all about the myths of humanity. No one can encompass all of knowledge. – The point is that these planetary rings aren't unusual. Almost every single gas giant has them, even if it's only a thin curve of dust. As it happens, the sun of Terminus has no true gas giant in its planetary family, so unless a Terminian is a space traveller, or has taken University instruction in astronomy, he's likely to know nothing about planetary rings. What *is* unusual is a ring that is sufficiently broad to be bright and noticeable, like that one. It's beautiful. It must be a couple of hundred kilometres wide at least.'

At this point, Pelorat snapped his fingers. '*That's* what it meant.'

Bliss looked startled. 'What is it, Pel?'

Pelorat said, 'I came across a scrap of poetry once, very ancient, and in an archaic version of Galactic that was hard to make out but that was good evidence of great age. – Though I shouldn't complain of the archaism, old chap. My work has made me an expert on various varieties of Old Galactic, which is quite gratifying even if it is of no use to me whatever outside my work. – What was I talking about?'

Bliss said, 'An old scrap of poetry, Pel dear.'

'Thank you, Bliss,' he said. And to Trevize, 'She keeps close track of what I say in order to pull me back whenever I get off-course, which is most of the time.'

'It's part of your charm, Pel,' said Bliss, smiling.

'Anyway, this scrap of poetry purported to describe the planetary system of which Earth was part. Why it should do so, I don't know, for the poem as a whole does not survive, at least, I was never able to locate it. Only this one portion survived, perhaps because of its astronomical content. In any case, it spoke of the brilliant triple ring of the sixth planet "both brade and large, sae the woruld shronk in comparisoun". I can still quote it, you see. I didn't understand what a planet's ring could be. I remember thinking of three circles on one side of the planet, all in a row. It seemed so nonsensical, I didn't bother to include it in my library. I'm sorry now I didn't inquire.' He shook his head. 'Being a mythologist in today's Galaxy is so solitary a job, one forgets the good of inquiring.'

Trevize said, consolingly, 'You were probably right to ignore it, Janov. It's a mistake to take poetic chatter literally.'

'But that's what was meant,' said Pelorat, pointing at the screen. 'That's what the poem was speaking of. Three wide rings, concentric, wider than the planet itself.'

Trevize said, 'I never heard of such a thing. I don't think rings can be that wide. Compared to the planet they circle, they are always very narrow.'

Pelorat said, 'We never heard of a habitable planet with a giant satellite, either. Or one with a radioactive crust. This is uniqueness number three. If we find a radioactive planet that might be otherwise habitable, with a giant satellite, and with another planet in the system that has a huge ring, there would be no doubt at all that we had encountered Earth.'

Trevize smiled. 'I agree, Janov. If we find all three, we will certainly have found Earth.'

'If!' said Bliss, with a sigh.

30

They were beyond the main worlds of the planetary system, plunging outwards between the positions of the two outermost planets so that there was now no significant mass within 1.5 billion kilometres. Ahead lay only the vast cometary cloud which, gravitationally, was insignificant.

The *Far Star* had accelerated to a speed of 0.1 c, one tenth the speed of light. Trevize knew well that, in theory, the ship could be accelerated to nearly the speed of light, but he also knew that, in practice, 0.1 c was the reasonable limit.

At that speed, any object with appreciable mass could be avoided, but there was no way of dodging the innumerable dust particles in space and, to a far greater extent even, individual atoms and molecules. At very fast speeds, even such small objects could do damage, scouring and scraping the ship's hull. At speeds near the speed of light, each atom smashing into the hull had the properties of a cosmic ray particle. Under that penetrating cosmic radiation, anyone on board ship would not long survive.

The distant stars showed no perceptible motion in the viewscreen, and even though the ship was moving at thirty thousand kilometres per second, there was every appearance of its standing still.

The computer scanned space to great distances for any oncoming object of small but significant size that might be on a collision course, and the ship veered gently to avoid it, in the extremely unlikely case that that would be necessary. Between the small size of any possible oncoming object, the speed with which it was passed, and the lack of inertial effect as the result of the course-change, there was no way of telling whether anything ever took place in the nature of what might be termed a 'close call'.

Trevize, therefore, did not worry about such things, or even give it the most casual thought. He kept his full attention on the three sets of co-ordinates he had been given by Deniador, and, particularly, on the set which indicated the object closest to themselves.

'Is there something wrong with the figures?' asked Pelorat, anxiously.

'I can't tell yet,' said Trevize. 'Co-ordinates in themselves aren't useful, unless you know the zero point and the conventions used in setting them up – the direction in which to mark off the distance, so to speak, what the equivalent of a prime meridian is, and so on.'

'How do you find out such things?' said Pelorat blankly.

'I obtained the co-ordinates of Terminus and a few other known points, relative to Comporellon. If I put them into the computer, it will calculate what the conventions must be for such co-ordinates if Terminus and the other points are to be correctly located. I'm only trying to organize things in my mind so that I can properly program the computer for this. Once the conventions are determined, the figures we have for the Forbidden Worlds might possibly have meaning.'

'Only possibly?' said Bliss.

'Only possibly, I'm afraid,' said Trevize. 'These are old figures after all – presumably Comporellian, but not definitely. What if they are based on other conventions?'

'In that case?'

'In that case, we have only meaningless figures. But – we just have to find out.'

His hands flickered over the softly glowing keys of the computer, feeding it the necessary information. He then placed his hands on the handmarks on the desk. He waited while the computer worked out the conventions of the known co-ordinates, paused a moment, then interpreted the co-ordinates of the nearest Forbidden World by the same conventions, and finally located those co-ordinates on the Galactic map in its memory.

A starfield appeared on the screen and moved rapidly as it adjusted itself. When it reached stasis, it expanded with stars bleeding off the edges in all directions until they were almost all gone. At no point could the eye follow the rapid change; it was all a speckled blur. Until finally, a space one tenth of a parsec on each side (according to the index figures below the screen) was all that remained. There was no further change, and only half a dozen dim sparks relieved the darkness of the screen.

'Which one is the Forbidden World?' asked Pelorat, softly.

'None of them,' said Trevize. 'Four of them are red dwarfs, one a near-red dwarf, and the last a white dwarf. None of them can possibly have a habitable world in orbit about them.'

'How do you know they're red dwarfs just by looking at them.'

Trevize said, 'We're not looking at real stars; we're looking at a section of the Galactic map stored in the computer's memory. Each one is labelled. You can't see it and ordinarily I couldn't see it, either, but as long as my hands are making contact, as they are, I am aware of a considerable amount of data on any star on which my eyes concentrate.'

Pelorat said, in a woebegone tone, 'Then the co-ordinates are useless.'

Trevize looked up at him, 'No, Janov. I'm not finished. There's still the matter of time. The co-ordinates for the Forbidden World are those of twenty thousand years ago. In that time, both it and Comporellon have been revolving about the Galactic Centre, and they may well be revolving at different speeds and in orbits of different inclinations and eccentricities. With time, therefore, the two worlds may be drifting closer together or further apart and, in twenty thousand years, the Forbidden World may have drifted anywhere from one-half to five parsecs off the mark. It certainly wouldn't be included in that tenth-parsec square.'

'What do we do, then?'

'We have the computer move the Galaxy twenty thousand years back in time relative to Comporellon.'

'Can it do that?' asked Bliss, sounding rather awe-struck.

'Well, it can't move the Galaxy itself back in time, but it can move the map in its memory banks back in time.'

Bliss said, 'Will we see anything happen?'

'Watch,' said Trevize.

Very slowly, the half-dozen stars crawled over the face of the screen. A new star, not hitherto on the screen, drifted in from the left hand edge, and Pelorat pointed in excitement. 'There! There!'

Trevize said, 'Sorry. Another red dwarf. They're very common. At least three-fourths of all the stars in the Galaxy are red dwarfs.'

The screen settled down and stopped moving.

'Well?' said Bliss.

Trevize said, 'That's it. That's the view of that portion of the Galaxy as it would have been twenty thousand years ago. At the very centre of the screen is a point where the Forbidden World ought to be if it had been drifting at some average velocity.'

'Ought to be, but isn't,' said Bliss sharply.

'It isn't,' agreed Trevize, with remarkably little emotion.

Pelorat released his breath in a long sigh. 'Oh, too bad, Golan.'

Trevize said, 'Wait, don't despair. I wasn't expecting to see the star there.'

'You weren't?' said Pelorat, astonished.

'No. I told you that this isn't the Galaxy itself, but the computer's map of the Galaxy. If a real star is not included in the map, we don't see it. If the planet is called "Forbidden" and has been called so for twenty thousand years, the chances are it wouldn't be included in the map. And it isn't, for we don't see it.'

Bliss said, 'We might not see it because it doesn't exist. The Comporellian legends may be false, or the co-ordinates may be wrong.'

'Very true. The computer, however, can now make an estimate as to what the co-ordinates ought to be at this time, now that it has located the spot where it may have been twenty thousand years ago. Using the co-ordinates corrected for time, a correction I could only have made through use of the star map, we can now switch to the real star field of the Galaxy itself.'

Bliss said, 'But you only assumed an average velocity for the Forbidden World. What if its velocity was *not* average? You would not now have the correct co-ordinates.'

'True enough, but a correction, assuming average velocity, is almost certain to be closer to its real position, than if we had made no time correction at all.'

'You hope!' said Bliss doubtfully.

'That's exactly what I do,' said Trevize. 'I hope. – And now let's look at the real Galaxy.'

The two onlookers watched tensely, while Trevize (perhaps to reduce his own tensions and delay the zero moment) spoke softly, almost as though he were lecturing.

'It's more difficult to observe the real Galaxy,' he said. 'The map in the computer is an artificial construction, with irrelevancies capable of being eliminated. If there is a nebula obscuring the view I can remove it. If the angle of view is inconvenient for what I have in mind, I can change the angle, and so on. The real Galaxy, however, I must take as I find it, and if I want a change I must move physically through space, which will take far more time than it would take to adjust a map.'

And as he spoke, the screen showed a star cloud so rich in individual stars as to seem an irregular heap of powder.

Trevize said, 'That's a large angle view of a section of the Milky Way, and I want the foreground, of course. If I expand the foreground, the background will tend to fade in comparison. The co-ordinate spot is close enough to Comporellon so that I should be able to expand it to about the situation I had on the view of the map. Just let me put in the necessary instructions, if I can hold on to my sanity long enough. *Now.*'

The star field expanded with a rush so that thousands of stars pushed off every edge, giving the watchers so real a sensation of moving towards the screen that all three automatically leaned backwards as though in response to a forward rush.

The old view returned, not quite as dark as it had been on the map, but with the half-dozen stars shown as they had been in the original view. And there, close to the centre, was another star, shining far more brightly than the others.

'There it is,' said Pelorat, in an awed whisper.

'It may be. I'll have the computer take its spectrum and analyse it.' There was a moderately long pause, then Trevize said, 'Spectral class, G-4, which makes it a trifle dimmer and smaller than Terminus's sun, but rather brighter than Comporellon's sun. And no G-class star should be omitted from the computer's Galactic map. Since this one is, that is a strong indication that it may be the sun about which the Forbidden World revolves.'

Bliss said, 'Is there any chance of its turning out that there is no habitable planet revolving about this star after all.'

'There's a chance, I suppose. In that case, we'll try to find the other two Forbidden Worlds.'

Bliss persevered. 'And if the other two are false alarms, too?'

'Then we'll try something else.'

'Like what?'

'I wish I knew,' said Trevize grimly.

Part III

Aurora

8

Forbidden World

31

'Golan,' said Pelorat. 'Does it bother you if I watch?'

'Not at all, Janov,' said Trevize.

'If I ask questions?'

'Go ahead.'

Pelorat said, 'What are you doing?'

Trevize took his eyes off the viewscreen. 'I've got to measure the distance of each star that seems to be near the Forbidden World on the screen, so that I can determine how near they are really. Their gravitational fields must be known and for that I need mass and distance. Without that knowledge, one can't be sure of a clean Jump.'

'How do you do that?'

'Well, each star I see has its co-ordinates in the computer's memory banks and these can be converted into co-ordinates on the Comporellian system. That can, in turn, be slightly corrected for the actual position of the *Far Star* in space relative to Comporellon's sun, and that gives me the distance of each. Those red dwarfs all look quite near the Forbidden World on the screen, but some might be much closer and some much further. We need their three-dimensional position, you see.'

Pelorat nodded, and said, 'And you already have the co-ordinates of the Forbidden World –'

'Yes, but that's not enough. I need the distances of the other stars to within a per cent or so. Their gravitational intensity in the neigh-bourhood of the Forbidden World is so small that a slight error makes no perceptible difference. The sun about which the Forbidden World revolves – or might revolve – possesses an enormously intense gravitational field in the neighbourhood of the Forbidden World and I must know its distance with perhaps a thousand times the accuracy of that of the other stars. The co-ordinates alone won't do.'

'Then what do you do?'

'I measure the apparent separation of the Forbidden World – or, rather, its star – from three nearby stars which are so dim it takes considerable magnification to make them out at all. Presumably, those three are *very* far away. We then keep one of those three stars centred on the screen and Jump a tenth of a parsec in a direction at right angles to the line of vision to the Forbidden World. We can do that safely enough even without knowing distances to comparatively far-off stars.

'The reference star which is centred would still be centred after the Jump. The two other dim stars, if all three are truly very distant, do not change their positions measurably. The Forbidden World, however, is close enough to change its apparent position in paralactic shift. From the size of the shift, we can determine its distance. If I want to make doubly certain, I choose three other stars and try again.'

Pelorat said, 'How long does all that take?'

'Not very long. The computer does the heavy work. I just tell it what to do. What really takes the time is that I have to study the results and make sure they look right and that my instructions aren't at fault somehow. If I were one of those daredevils with utter faith in themselves and the computer, it could be done in a few minutes.'

Pelorat said, 'It's really astonishing. Think how much the computer does for us.'

'I think of it all the time.'

'What would you do without it?'

'What would I do without a gravitic ship? What would I do without my astronautic training? What would I do without twenty thousand years of hyperspatial technology behind me? The fact is that I'm myself – here – now. Suppose we were to imagine ourselves twenty thousand additional years into the future. What technological marvels would we have to be grateful for? Or might it be that twenty thousand years hence humanity would not exist?'

'Scarcely that,' said Pelorat. 'Scarcely not exist. Even if we don't become part of Galaxia, we would still have psychohistory to guide us.'

Trevize turned in his chair, releasing his hand-hold on the computer. 'Let it work out distances,' he said, 'and let it check the matter a number of times. There's no hurry.'

He looked quizzically at Pelorat, and said, 'Psychohistory! You know, Janov, twice that subject came up on Comporellon, and twice it was described as a superstition. I said so once, and then Deniador said it also. After all, how can you define psychohistory but as a superstition of the Foundation. Isn't it a belief without proof or evidence? What do you think, Janov? It's more your field than mine.'

Pelorat said, 'Why do you say there's no evidence, Golan? The simulacrum of Hari Seldon has appeared in the Time Vault a dozen times and has discussed events as they happened. He could not have known what those events would be, in his time, had he not been able to predict them psychohistorically.'

Trevize nodded. 'That sounds impressive. He was wrong about the Mule, but even allowing for that, it's impressive. Still, it has an uncomfortable magical feel to it. Any conjurer can do tricks.'

'No conjurer could predict centuries into the future.'

'No conjurer could really do what he makes you think he does.'

'Come, Golan. I can't think of any trick that would allow me to predict what will happen five centuries from now.'

'Nor can you think of a trick that will allow a conjurer to read the contents of a message hidden in a pseudotesseract on an unmanned orbiting satellite. Just the same, I've seen a conjurer do it. Has it ever occurred to you that the Time Capsule, along with the Hari Seldon simulacrum, may be rigged by the government?'

Pelorat looked as though he were revolted by the suggestion. 'They wouldn't do that.'

Trevize made a scornful sound.

Pelorat said, 'And they'd be caught if they tried.'

'I'm not at all sure of that. The point is, though, that we don't know how psychohistory works at all.'

'I don't know how that computer works, but I know it works.'

'That's because others know how it works. How would it be if *no one* knew how it worked. Then, if it stopped working for any reason, we would be helpless to do anything about it. And if psychohistory suddenly stopped working –'

'The Second Foundationers know the workings of psychohistory.'

'How do you know that, Janov?'

'So it is said.'

'Anything can be said. – Ah, we have the distance of the Forbidden World's star, and, I hope, very accurately. Let's consider the figures.'

He stared at them for a long time, his lips moving occasionally, as though he were doing some rough calculations in his head. Finally, he said, without lifting his eyes, 'What's Bliss doing?'

'Sleeping, old chap,' said Pelorat. Then, defensively, 'She *needs* sleep, Golan. Maintaining herself as part of Gaia across hyperspace is energy-consuming.'

'I suppose so,' said Trevize, and turned back to the computer. He placed his hands on the desk and muttered, 'I'll let it go in several Jumps and have it recheck each time.' Then he withdrew them again and said, 'I'm serious, Janov. What *do* you know about psychohistory?'

Pelorat looked taken aback. 'Nothing. Being a historian, which I am, after a fashion, is worlds different from being a psychohistorian. – Of course, I know the two fundamental basics of psychohistory, but everyone knows that.'

'Even I do. The first requirement is that the number of human beings involved must be large enough to make statistical treatment valid. But how large is "large enough"?'

Pelorat said, 'The latest estimate of the Galactic population is something like ten quadrillion, and that's probably an underestimate. Surely, that's large enough.'

'How do you know.'

'Because psychohistory *does* work, Golan. No matter how you chop logic, it *does* work.'

'And the second requirement,' said Trevize, 'is that human beings not be aware of psychohistory, so that the knowledge does not skew their reactions. – But they *are* aware of psychohistory.'

'Only of its bare existence, old chap. That's not what counts. The second requirement is that human beings not be aware of the *predictions* of psychohistory and that they are not – except that the Second Foundationers are supposed to be aware of them, but they're a special case.'

'And upon those two requirements alone, the science of psychohistory has been developed. That's hard to believe.'

'Not out of those two requirements *alone*,' said Pelorat. 'There are advanced mathematics and elaborate statistical methods. The story is – if you want tradition – that Hari Seldon devised psychohistory by modelling it upon the kinetic theory of gases. Each atom or molecule in a gas moves randomly so that we can't know the position or velocity of any one of them. Nevertheless, using statistics, we can work out the rules governing their overall behaviour with great precision. In the same way, Seldon intended to work out the overall behaviour of human societies even though the solutions would not apply to the behaviour of individual human beings.'

'Perhaps, but human beings aren't atoms.'

'True,' said Pelorat. 'A human being has consciousness and his behaviour is sufficiently complicated to make it appear to be free will. How Seldon handled that I haven't any idea, and I'm sure I couldn't understand it even if someone who knew tried to explain it to me – but he did it.'

Trevize said, 'And the whole thing depends on dealing with people who are both numerous and unaware. Doesn't that seem to you a quicksandish foundation on which to build an enormous mathematical structure. If those requirements are not truly set, then everything collapses.'

'But since the Plan hasn't collapsed –'

'Or, if the requirements are not exactly false or inadequate but simply weaker than they should be, psychohistory might work adequately for centuries and then, upon reaching some particular crisis, would collapse – as it did temporarily in the time of the Mule. – Or what if there is a third requirement?'

'What third requirement?' asked Pelorat, frowning slightly.

'I don't know,' said Trevize. 'An argument may seem thoroughly logical and elegant and yet contain unexpressed assumptions. Maybe the third requirement is an assumption so taken for granted that no one ever thinks of mentioning it.'

'An assumption that is so taken for granted is usually valid enough, or it wouldn't be so taken for granted.'

Trevize snorted. 'If you knew scientific history as well as you know traditional history, Janov, you would know how wrong that is. – But I see that we are now in the neighbourhood of the sun of the Forbidden World.'

And, indeed, centred on the screen, was a bright star – one so bright that the screen automatically filtered its light to the point where all other stars were washed out.

32

Facilities for washing and for personal hygiene on board the *Far Star* were compact, and the use of water was always held to a reasonable minimum to avoid overloading the recycling facilities. Both Pelorat and Bliss had been sternly reminded of this by Trevize.

Even so, Bliss maintained an air of freshness at all times and her dark, long hair could be counted on to be glossy, her fingernails to sparkle.

She walked into the pilot-room and said, 'There you are!'

Trevize looked up and said, 'No need for surprise. We could scarcely have left the ship, and a thirty-second search would be bound to uncover us inside the ship, even if you couldn't detect our presence mentally.'

Bliss said, 'The expression was purely a form of greeting and not meant to be taken literally, as you well know. Where are we? – And don't say "in the pilot-room".'

'Bliss, dear,' said Pelorat, holding out one arm, 'we're at the outer regions of the planetary system of the nearest of the three Forbidden Worlds.'

She walked to his side, placing her hand lightly on his shoulder, while his arm moved about her waist. She said, 'It can't be very Forbidden. Nothing has stopped us.'

Trevize said, 'It is only Forbidden because Comporellon and the other worlds of the second wave of settlement have voluntarily placed the worlds of the first wave – the Spacers – out of bounds. If we ourselves don't feel bound by that voluntary agreement, what is to stop us?'

'The Spacers, if any are left, might have voluntarily placed the worlds of the second wave out of bounds, too. Just because we don't mind intruding upon them doesn't mean that they don't mind it.'

'True,' said Trevize, '*if* they exist. But so far we don't even know if any planet exists for them to live on. So far, all we see are the usual gas giants. Two of them, and not particularly large ones.'

Pelorat said hastily, 'But that doesn't mean the Spacer world doesn't exist. Any habitable world would be much closer to the sun and much smaller and very hard to detect in the solar glare from this distance. We'll have to micro-Jump inward to detect such a planet.' He seemed rather proud to be speaking like a seasoned space traveller.

'In that case,' said Bliss, 'why aren't we moving inwards?'

'Not just yet,' said Trevize. 'I'm having the computer check as far as it can for any sign of an artificial structure. We'll move inwards by stages – a dozen, if necessary – checking at each stage. I don't want to be trapped this time as we were when we first approached Gaia. Remember, Janov?'

'Traps like that could catch us every day. The one at Gaia brought me Bliss.' Pelorat gazed at her fondly.

Trevize grinned. 'Are you hoping for a new Bliss every day?'

Pelorat looked hurt, and Bliss said, with a trace of annoyance, 'My good chap – or whatever it is that Pel insists on calling you – you might as well move in more quickly. While I am with you, you will not be trapped.'

'The power of Gaia?'

'To detect the presence of other minds? Certainly.'

'Are you sure you are strong enough, Bliss. I gather you must sleep quite a bit to regain strength expended at maintaining contact with the main body of Gaia. How far can I rely on the perhaps narrow limits of your abilities at this distance from the source?'

Bliss flushed. 'The strength of the connection is ample.'

Trevize said, 'Don't be offended. I'm simply asking. – Don't you see this as a disadvantage of being Gaia? I am not Gaia. I am a complete and independent individual. That means I can travel as far as I wish from my world and my people, and remain Golan Trevize. What powers I have, and such as they are, I continue to have, and they remain wherever I do. If I were alone in space, parsecs away from any human being, and unable, for some reason, to communicate with anyone in any way, or even to see the spark of a single star in the sky, I would be and remain Golan Trevize. I might not be able to survive, and I might die, but I would die Golan Trevize.'

Bliss said, 'Alone in space and far from all others, you would be unable to call on the help of your fellows, on their different talents and knowledge. Alone, as an isolated individual, you would be sadly diminished as compared with yourself as part of an integrated society. You know that.'

Trevize said, 'There would nevertheless not be the same diminution as in your case. There is a bond between you and Gaia that is far stronger than the one between me and my society, and that bond stretches through hyperspace and requires energy for maintenance, so that you must gasp, mentally, with the effort, and feel yourself to be a diminished entity far more than I must.'

Bliss's young face set hard and, for a moment, she looked young no more or, rather, she appeared ageless – more Gaia than Bliss, as though to refute Trevize's contention. She said, 'Even if everything you say is so, Golan Trevize – that is, was, and will be, that cannot perhaps be less, but certainly cannot be more – even if everything you say is so, do you expect there is no price to be paid for a benefit gained? Is it not better to be a warm-blooded creature such as yourself than a cold-blooded creature such as a fish, or whatever?'

Pelorat said, 'Tortoises are cold-blooded. Terminus doesn't have any, but some worlds do. They are shelled creatures, very slow moving but long-living.'

'Well, then, isn't it better to be a human being than a tortoise; to move quickly whatever the temperature, rather than slowly? Isn't it better to support high-energy activities, quickly contracting muscles, quickly working nerve fibres, intense and long-sustained thought – than to creep slowly, and sense gradually, and have only a blurred awareness of the immediate surroundings? Isn't it?'

'Granted,' said Trevize. 'It is. What of it?'

'Well, don't you know you must pay for warm-bloodedness? To maintain your temperature above that of your surroundings, you must expend energy far more wastefully than a tortoise must. You must be eating almost constantly so that you can pour energy into your body as quickly as it leaks out. You would starve far more quickly than a tortoise would, and die more quickly, too. Would you rather be a tortoise, and live more slowly and longer? Or would you rather pay the price and be a quick-moving, quick-sensing, thinking organism?'

'Is this a true analogy, Bliss?'

'No, Trevize, for the situation with Gaia is more favourable. We don't expend unusual quantities of energy when we are compactly together. It is only when part of Gaia is at hyperspatial distances from the rest of Gaia that energy expenditure rises. – And remember that what you have voted for is not merely a larger Gaia, not just a larger individual world. You have decided for Galaxia, for a vast complex of worlds. Anywhere in the Galaxy, you will be part of Galaxia and you will be closely surrounded by parts of something that extends from each interstellar atom to the central black hole. It would then require small amounts of energy to remain a whole. No part would be at any great distance from all other parts. It is all this you have decided for, Trevize. How can you doubt that you have chosen well?'

Trevize's head was bent in thought. Finally, he looked up and said, 'I may have chosen well, but I must be *convinced* of that. The decision I have made is the most important in the history of humanity and it is not enough that it is a good one. I must *know* it to be a good one.'

'What more do you need than what I have told you?'

'I don't know, but I will find it on Earth.' He spoke with absolute conviction.

Pelorat said, 'Golan, the star shows a disc.'

It did. The computer, busy about its own affairs and not the least concerned with any discussion that might swirl about it, had been approaching the star in stages, and had reached the distance Trevize had set for it.

They continued to be well outside the planetary plane and the computer split the screen to show each of three small inner planets.

It was the innermost that had a surface temperature in the liquid-water range, and that had an oxygen atmosphere as well. Trevize waited for its orbit to be computed and the first crude estimate seemed reasonable. He kept that computation going, for the longer the planetary movement was observed, the more accurate the com-putation of its orbital elements.

Trevize said quite calmly, 'We have a habitable planet in view. Very likely habitable.'

'Ah.' Pelorat looked as nearly delighted as his solemn expression would allow.

'I'm afraid, though,' said Trevize, 'that there's no giant satellite. In fact, no satellite of any kind has been detected so far. So it isn't Earth. At least, not if we go by tradition.'

'Don't worry about that, Golan,' said Pelorat. 'I rather suspected we weren't going to encounter Earth here when I saw that neither of the gas giants had an unusual ring system.'

'Very well then,' said Trevize. 'The next step is to find out the nature of the life inhabiting it. From the fact that it has an oxygen atmosphere, we can be absolutely certain that there is plant life upon it, but –'

'Animal life, too,' said Bliss abruptly. 'And in quantity.'

'What?' Trevize turned to her.

'I can sense it. Only faintly at this distance, but the planet is unquestionably not only habitable, but inhabited.'

33

The *Far Star* was in polar orbit about the Forbidden World, at a distance great enough to keep the orbital period at a little in excess of six days. Trevize seemed in no hurry to come out of orbit.

'Since the planet is inhabited,' he explained, 'and since, according to Deniador, it was once inhabited by human beings who were technologically advanced and who represent a first wave of Settlers – the so-called Spacers – they may be technologically advanced still and may have no great love for us of the second wave who have replaced them. I would like them to show themselves, so that we can learn a little about them before risking a landing.'

'They may not know we are here,' said Pelorat.

'*We* would, if the situation were reversed. I must assume, then, that, if they exist, they are likely to try to make contact with us. They might even want to come out and get us.'

'But if they did come out after us and were technologically advanced, we might be helpless to –'

'I can't believe that,' said Trevize. 'Technological advancement is not necessarily all one piece. They might conceivably be far beyond us in some ways, but it's clear they don't indulge in interstellar travel. It is we, not they, who have settled the Galaxy, and in all the history of the Empire, I know of nothing that would indicate that they left their worlds and made themselves evident to us. If they haven't been space travelling, how could they be expected to have made serious advances in astronautics? And if they haven't, they can't possibly have anything like a gravitic ship. We may be essentially unarmed but even if they come lumbering after us with a battleship, they couldn't possibly catch us. – No, we wouldn't be helpless.'

'Their advance may be in mentalics. It may be that the Mule was a Spacer –'

Trevize shrugged in clear irritation. 'The Mule can't be everything. The Gaians have described him as an aberrant Gaian. He's also been considered a random mutant.'

Pelorat said, 'To be sure, there have also been speculations – not taken very seriously, of course – that he was a mechanical artifact. A robot, in other words, though that word wasn't used.'

'If there *is* something that seems mentally dangerous, we will have to depend on Bliss to neutralize that. She can – Is she asleep now, by the way?'

'She has been,' said Pelorat, 'but she was stirring when I came out here.'

'Stirring, was she? Well, she'll have to be awake on short notice if anything starts happening. You'll have to see to that, Janov.'

'Yes, Golan,' said Pelorat quietly.

Trevize shifted his attention to the computer. 'One thing that bothers me are the entry stations. Ordinarily, they are a sure sign of a planet inhabited by human beings with a high technology. But these –'

'Is there something wrong with them?'

'Several things. In the first place, they're very archaic. They might be thousands of years old. In the second, there's no radiation, but thermals.'

'What are thermals?'

'Thermal radiation is given off by any object warmer than its surroundings. It's a familiar signature that everything yields and it consists of a broad band of radiation following a fixed pattern depending on temperature. That is what the entry stations are radiating. If there are working human devices aboard the stations, there is bound to be a leakage of non-thermal, non-random radiation. Since only thermals are present we can assume that either the stations are empty, and have been, perhaps, for thousands of years; or, if occupied, it is by people with a technology so advanced in this direction that they leak no radiation.'

'Perhaps,' said Pelorat, 'the planet has a high civilization, but the entry stations are empty because the planet has been left so strictly alone for so long by our kind of settlers that they are no longer concerned about any approach.'

'Perhaps. – Or perhaps it is a lure of some sort.'

Bliss entered, and Trevize, noting her out of the corner of his eyes, said grumpily 'Yes, here we are.'

'So I see,' said Bliss, 'and still in an unchanged orbit. I can tell that much.'

Pelorat explained hastily. 'Golan is being cautious, dear. The entry stations seem unoccupied and we're not sure of the significance of that.'

'There's no need to worry about it,' said Bliss indifferently. 'There are no detectable signs of intelligent life on the planet we're orbiting.'

Trevize bent an astonished glare at her. 'What are you talking about? You said –'

'I said there was animal life on the planet, and so there is, but where in the Galaxy were you taught that animal life necessarily implies human life?'

'Why didn't you say this when you first detected animal life?'

'Because at that distance, I couldn't tell. I could barely detect the unmistakable wash of animal neural activity, but there was no way I could, at that intensity, tell butterflies from human beings.'

'And now?'

'We're much closer now, and you may have thought I was asleep, but I wasn't – or, at least, only briefly. I was, to use an inappropriate word, listening as hard as I could for any sign of mental activity complex enough to signify the presence of intelligence.'

'And there isn't any?'

'I would suppose,' said Bliss, with sudden caution, 'that if I detect nothing at this distance, there can't possibly be more than a few thousand human beings on the planet. If we come closer, I can judge it still more delicately.'

'Well, that changes things,' said Trevize, with some confusion.

'I suppose,' said Bliss, who looked distinctly sleepy and, therefore, irritable. 'You can now discard all this business of analysing radiation and inferring and deducing and who knows what else you may have been doing. My Gaian senses do the job much more efficiently and surely. Perhaps you see what I mean when I say it is better to be a Gaian than an Isolate.'

Trevize waited before answering, clearly labouring to hold his temper. When he spoke, it was with a polite, and almost formal tone, 'I am grateful to you for the information. Nevertheless, you must understand that, to use an analogy, the thought of the advantage of improving my sense of smell would be insufficient motive for me to decide to abandon my humanity and become a blood-hound.'

34

They could see the Forbidden World now, as they moved below the cloud layer and drifted through the atmosphere. It looked curiously moth-eaten.

The polar regions were icy, as might be expected, but they were not large in extent. The mountainous regions were barren, with occasional glaciers, but they were not large in extent, either. There were small desert areas, well scattered.

Putting all that aside, the planet was, in potential, beautiful. Its continental areas were quite large, but sinuous, so that there were long shorelines, and rich coastal plains of generous extent. There were lush tracts of both tropical and temperate forests, rimmed by grasslands – and yet the moth-eaten nature of it all was evident.

Scattered through the forests were semi-barren areas, and parts of the grasslands were thin and sparse.

'Some sort of plant disease?' said Pelorat, wonderingly.

'No,' said Bliss slowly. 'Something worse than that, and more permanent.'

'I've seen a number of worlds,' said Trevize, 'but nothing like this.'

'I have seen very few worlds,' said Bliss, 'but I think the thoughts of Gaia and this is what you might expect of a world from which humanity has disappeared.'

'Why?' said Trevize.

'Think about it,' said Bliss tartly. 'No inhabited world has a true ecological balance. Earth must have had one originally, for if that was the world on which humanity evolved, there must have been long ages when humanity did not exist, or any species capable of developing an advanced technology and the ability to modify the environment. In that case, a natural balance – ever-changing, of course – must have existed. On all other inhabited worlds, however, human beings have carefully terraformed their new environments and established plant and animal life, but the ecological system they introduce is bound to be unbalanced. It would possess only a limited number of species and only those that human beings wanted, or couldn't help introducing –'

Pelorat said, 'You know what that reminds me of? – Pardon me, Bliss, for interrupting, but it so fits that I can't resist telling you right now before I forget. There's an old creation myth I once came across; a myth in which life was formed on a planet and consisted of only a limited assortment of species, just those useful to or pleasant for humanity. The first human beings then did something silly – never mind what, old fellow, because those old myths are usually

symbolic and only confusing if they are taken literally – and the
planet's soil was cursed. "Thorns also and thistles shall it bring forth
to thee", is the way the curse was quoted though the passage sounds
much better in the archaic Galactic in which it was written. The
point is, though, was it really a curse? Things human beings don't
like and don't want, such as thorns and thistles, may be needed to
balance the ecology.'

Bliss smiled. 'It's really amazing, Pel, how everything reminds you
of a legend, and how illuminating they are sometimes. Human beings,
in terraforming a world leave out the thorns and thistles, whatever
they may be, and human beings then have to labour to keep the
world going. It isn't a self-supporting organism as Gaia is. It is rather
a miscellaneous collection of Isolates and the collection isn't miscellaneous enough to allow the ecological balance to persist indefinitely.
If humanity disappears, and if its guiding hands are removed, the
world's pattern of life inevitably begins to fall apart. The planet
un-terraforms itself.'

Trevize said, sceptically, 'If that's what's happening, it doesn't
happen quickly. This world may have been free of human beings
for twenty thousand years and yet most of it still seems to be very
much a going concern.'

'Surely,' said Bliss, 'that depends on how well the ecological
balance was set up in the first place. If it is a fairly good balance to
begin with, it might last for a long time without human beings. After
all, twenty thousand years, though very long in terms of human
affairs, is just overnight when compared to a planetary lifetime.'

'I suppose,' said Pelorat, staring intently at the planetary vista,
'that if the planet is degenerating, we can be sure that the human
beings are gone.'

Bliss said, 'I still detect no mental activity at the human level and
I am willing to suppose that the planet is safely free of humanity.
There is the steady hum and buzz of lower levels of consciousness,
however, levels high enough to represent birds and mammals. Just
the same, I'm not sure that unterraforming is enough to show human

beings are gone. A planet might deteriorate even if human beings existed upon it, if the society were itself abnormal and did not understand the importance of preserving the environment.'

'Sure,' said Pelorat, 'such a society would quickly be destroyed. I don't think it would be possible for human beings to fail to understand the importance of retaining the very factors that are keeping them alive.'

Bliss said, 'I don't have your pleasant faith in human reason, Pel. It seems to me to be quite conceivable that when a planetary society consists only of Isolates, local and even individual concerns might easily be allowed to overcome planetary concerns.'

'I don't think that's conceivable,' said Trevize, 'any more than Pelorat does. In fact, since human-occupied worlds exist by the million and none of them have deteriorated in an un-terraforming fashion, your fear of Isolatism may be exaggerated, Bliss.'

The ship now moved out of the daylit hemisphere into the night. The effect was that of a rapidly deepening twilight, and then utter darkness outside, except for starlight where the sky was clear.

The ship maintained its height by accurately monitoring the atmospheric pressure and gravitational intensity. They were at a height too great to encounter any upthrusting mountainous massif, for the planet was at a stage when a mountain-building had not recently taken place. Still the computer felt its way forward with its microwave fingertips, just in case.

Trevize regarded the velvety darkness and said, thoughtfully, 'Somehow what I find most convincing as the sign of a deserted planet is the absence of visible light on the dark side. No technological society could possibly endure darkness. – As soon as we get into the dayside, we'll go lower.'

'What would be the use of that?' said Pelorat. 'There's nothing there.'

'Who said there's nothing there?'

'Bliss did. And you did.'

'No, Janov. I said there's no radiation of technological origin and

Bliss said there's no sign of human mental activity, but that doesn't mean there's nothing there. Even if there are no human beings on the planet, there would surely be relics of some sort. I'm after information, Janov, and the remainders of a technology may have its uses in that direction.'

'After twenty thousand years?' Pelorat's voice climbed in pitch. 'What do you think can survive twenty thousand years? There will be no films, no paper, no print; metal will have rusted, wood will have decayed, plastic will be in shattered grains. Even stone will have crumbled and eroded.'

'It may not be twenty thousand years,' said Trevize patiently. 'I mentioned that time as the longest period the planet may have been left empty of human beings because Comporellian legend has this world flourishing at that time. But suppose the last human beings had died or vanished or fled only a thousand years ago.'

They arrived at the other end of the night side and the dawn came and brightened into sunlight almost instantaneously.

The *Far Star* sank downwards and slowed its progress until the details of the land surface were clearly visible. The small islands that dotted the continental shores could now be clearly seen. Most were green with vegetation.

Trevize said, 'It's my idea that we ought to study the spoiled areas particularly. It seems to me that those places where human beings were most concentrated would be where the ecological balance was most lacking. Those areas might be the nucleus of the spreading blight of unterraforming. What do you think, Bliss?'

'It's possible. In any case, in the absence of definite knowledge, we might as well look where it's easiest to see. The grasslands and forest would have swallowed most signs of human habitation so that looking there might prove a waste of time.'

'It strikes me,' said Pelorat, 'that a world might eventually establish a balance with what it has; that new species might develop; and that the bad areas might be recolonized on a new basis.'

'Possibly, Pel,' said Bliss. 'It depends on how badly out of balance the world was in the first place. And for a world to heal itself and achieve a new balance through evolution would take far more than twenty thousand years. We'd be talking millions of years.'

The *Far Star* was no longer circling the world. It was drifting slowly across a five-hundred-kilometre-wide stretch of scattered heath and furze, with occasional clumps of trees.

'What do you think of that?' said Trevize suddenly, pointing. The ship came to a drifting halt and hovered in mid-air. There was a low, but persistent, hum as the gravitic engines shifted into high, neutralizing the planetary gravitational field almost entirely.

There was nothing much to see where Trevize pointed. Tumbled mounds bearing soil and sparse grass were all that was visible.

'It doesn't look like anything to me,' said Pelorat.

'There's a straight-line arrangement to that junk. Parallel lines, and you can make out some faint lines at right angles, too. See? See? You can't get that in any natural formation. That's human architecture, marking out foundations and walls, just as clearly as though they were still standing there to be looked at.'

'Suppose it is,' said Pelorat. 'That's just a ruin. If we're going to do archaeological research, we're going to have to dig and dig. Professionals would take years to do it properly –'

'Yes, but we can't take the time to do it properly. That may be the faint outline of an ancient city and something of it may still be standing. Let's follow those lines and see where they take us.'

It was towards one end of the area, at a place where the trees were somewhat more thickly clumped, that they came to standing walls – or partially standing ones.

Trevize said, 'Good enough for a beginning. We're landing.'

9

Facing the Pack

35

The *Far Star* came to rest at the bottom of a small rise, a hill in the generally flat countryside. Almost without thought, Trevize had taken it for granted that it would be best for the ship not to be visible for miles in every direction.

He said, 'The temperature outside is 24°C, the wind is about 11 kilometres per hour from the west, and it is partly cloudy. The computer does not know enough about the general air circulation to be able to predict the weather. However, since the humidity is some 40 per cent, it seems scarcely about to rain. On the whole, we seem to have chosen a comfortable latitude or season of the year, and after Comporellon that's a pleasure.'

'I suppose,' said Pelorat, 'that as the planet continues to unterraform, the weather will become more extreme.'

'I'm sure of that,' said Bliss.

'Be as sure as you like,' said Trevize. 'We have thousands of years of leeway. Right now, it's still a pleasant planet and will continue to be so for our lifetimes and far beyond.'

He was clasping a broad belt about his waist as he spoke, and Bliss said sharply, 'What's that, Trevize?'

'Just my old navy training,' said Trevize. 'I'm not going into an unknown world unarmed.'

'Are you seriously intending to carry weapons.'

'Absolutely. Here on my right,' he slapped a holster that contained a massive weapon with a broad muzzle, 'is my blaster, and here on my left' (a smaller weapon with a thin muzzle that contained no opening), 'is my neuronic whip.'

'Two varieties of murder,' said Bliss, with distaste.

'Only one. The blaster kills. The neuronic whip doesn't. It just stimulates the pain nerves, and it hurts so that you can wish you were dead, I'm told. Fortunately, I've never been at the wrong end of one.'

'Why are you taking them?'

'I told you. It's an enemy world.'

'Trevize, it's an *empty* world.'

'Is it? There's no technological society, it would seem, but what if there are post-technological primitives. They may not possess anything worse than clubs or rocks, but those can kill, too.'

Bliss looked exasperated, but lowered her voice in an effort to be reasonable. 'I detect no human neuronic activity, Trevize. That eliminates primitives of any type, post-technological or otherwise.'

'Then I won't have to use my weapons,' said Trevize. 'Still, what harm would there be in carrying them? They'll just make me a little heavier, and since the gravitational pull at the surface is about 91 per cent that of Terminus, I can afford the weight. – Listen, the ship may be unarmed as a ship, but it has a reasonable supply of hand-weapons. I suggest that you two also –'

'No,' said Bliss at once. 'I will not make even a gesture in the direction of killing – or of inflicting pain, either.'

'It's not a question of killing, but of avoiding being killed, if you see what I mean.'

'I can protect myself in my own way.'

'Janov?'

Pelorat hesitated. 'We didn't have arms on Comporellon.'

'Come, Janov, Comporellon was a known quantity, a world associated with the Foundation. Besides, we were at once taken into custody. If we had had weapons they would have been taken away. Do you want a blaster?'

Pelorat shook his head. 'I've never been in the navy, old chap. I wouldn't know how to use one of those things and, in an emergency, I would never think of it in time. I'd just run and – and get killed.'

'You won't get killed, Pel,' said Bliss energetically. 'Gaia has you in my/its protection, and that posturing naval hero as well.'

Trevize said, 'Good. I have no objection to being protected, but I am not posturing. I am simply making assurance doubly sure, and if I never have to make a move towards these things, I'll be completely pleased, I promise you. Still I *must* have them.'

He patted both weapons affectionately and said, 'Now let's step out on this world which may not have felt the weight of human beings upon its surface for thousands of years.'

36

'I have a feeling,' said Pelorat, 'that it must be rather late in the day, but the sun is high enough to make it near noon, perhaps.'

'I suspect,' said Trevize, looking about the quiet panorama, 'that your feeling originates out of the sun's orange tint, which gives it a sunset feel. If we're still here at actual sunset and the cloud formations are proper, we ought to experience a deeper red than we're used to. I don't know whether you'll find it beautiful or depressing. – For that matter it was probably even more extreme on Comporellon, but there we were indoors virtually all the time.'

He turned slowly, considering the surroundings in all directions. In addition to the almost subliminal oddness of the light, there was the distinctive smell of the world – or this section of it. It seemed a little musty, but far from actively unpleasant.

The trees nearby were of middling height, and looked old, with gnarled bark and trunks a little off the vertical, though because of a prevailing wind or something off-colour about the soil he couldn't tell. Was it the trees that lent a somehow menacing ambience to the world or was it something else – less material.

Bliss said, 'What do you intend to do, Trevize? Surely we didn't come all this distance to enjoy the view?'

Trevize said, 'Actually, perhaps that ought to be my part of it just now. I would suggest that Janov explore this place. There are ruins off in that direction and he's the one who can judge the value of any records he might find. I imagine he can understand writings or films in archaic Galactic and I know quite well I wouldn't. And I suppose, Bliss, you want to go with him in order to protect him. As for me, I will stay here as a guard on the outer rim.'

'A guard against what? Primitives with rocks and clubs?'

'Perhaps.' And then the smile that had hovered about his lips faded and he said, 'Oddly enough, Bliss, I'm a little uneasy about this place. I can't say why.'

Pelorat said, 'Come, Bliss. I've been a home-body collector of old tales all my life, so I've never actually put my hands on ancient documents. Just imagine if we could find –'

Trevize watched them walk away, Pelorat's voice fading as he walked eagerly towards the ruins; Bliss swinging along at his side.

Trevize listened absently and then turned back to continue his study of the surroundings. What could there be to rouse apprehension?

He had never actually set foot upon a world without a human population, but he had viewed many from space. Usually, they were small worlds, not large enough to hold either water or air, but they had been useful as marking a meeting site during naval manoeuvres (there had been no war in his life-time, or for a century before his birth – but manoeuvres went on), or as an exercise in simulated emergency repairs. Ships he had been on had been in orbit about such worlds, or had even rested on them, but he had never had occasion to step off the ships at those times.

Was it that he was now actually standing on an empty world? Would he have felt the same if he had been standing on one of the many small, airless worlds he had encountered in his student days – and even since?

He shook his head. It wouldn't have bothered him. He was sure of that. He would have been in a space suit, as he had been innumerable times when he was free of his ship in space. It was a familiar situation and contact with a mere lump of rock would have produced no alteration in the familiarity. Surely!

Of course – He was not wearing a space suit now.

He was standing on a habitable world, as comfortable to the feel as Terminus would be – far more comfortable than Comporellon had been. He experienced the wind against his cheek, the warmth of the sun on his back, the rustle of vegetation in his ears. Everything was familiar, except that there were no human beings on it – at least, not any longer.

Was that it? Was it that that made the world seem so eerie? Was it that it was not merely an uninhabited world, but a *deserted* one?

He had never been on a deserted world before; never heard of a deserted world before; never thought a world *could* be deserted. All the worlds he had known of till now, once they had been populated by human beings, remained so populated forever.

He looked up towards the sky. Nothing else had deserted it. An occasional bird flew across his line of vision, seeming more natural, somehow, than the slate-blue sky between the orange-tinted fairweather clouds. (Trevize was certain that, given a few days on the planet, he would become accustomed to the off-colour so that sky and clouds would grow to seem normal to him.)

He heard birdsongs from the trees, and the softer noise of insects. Bliss had mentioned butterflies earlier and here they were – in surprising numbers and in several colourful varieties.

There were also occasional rustlings in the clumps of grass that surrounded the trees, but he could not quite make out what was causing them.

Nor did the obvious presence of life in his vicinity rouse fear in him. As Bliss had said, terraformed worlds had, from the very first, lacked dangerous animals. The fairy tales of childhood, and the heroic fantasies of his teenage years were invariably set on a legendary world that must have been derived from the vague myths of Earth. The hyperdrama holoscreen had been filled with monsters – lions, unicorns, dragons, whales, brontosaurs, bears. There were dozens of them with names he could not remember; some of them surely mythical, and perhaps all of them. There were smaller animals that bit and stung, even plants that were fearful to the touch – but only in fiction. He had once heard that primitive honeybees were able to sting, but certainly no real bees were in any way harmful.

Slowly, he walked to the right, skirting the border of the hill. The grass was tall and rank, but sparse, growing in clumps. He made his way among the trees, also growing in clumps.

Then he yawned. Certainly, nothing exciting was happening, and he wondered if he might not retreat to the ship and take a nap. No, unthinkable. Clearly, he had to stand on guard.

Perhaps he ought to do sentry duty – marching, one, two, one, two, swinging about with a snap and performing complicated manoeuvrings with a parade electro-rod. (It was a weapon no warrior had used in three centuries, but it was still absolutely essential at drill, for no reason anyone could ever advance.)

He grinned at the thought of it, then wondered if he ought to join Pelorat and Bliss in the ruins. Why? What good would he do?

Suppose he saw something that Pelorat had happened to overlook? – Well, time enough to make the attempt after Pelorat returned. If there was anything that might be found easily, by all means let Pelorat make the discovery.

Might the two be in trouble? Foolish! What possible kind of trouble?

And if there *were* trouble, they would call out.

He stopped to listen. He heard nothing.

And then the irresistible thought of sentry duty recurred to him and he found himself marching, feet moving up and down with a stamp, an imaginary electro-rod coming off one shoulder, whirling, and being held out straight before him, exactly vertical – whirling again, end over end, and back over the other shoulder. Then, with a smart about-face, he was looking towards the ship (rather far-off now) once more.

And when he did that, he froze in reality, and not in sentry make-believe.

He was not alone.

Until then, he had not seen any living creature other than plant growth, insects, and an occasional bird. He had neither seen nor heard anything approach – but now an animal stood between him and the ship.

Sheer surprise at the unexpected event deprived him, for a moment, of the ability to interpret what he saw. It was not till after a perceptible interval that he knew what he was looking at.

It was only a dog.

Trevize was not a dog person. He had never owned a dog and he felt no surge of friendliness towards one when he encountered it. He felt no such surge this time, either. He thought, rather impatiently, that there was no world on which these creatures had not accompanied men. They existed in countless varieties and Trevize had long had the weary impression that each world had at least one variety characteristic of itself. Nevertheless, all varieties were constant in this: whether they were kept for entertainment, show, or some form of useful work – they were bred to love and trust human beings.

It was a love and trust Trevize had never appreciated. He had once lived with a woman who had had a dog. That dog, whom Trevize tolerated for the sake of the woman, conceived a deep-seated adoration of him, followed him about, leaned against him when relaxing (all fifty pounds of him), covered him with saliva and hair at unexpected moments, and squatted outside the door and moaned, whenever he and the woman were trying to engage in sex.

From that experience, Trevize had emerged with the firm conviction that for some reason known only to the canine mind and its odour-analysing ability, he was a fixed object of doggish devotion.

Therefore, once the initial surprise was over, he surveyed the dog without concern. It was a large dog, lean and rangy, and with long legs. It was staring at him with no obvious sign of adoration. Its mouth was open in what might have been taken as a welcoming grin, but the teeth displayed were somehow large and dangerous, and Trevize decided that he would be more comfortable without the dog in his line of view.

It occurred to him, then, that the dog had never seen a human being, and that countless canine generations preceding had never seen one. The dog might have been as astonished and uncertain at the sudden appearance of a human being as Trevize had been at that of the dog. Trevize, at least, had quickly recognized the dog for what it was, but the dog did not have that advantage. It was still puzzled, and perhaps alarmed.

Clearly, it would not be safe to leave an animal that large, and with such teeth, in an alarmed state. Trevize realized that it would be necessary to establish a friendship at once.

Very slowly, he approached the dog (no sudden motions, of course). He held out his hand, ready to allow it to be sniffed, and made soft, soothing sounds, most of which consisted of 'Nice doggie' – something he found intensely embarrassing.

The dog, eyes fixed on Trevize, backed away a step or two, as though in distrust, and then its upper lip wrinkled into a snarl and from its mouth there issued a rasping growl. Although Trevize had never seen a dog behave so, there was no way of interpreting the action as representing anything but menace.

Trevize therefore stopped advancing and froze. His eyes caught motion to one side, and his head turned slowly. There were two other dogs advancing from that direction. They looked just as deadly as the first.

Deadly? That adjective occurred to him only now, and its dreadful appropriateness was unmistakable.

His heart was suddenly pounding. The way to the ship was blocked. He could not run aimlessly, for those long canine legs would reach him in yards. If he stood his ground and used his blaster, then while he killed one, the other two would be upon him. Off in the distance, he could see other dogs approaching. Was there some way in which they communicated? Did they hunt in packs?

Slowly, he shifted ground leftwards, in a direction in which there were no dogs – as yet. Slowly. Slowly.

The dogs shifted ground with him. He felt certain that all that saved him from instant attack was the fact that the dogs had never seen or smelled anything like himself before. They had no established behaviour pattern they could follow in his case.

If he ran, of course, that would represent something familiar to the dogs. They would know what to do if something the size of Trevize showed fear and ran. They would run, too. Faster.

Trevize kept sidling towards a tree. He had the wildest desire to move upwards where the dogs could not follow. They moved with him, snarling softly, coming closer. All three had their eyes fixed unwinkingly upon him. Two more were joining them and, further off, Trevize could see still other dogs approaching. At some point, when he was close enough, he would have to make the dash. He could not wait too long, or run too soon. Either might be fatal.

Now!

He probably set a personal record for acceleration and even so it was a near thing. He felt the snap of jaws close on the heel of one foot, and for just a moment he was held fast before the teeth slid off the tough ceramoid.

He was not skilled at climbing trees. He had not climbed one since he was ten and, as he recalled, that had been a clumsy effort. In this case, though, the trunk was not quite vertical, and the bark was gnarled and offered handholds. What was more, he was driven by necessity, and it is remarkable what one can do if the need is great enough.

Trevize found himself sitting in a crotch, perhaps ten metres above the ground. For the moment he was totally unaware that he had scraped one hand and that it was oozing blood. At the base of the tree, five dogs now sat on their haunches, staring upwards, tongues lolling, all looking patiently expectant.

What now?

37

Trevize was not in a position to think about the situation in logical detail. Rather, he experienced flashes of thought in odd and distorted sequence which, if he had eventually sorted them out, would have come to this –

Bliss had earlier maintained that in terraforming a planet, human beings would establish an unbalanced ecology, which they would be able to keep from falling apart only by unending effort. For instance, no settlers had ever brought with them any of the large predators. Small ones could not be helped. Insects, parasites – even small hawks, shrews and so on.

Those dramatic animals of legend and vague literary accounts – tigers, grizzly bears, orcs, crocodiles? Who would carry them from world to world even if there were sense to it? And where would there be sense to it?

It meant that human beings were the only large predators, and it was up to them to cull those plants and animals that, left to themselves, would smother in their own over-plenty.

And if human beings somehow vanished, then other predators must take their place. But what predators? The most sizeable predators tolerated by human beings were dogs and cats, tamed and living on human bounty.

What if no human beings remained to feed them? They must then find their own food – for their survival and, in all truth, for the survival of those they preyed on, whose numbers had to be kept in check lest overpopulation do a hundred times the damage that predators would do.

So dogs would multiply, in their variations, with the large ones attacking the large, untended herbivores; the smaller ones preying on birds and rodents. Cats would prey by night as dogs did by day; the former singly, the latter in packs.

And perhaps evolution would eventually produce more varieties, to fill additional environmental niches. Would some dogs eventually develop sea-going characteristics to enable them to live on fish; and would some cats develop gliding abilities to hunt the clumsier birds in the air as well as on the ground?

In flashes, all this came to Trevize while he struggled with more systematic thought to tell him what he might do.

The number of dogs kept growing. He counted twenty-three now surrounding the tree and there were others approaching. How large was the pack? What did it matter? It was large enough already.

He withdrew his blaster from its holster, but the solid feel of the butt in his hand did not give him the sense of security he would have liked. When had he last inserted an energy unit into it and how many charges could he fire? Surely not twenty-three.

What about Pelorat and Bliss? If they emerged, would the dogs turn on them? Were they safe even if they did not emerge? If the dogs sensed the presence of two human beings inside the ruins, what could stop them from attacking them there. Surely there would be no doors or barriers to hold them off.

Could Bliss stop them, and even drive them away? Could she concentrate her powers through hyperspace to the desired pitch of intensity? For how long could she maintain them?

Should he call for help then? Would they come running if he yelled, and would the dogs flee under Bliss's glare? (Would it take a glare or was it simply a mental action undetectable to onlookers without the ability?) Or, if they appeared, would they then be torn apart under the eyes of Trevize, who would be forced to watch, helplessly, from the relative safety of his post in the tree?

No, he would have to use his blaster. If he could kill one dog and frighten them off for just a while, he could scramble down the tree, yell for Pelorat and Bliss, kill a second dog if they showed signs of returning, and all three could then hustle into the ship.

He adjusted the intensity of the microwave beam to the three-quarter mark. That should be ample to kill a dog with a loud report. The report would serve to frighten the dogs away, and he would be conserving energy.

He aimed carefully at a dog in the middle of the pack, one who seemed (in Trevize's own imagination, at least) to exude a greater malignancy than the rest – perhaps only because he sat more quietly and, therefore, seemed more cold-bloodedly intent on his prey. The dog was staring directly at the weapon now, as though it scorned the worst Trevize could do.

It occurred to Trevize that he had never himself fired a blaster at a human being, or seen anyone else do it. There had been firing at water-filled dummies of leather and plastic during training; with the water almost instantaneously heated to the boiling point, and shredding the covering as it exploded.

But who, in the absence of war, would fire at a human being? And what human being would withstand a blaster and force its use? Only here, on a world made pathological by the disappearance of human beings –

With that odd ability of the brain to note something utterly beside the point, Trevize was aware of the fact that a cloud had hidden the sun – and then he fired.

There was an odd shimmer of the atmosphere on a straight line from the muzzle of the blaster to the dog; a vague sparkle that might have gone unnoticed if the sun were still shining unhindered.

The dog must have felt the initial surge of heat, and made the smallest motion as though it were about to leap. And then it exploded, as a portion of its blood and cellular contents vaporized.

The explosion made a disappointingly small noise, for the dog's integument was simply not as tough as that of the dummies they had practised on. Flesh, skin, blood, and bone were scattered, however, and Trevize felt his stomach heave.

The dogs started back, some having been bombarded with uncomfortably warm fragments. That was only a momentary hesitation, however. They crowded against each other suddenly, in order to eat what had been provided. Trevize felt his sickness increase. He was not frightening them; he was feeding them. At that rate, they would never leave. In fact, the smell of fresh blood and warm meat would attract still more dogs, and perhaps other smaller predators as well.

A voice called out, 'Trevize. What –'

Trevize looked outwards. Bliss and Pelorat had emerged from the ruins. Bliss had stopped short, her arms thrown out to keep Pelorat back. She stared at the dogs. The situation was obvious and clear. She had to ask nothing.

Trevize shouted, 'I tried to drive them off without involving you and Janov. Can you hold them off?'

'Barely,' said Bliss, not shouting, so that Trevize had trouble hearing her even though the dogs' snarling had quieted as though a soothing sound-absorbent blanket had been thrown over them.

Bliss said, 'There are too many of them, and I am not familiar with their pattern of neuronic activity. We have no such savage things on Gaia.'

'Or on Terminus. Or on any civilized world,' shouted Trevize. 'I'll shoot as many of them as I can and you try to handle the rest. A smaller number will give you less trouble.'

'No, Trevize. Shooting them will just attract others. – Stay behind me, Pel. There's no way you can protect me. – Trevize, your other weapon.'

'The neuronic whip?'

'Yes. That produces pain. Low power. Low power!'

'Are you afraid of hurting them?' called out Trevize in anger. 'Is this a time to consider the sacredness of life?'

'I'm considering Pel's. Also mine. Do as I say. Low power, and shoot at one of the dogs. I can't hold them much longer.'

The dogs had drifted away from the tree and had surrounded Bliss and Pelorat, who stood with their backs to a crumbling wall. The dogs nearest the two made hesitant attempts to come closer still, whining a bit as though trying to puzzle out what it was that held them off when they could sense nothing that would do it. Some tried uselessly to scramble up the wall and attack from behind.

Trevize's hand was trembling as he adjusted the neuronic whip to low power. The neuronic whip used much less energy than the blaster did, and a single power-cartridge could produce hundreds of whip-like strokes but, come to think of it, he didn't remember when he had last charged this weapon, either.

It was not so important to aim the whip. Since conserving energy was not as critical, he could use it in a sweep across the mass of dogs. That was the traditional method of controlling crowds that showed signs of turning dangerous.

However, he followed Bliss's suggestion. He aimed at one dog and fired. The dog fell over, its legs twitching. It emitted loud, high-pitched squeals.

The other dogs backed away from the stricken beast, ears flattening backwards against their heads. Then, squealing in their turn, they turned and left, at first slowly, then more rapidly, and finally, at a full race. The dog who had been hit, scrambled painfully to its legs, and limped away whimpering, much the last of them.

The noise vanished in the distance, and Bliss said, 'We had better get into the ship. They will come back. Or others will.'

Trevize thought that never before had he manipulated the ship's entry mechanism so rapidly. And it was possible he might never do so again.

38

Night had fallen before Trevize felt something approaching the normal. The small patch of syntho-skin on the scrape on his hand had soothed the physical pain, but there was a scrape on his psyche for which soothing was not so easy.

It was not the mere exposure to danger. He could react to that as well as any ordinarily brave person might. It was the totally unlooked-for direction from which the danger had come. It was the feeling of the ridiculous. How would it look if people were to find out he had been treed by snarling *dogs*? It would scarcely be worse if he had been put to flight by the whirring of angry canaries.

For hours, he kept listening for a new attack on the part of the dogs, for the sound of howls, for the scratch of claws against the outer hull.

Pelorat, by comparison, seemed quite cool. 'There was no question in my mind, old chap, that Bliss would handle it, but I must say you fired the weapon well.'

Trevize shrugged. He was in no mood to discuss the matter.

Pelorat was holding his library – the one compact disc on which his lifetime of research into myths and legends were stored – and with it he retreated into his bedroom where he kept his small reader.

He seemed quite pleased with himself. Trevize noticed that but didn't follow it up. Time for that later when his mind wasn't quite as taken up with dogs.

Bliss said, rather tentatively, when the two were alone, 'I presume you were taken by surprise.'

'Quite,' said Trevize gloomily. 'Who would think that at the sight of a dog – a *dog* – I should run for my life.'

'Twenty thousand years without men and it would not be quite a dog. Those beasts must now be the dominant large predators.'

Trevize nodded. 'I figured that out while I was sitting on the tree branch being a dominated prey. You were certainly right about an unbalanced ecology.'

'Unbalanced, certainly, from the human standpoint – but considering how efficiently the dogs seem to be going about their business, I wonder if Pel may be right in his suggestion that the ecology could balance itself, with various environmental niches being filled by evolving variations of the relatively few species that were once brought to the world.'

'Oddly enough,' said Trevize, 'the same thought occurred to me.'

'Provided, of course, the unbalance is not so great that the process of righting itself takes too long. The planet might become completely non-viable before that.'

Trevize grunted.

Bliss looked at him thoughtfully. 'How is it that you thought of arming yourself?'

Trevize said, 'It did me little good. It was your ability –'

'Not entirely. I needed your weapon. At short notice, with only hyperspatial contact with the rest of Gaia, with so many individual minds of so unfamiliar a nature, I could have done nothing without your neuronic whip.'

'My blaster was useless. I tried that.'

'With a blaster, Trevize, a dog merely disappears. The rest may be surprised, but not frightened.'

'Worse than that,' said Trevize. 'They ate the remnants. I was bribing them to stay.'

'Yes, I see that might be the effect. The neuronic whip is different. It inflicts pain, and a dog in pain emits cries of a kind that are well understood by other dogs who, by conditioned reflex, if nothing else, begin to feel frightened themselves. With the dogs already disposed towards fright, I merely nudged their minds, and off they went.'

'Yes, but you realized the whip was the more deadly of the two in this case, I did not.'

'I am accustomed to dealing with minds. You are not. That's why I insisted on low power and aiming at one dog. I did not want so much pain that it killed a dog and left him silent. I did not want the pain so dispersed as to cause mere whimpering. I wanted strong pain concentrated at one point.'

'And you got it, Bliss,' said Trevize. 'It worked perfectly. I owe you considerable gratitude.'

'You begrudge that,' said Bliss thoughtfully, 'because it seems to you that you played a ridiculous role. And yet, I repeat, I could have done nothing without your weapons. What puzzles me is how you can explain your arming yourself in the face of my assurance that there were no human beings on this world, something I am still certain is a fact. Did you foresee the dogs?'

'No,' said Trevize. 'I certainly didn't. Not consciously, at least. And I don't habitually go armed, either. It never even occurred to me to put on weapons at Comporellon. – But I can't allow myself to trip into the trap of feeling it was magic, either. It couldn't have been. I suspect that once we began talking about unbalanced ecologies earlier, I somehow had an unconscious glimpse of animals grown dangerous in the absence of human beings. That is clear enough in hindsight, but I *might* have had a whiff of it in foresight. Nothing more than that.'

Bliss said, 'Don't dismiss it that casually. I participated in the same conversation concerning unbalanced ecologies and I didn't have that same foresight. It is that special trick of foresight in you that Gaia values. I can see, too, that it must be irritating to you to have a hidden foresight the nature of which you cannot detect; to act with decision, but without clear reason.'

'The usual expression on Terminus is "to act on a hunch".'

'On Gaia we say, "to know without thought". You don't like knowing without thought, do you?'

'It bothers me, yes. I don't like being driven by hunches. I assume the hunch has reason behind it, but not knowing the reason makes me feel I'm not in control of my own mind – a kind of mild madness.'

'And when you decided in favour of Gaia and Galaxia, you were acting on a hunch, and now you seek the reason.'

'I have said so at least a dozen times.'

'And I have refused to accept your statement as literal truth. For that I am sorry. I will oppose you in this no longer. I hope, though, that I may continue to point out items in Gaia's favour.'

'Always,' said Trevize, 'if you, in turn, recognize that I may not accept them.'

'Does it occur to you, then, that this Unknown World is reverting to a kind of savagery, and perhaps to eventual desolation and uninhabitability, because of the removal of a single species that is capable of acting as a guiding intelligence? If the world were Gaia, or better yet, a part of Galaxia, this could not happen. The guiding intelligence would still exist in the form of the Galaxy as a whole, and ecology, whenever unbalanced, and for whatever reason, would move towards balance again.'

'Does that mean that dogs would no longer eat?'

'Of course they would eat, just as humans do. They would eat, however, with purpose, in order to balance the ecology under deliberate direction, and not as a result of random circumstance.'

Trevize said, 'The loss of individual freedom might not matter to dogs, but it must matter to human beings. – And what if *all* human beings were removed from existence, everywhere, and not merely on one world or on several? What if Galaxia were left without human beings at all? Would there still be a guiding intelligence? Would all other life forms and inanimate matter be able to put together a common intelligence adequate for the purpose?'

Bliss hesitated. 'Such a situation,' she said, 'has never been experienced. Nor does there seem any likelihood that it will ever be experienced in the future.'

Trevize said, 'But doesn't it seem obvious to you, that the human mind is qualitatively different from everything else, and that if it were absent, the sum total of all other consciousness could not replace it. Would it not be true, then, that human beings are a special case and must be treated as such? They should not be fused even with one another, let alone with non-human objects.'

'Yet you decided in favour of Galaxia.'

'For an overriding reason I cannot make out.'

'Perhaps that overriding reason was a glimpse of the effect of unbalanced ecologies? Might it not have been reasoning that every world in the Galaxy is on a knife-edge, with instability on either side, and that only Galaxia could prevent such disasters as are taking place on this world – to say nothing of the continuing interhuman disasters of war and administrative failure.'

'No. Unbalanced ecologies were not in my mind at the time of my decision.'

'How can you be sure?'

'I may not know what it is I'm foreseeing, but if something is suggested afterwards, I would recognize it if that were indeed what I foresaw. – As it seems to me I may have foreseen dangerous animals on this world.'

'Well,' said Bliss soberly, 'we might have been dead as a result of those dangerous animals if it had not been for a combination of our powers, your foresight and my mentalism. Come, then, let us be friends.'

Trevize nodded. 'If you wish.'

There was a chill in his voice that caused Bliss's eyebrows to rise, but at this point Pelorat burst in, nodding his head as though prepared to shake it off its foundations.

'I think,' he said, 'we have it.'

39

Trevize did not, in general, believe in easy victories, and yet it was only human to fall into belief against one's better judgement. He felt the muscles in his chest and throat tighten, but managed to say, 'The location of Earth? Have you discovered that, Janov?'

Pelorat stared at Trevize for a moment, and deflated. 'Well, no,' he said, visibly abashed. 'Not quite that. – Actually, Golan, not that at all. I had forgotten about that. It was something else that I discovered in the ruins. I suppose it's not really important.'

Trevize managed a long breath and said, 'Never mind, Janov. Every finding is important. What was it you came in to say?'

'Well,' said Pelorat, 'it's just that almost nothing survived, you understand. Twenty thousand years of storm and wind don't leave much. What's more, plant life is gradually destructive and animal life – but never mind all that. The point is that "almost nothing" is not the same as "nothing".

'The ruins must have included a public building, for there was some fallen stone, or concrete, with incised lettering upon it. There was hardly anything visible, you understand, old chap, but I took photographs with one of those cameras we have on board ship, the kind with built-in computer enhancement – I never got round to asking permission to take one, Golan, but it was important, and I –'

Trevize waved his hand in impatient dismissal. 'Go on.'

'I could make out some of the lettering, which was very archaic. Even with computer enhancement and with my own fair skill at reading Archaic, it was impossible to make out much except for one short phrase. The letters there were larger and a bit clearer than the rest They may have been incised more deeply because they identified the world itself. The phrase reads, "Planet Aurora", so I imagine this world we rest upon is named Aurora, or was named Aurora.'

'It had to be named something,' said Trevize.

'Yes, but names are very rarely chosen at random. I made a careful search of my library just now and there are two old legends, from two widely-spaced worlds, as it happens, so that one can reasonably suppose them to be of independent origin, if one remembers that . . . but never mind that. In both legends, Aurora is used as a name for the dawn. We can suppose that Aurora may have actually meant dawn in some pre-Galactic language.

'As it happens some word for dawn or daybreak is often used as a name for space stations or other structures that are the first built of their kind. If this world is called dawn in whatever language, it may be the first of its kind, too.'

Trevize said, 'Are you getting ready to suggest that this planet is Earth and that Aurora is an alternative name for it because it represents the dawn of life and of man?'

Pelorat said, 'I couldn't go that far, Golan.'

Trevize said, with a trace of bitterness, 'There is, after all, no radioactive surface, no giant satellite, no gas giant with huge rings.'

'Exactly. But Deniador, back on Comporellon, seemed to think this was one of the worlds that was once inhabited by the first wave of settlers – the Spacers. If it were, then its name, Aurora, might indicate it to have been the first of those Spacer worlds. We might, at this very moment, be resting on the oldest human world in the Galaxy except for Earth itself. Isn't that exciting?'

'Interesting, at any rate, Janov, but isn't that a great deal to infer merely from the name, Aurora?'

'There's more,' said Pelorat excitedly. 'As far as I could check in my records there is no world in the Galaxy today with the name of "Aurora", and I'm sure your computer will verify that. As I said, there are all sorts of worlds and other objects named "Dawn" in various ways, but no one uses the actual word "Aurora".'

'Why should they? If it's a pre-Galactic word, it wouldn't be likely to be popular.'

'But names *do* remain, even when they're meaningless. If this were the first settled world, it would be famous; it might even, for a while, have been the dominant world of the Galaxy. Surely, there would be other worlds calling themselves "New Aurora", or "Aurora Minor", or something like that. And then others –'

Trevize broke in. 'Perhaps it wasn't the first settled world. Perhaps it was never of any importance.'

'There's a better reason in my opinion, my dear chap.'

'What would that be, Janov?'

'If the first wave of settlements was overtaken by a second wave to which all the worlds of the Galaxy now belong – as Deniador said – then there is very likely to have been a period of hostility between the two waves. The second wave – making up the worlds that now exist – would not use the names given to any of the worlds of the first wave. In that way, we can infer from the fact that the name "Aurora" has never been repeated that there *were* two waves of settlers, and that this is a world of the first wave.'

Trevize smiled. 'I'm getting a glimpse of how you mythologists work, Janov. You build a beautiful superstructure, but it may be standing on air. The legends tell us that the settlers of the first wave were accompanied by numerous robots, and that these were supposed to be their undoing. Now if we could find a robot on this world, I'd be willing to accept all this first-wave supposition, but we can't expect after twenty thou –'

Pelorat, whose mouth had been working, managed to find his voice. 'But, Golan, haven't I told you? – No, of course I haven't. I'm so excited I can't put things in the right order. There *was* a robot.'

40

Trevize rubbed his forehead, almost as though he were in pain. He said, 'A robot? There was a robot?'

'Yes,' said Pelorat, nodding his head emphatically.

'How do you know?'

'Why, it was a robot. How could I fail to know one if I see one?'

'Have you ever seen a robot before?'

'No, but it was a metal object that looked like a human being. Head, arms, legs, torso. Of course, when I say metal, it was mostly rust, and when I walked towards it, I suppose the vibration of my tread damaged it further, so that when I reached to touch it –'

'Why should you touch it?'

'Well, I suppose I couldn't quite believe my eyes. It was an automatic response. As soon as I touched it, it crumbled. But –'

'Yes?'

'Before it quite did, its eyes seemed to glow very faintly and it made a sound as though it were trying to say something.'

'You mean it was still *functioning*?'

'Just barely, Golan. Then it collapsed.'

Trevize turned to Bliss. 'Do you corroborate all this, Bliss.'

'It was a robot, and we saw it,' said Bliss.

'And was it still functioning?'

Bliss said tonelessly, 'As it crumbled I caught a faint sense of neuronic activity.'

'How can there have been neuronic activity? A robot doesn't have an organic brain built of cells.'

'It has the computerized equivalent, I imagine,' said Bliss, 'and I would detect that.'

'Did you detect a robotic rather than a human mentality?'

Bliss pursed her lips and said, 'It was too feeble to decide anything about it except that it was there.'

Trevize looked at Bliss, then at Pelorat, and said, in a tone of exasperation, 'This changes everything.'

Part IV

Solaria

10

Robots

41

Trevize seemed lost in thought during dinner, and Bliss concentrated on the food.

Pelorat, the only one who seemed anxious to speak, pointed out that if the world they were on was Aurora and if it was the first settled world, it ought to be fairly close to Earth.

'It might pay to scour the immediate stellar neighbourhood,' he said. 'It would only mean sifting through a few hundred stars at most.'

Trevize muttered that hit-and-miss was a last resort and he wanted as much information about Earth as possible before attempting to approach it even if he found it. He said no more and Pelorat, clearly squelched, dwindled into silence as well.

After the meal, as Trevize continued to volunteer nothing, Pelorat said tentatively, 'Are we to be staying here, Golan?'

'Overnight, anyway,' said Trevize. 'I need to do a bit more thinking.'

'Is it safe?'

'Unless there's something worse than dogs about,' said Trevize, 'we're quite safe here in the ship.'

Pelorat said, 'How long would it take to lift off, if there *is* something worse than dogs about?'

Trevize said, 'The computer is on launch alert. I think we can manage to take off in between two and three minutes. And it will warn us quite effectively if anything unexpected takes place, so I suggest we all get some sleep. Tomorrow morning, I'll come to a decision as to the next move.'

Easy to say, thought Trevize, as he found himself staring at the darkness. He was curled up, partly dressed, on the floor of the computer room. It was quite uncomfortable, but he was sure that his bed would be no more conducive to sleep at this time and here at least he could take action at once if the computer sounded an alarm.

Then he heard footsteps and automatically sat up, hitting his head against the edge of the desk – not hard enough to do damage, but hard enough to make rubbing and grimacing a necessity.

'Janov?' he said in a muffled voice, eyes tearing.

'No. It's Bliss.'

Trevize reached over the edge of the table with one hand to make at least semicontact with the computer, and a soft light showed Bliss in a light pink wraparound.

Trevize said, 'What is it?'

'I looked in your bedroom and you weren't there. There was no mistaking your neuronic activity, however, and I followed it. You were clearly awake so I walked in.'

'Yes, but what is it you want?'

She sat down against the wall, knees up, and cradled her chin against them. She said, 'Don't be concerned. I have no designs on what's left of your virginity.'

'I don't imagine you do,' said Trevize sardonically. 'Why aren't you asleep? You need it more than we do.'

'Believe me,' she said in a low, heartfelt tone, 'that episode with the dogs was very draining.'

'I believe that.'

'But I had to talk to you when Pel was sleeping.'

'About what?'

Bliss said, 'When he told you about the robot, you said that that changes everything. What did you mean?'

Trevize said, 'Don't you see that for yourself? We have three sets of co-ordinates; three Forbidden Worlds. I want to visit all three to learn as much as possible about Earth before trying to reach it.'

He edged a bit closer so that he could speak lower still, then drew away sharply. He said, 'Look, I don't want Janov coming in here looking for us. I don't know what *he*'d think.'

'It's not likely. He's sleeping and I've encouraged that just a bit. If he stirs, I'll know. – Go on. You want to visit all three. What's changed?'

'It wasn't part of my plan to waste time on any world needlessly. If this world, Aurora, has been without human occupation for twenty thousand years then it is doubtful that any information of value has survived. I don't want to spend weeks or months scrabbling uselessly about the planetary surface, fighting off dogs and cats and bulls or whatever else may have become wild and dangerous, just on the hope of finding a scrap of reference material amid the dust, rust, and decay. It may be that on one or both of the other Forbidden Worlds there may be human beings and intact libraries. – So it was my intention to leave this world at once. We'd be out in space now, if I had done so, sleeping in perfect security.'

'But?'

'But if there are robots still functioning on this world, they may have important information that we could use. They would be safer to deal with than human beings would be, since, from what I've heard, they must follow orders and can't harm human beings.'

'So you've changed your plan and now you're going to spend time on this world searching for robots.'

'I don't want to, Bliss. It seems to me that robots can't last twenty thousand years without maintenance. – Yet since you've seen one with a spark of activity still, it's clear I can't rely on my commonsense guesses about robots. I mustn't lead out of ignorance. Robots may be more enduring than I imagine, or they may have a certain capacity for self-maintenance.'

Bliss said, 'Listen to me, Trevize, and please keep this confidential.'

'Confidential?' said Trevize, raising his voice in surprise. 'From whom?'

'Sh! From Pel, of course. Look, you don't have to change your plans. You were right the first time. There are no functioning robots on this world. I detect nothing.'

'You detected that one, and one is as good as –'

'I did not detect that one. It was non-functioning; *long* non-functioning.'

'You said –'

'I know what I said. Pel thought he saw motion and heard sound. Pel is a romantic. He's spent his working life gathering data, but that is a difficult way of making one's mark in the scholarly world. He would dearly love to make an important discovery of his own. His finding of the word "Aurora" was legitimate and made him happier than you can imagine. He wanted desperately to find more.'

Trevize said, 'Are you telling me he wanted to make a discovery so badly he convinced himself he had come upon a functioning robot when he hadn't?'

'What he came upon was a lump of rust containing no more consciousness than the rock against which it rested.'

'But you supported his story.'

'I could not bring myself to rob him of his discovery. He means so much to me.'

Trevize stared at her for a full minute, then he said, 'Do you mind explaining *why* he means so much to you? I want to know. I really want to know. To you he must seem an elderly man with nothing romantic about him. He's an Isolate, and you despise Isolates. You're young and beautiful and there must be other parts of Gaia that have the bodies of vigorous and handsome young men. With them you can have a physical relationship that can resonate through Gaia and bring peaks of ecstasy. So what do you see in Janov?'

Bliss looked at Trevize solemnly, 'Don't you love him?'

Trevize shrugged and said, 'I'm fond of him. I suppose you could say, in a non-sexual way, that I love him.'

'You haven't known him very long, Trevize. Why do you love him, in that non-sexual way of yours?'

Trevize found himself smiling without being aware of it. 'He's such an *odd* fellow. I honestly think that never in his life has he given a single thought to himself. He was ordered to go along with me, and he went. No objection. He wanted me to go to Trantor, but when I said I wanted to go to Gaia, he never argued. And now he's come along with me in this search for Earth, though he must know it's dangerous. I feel perfectly confident that if he had to sacrifice his life for me – or for anyone – he would, and without repining.'

'Would you give your life for him, Trevize?'

'I might, if I didn't have time to think. If I did have time to think, I would hesitate and I might funk it. I'm not as *good* as he is. And because of that, I have this terrible urge to protect and keep him good. I don't want the Galaxy to teach him *not* to be good. Do you understand? And I have to protect him from *you* particularly. I can't bear the thought of you tossing him aside when whatever nonsense amuses you now is done with.'

'Yes, I thought you'd think something like that. Don't you suppose I see in Pel what you see in him – and even more so, since I can contact his mind directly? Do I act as though I want to hurt him? Would I support his fantasy of having seen a functioning robot, if it weren't that I couldn't bear to hurt him? Trevize, I am used to what you would call goodness, for every part of Gaia is ready to be sacrificed for the whole. We know and understand no other course of action. But we give up nothing in so doing, for each part *is* the whole, though I don't expect you to understand that. Pel is something different.'

Bliss was no longer looking at Trevize. It was as though she were talking to herself. 'He is an Isolate. He is not selfless because he is a part of a greater whole. He is selfless because he is selfless. Do you understand me? He has all to lose and nothing to gain, and yet he is what he is. He shames me for being what I am without fear of loss, when he is what he is without hope of gain.'

She looked up at Trevize again, now, very solemnly. 'Do you know how much more I understand about him than you possibly can? And do you think I would harm him in any way?'

Trevize said, 'Bliss, earlier today, you said, "Come, let us be friends," and all I replied was, "If you wish." That was grudging of me, for I was thinking of what you might do to Janov. It is my turn, now. Come, Bliss, let us be friends. You can keep on pointing out the advantage of Galaxia and I may keep on refusing to accept your arguments, but even so, and despite that, let us be friends.' And he held out his hand.

'Of course, Trevize,' she said, and their hands gripped each other strongly.

42

Trevize grinned quietly to himself. It was an internal grin for the line of his mouth didn't budge.

When he had worked with the computer to find the star (if any) of the first set of co-ordinates, both Pelorat and Bliss had watched intently and had asked questions. Now they stayed in their room and slept or, at any rate, relaxed, and left the job entirely to Trevize.

In a way, it was flattering, for it seemed to Trevize that by now they had simply accepted the fact that Trevize knew what he was doing and required no supervision or encouragement. For that matter, Trevize had gained enough experience from the first episode to rely more thoroughly on the computer and to feel that it needed, if not none, then at least less supervision.

Another star – luminous and unrecorded on the Galactic map – showed up. This second star was more luminous than the star about which Aurora circled, and that made it all the more significant that the star was unrecorded in the computer.

Trevize marvelled at the peculiarities of ancient tradition. Whole centuries might be telescoped or dropped out of consciousness altogether. Entire civilizations might be banished into forgetfulness.

Yet out of the midst of these centuries, snatched from those civilizations, might be one or two factual items that would be remembered undistorted – such as these co-ordinates.

He had remarked on this to Pelorat some time before, and Pelorat had at once told him that it was precisely this that made the study of myths and legends so rewarding. 'The trick is,' Pelorat had said, 'to work out or decide which particular components of a legend represent accurate underlying truth. That isn't easy and different mythologists are likely to pick different components, depending, usually, on which happen to suit their particular interpretations.'

In any case, the star was right where Deniador's co-ordinates, corrected for time, said it would be. Trevize was prepared, at this moment, to wager a considerable sum that the third star would be in place as well. And if it was, Trevize was prepared to suspect that the legend was further correct in stating that there were fifty Forbidden Worlds altogether (despite the suspiciously even number) and to wonder where the other forty-seven might be.

A habitable world, Forbidden World, was found circling the star – and by this time its presence didn't cause even a ripple of surprise in Trevize's bosom. He had been absolutely sure it would be there. He set the *Far Star* into a slow orbit about it.

The cloud layer was sparse enough to allow a reasonable view of the surface from space. The world was a watery one as almost all habitable worlds were. There was an unbroken tropical ocean and two unbroken polar oceans. In one set of middle latitudes, there was a more or less serpentine continent encircling the world with bays on either side producing an occasional narrow isthmus. In the other set of middle latitudes, the land surface was broken into three large parts and each of the three was thicker north—south than the opposite continent was.

Trevize wished he knew enough climatology to be able to predict, from what he saw, what the temperatures and seasons might be like. For a moment, he toyed with the idea of having the computer work on the problem. The trouble was that climate was not the point at issue.

Much more important was that, once again, the computer detected no radiation that might be of technological origin. What his telescope told him was that the planet was not moth-eaten and that there were no signs of desert. The land moved backwards in various shades of green, but there were no signs of urban areas on the day side, no lights on the night side.

Was this another planet filled with every kind of life but human?

He rapped at the door of the other bedroom.

'Bliss?' he called out in a loud whisper, and rapped again.

There was a rustling, and Bliss's voice said, 'Yes?'

'Could you come out here? I need your help.'

'If you wait just a bit, I'll make myself a bit presentable.'

When she finally appeared, she looked as presentable as Trevize had ever seen her. He felt a twinge of annoyance at having been made to wait, however, for it made little difference to him what she looked like. But they were friends now, and he suppressed the annoyance.

She said with a smile and in a perfectly pleasant tone, 'What can I do for you, Trevize?'

Trevize waved at the viewscreen. 'As you can see we're passing over the surface of what looks like a perfectly healthy world with a quite solid vegetation cover over its land area. No lights at night, however, and no technological radiation. Please listen and tell me if there's any animal life. There was one point at which I thought I could see herds of grazing animals, but I wasn't sure. It might be a case of seeing what one desperately wants to see.'

Bliss 'listened'. At least, a curiously intent look came across her face. She said, 'Oh yes – rich in animal life.'

'Mammalian?'

'Must be.'

'Human?'

Now she seemed to concentrate harder. A full minute passed, and then another, and finally she relaxed. 'I can't quite tell. Every once in a while it seemed to me that I detected a whiff of intelligence sufficiently intense to be considered human. But it was so feeble and so occasional that perhaps I, too, was only sensing what I desperately wanted to sense. You see –'

She paused in thought, and Trevize nudged her with a 'Well?'

She said, 'The thing is I seem to detect something else. It is not something I'm familiar with, but I don't see how it can be anything but –'

Her face tightened again as she began to 'listen' with still greater intensity.

'Well,' said Trevize again.

She relaxed. 'I don't see how it can be anything but robots.'

'Robots!'

'Yes, and if I detect them, surely I ought to be able to detect human beings, too. But I don't.'

'Robots!' said Trevize again, frowning.

'Yes,' said Bliss, 'and I should judge, in great numbers.'

43

Pelorat also said 'Robots!' in almost exactly Trevize's tone when he was told of them. Then he smiled slightly. 'You were right, Golan, and I was wrong to doubt you.'

'I don't remember your doubting me, Janov.'

'Oh, well, old man, I didn't think I ought to *express* it. I just thought, in my heart, that it was a mistake to leave Aurora while there was a chance we might interview some surviving robot. But then it's clear you knew there would be a richer supply of robots here.'

'Not at all, Janov. I didn't know. I merely chanced it. Bliss tells me their mental fields seem to imply they are fully functioning, and it seems to me they can't very well be fully functioning without human beings about for care and maintenance. However, she can't spot anything human so we're still looking.'

Pelorat studied the viewscreen thoughtfully. 'It seems to be all forest, doesn't it?'

'Mostly forest. But there are clear patches that may be grasslands. The thing is that I see no cities, or any lights at night, or anything but thermal radiation at any time.'

'So no human beings after all?'

'I wonder. Bliss is in the galley trying to concentrate. I've set up an arbitrary prime meridian for the planet which means that it's divided into latitude and longitude in the computer. Bliss has a little device which she presses whenever she encounters what seems an unusual concentration of robotic mental activity – I suppose you can't say "neuronic activity" in connection with robots – or any whiff of human thought. The device is linked to the computer, which thus gets a fix on all the latitudes and longitudes, and we'll let it make the choice among them and pick a good place for landing.'

Pelorat looked uneasy. 'Is it wise to leave the matter of choice to the computer?'

'Why not, Janov? It's a very competent computer. Besides, when you have no basis on which to make a choice yourself, where's the harm in at least considering the computer's choice?'

Pelorat brightened up. 'There's something to that, Golan. Some of the oldest legends include tales of people making choices by tossing cubes to the ground.'

'Oh? What does that accomplish?'

'Each face of the cube has some decision on it – yes – no – perhaps – postpone – and so on. Whichever face happens to come upwards on landing would be taken as bearing the advice to be followed. Or they would set a ball rolling about a slotted disc with different decisions scattered among the slots. The decision written on the slot in which the ball ends is to be taken. Some mythologists think such activities represented games of chance rather than lotteries, but the two are much the same thing in my opinion.'

'In a way,' said Trevize, 'we're playing a game of chance in choosing our place of landing.'

Bliss emerged from the galley in time to hear the last comment. She said, 'No game of chance. I pressed several "maybes" and then one sure-fire "yes", and it's to the "yes" that we'll be going.'

'What made it a "yes"?' asked Trevize.

'I caught a whiff of human thought. Definite. Unmistakable.'

44

It had been raining, for the grass was wet. Overhead, the clouds were scudding by and showing signs of breaking up.

The *Far Star* had come to a gentle rest near a small grove of trees. (In case of wild dogs, Trevize thought, only partly in jest.) All about was what looked like pasture land, and coming down from the greater height at which a better and wider view had been possible, Trevize had seen what looked like orchards and grain fields – and this time, an unmistakable view of grazing animals.

There were no structures, however. Nothing artificial, except that the regularity of the trees in the orchard and the sharp boundaries that separated fields, were themselves as artificial as a microwave-receiving power station would have been.

Could that level of artificiality have been produced by robots, however? Without human beings?

Quietly, Trevize was putting on his holsters. This time, he knew that both weapons were in working order and that both were fully charged. For a moment, he caught Bliss's eye and paused.

She said, 'Go ahead. I don't think you'll have any use for them, but I thought as much once before, didn't I?'

Trevize said, 'Would you like to be armed, Janov?'

Pelorat shuddered. 'No, thank you. Between you and your physical defence, and Bliss and her mental defence, I feel in no danger at all. I suppose it is cowardly of me to hide in your protective shadows, but I can't feel proper shame when I'm too busy feeling grateful that I needn't be in a position of possibly having to use force.'

Trevize said, 'I understand. Just don't go anywhere alone. If Bliss and I separate, you stay with one of us and don't dash off somewhere under the spur of a private curiosity.'

'You needn't worry, Trevize,' said Bliss. 'I'll see to that.'

Trevize stepped out of the ship first. The wind was brisk and just a trifle cool in the aftermath of the rain, but Trevize found that welcome. It had probably been uncomfortably warm and humid before the rain.

He took in his breath with surprise. The smell of the planet was delightful. Every planet had its own odour, he knew, an odour always strange and usually distasteful – perhaps only because it was strange. Might not strange be pleasant as well? Or was this the accident of catching the planet just after the rain at a particular season of the year. Whichever it was –

'Come on,' he called. 'It's quite pleasant out here.'

Pelorat emerged and said, 'Pleasant is definitely the word for it. Do you suppose it always smells like this?'

'It doesn't matter. Within the hour, we'll be sufficiently accustomed to the aroma, and our nasal receptors will be sufficiently saturated, for us to smell nothing.'

'Pity,' said Pelorat.

'The grass is wet,' said Bliss, with a shade of disapproval.

'Why not? After all, it rains on Gaia too,' said Trevize, and as he spoke a shaft of yellow sunlight reached them momentarily through a small break in the clouds. There would soon be more of it.

'Yes,' said Bliss, 'but we know when and we're prepared for it.'

'Too bad,' said Trevize, 'you lose the thrill of the unexpected.'

Bliss said, 'You're right. I'll try not to be provincial.'

Pelorat looked about and said, in a disappointed tone, 'There seems to be nothing about.'

'Only seems to be,' said Bliss. 'They're approaching from beyond that rise.' She looked towards Trevize. 'Do you think we ought to go to meet them?'

Trevize shook his head. 'No. We've come to meet them across many parsecs. Let them walk the rest of the way. We'll wait for them here.'

Only Bliss could sense the approach until, from the direction of her pointing finger, a figure appeared over the brow of the rise. Then a second, and a third.

'I believe that is all at the moment,' said Bliss.

Trevize watched curiously. Though he had never seen robots, there was not a particle of doubt in him that that was what they were. They had the schematic and impressionistic shape of human beings and yet were not obviously metallic in appearance. The robotic surface was dull and gave the illusion of softness, as though it were covered in plush.

But how did he know the softness was an illusion. Trevize felt a sudden desire to feel those figures who were approaching so stolidly. If it were true that this was a Forbidden World and that spaceships never approached it – and surely that must be so since the sun was not included in the Galactic map – then the *Far Star* and the people it carried must represent something the robots had never experienced. Yet they were reacting with steady certainty, as though they were working their way through a routine exercise.

Trevize said, in a low voice, 'Here we may have information we can get nowhere else in the Galaxy. We could ask them for the location of Earth with reference to this world, and if they know, they will tell us. Who knows how long these things have functioned and endured? They may answer out of personal memory. Think of that.'

'On the other hand,' said Bliss, 'they may be recently manufactured and may know nothing.'

'Or,' said Pelorat, 'they may know, but may refuse to tell us.'

Trevize said, 'I suspect they can't refuse unless they've been ordered not to tell us, and why should such orders be issued when surely no one on this planet could have expected our coming?'

At a distance of about three metres, the robots stopped. They said nothing and made no further movement.

Trevize, his hand on his blaster, said to Bliss, without taking his eyes from the robots. 'Can you tell whether they are hostile?'

'You'll have to allow for the fact that I have no experience whatsoever with their mental workings, Trevize, but I don't detect anything that seems hostile.'

Trevize took his right hand away from the butt of the weapon, but kept it near. He raised his left hand, palm towards the robots and said, speaking slowly, 'I greet you. We come to this world as friends.'

The central robot of the three ducked his head in a kind of abortive bow that might also have been taken as a gesture of peace by an optimist, and replied.

Trevize's jaw dropped in astonishment. In a world of Galactic communication, one did not think of failure in so fundamental a need. However, the robot did not speak in Galactic Standard or anything approaching it. In fact, Trevize could not understand a word.

45

Pelorat's surprise was as great as that of Trevize, but there was an obvious element of pleasure in it, too.

'Isn't that strange?' he said.

Trevize turned to him and said, with more than a touch of asperity in his voice, 'It's not strange. It's gibberish.'

Pelorat said, 'Not gibberish at all. It's Galactic, but very archaic. I catch a few words. I could probably understand it easily if it were written down. It's the pronunciation that's the real puzzle.'

'Well, what did it say?'

'I think it told you it didn't understand what you said.'

Bliss said, 'I can't tell what it said, but what I sense is puzzlement, which fits. That is, if I can trust my analysis of robotic emotion – or if there is such a thing as robotic emotion.'

Speaking very slowly, and with difficulty, Pelorat said something, and the three robots ducked their heads in unison.

'What was that?' said Trevize.

Pelorat said, 'I said I couldn't speak well, but I would try. I asked for a little time. Dear me, old chap, this is fearfully interesting.'

'Fearfully disappointing,' muttered Trevize.

'You see,' said Pelorat, 'every habitable planet in the Galaxy manages to work out its own variety of Galactic so that there are a million dialects that are sometimes barely intercomprehensible, but they're all pulled together by the development of Galactic Standard. Assuming this world to have been isolated for twenty thousand years, the language would ordinarily drift so far from that of the rest of the Galaxy as to be an entirely different language. That it isn't may be because the world has a social system that depends upon robots which can only understand the language as spoken in the fashion in which they were programmed. Rather than re-programming, the language remained static and we now have what is to us merely a very archaic form of Galactic.'

'There's an example,' said Trevize, 'of how a robotized society can be held static and made to turn degenerate.'

'But, my dear fellow,' protested Pelorat, 'keeping a language relatively unchanged is not necessarily a sign of degeneration. There are advantages to it. Documents preserved for centuries and millennia retain their meaning and give greater longevity and authority to historical records. In the rest of the Galaxy, the language of Imperial edicts of the time of Hari Seldon already begins to sound quaint.'

'And do you know this archaic Galactic?'

'Not to say *know*, Golan. It's just that in studying ancient myths and legends I've picked up the trick of it. The vocabulary is not entirely different, but it is inflected differently, and there are idiomatic expressions we don't use any longer and, as I have said, the pronunciation is totally changed. I can act as interpreter, but not as a very good one.'

Trevize heaved a tremulous sigh. 'A small stroke of good fortune is better than none. Carry on, Janov.'

Pelorat turned to the robots, waited a moment, then looked back at Trevize. 'What am I supposed to say?'

'Let's go all the way. Ask them where Earth is.'

Pelorat said the words one at a time, with exaggerated gestures of his hands.

The robots looked at each other and made a few sounds. The middle one then spoke to Pelorat, who replied while moving his hands apart as though he were stretching a length of rubber. The robot responded by spacing his words as carefully as Pelorat had.

Pelorat said to Trevize, 'I'm not sure I'm getting across what I mean by "Earth". I suspect they think I'm referring to some region on their planet and they say they don't know of any such region.'

'Do they use the name of this planet, Janov?'

'The closest I can come to what I think they are using as the name is "Solaria".'

'Have you ever heard of it in your legends?'

'No – any more than I had ever heard of Aurora.'

'Well, ask them if there is any place named Earth in the sky – among the stars. Point upwards.'

Again an exchange, and finally Pelorat turned and said, 'All I can get from them, Golan, is that there are no places in the sky.'

Bliss said, 'Ask those robots how old they are; or rather, how long they have been functioning.'

'I don't know how to say "functioning",' said Pelorat, shaking his head. 'In fact, I'm not sure if I can say "how old". I'm *not* a very good interpreter.'

'Do the best you can, Pel dear,' said Bliss.

And after several exchanges, Pelorat said, 'They've been functioning for twenty-six years.'

'Twenty-six years,' muttered Trevize in disgust. 'They're hardly older than you are, Bliss.'

Bliss said, with sudden pride, 'It so happens –'

'I know. You're Gaia which is thousands of years old. – In any case, these robots cannot talk about Earth from personal experience, and their memory-banks clearly do not include anything not necessary to their functioning. So they know nothing about astronomy.'

Pelorat said, 'There may be other robots somewhere on the planet that are primordial, perhaps.'

'I doubt it,' said Trevize, 'but ask them, if you can find the words for it, Janov.'

This time there was quite a long conversation and Pelorat eventually broke it off with a flushed face and a clear air of frustration.

'Golan,' he said, 'I don't understand part of what they're trying to say, but I gather that the older robots are used for manual labour and don't know anything. If this robot were a human, I'd say he spoke of the older robots with contempt. These three are house robots, they say, and are not allowed to grow old before being replaced. They're the ones who really know things – their words, not mine.'

'They don't know much,' growled Trevize. 'At least of the things we want to know.'

'I now regret,' said Pelorat, 'that we left Aurora so hurriedly. If we had found a robot survivor there, and we surely would have, since the very first one I encountered still had a spark of life left in it, they would know of Earth through personal memory.'

'Provided their memories were intact, Janov,' said Trevize. 'We can always go back there and, if we have to, dog packs or not, we will. – But if these robots are only a couple of decades old, there must be those who manufacture them, and the manufacturers must be human, I should think.' He turned to Bliss. 'Are you *sure* you sensed –'

But she raised a hand to stop him and there was a strained and intent look on her face. 'Coming now,' she said, in a low voice.

Trevize turned his face towards the rise and there, first appearing from behind it, and then striding towards them, was the unmistakable figure of a human being. His complexion was pale and his hair light and long, standing out slightly from the sides of his head. His face was grave but quite young in appearance. His bare arms and legs were not particularly muscled.

The robots stepped aside for him, and he advanced till he stood in their midst.

He then spoke in a clear, pleasant voice and his words, although used archaically, were in Galactic Standard, and easily understood.

'Greetings, wanderers from space,' he said. 'What would you with my robots?'

46

Trevize did not cover himself with glory. He said foolishly, 'You speak Galactic?'

The Solarian said, with a grim smile, 'And why not, since I am not mute?'

'But these?' Trevize gestured towards the robots.

'These are robots. They speak our language, as I do. But I am Solarian and hear the hyperspatial communications of the worlds beyond so that I have learned your way of speaking, as have my predecessors. My predecessors have left descriptions of the language, but I constantly hear new words and expressions that change with the years, as though you Settlers can settle worlds, but not words. How is it you are surprised at my understanding of your language?'

'I should not have been,' said Trevize. 'I apologize. It was just that speaking to the robots, I had not thought to hear Galactic on this world.'

He studied the Solarian. He was wearing a thin white robe, draped loosely over his shoulder, with large openings for his arms. It was open in front, exposing a bare chest and loincloth below. Except for a pair of light sandals, he wore nothing else.

It occurred to Trevize that he could not tell whether the Solarian was male or female. The breasts were male, certainly, but the chest was hairless and the thin loincloth showed no bulge of any kind.

He turned to Bliss and said in a low voice, 'This might still be a robot, but very like a human being in –'

Bliss said, her lips hardly moving, 'The mind is that of a human being, not a robot.'

The Solarian said, 'Yet you have not answered my original question.

I shall excuse the failure and put it down to your surprise. I now ask again and you must not fail a second time. What would you with my robots?'

Trevize said, 'We are travellers who seek information to reach our destination. We asked your robots for information that would help us, but they lacked the knowledge.'

'What is the information you seek? Perhaps I can help you.'

'We seek the location of Earth. Could you tell us that?'

The Solarian's eyebrows lifted. 'I would have thought that your first object of curiosity would have been myself. I will supply that information although you have not asked for it. I am Sarton Bander and you stand upon the Bander estate, which stretches as far as your eye can see in every direction and far beyond. I cannot say that you are welcome here, for in coming here, you have violated a trust. You are the first Settlers to touch down upon Solaria in many thousands of years and, as it turns out, you have come here merely to inquire as to the best way of reaching another world. In the old days, Settlers, you and your ship would have been destroyed on sight.'

'That would be a barbaric way of treating people who mean no harm and offer none,' said Trevize cautiously.

'I agree, but when members of an expanding society set foot upon an inoffensive and static one, that mere touch is filled with potential harm. While we feared that harm, we were ready to destroy those who came at the instant of their coming. Since we no longer have reason to fear, we are, as you see, ready to talk.'

Trevize said, 'I appreciate the information you have offered us so freely, and yet you failed to answer the question I did ask. I will repeat it. Could you tell us the location of the planet Earth?'

'By Earth, I take it you mean the world on which the human species, and the various species of plants and animals' (his hand moved gracefully about as though to indicate all the surroundings about them), 'originated.'

'Yes, I do, sir.'

A queer look of repugnance flitted over the Solarian's face. He said, 'Please address me simply as Bander, if you must use a form of address. Do not address me by any word that includes a sign of gender. I am neither male nor female. I am *whole*.'

Trevize nodded (he had been right). 'As you wish, Bander. What, then, is the location of Earth, the world of origin of all of us?'

Bander said, 'I do not know. Nor do I wish to know. If I did know, or if I did find out, it would do you no good, for Earth no longer exists as a world. – Ah,' he went on, stretching out his arms. 'The sun feels good. I am not often on the surface, and never when the sun does not show itself. My robots were sent to greet you while the sun was yet hiding behind the clouds. I followed only when the clouds cleared.'

'Why is it that Earth no longer exists as a world?' said Trevize, insistently, steeling himself for the tale of radioactivity once again.

Bander, however, ignored the question or, rather, put it to one side carelessly. 'The story is too long,' he said. 'You told me that you came with no intent of harm.'

'That is correct.'

'Why then did you come armed?'

'That is merely a precaution. I did not know what I might meet.'

'It doesn't matter. Your little weapons represent no danger to me. Yet I am curious. I have, of course, heard much of your arms, and of your curiously barbaric history that seems to depend so entirely upon arms. Even so, I have never actually seen a weapon. May I see yours?'

Trevize took a step backwards. 'I'm afraid not, Bander.'

Bander seemed amused. 'I asked only out of politeness. I need not have asked at all.'

It held out its hand and from Trevize's right holster, there emerged his blaster, while from his left holster, there rose up his neuronic whip. Trevize snatched at his weapons but felt his arms held back as though by stiffly elastic bonds. Both Pelorat and Bliss started forward and it was clear that they were held as well.

Bander said, 'Don't bother trying to interfere. You cannot.' The weapons flew to its hands and it looked them over carefully. 'This one,' it said, indicating the blaster, 'seems to be a microwave beamer that produces heat, thus exploding any fluid-containing body. The other is more subtle, and, I must confess, I do not see at a glance what it is intended to do. However, since you mean no harm and offer no harm, you don't need arms. I can, and I do, bleed the energy content of the units of each weapon. That leaves them harmless unless you use one or the other as a club, and they would be clumsy indeed if used for that purpose.'

The Solarian released the weapons and again they drifted through the air, this time back towards Trevize. Each settled neatly into its holster.

Trevize, feeling himself released, pulled out his blaster, but there was no need to use it. The contact hung loosely, and the energy unit had clearly been totally drained. That was precisely the case with the neuronic whip as well.

He looked up at Bander, who said, smiling, 'You are quite helpless, Outworlder. I can as easily, if I so desired, destroy your ship and, of course, you.'

11

Underground

47

Trevize felt frozen. Trying to breathe normally, he turned to look at Bliss.

She was standing with her arm protectively about Pelorat's waist, and, to all appearances, was quite calm. She smiled slightly and, even more slightly, nodded her head.

Trevize turned back to Bander. Having interpreted Bliss's actions as signifying confidence, and hoping with dreadful earnestness that he was correct, he said grimly, 'How did you do that. Bander?'

Bander smiled, obviously in high good humour. 'Tell me, little Outworlders, do you believe in sorcery? In magic?'

'No, we do not, little Solarian,' snapped Trevize.

Bliss tugged at Trevize's sleeve and whispered, 'Don't irritate him. He's dangerous.'

'I can see he is,' said Trevize, keeping his voice low with difficulty. 'You do something, then.'

Her voice barely heard, Bliss said, 'Not yet. He will be less dangerous if he feels secure.'

Bander paid no attention to the brief whispering among the Outworlders. It moved away from them uncaringly, the robots separating to let it pass.

Then it looked back and crooked a finger languidly. 'Come. Follow me. All three of you. I will tell you a story that may not interest you, but that interests me.' It continued to walk forward leisurely.

Trevize remained in place for a while, uncertain as to the best course of action. Bliss walked forward, however, and the pressure of her arm led Pelorat forward as well. Eventually, Trevize moved; the alternative was to be left standing alone with the robots.

Bliss said lightly, 'If Bander will be so kind as to tell the story that may not interest us –'

Bander turned and looked intently at Bliss as though it were truly aware of her for the first time. 'You are the feminine half-human,' it said, 'aren't you? The lesser half?'

'The smaller half, Bander. Yes.'

'These other two are masculine half-humans, then?'

'So they are.'

'Have you had your child yet, feminine?'

'My name, Bander, is Bliss. I have not yet had a child. This is Trevize. This is Pel.'

'And which of these two masculines is to assist you when it is your time? Or will it be both? Or neither?'

'Pel will assist me, Bander.'

Bander turned its attention to Pelorat. 'You have white hair, I see.'

Pelorat said, 'I have.'

'Was it always that colour?'

'No, Bander, it became so with age.'

'And how old are you?'

'I am fifty-two years old, Bander,' Pelorat said, then added hastily. 'That's Galactic Standard Years.'

Bander continued to walk (towards the distant mansion, Trevize assumed), but more slowly. It said, 'I don't know how long a Galactic Standard Year is, but it can't be very different from our year. And how old will you be when you die, Pel?'

'I can't say. I may live thirty more years.'

'Eighty-two years, then. Short-lived, and divided in halves. Unbelievable, and yet my distant ancestors were like you and lived on Earth. – But some of them left Earth to establish new worlds around other stars, wonderful worlds, well organized, and many.'

Trevize said loudly, 'Not many. Fifty.'

Bander turned a lofty eye on Trevize. There seemed less humour in it now. 'Trevize. That's your name.'

'Golan Trevize in full. I say there were fifty Spacer worlds. *Our* worlds number in the millions.'

'Do you know, then, the story that I wish to tell you?' said Bander softly.

'If the story is that there were once fifty Spacer worlds, we know it.'

'We count not in numbers only, little half-human,' said Bander. 'We count the quality, too. There were fifty, but such a fifty that not all your millions could make up one of them. And Solaria was the fiftieth and, therefore, the best. Solaria was as far beyond the other Spacer worlds, as they were beyond Earth.

'We of Solaria alone learned how life was to be lived. We did not herd and flock like animals, as they did on Earth, as they did on other worlds, as they did even on the other Spacer worlds. We lived each alone, with robots to help us, viewing each other electronically as often as we wished, but coming within natural sight of one another only rarely. It is many years since I have gazed at human beings as I now gaze at you but, then, you are only half-humans and your presence, therefore, does not limit my freedom any more than a cow would limit it, or a robot.

'Yet we were once half-human, too. No matter how we perfected our freedom; no matter how we developed as solitary masters over countless robots; the freedom was never absolute. In order to produce young there had to be two individuals in co-operation. It was possible, of course, to contribute sperm cells and egg cells, to have the fertilization process and the consequent embryonic growth take place artificially in automated fashion. It was possible for the infant to live adequately under robotic care. It could all be done, but the half-humans would not give up the pleasure that went with biological impregnation. Perverse emotional attachments would develop in consequence and freedom vanished. Do you see that that had to be changed?'

Trevize said, 'No, Bander, because we do not measure freedom by your standards.'

'That is because you do not know what freedom is. You have never lived but in swarms, and you know no way of life but to be constantly forced, in even the smallest things, to bend your wills to those of others or, which is equally vile, to spend your days struggling to force others to bend their wills to yours. Where is any possible freedom there? Freedom is nothing if it is not to live as you wish! Exactly as you wish!

'Then came the time when the Earthpeople began to swarm outwards once more, when their clinging crowds again swirled through space. The other Spacers, who did not flock as the Earthpeople did, but who flocked nevertheless, if to a lesser degree, tried to compete.

'We Solaiians did not. We foresaw inevitable failure in swarming. We moved underground and broke off all contact with the rest of the Galaxy. We were determined to remain ourselves at all costs. We developed suitable robots and weapons to protect our apparently empty surface, and they did the job admirably. Ships came and were destroyed, and stopped coming. The planet was considered deserted, and was forgotten, as we hoped it would be.

'And meanwhile underground, we worked to solve our problems. We adjusted our genes gingerly, delicately. We had failures, but some successes, and we capitalized on the successes. It took us many centuries, but we finally became whole human beings, incorporating both the masculine and feminine principles in one body, supplying our own complete pleasure at will and producing, when we wished, fertilized eggs for development under skilled robotic care.'

'Hermaphrodites,' said Pelorat.

'Is that what it is called in your language?' asked Bander indifferently. 'I have never heard the word.'

'Hermaphroditism stops evolution dead in its tracks,' said Trevize. 'Each child is the genetic duplicate of its hermaphroditic parent.'

'Come,' said Bander, 'you treat evolution as a hit-and-miss affair. We can design our children if we wish. We can change and adjust the genes and, on occasion, we do. – But we are almost at my dwelling. Let us enter. It grows late in the day. The sun already fails to give its warmth adequately and we will be more comfortable indoors.'

They passed through a door that had no locks of any kind but that opened as they approached and closed behind them as they passed through. There were no windows, but as they entered a cavernous room, the walls glowed to luminous life and brightened. The floor seemed bare, but was soft and springy to the touch. In each of the four corners of the room, a robot stood motionless.

'That wall,' said Bander, pointing to the wall opposite the door – a wall that seemed no different in any way from the other three – 'is my vision-screen. The world opens before me through that screen but it in no way limits my freedom for I cannot be compelled to use it.'

Trevize said, 'Nor can you compel another to use his if you wish to see him through that screen and he does not.'

'Compel?' said Bander haughtily. 'Let another do as it pleases, if it is but content that I do as I please. Please note that we do not use gendered pronouns in referring to each other.'

There was one chair in the room, facing the vision-screen, and Bander sat down in it.

Trevize looked about, as though expecting additional chairs to spring from the floor. 'May we sit, too?' he said.

'If you wish,' said Bander.

Bliss, smiling, sat down on the floor. Pelorat sat down beside her. Trevize stubbornly continued to stand.

Bliss said, 'Tell me, Bander, how many human beings live on this planet?'

'Say Solarians, half-human Bliss. The phrase "human being" is contaminated by the fact that half-humans call themselves that. We might call ourselves whole-humans, but that is clumsy. Solarian is the proper term.'

'How many Solarians, then, live on this planet?'

'I am not certain. We do not count ourselves. Perhaps twelve hundred.'

'Only twelve hundred on the entire world?'

'Fully twelve hundred. You count in numbers again, while we count in quality. – Nor do you understand freedom. If one other Solarian exists to dispute my absolute mastery over any part of my land, over any robot or living thing or object, my freedom is limited. Since other Solarians exist, the limitation on freedom must be removed as far as possible by separating them all to the point where contact is virtually non-existent. Solaria will hold twelve hundred Solarians under conditions approaching the ideal. Add more, and liberty will be palpably limited so that the result will be unendurable.'

'That means each child must be counted and must balance deaths,' said Pelorat suddenly.

'Certainly. That must be true of any world with a stable population – even yours, perhaps.'

'And since there are probably few deaths, there must therefore be few children.'

'Indeed.'

Pelorat nodded his head and was silent.

Trevize said, 'What I want to know is how you made my weapons fly through the air. You haven't explained that.'

'I offered you sorcery or magic as an explanation. Do you refuse to accept that?'

'Of course I refuse. What do you take me for?'

'Will you, then, believe in the conservation of energy, and in the necessary increase of entropy?'

'That I do. Nor can I believe that even in twenty thousand years you have changed these laws, or modified them a micrometre.'

'Nor have we, half-person. But now consider. Outdoors, there is sunlight.' There was its oddly graceful gesture, as though marking out sunlight all about. 'And there is shade. It is warmer in the sunlight than in the shade, and heat flows spontaneously from the sunlit area into the shaded area.'

'You tell me what I know,' said Trevize.

'But perhaps you know it so well that you no longer think about it. And at night, Solaria's surface is warmer than the objects beyond its atmosphere, so that heat flows spontaneously from the planetary surface into outer space.'

'I know that, too.'

'And day or night, the planetary interior is warmer than the planetary surface. Heat therefore flows spontaneously from the interior to the surface. I imagine you know that, too.'

'And what of all that, Bander?'

'The flow of heat from hotter to colder, which must take place by the second law of thermodynamics, can be used to do work.'

'In theory, yes, but sunlight is dilute, the heat of the planetary surface is even more dilute, and the rate at which heat escapes from the interior makes that the most dilute of all. The amount of heat-flow that can be harnessed would probably not be enough to lift a pebble.'

'It depends on the device you use for the purpose,' said Bander. 'Our own tool was developed over a period of thousands of years and it is nothing less than a portion of our brain.'

Bander lifted the hair on either side of its head, exposing that portion of its skull behind its ears. It turned its head this way and that, and behind each ear was a bulge the size and shape of the blunt end of a hen's egg.

'That portion of my brain, and its absence in you, is what makes the difference between a Solarian and you.'

48

Trevize glanced now and then at Bliss's face, which seemed entirely concentrated on Bander. Trevize had grown quite certain he knew what was going on.

Bander, despite its paean to freedom, found this unique opportunity irresistible. There was no way it could speak to robots on a basis of intellectual equality, and certainly not to animals. To speak to its fellow-Solarians would be, to it, unpleasant, and what communication there must be would be forced, and never spontaneous.

As for Trevize, Bliss and Pelorat, they might be half-human to Bander, and it might regard them as no more an infringement on its liberty than a robot or a goat would be – but they were its intellectual equals (or near equals) and the chance to speak to them was a unique luxury it had never experienced before.

No wonder, Trevize thought, it was indulging itself in this way. And Bliss (Trevize was doubly sure) was encouraging this, just pushing Bander's mind ever so gently in order to urge it to do what it very much wanted to do in any case.

Bliss, presumably, was working on the supposition that if Bander spoke enough, it might tell them something useful concerning Earth. That made sense to Trevize, so that even if he had not been truly curious about the subject under discussion, he would nevertheless have endeavoured to continue the conversation.

'What do these brain-lobes do?' Trevize asked.

Bander said, 'They are transducers. They are activated by the flow of heat and they convert the heat-flow into mechanical energy.'

'I cannot believe that. The flow of heat is insufficient.'

'Little half-human, you do not think. If there were many Solarians crowded together, each trying to make use of the flow of heat, then, yes, the supply would be insufficient. I, however, have over forty thousand square kilometres that are mine, mine alone. I can collect heat-flow from any quantity of those square kilometres with no one to dispute me, so the quantity is sufficient. Do you see?'

'Is it that simple to collect heat-flow over a wide area? The mere act of concentration takes a great deal of energy.'

'Perhaps, but I am not aware of it. My transducer-lobes are constantly concentrating heat-flow so that as work is needed, work is done. When I drew your weapons into the air, a particular volume of the sunlit atmosphere lost some of its excess heat to a volume of the shaded area, so that I was using solar energy for the purpose. Instead of using mechanical or electronic devices to bring that about, however, I used a neuronic device.' It touched one of the transducer-lobes gently. 'It does it quickly, efficiently, constantly – and effortlessly.'

'Unbelievable,' muttered Pelorat.

'Not at all unbelievable,' said Bander. 'Consider the delicacy of the eye and ear, and how they can turn small quantities of photons and air vibrations into information. That would seem unbelievable if you had never come across it before. The transducer-lobes are no more unbelievable, and would not be so to you, were they not unfamiliar.'

Trevize said, 'What do you do with these constantly operating transducer-lobes?'

'We run the world,' said Bander. 'Every robot on this vast estate obtains its energy from me; or, rather, from natural heat-flow. Whether a robot is adjusting a contact, or felling a tree, the energy is derived from mental transduction – *my* mental transduction.'

'And if you are asleep?'

'The process of transduction continues waking or sleeping, little half-human,' said Bander. 'Do you cease breathing when you sleep? Does your heart stop beating? At night, my robots continue working at the cost of cooling Solaria's interior a bit. The change is immeasurably small on a global scale and there are only twelve hundred of us, so that all the energy we use does not appreciably shorten our sun's life or drain the world's internal heat.'

'Has it occurred to you that you might use it as a weapon?'

Bander stared at Trevize as though he were something peculiarly incomprehensible. 'I suppose by that,' it said, 'you mean that Solaria might confront other worlds with energy weapons based on transduction? Why should we? Even if we could beat their energy weapons based on other principles – which is anything but certain – what would we gain? The control of other worlds? What do we want with other worlds when we have an ideal world of our own? Do we want to establish our domination over half-humans and use them in forced labour? We have our robots that are far better than half-humans for the purpose. We have everything. We want nothing – except to be left to ourselves. See here – I'll tell you another story.'

'Go ahead,' said Trevize.

'Twenty thousand years ago when the half-creatures of Earth began to swarm into space and we ourselves withdrew underground, the other Spacer worlds were determined to oppose the new Earth-settlers. So they struck at Earth.'

'At Earth,' said Trevize, trying to hide his satisfaction over the fact that the subject had come up at last.

'Yes, at the centre. A sensible move, in a way. If you wish to kill a person, you strike not at a finger or a heel, but at the heart. And our fellow-Spacers, not too far removed from human beings themselves in passions, managed to set Earth's surface radioactively aflame, so that the world became largely uninhabitable.'

'Ah, that's what happened,' said Pelorat, clenching a fist and moving it rapidly, as though nailing down a thesis. 'I knew it could not be a natural phenomenon. How was it done?'

'I don't know how it was done,' said Bander indifferently, 'and in any case it did the Spacers no good. That is the point of the story. The Settlers continued to swarm and the Spacers – died out. They had tried to compete, and vanished. We Solarians retired and refused to compete, and so we are still here.'

'And so are the Settlers,' said Trevize grimly.

'Yes, but not forever. Swarmers must fight, must compete, and eventually must die. That may take tens of thousands of years, but we can wait. And when it happens, we Solarians, whole, solitary, liberated, will have the Galaxy to ourselves. We can then use, or not use, any world we wish to in addition to our own.'

'But this matter of Earth,' said Pelorat, snapping his fingers impatiently. 'Is what you tell us legend or history?'

'How does one tell the difference, half-Pelorat?' said Bander. 'All history is legend, more or less.'

'But what do your records say? May I see the records on the subject, Bander? – Please understand that this matter of myths, legends and primeval history is my field. I am a scholar dealing with such matters and particularly with those matters as related to Earth.'

'I merely repeat what I have heard,' said Bander. 'There are no records on the subject. Our records deal entirely with Solarian affairs and other worlds are mentioned in them only insofar as they impinge on us.'

'Surely, Earth has impinged on you,' said Pelorat.

'That may be, but, if so, it was long, long ago, and Earth, of all worlds, was most repulsive to us. If we had any records of Earth, I am sure they were destroyed out of sheer revulsion.'

Trevize gritted his teeth in chagrin. 'By yourselves?' he asked.

Bander turned his attention to Trevize. 'There is no one else to destroy them.'

Pelorat would not let go of the matter. 'What else have you heard concerning Earth?'

Bander thought. It said, 'When I was young, I heard a tale from a robot about an Earthman who once visited Solaria; about a Solarian woman who left with him and became an important figure in the Galaxy. That, however, was, in my opinion, an invented tale.'

Pelorat bit at his lip. 'Are you sure?'

'How can I be sure of anything in such matters?' said Bander. 'Still, it passes the bounds of belief that an Earthman would dare come to Solaria, or that Solaria would allow the intrusion. It is even less likely that a Solarian woman – we were half-humans then, but even so – should voluntarily leave this world. – But come, let me show you my home.'

'Your home?' said Bliss, looking about. 'Are we not in your home?'

'Not at all,' said Bander. 'This is an anteroom. It is a viewing room. In it I see my fellow-Solarians when I must. Their images appear on that wall, or three-dimensionally in the space before the wall. This room is a public assembly, therefore, and not part of my home. Come with me.'

It walked on ahead, without turning to see if it were followed, but the four robots left their corners, and Trevize knew that if he and his companions did not follow spontaneously, the robots would gently coerce them into doing so.

The other two got to their feet and Trevize whispered lightly to Bliss, 'Have you been keeping him talking?'

Bliss pressed his hand, and nodded. 'Just the same, I wish I knew what his intentions were,' she added, with a note of uneasiness in her voice.

49

They followed Bander. The robots remained at a polite distance, but their presence was a constantly-felt threat.

They were moving through a corridor, and Trevize mumbled low-spiritedly, 'There's nothing helpful about Earth on this planet. I'm sure of it. Just another variation on the radioactivity theme.' He shrugged. 'We'll have to go on to the third set of co-ordinates.'

A door opened before them, revealing a small room. Bander said, 'Come, half-humans, I want to show you how we live.'

Trevize whispered, 'He gets infantile pleasure out of display. I'd love to knock him down.'

'Don't try to compete in childishness,' said Bliss.

Bander ushered all three into the room. One of the robots followed as well. Bander gestured the other robots away and entered itself. The door closed behind him.

'It's an elevator,' said Pelorat, with a pleased air of discovery.

'So it is,' said Bander. 'Once we went underground, we never truly emerged. Nor would we want to, though I find it pleasant to feel the sunlight on occasion. I dislike clouds or night in the open, however. That gives one the sensation of being underground without truly being underground, if you know what I mean. That is cognitive dissonance, after a fashion, and I find it very unpleasant.'

'Earth built underground,' said Pelorat. 'The Caves of Steel, they called their cities. And Trantor built underground, too, even more extensively, in the old Imperial days. – And Comporellon builds underground right now. It is a common tendency, when you come to think of it.'

'Half-humans swarming underground and we living underground in isolated splendour are two widely different things,' said Bander.

Trevize said, 'On Terminus, dwelling places are on the surface.'

'And exposed to the weather,' said Bander. 'Very primitive.'

The elevator, after the initial feeling of lower gravity that had given away its nature to Pelorat, gave no sensation of motion whatsoever. Trevize was wondering how far down it would penetrate, when there was a brief feeling of higher gravity and the door opened.

Before them was a large and elaborately furnished room. It was dimly lit, though the source of the light was not apparent. It almost seemed as though the air itself were faintly luminous.

Bander pointed its finger and where it pointed the light grew a bit more intense. It pointed it elsewhere and the same thing happened. It placed its left hand on a stubby rod to one side of the doorway and, with its right hand, made an expansive circular gesture so that the whole room lit up as though it were in sunlight, but with no sensation of heat.

Trevize grimaced and said, half-aloud, 'The man's a charlatan.'

Bander said sharply, 'Not "the man", but "the Solarian". I'm not sure what the word "charlatan" means, but if I catch the tone of voice, it is opprobrious.'

Trevize said, 'It means one who is not genuine, who arranges effects to make what is done seem more impressive than it really is.'

Bander said, 'I admit that I love the dramatic, but what I have shown you is not an effect. It is real.'

It tapped the rod on which its left hand was resting. 'This heat-conducting rod extends several kilometres downwards, and there are similar rods in many convenient places throughout my estate. I know there are similar rods on other estates. These rods increase the rate at which heat leaves Solaria's lower regions for the surface and eases its conversion into work. I do not need the gestures of the hand to produce the light, but it does lend an air of drama or, perhaps, as you point out, a slight touch of the not-genuine. I enjoy that sort of thing.'

Bliss said, 'Do you have much opportunity to experience the pleasure of such little dramatic touches?'

'No,' said Bander, shaking its head. 'My robots are not impressed with such things. Nor would my fellow-Solarians be. This unusual chance of meeting half-humans and displaying for them is most – amusing.'

Pelorat said, 'The light in this room shone dimly when we entered. Does it shine dimly at all times?'

'Yes, a small drain of power – like keeping the robots working. My entire estate is always running, and those parts of it not engaged in active labour are idling.'

'And you supply the power constantly for all this vast estate?'

'The sun and the planet's core supply the power. I am merely the conduit. Nor is all the estate productive. I keep most of it as wilderness and well stocked with a variety of animal life; first, because that protects my boundaries, and second, because I find aesthetic value in it. In fact, my fields and factories are small. They need only supply my own needs, plus some specialities to exchange for those of others. I have robots, for instance, that can manufacture and install the heat-conducting rods at need. Many Solarians depend upon me for that.'

'And your home?' asked Trevize. 'How large is that?'

It must have been the right question to ask for Bander beamed. 'Very large. One of the largest on the planet, I believe. It goes on for kilometres in every direction. I have as many robots caring for my home underground, as I have in all the thousands of square kilometres of surface.'

'You don't live in all of it, surely,' said Pelorat.

'It might conceivably be that there are chambers I have never entered, but what of that?' said Bander. 'The robots keep every room clean, well-ventilated, and in order. But come, step out here.'

They emerged through a door that was not the one through which they had entered and found themselves in another corridor. Before them was a little topless ground-car that ran on tracks.

Bander motioned them into it, and one by one they clambered aboard. There was not quite room for all four, plus the robot, but Pelorat and Bliss squeezed together tightly to allow room for Trevize. Bander sat in the front with an air of easy comfort, the robot at its side, and the car moved along with no sign of overt manipulation of controls other than Bander's smooth hand motions now and then.

'This is a car-shaped robot, actually,' said Bander, with an air of negligent indifference.

They progressed at a stately pace, very smoothly past doors that opened as they approached, and closed as they receded. The decorations in each were of widely different kinds as though robots had been ordered to devise combinations at random.

Ahead of them the corridor was gloomy, and behind them as well. At whatever point they actually found themselves, however, they were in the equivalent of cool sunlight. The rooms, too, would light as the doors opened. And each time, Bander moved its hand slowly and gracefully.

There seemed no end to the journey. Now and then they found themselves curving in a way that made it plain that the underground mansion spread out in two dimensions. (No, three, thought Trevize, at one point, as they moved steadily down a shallow declivity.)

Wherever they went, there were robots, by the dozens – scores – hundreds – engaged in unhurried work whose nature Trevize could not easily divine. They passed the open door of one large room in which rows of robots were bent quietly over desks.

Pelorat asked, 'What are they doing, Bander?'

'Bookkeeping,' said Bander. 'Keeping statistical records, financial accounts, and all sorts of things that, I am very glad to say, I don't have to bother with. This isn't just an idle estate. About a quarter of its growing area is given over to orchards. An additional tenth are grain fields, but it's the orchards that are really my pride. We grow the best fruit in the world and grow them in the largest number of varieties, too. A Bander peach is *the* peach on Solaria. Hardly anyone else even bothers to grow peaches. We have twenty-seven varieties of apples and – and so on. The robots could give you full information.'

'What do you do with all the fruit?' asked Trevize. 'You can't eat it all yourself.'

'I wouldn't dream of it. I'm only moderately fond of fruit. It's traded to the other estates.'

'Traded for what?'

'Mineral material mostly. I have no mines worth mentioning on my estates. Then, too, I trade for whatever is required to maintain a healthy ecological balance. I have a very large variety of plant and animal life on the estate.'

'The robots take care of all that, I suppose,' said Trevize.

'They do. And very well, too.'

'All for one Solarian.'

'All for the estate and its ecological standards. I happen to be the only Solarian who visits the various parts of the estate – when I choose – but that is part of my absolute freedom.'

Pelorat said, 'I suppose the others – the other Solarians – also maintain a local ecological balance and have marshlands, perhaps, or mountainous areas or seafront estates.'

Bander said, 'I suppose so. Such things occupy us in the conferences that world affairs sometimes make necessary.'

'How often do you have to get together?' asked Trevize. (They were going through a rather narrow passageway, quite long, and with no rooms on either side. Trevize guessed that it might have been built through an area that did not easily allow anything wider to be constructed, so that it served as a connecting link between two wings that could each spread out more widely.)

'Too often. It's a rare month when I don't have to pass some time in conference with one of the committees I am a member of. Still, although I may not have mountains or marshlands on my estate, my orchards, my fishponds, and my botanical gardens are the best in the world.'

Pelorat said, 'But my dear fellow – I mean, Bander – I would assume you have never left your estate and visited those of others –'

'Certainly *not*,' said Bander, with an air of outrage.

'I said I assumed that,' said Pelorat, mildly. 'But in that case, how can you be certain that yours are best, never having investigated, or even seen the others?'

'Because,' said Bander, 'I can tell from the demand for my products in inter-estate trade.'

Trevize said, 'What about manufacturing?'

Bander said, 'There are estates where they manufacture tools and machinery. As I said, on my estate we make the heat-conducting rods, but those are rather simple.'

'And robots.'

'Robots are manufactured here and there. Throughout history, Solaria has led all the Galaxy in the cleverness and subtlety of robot design.'

'Today also, I imagine,' said Trevize, carefully having the intonation make the remark a statement and not a question.

Bander said, 'Today? With whom is there to compete today? Only Solaria makes robots nowadays. Your worlds do not, if I interpret what I hear on the hyperwave correctly.'

'But the other Spacer worlds?'

'I told you. They no longer exist.'

'At all?'

'I don't think there is a Spacer alive anywhere but on Solaria.'

'Then is there no one who knows the location of Earth?'

'Why should anyone want to know the location of Earth?'

Pelorat broke in, 'I want to know. It's my field of study.'

'Then,' said Bander, 'you will have to study something else. I know nothing about the location of Earth, nor have I heard of anyone who ever did, nor do I care a sliver of robot-metal about the matter.'

The car came to a halt, and, for a moment, Trevize thought that Bander was offended. The halt was a smooth one, however, and Bander, getting out of the car, looked his usual amused self as he motioned the others to get out also.

The lighting in the room they entered was subdued, even after Bander had brightened it with a gesture. It opened into a side corridor, on both sides of which were smaller rooms. In each one of the smaller rooms were one or two ornate vases, sometimes flanked by objects that might have been film projectors.

'What is all this, Bander?' asked Trevize.

Bander said, 'The ancestral death chambers, Trevize.'

50

Pelorat looked about with interest. 'I suppose you have the ashes of your ancestors interred here?'

'If you mean by "interred",' said Bander, 'buried in the ground, you are not quite right. We may be underground, but this is my mansion, and the ashes are in it, as we are right now. In our language we say that the ashes are "inhoused".' It hesitated, then said, '"House" is an archaic word for "mansion".'

Trevize looked about him perfunctorily. 'And these are all your ancestors? How many?'

'Nearly a hundred,' said Bander, making no effort to hide the pride in his voice. 'Ninety-four, to be exact. Of course, the earliest are not true Solarians – not in the present sense of the word. They were half-people, masculine and feminine. Such half-ancestors were placed in adjoining urns by their immediate descendants. I don't go into those rooms, of course. It's rather "shamiferous". At least, that's the Solarian word for it; but I don't know your Galactic equivalent. You may not have one.'

'And the films?' asked Bliss. 'I take it those are film projectors?'

'Diaries,' said Bander, 'the history of their lives. Scenes of themselves in their favourite parts of the estate. It means they do not die in every sense. Part of them remains, and it is part of my freedom that I can join them whenever I choose; I can watch this bit of film or that, as I please.'

'But not the – shamiferous ones.'

Bander's eyes slithered away. 'No,' he admitted, 'but then we all have that as part of the ancestry. It is a common wretchedness.'

'Common? Then other Solarians also have these death chambers?' asked Trevize.

'Oh yes, we all do, but mine is the best, the most elaborate, the most perfectly preserved.'

Trevize said, 'Do you have your own death chamber already prepared?'

'Certainly. It is completely constructed and appointed. That was done as my first duty when I inherited the estate. And when I am laid to ash – to be poetic – my successor will go about the construction of its own as *its* first duty.'

'And do you have a successor?'

'I will have when the time comes. There is as yet ample scope for life. When I must leave, there will be an adult successor, ripe enough to enjoy the estate, and well lobed for power-transduction.'

'It will be your offspring, I imagine.'

'Oh yes.'

'But what if,' said Trevize, 'something untoward takes place? I presume accidents and misfortunes take place even on Solaria. What happens if a Solarian is laid to ash prematurely and it has no successor to take its place, or at least not one who is ripe enough to enjoy the estate?'

'That rarely happens. In my line of ancestors, that happened only once. When it does, however, one need only remember that there are other successors waiting for other estates. Some of those are old enough to inherit, and yet have parents who are young enough to produce a second descendant and to live on till that second descendant is ripe enough for the succession. One of these old/young successors, as they are called, would be assigned to the succession of my estate.'

'Who does the assigning?'

'We have a ruling board that has this as one of its few functions – the assignment of a successor in case of premature ashing. It is all done by holovision, of course.'

Pelorat said, 'But see here, if Solarians never see each other, how would anyone know that some Solarian somewhere has unexpectedly – or expectedly, for that matter – been laid to ash.'

Bander said, 'When one of us is laid to ash, all power at the estate ceases. If no successor takes over at once, the abnormal situation is eventually noticed and corrective measures are taken. I assure you that our social system works smoothly.'

Trevize said, 'Would it be possible to view some of these films you have here?'

Bander froze. Then it said, 'It is only your ignorance that excuses you. What you have said is crude and obscene.'

'I apologize for that,' said Trevize. 'I do not wish to intrude on you, but we've already explained that we are very interested in obtaining information on Earth. It occurs to me that the earliest films you have would date back to a time before Earth was radioactive. Earth might therefore be mentioned. There might be details given about it. We certainly do not wish to intrude on your privacy, but would there be any way in which you yourself could explore those films, or have a robot do so, perhaps, and then allow any relevant information to be passed on to us? Of course, if you can respect our motives and understand that we will try our best to respect your feelings in return, you might allow us to do the viewing ourselves.'

Bander said frigidly, 'I imagine you have no way of knowing that you are becoming more and more offensive. However, we can end all this at once, for I can tell you that there are no films accompanying my early half-human ancestors.'

'None?' Trevize's disappointment was heart-felt.

'They existed once. But even you can imagine what might have been on them. Two half-humans showing interest in each other or, even,' Bander cleared his throat, and said, with an effort, 'interacting. Naturally, all half-human films were destroyed many generations ago.'

'What about the records of other Solarians?'

'All destroyed.'

'Can you be sure?'

'It would be mad not to destroy them.'

'It might be that some Solarians *were* mad, or sentimental, or forgetful. We presume you will not object to directing us to neighbouring estates.'

Bander looked at Trevize in surprise. 'Do you suppose others will be as tolerant of you as I have been?'

'Why not, Bander?'

'You'll find they won't be.'

'It's a chance we'll have to take.'

'No, Trevize. No, any of you. Listen to me.' There were robots in the background, and Bander was frowning.

'What is it, Bander,' said Trevize, suddenly uneasy.

Bander said, 'I have enjoyed speaking to all of you, and observing you in all your – strangeness. It was a unique experience, which I have been delighted with, but I cannot record it in my diary, nor memorialize it in film.'

'Why not?'

'My speaking to you; my listening to you; my bringing you into my mansion; my bringing you here into the ancestral death chambers; are shameful acts.'

'We are not Solarians. We matter to you as little as these robots do, do we not?'

'I excuse the matter to myself in that way. It may not serve as an excuse to others.'

'What do you care? You have absolute liberty to do as you choose, don't you?'

'Even as we are, freedom is not truly absolute. If I were the *only* Solarian on the planet, I could do even shameful things in absolute freedom. But there are other Solarians on the planet, and, because of that, ideal freedom, though approached, is not actually reached. There are twelve hundred Solarians on the planet who would despise me if they knew what I had done.'

'There is no reason they need know about it.'

'That is true. I have been aware of that since you've arrived. I've been aware of it all this time that I've been amusing myself with you. The others must not find out.'

Pelorat said, 'If that means you fear complications as a result of our visits to other estates in search of information about Earth, why, naturally, we will mention nothing of having visited you first. That is clearly understood.'

Bander shook his head. 'I have taken enough chances. I will not speak of this, of course. My robots will not speak of this, and will even be instructed not to remember it. Your ship will be taken underground and explored for what information it can give us –'

'Wait,' said Trevize, 'how long do you suppose we can wait here while you inspect our ship? That is impossible.'

'Not at all impossible, for you will have nothing to say about it. I am sorry. I would like to speak to you longer and to discuss many other things with you, but you see the matter grows more dangerous.'

'No, it does not,' said Trevize emphatically.

'Yes, it does, little half-human. I'm afraid the time has come when I must do what my ancestors would have done at once. I must kill you, all three.'

12

To the Surface

51

Trevize turned his head at once to look at Bliss. Her face was expressionless, but taut, and her eyes were fixed on Bander with an intensity that made her seem oblivious to all else.

Pelorat's eyes were wide, disbelieving.

Trevize, not knowing what Bliss would – or could – do, struggled to fight down an overwhelming sense of loss (not so much at the thought of dying, as of dying without knowing where Earth was, without knowing why he had chosen Gaia as humanity's future). He had to play for time.

He said, striving to keep his voice steady, and his words clear, 'You have shown yourself a courteous and gentle Solarian, Bander. You have not grown angry at our intrusion into your world. You have been kind enough to show us over your estate and mansion, and you have answered our questions. It would suit your character better to allow us to leave now. No one need ever know we were on this world and we would have no cause to return. We arrived in all innocence, seeking merely information.'

'What you say is so,' said Bander lightly, 'and, so far, I have given you life. Your lives were forfeit the instant you entered our atmosphere. What I might have done – and should have done – on making close contact with you, would be to have killed you at once. I should then have ordered the appropriate robot to dissect your bodies for what information on Outworlders that might yield me.

'I have not done that. I have pampered my own curiosity and given in to my own easygoing nature, but it is enough. I can do it no longer. I have, in fact, already compromised the safety of Solaria, for if, through some weakness, I were to let myself be persuaded to let you go, others of your kind would surely follow however much you might promise that they would not.

'There is, however, at least this. Your death will be painless. I will merely heat your brains mildly and drive them into inactivation. You will experience no pain. Life will merely cease. Eventually, when dissection and study are over, I will convert you to ashes in an intense flash of heat and all will be over.'

Trevize said, 'If we must die, then I cannot argue against a quick and painless death, but why must we die at all, having given no offence?'

'Your arrival was an offence.'

'Not on any rational ground, since we could not know it was an offence.'

'Society defines what constitutes an offence. To you, it may seem irrational and arbitrary, but to us it is not, and this is our world on which we have the full right to say that in this and that, you have done wrong and deserve to die.'

Bander smiled as though he were merely making pleasant conversation and went on, 'Nor have you any right to complain on the ground of your own superior virtue. You have a blaster which uses a beam of microwaves to induce intense killing heat. It does what I intend to do, but does it, I am sure, much more crudely and painfully. You would have no hesitation in using it on me right now, had I not drained its energy, and if I were to be so foolish as to allow you the freedom of movement that would enable you to remove the weapon from its holster.'

Trevize said despairingly, afraid even to glance again at Bliss, lest Bander's attention be diverted to her, 'I ask you, as an act of mercy, not to do this.'

Bander said, turning suddenly grim, 'I must first be merciful to myself and to my world, and to do that, you must die.'

He raised his hand and instantly darkness descended upon Trevize.

52

For a moment, Trevize felt the darkness choking him and thought wildly, Is this death?

And as though his thoughts had given rise to an echo, he heard a whispered, 'Is this death?' It was Pelorat's voice.

Trevize tried to whisper, and found he could. 'Why ask?' he said, with a sense of vast relief. 'The mere fact that you can ask shows it is not death.'

'There are old legends that there is life after death.'

'Nonsense,' muttered Trevize. 'Bliss? Are you here, Bliss?'

There was no answer to that.

Again Pelorat echoed. 'Bliss? Bliss? What happened, Golan?'

Trevize said, 'Bander must be dead. He would, in that case, be unable to supply the power for his estate. The lights would go out.'

'But how could –? You mean Bliss did it?'

'I suppose so. I hope she did not come to harm in the process.'
He was on his hands and knees crawling about in the total darkness of the underground (if one did not count the occasional
subvisible flashing of a radioactive atom breaking down in the
walls).

Then his hand came on something warm and soft. He felt along
it and recognized a leg, which he seized. It was clearly too small to
be Bander's. 'Bliss?'

The leg kicked out, forcing Trevize to let go.

He said, 'Bliss? Say something!'

'I am alive,' came Bliss's voice, curiously distorted.

Trevize said, 'But are you well?'

'No.' And, with that, light returned to their surroundings – weakly.
The walls gleamed faintly, brightening and dimming erratically.

Bander lay crumpled in a shadowy heap. At his side, holding his
head, was Bliss.

She looked up at Trevize and Pelorat. 'The Solarian is dead,' she
said, and her cheeks glistened with tears in the weak light.

Trevize was dumbfounded. 'Why are you crying?'

'Should I not cry at having killed a living thing of thought and
intelligence? That was not my intention.'

Trevize leant down to help her to her feet, but she pushed him
away.

Pelorat knelt in his turn, saying softly, 'Please, Bliss, even you
can't bring him back to life. Tell us what happened.'

She allowed herself to be pulled upwards and said dully, 'Gaia
can do what Bander could do. Gaia can make use of the unevenly
distributed energy of the Universe and translate it into chosen work
by mental power alone.'

'I knew that,' said Trevize, attempting to be soothing without
quite knowing how to go about it. 'I remember well our meeting
in space when you – or Gaia, rather – held our spaceship captive. I

thought of that when he held me captive after he had taken my weapons. He held you captive, too, but I was confident you could have broken free if you had wished.'

'No. I would have failed if I had tried. When your ship was in my/our/Gaia's grip,' she said sadly, 'I and Gaia were truly one. Now there is a hyperspatial separation that limits my/our/Gaia's efficiency. Besides, Gaia does what it does by the sheer power of massed brains. Even so, all those brains together lack the transducer-lobes this one Solarian has. We cannot make use of energy as delicately, as efficiently, as tirelessly as he could. – You see that I cannot make the lights gleam more brightly, and I don't know how long I can make them gleam at all before tiring. He could supply the power for an entire vast estate, even when he was sleeping.'

'But you stopped him,' said Trevize.

'Because he didn't suspect my powers,' said Bliss, 'and because I did nothing that would give him evidence of them. He was therefore without suspicion of me and gave me none of his attention. He concentrated entirely on you, Trevize, because it was you who bore the weapons – again, how well it has served that you armed yourself – and I had to wait my chance to stop him with one quick and unexpected blow. When he was on the point of killing us, when his whole mind was concentrated on that, and on you, I was able to strike.'

'And it worked beautifully.'

'How can you say something so cruel, Trevize? It was only my intention to stop him. I merely wished to block his use of his transducer. In the moment of surprise when he tried to blast us and found he could not, but found, instead, that the very illumination about us was fading into darkness, I would tighten my grip and send him into prolonged normal sleep and release the transducer. The power would then remain on, and we could get out of this mansion, into our ship, and leave the planet. I hoped so to arrange things that, when he finally woke, he would have forgotten all that had happened from the instant of his sighting us. Gaia has no desire to kill in order to accomplish what can be brought about without killing.'

'What went wrong, Bliss?' said Pelorat softly.

'I had never encountered any such thing as those transducer-lobes and I lacked any time to work with them and learn about them. I merely struck out forcefully with my blocking manœuvre and, apparently, it didn't work correctly. It was not the entry of energy into the lobes that was blocked, but the exit of that energy. Energy is always pouring into those lobes at a reckless rate but, ordinarily, the brain safeguards itself by pouring out that energy just as quickly. Once I blocked the exit, however, energy piled up within the lobes at once and, in a tiny fraction of a second, the temperature had risen to the point where the brain protein inactivated explosively and he was dead. The lights went out and I removed my block immediately, but, of course, it was too late.'

'I don't see that you could have done anything other than that which you did, dear,' said Pelorat.

'Of what comfort is that considering that I have killed.'

'Bander was on the point of killing us,' said Trevize.

'That was cause for stopping him, not for killing him.'

Trevize hesitated. He did not wish to show the impatience he felt for he was unwilling to offend or further upset Bliss, who was, after all, their only defence against a supremely hostile world.

He said, 'Bliss, it is time to look beyond Bander's death. Because he is dead, all power on the estate is blanked out. This will be noticed, sooner or later, probably sooner, by other Solarians. They will be forced to investigate. I don't think you will be able to hold off the perhaps combined attack of several. And, as you have admitted yourself, you won't be able to supply for very long the limited power you are managing to supply now. It is important, therefore, that we get back to the surface, and to our ship, without delay.'

'But, Golan,' said Pelorat, 'how do we do that? We came for many kilometres along a winding path. I imagine it's quite a maze down here and, for myself, I haven't the faintest idea of where to go to reach the surface. I've always had a poor sense of direction.'

Trevize, looking about, realized that Pelorat was correct. He said, 'I imagine there are many openings to the surface, and we needn't find the one we entered.'

'But we don't know where any of the openings are. How do we find them?'

Trevize turned again to Bliss. 'Can you detect anything, mentally, that will help us find our way out.'

Bliss said, 'The robots on this estate are all inactive. I can detect a thin whisper of subintelligent life straight up, but all that tells us is that the surface is straight up, which we know.'

'Well, then,' said Trevize, 'we'll just have to look for some opening.'

'Hit and miss,' said Pelorat, appalled. 'We'll never succeed.'

'We might, Janov,' said Trevize. 'If we search, there will be a chance, however small. The alternative is simply to stay here, and if we do *that* then we will never succeed. Come, a small chance is better than none.'

'Wait,' said Bliss. 'I *do* sense something.'

'What?' said Trevize.

'A mind.'

'Intelligence?'

'Yes, but limited, I think. What reaches me most clearly, though, is something else.'

'What?' said Trevize, again fighting impatience.

'Fright! Intolerable fright!' said Bliss, in a whisper.

53

Trevize looked about ruefully. He knew where they had entered but he had no illusion on the score of being able to retrace the path by which they had come. He had, after all, paid little attention to the turnings and windings. Who would have thought they'd be in the position of having to retrace the route alone and without help, and with only a flickering, dim light to be guided by?

He said, 'Do you think you can activate the car, Bliss?'

Bliss said, 'I'm sure I could, Trevize, but that doesn't mean I can run it.'

Pelorat said, 'I think that Bander ran it mentally. I didn't see him touch anything when it was moving.'

Bliss said gently, 'Yes, he did it mentally, Pel, but *how*, mentally? You might as well say that he did it by using the controls. Certainly, but if I don't know the details of using the controls, that doesn't help, does it?'

'You might try,' said Trevize.

'If I try, I'll have to put my whole mind to it, and if I do that, then I doubt that I'll be able to keep the lights on. The car will do us no good in the dark even if I learn how to control it.'

'Then we must wander about on foot, I suppose?'

'I'm afraid so.'

Trevize peered at the thick and gloomy darkness that lay beyond the dim light in their immediate neighbourhood. He saw nothing, heard nothing.

He said, 'Bliss, do you still sense this frightened mind?'

'Yes, I do.'

'Can you tell where it is? Can you guide us to it?'

'The mental sense is a straight line. It is not refracted sensibly by ordinary matter, so I can tell it is coming from that direction.'

She pointed to a spot on the dusky wall, and said, 'But we can't walk through the wall to it. The best we can do is follow the corridors and try to find our way in whatever direction will keep the sensation growing stronger. In short, we will have to play the game of hot-and-cold.'

'Then let's start right now.'

Pelorat hung back. 'Wait, Golan, are we sure we want to find this thing, whatever it is. If it is frightened, it may be that we will have reason to be frightened, too.'

Trevize shook his head impatiently. 'We have no choice, Janov. It's a mind, frightened or not, and it may be willing to – or may be made to – direct us to the surface.'

'And do we just leave Bander lying here?' said Pelorat uneasily.

Trevize took his elbow. 'Come, Janov. We have no choice in that, either. Eventually some Solarian will reactivate the place, and a robot will find Bander and take care of him – I hope not before we are safely away.'

He allowed Bliss to lead the way. The light was always strongest in her immediate neighbourhood and she paused at each doorway, at each fork in the corridor, trying to sense the direction from which the fright came. Sometimes she would walk through a door, or move around a curve, then come back and try an alternate path, while Trevize watched helplessly.

Each time Bliss came to a decision and moved firmly in a particular direction, the light came on ahead of her. Trevize noticed that it seemed a bit brighter now – either because his eyes were adapting to the dimness, or because Bliss was learning how to handle the transduction more efficiently. At one point, when she passed one of the metal rods that were inserted into the ground, she put her hand on it and the lights brightened noticeably. She nodded her head as though she were pleased with herself.

Nothing looked in the least familiar; it seemed certain they were wandering through portions of the rambling underground mansion they had not passed through on the way in.

Trevize kept looking for corridors that led upwards sharply, and he varied that by studying the ceilings for any sign of a trapdoor. Nothing of the sort appeared, and the frightened mind remained their only chance of getting out.

They walked through silence, except for the sound of their own steps; through darkness, except for the light in their immediate vicinity; through death except for their own lives. Occasionally, they made out the shadowy bulk of a robot, sitting or standing in the dusk, with no motion. Once they saw a robot lying on its side, with legs and arms in queer frozen positions. It had been caught off-balance, Trevize thought, at the moment when power had been turned off, and it had fallen. Bander, either alive or dead, could not affect the force of gravity. Perhaps all over the vast Bander estate, robots were standing and lying inactive and it would be that that would quickly be noted at the borders.

Or perhaps not, he thought suddenly. Solarians would know when one of their number would be dying of old age and physical decay. The world would be alerted and ready. Bander, however, had died suddenly, without possible foreknowledge, in the prime of his existence. Who would know? Who would expect? Who would be watching for inactivation?

But no (and Trevize thrust back optimism and consolation as dangerous lures into overconfidence). The Solarians would note the cessation of all activity by the Bander estate and take action at once. They all had too great an interest in the succession to estates to leave death to itself.

Pelorat murmured, unhappily, 'Ventilation has stopped. A place like this, underground, must be ventilated, and Bander supplied the power. Now it has stopped.'

'It doesn't matter, Janov,' said Trevize. 'We've got enough air down in this empty underground place to last us for years.'

'It's close just the same. It's psychologically bad.'

'Please, Janov, don't get claustrophobic. – Bliss, are we any closer?'

'Much, Trevize,' she replied. 'The sensation is stronger and I am clearer as to its location.'

She was stepping forward more surely, hesitating less at points of choice of direction.

'There! There!' she said. 'I can sense it intensely.'

Trevize said, drily, 'Even I can hear it now.'

All three stopped and, automatically, held their breaths. They could hear a soft moaning, interspersed with gasping sobs.

They walked into a large room and, as the lights went on, they saw that, unlike all those they had hitherto seen, it was rich and colourful in furnishings.

In the centre of the room was a robot, stooping slightly, its arms stretched out in what seemed an almost affectionate gesture and, of course, it was absolutely motionless.

Behind the robot was a flutter of garments. A round frightened eye edged to one side of it, and there was still the sound of a broken-hearted sobbing.

Trevize darted around the robot and, from the other side, a small figure shot out, shrieking. It stumbled, fell to the ground, and lay there, covering its eyes, kicking its legs in all directions, as though to ward off some threat from whatever angle it might approach, and shrieking, shrieking –

Bliss said, quite unnecessarily, 'It's a child!'

54

Trevize drew back, puzzled. What was a child doing here? Bander had been so proud of his absolute solitude, so insistent upon it.

Pelorat, less apt to fall back on iron reasoning in the face of an obscure event, seized upon the solution at once, and said, 'I suppose this is the successor.'

'Bander's child,' said Bliss, agreeing, 'but too young, I think, to be a successor. The Solarians will have to find one elsewhere.'

She was gazing at the child, not in a fixed glare, but in a soft, mesmerizing way, and slowly the noise the child was making lessened. It opened its eyes and looked at Bliss in return. Its outcry was reduced to an occasional soft whimper.

Bliss made sounds of her own, now, soothing ones, broken words that made little sense in themselves but were meant only to reinforce the calming effect of her thoughts. It was as though she were mentally fingering the child's unfamiliar mind and seeking to even out its dishevelled emotions.

Slowly, never taking its eyes off Bliss, the child got to its feet, stood there swaying a moment, then made a dash for the silent, frozen robot. It threw its arms about the sturdy robotic leg as though avid for the security of its touch.

Trevize said, 'I suppose that the robot is its – nursemaid – or caretaker. I suppose a Solarian can't care for another Solarian, not even a parent for a child.'

Pelorat said, 'And I suppose the child is hermaphroditic.'

'It would have to be,' said Trevize.

Bliss, still entirely preoccupied with the child, was approaching it slowly, hands held half upwards, palms towards herself, as though emphasizing that there was no intention of seizing the small creature. The child was now silent, watching the approach, and holding on the more tightly to the robot.

Bliss said, 'There, child – warm, child – soft, warm, comfortable, safe, child – safe – safe.'

She stopped and, without looking round, said in a low voice, 'Pel, speak to it in its language. Tell it we're robots come to take care of it because the power failed.'

'Robots!' said Pelorat, shocked.

'We must be presented as robots. It's not afraid of robots. And it's never seen a human being, maybe can't even conceive of them.'

Pelorat said, 'I don't know if I can think of the right expression. I don't know the archaic word for "robot".'

'Say "robot", then, Pel. If that doesn't work, try saying "iron thing". Say whatever you can.'

Slowly, word by word, Pelorat spoke archaically. The child looked at him, frowning intensely, as though trying to understand.'

Trevize said, 'You might as well ask it how to get out, while you're at it.'

Bliss said, 'No. Not yet. Confidence first, then information.'

The child, looking now at Pelorat, slowly released its hold on the robot and spoke in a high-pitched musical voice.

Pelorat said anxiously, 'It's speaking too quickly for me.'

Bliss said, 'Ask it to repeat more slowly. I'm doing my best to calm it and remove its fears.'

Pelorat, listening again to the child, said, 'I think it's asking what made Jemby stop. Jemby must be the robot.'

'Check and make sure, Pel.'

Pelorat spoke, then listened, and said, 'Yes, Jemby is the robot. The child calls itself Fallom.'

'Good!' Bliss smiled at the child, a luminous, happy smile, pointed to it, and said, 'Fallom. Good Fallom. Brave Fallom.' She placed a hand on her chest and said, 'Bliss.'

The child smiled. It looked very attractive when it smiled. 'Bliss,' it said, hissing the 's' a bit imperfectly.

Trevize said, 'Bliss, if you can activate the robot, Jemby, it might be able to tell us what we want to know. Pelorat can speak to it as easily as to the child.'

'No,' said Bliss. 'That would be wrong. The robot's first duty is to protect the child. If it is activated and instantly becomes aware of us, aware of strange human beings, it may as instantly attack us. No strange human beings belong here. If I am then forced to inactivate it, it can give us no information, and the child, faced with a second inactivation of the only parent it knows – Well, I just won't do it.'

'But we were told,' said Pelorat mildly, 'that robots can't harm human beings.'

'So we were,' said Bliss, 'but we were not told what kind of robots these Solarians have designed. And even if this robot were designed to do no harm, it would have to make a choice between its child, or the nearest thing to a child it can have, and three objects whom it might not even recognize as human beings, merely as illegal intruders. Naturally, it would choose the child and attack us.'

She turned to the child again. 'Fallom,' she said, 'Bliss.' She pointed, 'Pel – Trev.'

'Pel. Trev,' said the child obediently.

She came closer to the child, her hands reaching towards it slowly. It watched her, then took a step backwards.

'Calm, Fallom,' said Bliss. 'Good, Fallom. Touch, Fallom. Nice, Fallom.'

It took a step towards her, and Bliss sighed. 'Good, Fallom.'

She touched Fallom's bare arm, for it wore, as its parent had, only a long robe, open in front, and with a loincloth beneath. The touch was gentle. She removed her hand, waited, and made contact again, stroking softly.

The child's eyes half-closed under the strong, calming effect of Bliss's mind.

Bliss's hands moved up slowly, softly, scarcely touching, to the child's shoulder, its neck, its ears, then under its long brown hair to a point just above and behind its ears.

Her hands dropped away then, and she said, 'The transducer-lobes are still small. The cranial bone hasn't developed yet. There's just a tough layer of skin there which will eventually expand outwards and be fenced in with bone after the lobes have fully grown. – Which means it can't, at the present time, control the estate or even activate its own personal robot. – Ask it how old it is, Pel.'

Pelorat said, after an exchange, 'It's fourteen years old, if I understand it rightly.'

Trevize said, 'It looks more like eleven.'

Bliss said, 'The length of the years used on this world may not correspond closely to Standard Galactic years. Besides, Spacers are supposed to have extended lifetimes and, if the Solarians are like the other Spacers in this, they may also have extended developmental periods. We can't go by years, after all.'

Trevize said, with an impatient click of his tongue, 'Enough anthropology. We must get to the surface and since we are dealing with a child, we may be wasting our time uselessly. It may not know the route to the surface. It may not ever have been on the surface.'

Bliss said, 'Pel!'

Pelorat knew what she meant and there followed the longest conversation he had yet had with Fallom.

Finally, he said, 'The child knows what the sun is. It says it's seen it. I *think* it's seen trees. It didn't act as though it were sure what the word meant – or at least what the word *I* used meant –'

'Yes, Janov,' said Trevize, 'but do get to the point.'

'I told Fallom that if it could get us out to the surface, that might make it possible for us to activate the robot. Actually, I said we *would* activate the robot. Do you suppose we might?'

Trevize said, 'We'll worry about that later. Did it say it would guide us?'

'Yes. I thought the child would be more anxious to do it, you see, if I made that promise. I suppose we're running the risk of disappointing it –'

'Come,' said Trevize, 'let's get started. All this will be academic if we are caught underground.'

Pelorat said something to the child, who began to walk, then stopped and looked back at Bliss.

Bliss held out her hand and the two then walked hand in hand.

'I'm the new robot,' she said, smiling slightly.

'It seems reasonably happy over that,' said Trevize.

Fallom skipped along and, briefly, Trevize wondered if it were happy simply because Bliss had laboured to make it so, or if, added to that, there was the excitement of visiting the surface or of having three new robots, or whether it was excitement at the thought of having its Jemby foster-parent back. Not that it mattered – as long as the child led them.

There seemed no hesitation in the child's progress. It turned without pause whenever there was a choice of paths. Did it really know where it was going, or was it all simply a matter of a child's indifference? Was it simply playing a game with no clear end in sight.

But Trevize was aware, from the slight burden on his progress, that he was moving uphill, and the child, bouncing self-importantly forward, was pointing ahead and chattering.

Trevize looked at Pelorat who cleared his throat and said, 'I *think* what he's saying is "doorway".'

'I hope your thought is correct,' said Trevize.

The child broke away from Bliss, and was running now. It pointed to a portion of the flooring that seemed darker than the sections immediately neighbouring it. The child stepped on it, jumping up and down a few times, and then turned with a clear expression of dismay, and spoke with shrill volubility.

Bliss said, with a grimace, 'I'll have to supply the power. – This is wearing me out.'

Her face reddened a bit and the lights dimmed, but a door opened just ahead of Fallom, who laughed in soprano delight.

The child ran out the door and the two men followed. Bliss came last, and looked back as the lights just inside darkened and the door closed. She then paused to catch her breath, looking rather worn out.

'Well,' said Pelorat, 'we're out. Where's the ship?'

All of them stood bathed in the still luminous twilight.

Trevize muttered, 'It seems to me that it was in that direction.'

'It seems so to me, too,' said Bliss. 'Let's walk,' and she held out her hand to Fallom.

There was no sound except those produced by the wind and by the motions and calls of living animals. At one point they passed a robot standing motionless near the base of a tree, holding some object of uncertain purpose.

Pelorat took a step towards it out of apparent curiosity, but Trevize said, 'Not our business, Janov. Move on.'

They passed another robot, at a greater distance, who had tumbled.

Trevize said, 'There are robots littered over many kilometres in all directions, I suppose.' And then, triumphantly, 'Ah, there's the ship.'

They hastened their steps now, then stopped suddenly. Fallom raised its voice in an excited squeak.

On the ground near the ship was what appeared to be an air-vessel of primitive design, with a rotor that looked energy-wasteful, and fragile besides. Standing next to the air-vessel, and between the little party of Outworlders and their ship, stood four human figures.

'Too late,' said Trevize, 'we wasted too much time. Now what?'

Pelorat said wonderingly, 'Four Solarians? It can't be. Surely they wouldn't come into physical contact like that. Do you suppose those are holo-images?'

'They are thoroughly material,' said Bliss. 'I'm sure of that. They're not Solarians either. There's no mistaking their minds. They're robots.'

55

'Well, then,' said Trevize wearily, 'onward!' He resumed his walk towards the ship at a calm pace and the others followed.

Pelorat said, rather breathlessly, 'What do you intend to do?'

'If they're robots, they've got to obey orders.'

The robots were awaiting them, and Trevize watched them narrowly as they came closer.

Yes, they must be robots. Their faces, which looked as though they were made of skin underlain with flesh, were curiously expressionless. They were dressed in uniforms that exposed no square centimetre of skin outside the face. Even the hands were covered by thin, opaque gloves.

Trevize gestured casually, in a fashion that was unquestionably a brusque request that they step aside.

The robots did not move.

In a low voice, Trevize said to Pelorat, 'Put it into words, Janov. Be firm.'

Pelorat cleared his throat and, putting an unaccustomed baritone into his voice, spoke slowly, gesturing them aside much as Trevize had done. At that, one of the robots, who was perhaps a shade taller than the rest, said something in a cold and incisive voice.

Pelorat turned to Trevize, 'I think he said we were Outworlders.'

'Tell him we are human beings and must be obeyed.'

The robot spoke, then, in peculiar but understandable Galactic. 'I understand you, Outworlder. I speak Galactic. We are Guardian robots.'

'Then you have heard me say that we are human beings and that you must therefore obey us.'

'We are programmed to obey Rulers only, Outworlder. You are not Rulers and not Solarian. Ruler Bander has not responded to the normal moment of Contact and we have come to investigate at close quarters. It is our duty to do so. We find a spaceship not of Solarian manufacture, several Outworlders present and all Bander robots inactivated. Where is Ruler Bander?'

Trevize shook his head and said slowly and distinctly, 'We know nothing of what you say. Our ship's computer is not working well. We found ourselves near this strange planet against our intentions. We landed to find our location. We found all robots inactivated. We know nothing of what might have happened.'

'That is not a credible account. If all robots on the estate are inactivated and all power is off, Ruler Bander must be dead. It is not logical to suppose that by coincidence he died just as you landed. There must be some sort of causal connection.'

Trevize said, with no set purpose but to confuse the issue and to indicate his own foreigner's lack of understanding and, therefore, of innocence, 'But the power is not off. You and the others are active.'

The robot said, 'We are Guardian Robots. We do not belong to any Ruler. We belong to all the world. We are not Ruler-controlled but are nuclear-powered. I ask again, where is Ruler Bander.'

Trevize looked about him. Pelorat appeared anxious; Bliss was tight-lipped but calm. Fallom was trembling, but Bliss's hand touched the child's shoulder and it stiffened somewhat and lost facial expression. (Was Bliss sedating it?)

The robot said, 'Once again, and for the last time, where is Ruler Bander?'

'I do not know,' said Trevize grimly.

The robot nodded and two of his companions left quickly. The robot said, 'My fellow Guardians will search the mansion. Meanwhile, you will be held for questioning. Hand me those objects you wear at your side.'

Trevize took a step backwards. 'They are harmless.'

'Do not move again. I do not question their nature, whether harmful or harmless. I ask for them.'

'No.'

The robot took a quick step forward, and its arm flashed out too quickly for Trevize to realize what was happening. The robot's hand was on his shoulder; the grip tightened and pushed downward. Trevize went to his knees.

The robot said, 'Those objects.' It held out his other hand.

'No,' gasped Trevize.

Bliss lunged forward, pulled the blaster out of its holster before Trevize, clamped in the robot's grip, could do anything to prevent her, and held it out towards the robot. 'Here, Guardian,' she said, 'and if you'll give me a moment – here's the other. Now release my companion.'

The robot, holding both weapons, stepped back, and Trevize rose slowly to his feet, rubbing his left shoulder vigorously, face wincing with pain.

(Fallom whimpered softly, and Pelorat picked it up in distraction, and held it tightly.)

Bliss said to Trevize, in a furious whisper, 'Why are you fighting him? He can kill you with two fingers.'

Trevize groaned and said, between gritted teeth, 'Why don't *you* handle him?'

'I'm trying to. It takes time. His mind is tight, intensely programmed, and leaves no handle. I must study it. You play for time.'

'Don't study his mind. Just destroy it,' said Trevize, almost soundlessly.

Bliss looked quickly towards the robot. It was studying the weapons intently, while the one other robot that still remained with it watched the Outworlders. Neither seemed interested in the whispering that was going on between Trevize and Bliss.

Bliss said, 'No. No destruction. We killed one dog and hurt another on the first world. You know what happened on this world.' (Another quick glance at the Guardian robots.) 'Gaia does not needlessly butcher life or intelligence. I need time to work it out peacefully.'

She stepped back and stared at the robot fixedly.

The robot said, 'These are weapons.'

'No,' said Trevize.

'Yes,' said Bliss, 'but they are no longer useful. They are drained of energy.'

'Is that indeed so? Why should you carry weapons that are drained of energy? Perhaps they are not drained.' The robot held one of the weapons in its fist and placed its thumb accurately. 'Is this the way it is activated.'

'Yes,' said Bliss, 'if you tighten the pressure, it would be activated, if it contained energy – but it does not.'

'Is that certain?' The robot pointed the weapon at Trevize. 'Do you still say that if I activate it now, it will not work?'

'It will not work,' said Bliss.

Trevize was frozen in place and unable to articulate. He had tested the blaster after Bander had drained it and it was totally dead, but the robot was holding the neuronic whip. Trevize had not tested that.

If the whip contained even a small residue of energy, there would be enough for a stimulation of the pain nerves, and what Trevize would feel would make the grip of the robot's hand seem to have been a pat of affection.

When he had been at the Naval Academy, Trevize had been forced to take a mild neuronic whipblow, as all cadets had had to. That was just to know what it was like. Trevize felt no need to know anything more.

The robot activated the weapon and, for a moment, Trevize stiffened painfully – and then slowly relaxed. The whip, too, was thoroughly drained.

The robot stared at Trevize and then tossed both weapons to one side. 'How do these come to be drained of energy?' it demanded. 'If they are of no use, why do you carry them.'

Trevize said, 'I am accustomed to the weight and carry them even when drained.'

The robot said, 'That does not make sense. You are all under custody. You will be held for further questioning, and, if the Rulers so decide, you will then be inactivated. – How does one open this ship? We must search it.'

'It will do you no good,' said Trevize. 'You won't understand it.'

'If not I, the Rulers will understand.'

'They will not understand, either.'

'Then you will explain so that they will understand.'

'I will not.'

'Then you will be inactivated.'

'My inactivation will give you no explanation, and I think I will be inactivated even if I explain.'

Bliss muttered, 'Keep it up. I'm beginning to unravel the workings of its brain.'

The robot ignored Bliss. (Did she see to that? thought Trevize, and hoped savagely that she had.)

Keeping its attention firmly on Trevize, the robot said, 'If you make difficulties, then we will partially inactivate you. We will damage you and you will then tell us what we want to know.'

Suddenly, Pelorat called out in a half-strangled cry. 'Wait, you cannot do this. – Guardian, you cannot do this.'

'I am under detailed instructions,' said the robot quietly. 'I can do this. Of course, I shall do as little damage as is consistent with obtaining information.'

'But you cannot. Not at all. I am an Outworlder, and so are these two companions of mine. But this child,' and Pelorat looked at Fallom, whom he was still carrying, 'is a Solarian. It will tell you what to do and you must obey it.'

Fallom looked at Pelorat with eyes that were open, but seemed empty.

Bliss shook her head, sharply, but Pelorat looked at her without any sign of understanding.

The robot's eyes rested briefly on Fallom. It said, 'The child is of no importance. It does not have transducer-lobes.'

'It does not yet have fully developed transducer-lobes,' said Pelorat, panting, 'but it will have them in time. It is a Solarian child.'

'It is a child, but without fully developed transducer-lobes it is not a Solarian. I am not compelled to follow its orders or to keep it from harm.'

'But it is the offspring of Ruler Bander.'

'Is it? How do you come to know that?'

Pelorat stuttered, as he sometimes did when over-earnest. 'Wh – what other child would be on this estate?'

'How do you know there aren't a dozen?'

'Have you seen any others?'

'It is I who will ask the questions.'

At this moment, the robot's attention shifted as the second robot touched its arm. The two robots who had been sent to the mansion were returning at a rapid run that, nevertheless, had a certain irregularity to it.

There was silence till they arrived and then one of them spoke in the Solarian language – at which all four of the robots seemed to lose their elasticity. For a moment, they appeared to wither, almost to deflate.

Pelorat said, 'They've found Bander,' before Trevize could wave him silent.

The robot turned slowly and said, in a voice that slurred the syllables, 'Ruler Bander is dead. By the remark you have just made, you show us you were aware of the fact. How did that come to be?'

'How can I know?' said Trevize defiantly.

'You knew it was dead. You knew it was there to be found. How could you know that, unless you had been there – unless it was you that had ended the life.' The robot's enunciation was already improving. It had endured and was absorbing the shock.

Then Trevize said, 'How could we have killed Bander? With its transducer-lobes it could have destroyed us in a moment.'

'How do you know what, or what not, transducer-lobes could do?'

'You mentioned the transducer-lobes just now.'

'I did no more than mention them. I did not describe their properties or abilities.'

'The knowledge came to us in a dream.'

'That is not a credible answer.'

Trevize said, 'To suppose that we have caused the death of Bander is not credible, either.'

Pelorat added, 'And in any case, if Ruler Bander is dead, then Ruler Fallom now controls this estate. Here the Ruler is, and it is it whom you must obey.'

'I have already explained,' said the robot, 'that an offspring with undeveloped transducer-lobes is not a Solarian. He cannot be a Successor, therefore another Successor, of the appropriate age, will be flown in as soon as we report this sad news.'

'What of Ruler Fallom?'

'There is no Ruler Fallom. There is only a child and we have an excess of children. It will be destroyed.'

Bliss said forcefully, 'You dare not. It is a child!'

'It is not I,' said the robot, 'who will necessarily do the act and it is certainly not I who will make the decision. That is for the consensus of the Rulers. In times of child-excess, however, I know well what the decision will be.'

'No. I say, no.'

'It will be painless. – But another ship is coming. It is important that we go into what was the Bander mansion and set up a holo-vision Council that will supply a Successor and decide on what to do with you. – Give me the child.'

Bliss snatched the semi-comatose figure of Fallom from Pelorat. Holding it tightly and trying to balance its weight on her shoulder, she said, 'Do not touch this child.'

Once again, the robot's arm shot out swiftly and it stepped forward, reaching for Fallom. Bliss moved quickly to one side, beginning her motion well before the robot had begun its own. The robot continued to move forward, however, as though Bliss were still standing before it. Curving stiffly downwards, with the forward tips of its feet as the pivot, it went down on its face. The other three stood motionless, eyes unfocused.

Bliss was sobbing, partly with rage. 'I almost had the proper method of control, and it wouldn't give me the time. I had no choice but to strike and now all four are inactivated. – Let's get on the ship before the other ship lands. I am too ill to face additional robots, now.'

Part V

Melpomenia

13

Away from Solaria

56

The leaving was a blur. Trevize had gathered up his futile weapons, had opened the airlock, and they had tumbled in. Trevize didn't notice until they were off the surface that Fallom had been brought in as well.

They probably would not have made it in time if the Solarian use of air-flight had not been so comparatively unsophisticated. It took the approaching Solarian vessel an unconscionable time to descend and land. On the other hand, it took virtually no time for the computer of the *Far Star* to take the gravitic ship vertically upwards.

And although the cut-off of the gravitational interaction and, therefore, of inertia wiped out the otherwise unbearable effects of acceleration that would have accompanied so speedy a takeoff, it did not wipe out the effects of air resistance. The outer hull temperature rose at a distinctly more rapid rate than navy regulations (or ship specifications, for that matter) would have considered suitable.

As they rose, they could see the second Solarian ship land and several more approaching. Trevize wondered how many robots Bliss could have handled, and decided they would have been overwhelmed if they had remained on the surface fifteen minutes longer.

Once out in space (or space enough, with only tenuous wisps of the planetary exosphere around them), Trevize made for the night side of the planet. It was a hop away, since they had left the surface as sunset was approaching. In the dark, the *Far Star* would have a chance to cool more rapidly, and there the ship continued to recede from the surface in a slow spiral.

Pelorat came out of the room he shared with Bliss. He said, 'The child is sleeping normally now. We've showed it how to use the toilet and it had no trouble understanding.'

'That's not surprising. It must have had similar facilities in the mansion.'

'I didn't see any there and I was looking,' said Pelorat, feelingly. 'We didn't get back on the ship a moment too soon for me.'

'Or any of us. But why did we bring that child on board?'

Pelorat shrugged apologetically. 'Bliss wouldn't let go. It was like saving a life in return for the one she took. She can't bear –'

'I know,' said Trevize.

Pelorat said, 'It's a very oddly shaped child.'

'Being hermaphroditic, it would have to be,' said Trevize.

'It has testicles, you know.'

'It could scarcely do without them.'

'And what I can only describe as a very small vagina.'

Trevize made a face. 'Disgusting.'

'Not really, Golan,' said Pelorat, protesting. 'It's adapted to its needs. It only delivers a fertilized egg-cell, or a very tiny embryo, which is then developed under laboratory conditions, tended, I dare say, by robots.'

'And what happens if their robot-system breaks down? If that happens, they would no longer be able to produce viable young.'

'Any world would be in serious trouble if its social structure broke down completely.'

'Not that I would weep uncontrollably over the Solarians.'

'Well,' said Pelorat, 'I admit it doesn't seem a very attractive world – to us, I mean. But that's only the people and the social structure, which are not our type at all, dear chap. But subtract the people and the robots, and you have a world which otherwise –'

'Might fall apart as Aurora is beginning to do,' said Trevize. 'How's Bliss, Janov?'

'Worn out, I'm afraid. She's sleeping now. She had a *very* bad time, Golan.'

'I didn't exactly enjoy myself either.'

Trevize closed his eyes, and decided he could use some sleep himself and would indulge in that relief as soon as he was reasonably certain the Solarians had no space capability – and so far the computer had reported nothing of artifactitious nature in space.

He thought bitterly of the two Spacer planets they had visited – hostile wild dogs on one – hostile hermaphroditic loners on the other – and in neither place the tiniest hint as to the location of Earth. All they had to show for the double visit was Fallom.

He opened his eyes. Pelorat was still sitting in place at the other side of the computer, watching him solemnly.

Trevize said, with sudden conviction, 'We should have left that Solarian child behind.'

Pelorat said, 'The poor thing. They would have killed it.'

'Even so,' said Trevize, 'it belonged there. It's part of that society. Being put to death because of being superfluous is the sort of thing it's born to.'

'Oh, my dear fellow, that's a hard-hearted way to look at it.'

'It's a *rational* way. We don't know how to care for it, and it may suffer more lingeringly with us and die anyway. What does it eat?'

'Whatever we do, I suppose, old man. Actually, the problem is what do *we* eat? How much do we have in the way of supplies?'

'Plenty. Plenty. Even allowing for our new passenger.'

Pelorat didn't look overwhelmed with happiness at this remark. He said, 'It's become a pretty monotonous diet. We should have taken some items on board at Comporellon – not that their cooking was excellent.'

'We couldn't. We left, if you remember, rather hurriedly, as we left Aurora, and as we left, in particular, Solaria. – But what's a little monotony. It spoils one's pleasure, but it keeps one alive.'

'Would it be possible to pick up fresh supplies if we need to?'

'Anytime, Janov. With a gravitic ship and hyperspatial engines, the Galaxy is a small place. In days, we can be anywhere. It's just that half the worlds in the Galaxy are alerted to watch for our ship and I would rather stay out of the way for a time.'

'I suppose that's so. – Bander didn't seem interested in the ship.'

'He probably wasn't even consciously aware of it. I suspect that the Solarians long ago gave up space flight. Their prime desire is to be left completely alone and they can scarcely enjoy the security of isolation if they are forever moving about in space and advertising their presence.'

'What are we going to do next, Golan?'

Trevize said, 'We have a third world to visit.'

Pelorat shook his head. 'Judging from the first two, I don't expect much from *that*.'

'Nor do I at the moment, but just as soon as I get a little sleep, I'm going to get the computer to plot our course to that third world.'

57

Trevize slept considerably longer than he had expected to, but that scarcely mattered. There was neither day nor night, in any natural sense, on board ship, and the circadian rhythm never worked absolutely perfectly. The hours were what they were made to be, and it wasn't uncommon for Trevize and Pelorat (and particularly Bliss) to be somewhat out-of-synch as far as the natural rhythms of eating and sleeping were concerned.

Trevize even speculated, in the course of his scrapedown (the importance of conserving water made it advisable to scrape off the suds rather than rinse them off) about sleeping another hour or two, when he turned and found himself staring at Fallom, who was as undressed as he was.

He could not help jumping back, which, in the restricted area of the Personal was bound to bring part of his body against something hard. He grunted.

Fallom was staring curiously at him and was pointing at Trevize's penis. What it said was incomprehensible but the whole bearing of the child seemed to bespeak a sense of disbelief. For his own peace of mind, Trevize had no choice but to put his hands over his penis.

Then Fallom said, in its high-pitched voice, 'Greetings.'

Trevize started slightly at the child's unexpected use of Galactic, but the word had the sound of having been memorized.

Fallom continued, a painstaking word at a time, 'Bliss – say – you – wash – me.'

'Yes?' said Trevize. He put his hands on Fallom's shoulders. 'You – stay – here.'

He pointed downwards at the floor and Fallom, of course, looked instantly at the place to which the finger pointed. It showed no comprehension of the phrase at all.

'Don't move,' said Trevize, holding the child tightly by both arms, pressing them towards the body as though to symbolize immobility. He hastily dried himself and put on his shorts, and over them his trousers.

He stepped out and roared, 'Bliss!'

It was difficult for anyone to be more than four metres from any one else on the ship and Bliss came to the door of her room at once. She said, smiling, 'Are you calling me, Trevize, or was that the soft breeze sighing through the waving grass?'

'Let's not be funny, Bliss. What is that?' He jerked his thumb over his shoulder.

Bliss looked past him and said, 'Well, it looks like the young Solarian we brought on board yesterday.'

'*You* brought on board. Why do you want me to wash it?'

'I should think you'd want to. It's a very bright creature. It's picking up Galactic words quickly. It never forgets once I explain something. Of course, I'm helping it do so.'

'Naturally.'

'Yes. I keep it calm. I kept it in a daze during most of the disturbing events on the planet. I saw to it that it slept on board ship and I'm trying to divert its mind just a little bit from its lost robot, Jemby, that, apparently, it loved very much.'

'So that it ends up liking it here, I suppose.'

'I hope so. It's adaptable because it's young, and I encourage that by as much as I dare influence its mind. I'm going to teach it to speak Galactic.'

'Then *you* wash it. Understood?'

Bliss shrugged. 'I will, if you insist, but I would want it to feel friendly with each of us. It would be useful to have each of us perform parental functions. Surely you can co-operate in that.'

'Not to this extent. And when you finish washing it, get rid of it. I want to talk to you.'

Bliss said, with a sudden edge of hostility, 'How do you mean, get rid of it?'

'I don't mean dump it through the airlock. I mean, put it in your room. Sit it down in a corner. I want to talk to you.'

'I'll be at your service,' she said coldly.

He stared after her, nursing his wrath for the moment, then moved into the pilot-room, and activated the viewscreen.

Solaria was a dark circle with a curving crescent of light at the left. Trevize placed his hands on the desk to make contact with the computer and found his anger cooling at once. One had to be calm to link mind and computer effectively and, eventually, conditioned reflex linked hand-hold and serenity.

There were no artifactitious objects about the ship in any direction, out as far as the planet itself. The Solarians (or their robots, most likely) could not, or would not, follow.

Good enough. He might as well get out of the night-shadow, then. If he continued to recede, it would, in any case, vanish as Solaria's disc grew smaller than that of the more distant, but much larger, sun that it circled.

He set the computer to move the ship out of the planetary plane as well, since that would make it possible to accelerate with greater safety. They would then more quickly reach a region where space curvature would be low enough to make the Jump secure.

And, as often on such occasions, he fell to studying the stars. They were almost hypnotic in their quiet changelessness. All their turbulence and instability were wiped out by the distance that left them only dots of light.

One of those dots might well be the sun about which Earth revolved – the original sun, under whose radiation life began, and under whose beneficence humanity evolved.

Surely, if the Spacer worlds circled stars that were bright and prominent members of the stellar family, and that were nevertheless unlisted in the computer's Galactic map, the same might be true of *the* sun.

Or was it only the suns of the Spacer worlds that were omitted because of some primeval treaty agreement that left them to themselves? Would Earth's sun be included in the Galactic map, but not marked off from the myriads of stars that were sun-like, yet had no habitable planet in orbit about itself.

There were after all, some thirty billion sun-like stars in the Galaxy, and only about one in a thousand had habitable planets in orbits about them. There might be a thousand such habitable planets within a few hundred parsecs of his present position. Should he sift through the sun-like stars one by one, searching for them?

Or was the original sun not even in this region of the Galaxy? How many other regions were convinced the sun was one of *their* neighbours, that *they* were primeval settlers –

He needed information, and so far he had none.

He doubted strongly whether even the closest examination of the millennial ruins on Aurora would give information concerning Earth's location. He doubted even more strongly that the Solarians could be made to yield information.

Then, too, if all information about Earth had vanished out of the great Library at Trantor; if no information about Earth remained in the great Collective Memory of Gaia; there seemed little chance that any information that might have existed on the lost worlds of the Spacers would have been overlooked.

And if he found Earth's sun and, then, Earth itself, by the sheerest good fortune – would something force him to be unaware of the fact? Was Earth's defence absolute? Was its determination to remain in hiding unbreakable?

What was he looking for anyway?

Was it Earth? Or was it the flaw in Seldon's Plan that he thought (for no clear reason) he might find on Earth?

Seldon's Plan had been working for five centuries now, and would bring the human species (so it was said) to safe harbour at last in the womb of a Second Galactic Empire, greater than the First, a nobler and a freer one – and yet he, Trevize, had voted against it, and for Galaxia.

Galaxia would be one large organism, while the Second Galactic Empire would, however great in size and variety, be a mere union of individual organisms of microscopic size in comparison to itself. The Second Galactic Empire would be another example of the kind of union of individuals that humanity had set up ever since it became humanity. The Second Galactic Empire might be the largest and best of the species, but it would still be but one more member of that species.

For Galaxia, a member of an entirely different species of organization, to be better than the Second Galactic Empire, there must be a flaw in the Plan, something the great Hari Seldon had himself overlooked.

But if it were something Seldon had overlooked, how could Trevize correct the matter? He was not a mathematician; knew nothing, absolutely nothing, about the details of the Plan; would understand nothing, furthermore, even if it were explained to him.

All he knew were the assumptions – that a great number of human beings be involved and that they not be aware of the conclusions reached. The first assumption was self-evidently true, considering the vast population in the Galaxy, and the second had to be true since only the Second Foundationers knew the details of the Plan, and they kept it to themselves securely enough.

That left an added unacknowledged assumption, a taken-for-granted assumption, one so taken for granted it was never mentioned nor thought of – and yet one that might be false. An assumption that, if it *were* false, would alter the grand conclusion of the Plan and make Galaxia preferable to Empire.

But if the assumption was so obvious and so taken for granted that it was never even expressed, how could it be false? And if no one ever mentioned it, or thought of it, how could Trevize know it was there, or have any idea of its nature even if he guessed its existence?

Was he truly Trevize, the man with the flawless intuition – as Gaia insisted? Did he know the right thing to do even when he didn't know why he was doing it?

Now he was visiting every Spacer world he knew about. – Was that the right thing to do? Did the Spacer worlds hold the answer? Or at least the beginning of the answer?

What was there on Aurora but ruins and wild dogs? (And, presumably, other feral creatures. Raging bulls? Overgrown rats? Stalking green-eyed cats?) Solaria was alive, but what was there on it but robots and energy-transducing human beings? What had either world to do with Seldon's Plan unless they contained the secret of the location of the Earth?

And if they did, what had *Earth* to do with Seldon's Plan? Was this all madness? Had he listened too long and too seriously to the fantasy of his own infallibility?

An overwhelming weight of shame came over him and seemed to press upon him to the point where he could barely breathe. He looked at the stars – remote, uncaring – and thought: I must be the Great Fool of the Galaxy.

58

Bliss's voice broke in on him. 'Well, Trevize, why do you want to see – Is anything wrong?' Her voice had twisted into sudden concern.

Trevize looked up and, for a moment, found it momentarily difficult to brush away his mood. He stared at her, then said, 'No, no. Nothing's wrong. I – I was merely lost in thought. Every once in a while, after all, I find myself thinking.'

He was uneasily aware that Bliss could read his emotions. He had only her word that she was voluntarily abstaining from any oversight of his mind.

She seemed to accept his statement, however. She said, 'Pelorat is with Fallom, teaching it Galactic phrases. The child seems to eat what we do without undue objection. – But what do you want to see me about?'

'Well, not here,' said Trevize. 'The computer doesn't need me at the moment. If you want to come into my room, the bed's made and you can sit on it while I sit on the chair. Or vice versa, if you prefer.'

'It doesn't matter.' They walked the short distance to Trevize's room. She eyed him narrowly. 'You don't seem furious, any more.'

'Checking my mind?'

'Not at all. Checking your face.'

'I'm not furious. I may lose my temper momentarily, now and then, but that's not the same as furious. If you don't mind, though, there are questions I must ask you.'

Bliss sat down on Trevize's bed, holding herself erect, and with a solemn expression on her wide-cheeked face and in her dark brown eyes. Her shoulder-length black hair was neatly arranged and her slim hands were clasped loosely in her lap. There was a faint trace of perfume about her.

Trevize smiled. 'You've dolled yourself up. I suspect you think I won't yell quite so hard at a young and pretty girl.'

'You can yell and scream all you wish if it will make you feel better. I just don't want you yelling and screaming at Fallom.'

'I don't intend to. In fact, I don't intend to yell and scream at you. Haven't we decided to be friends?'

'Gaia has never had anything but feelings of friendship towards you, Trevize.'

'I'm not talking about Gaia. I know you're part of Gaia and that you *are* Gaia. Still there's part of you that's an individual, at least after a fashion. I'm talking to the individual. I'm talking to someone named Bliss without regard – or with as little regard as possible – to Gaia. Haven't we decided to be friends, Bliss?'

'Yes, Trevize.'

'Then how is it you delayed dealing with the robots on Solaria after we had left the mansion and reached the ship? I was humiliated and physically hurt, yet you did nothing. Even though every moment might bring additional robots to the scene and the number might overwhelm us, you did nothing.'

Bliss looked at him seriously, and spoke as though she were intent on explaining her actions rather than defending them. 'I was not doing nothing, Trevize. I was studying the Guardian robots' minds, and trying to learn how to handle them.'

'I know that's what you were doing. At least you said you were at the time. I just don't see the sense of it. Why handle the minds when you were perfectly capable of destroying them – as you finally did?'

'Do you think it so easy to destroy an intelligent being?'

Trevize's lips twisted into an expression of distaste. 'Come, Bliss. An intelligent *being*? It was just a robot.'

'Just a robot?' A little passion entered her voice. 'That's the argument always. Just. Just! Why should the Solarian, Bander, have hesitated to kill us? We were just human beings without transducers. Why should there be any hesitation about leaving Fallom to its fate? It was just a Solarian, and an immature specimen at that. If you start dismissing anyone or anything you want to do away with as just a this or just a that, you can destroy anything you wish. There are always categories you can find for them.'

Trevize said, 'Don't carry a perfectly legitimate remark to extremes just to make it seem ridiculous. The robot was just a robot. You can't deny that. It was not human. It was not intelligent in our sense. It was a machine mimicking an appearance of intelligence.'

Bliss said, 'How easily you can talk when you know nothing about it. I am Gaia. Yes, I am Bliss, too, but I am Gaia. I am a world that finds every atom of itself precious and meaningful, and every organization of atoms even more precious and meaningful. I/we/Gaia would not lightly break down an organization, though we would gladly build it into something still more complex, provided always that that would not harm the whole.

'The highest form of organization we know produces intelligence, and to be willing to destroy intelligence requires the sorest need. Whether it is machine intelligence or biochemical intelligence scarcely matters. In fact, the Guardian robot represented a kind of intelligence I/we/Gaia had never encountered. To study it was wonderful. To destroy it, unthinkable – except in a moment of crowning emergency.'

Trevize said drily, 'There were three greater intelligences at stake: your own, that of Pelorat, the human being you love, and, if you don't mind my mentioning it, mine.'

'Four! You still keep forgetting to include Fallom. – They were not yet at stake. So I judged. See here – Suppose you were faced with a painting, a great artistic masterpiece, the existence of which meant death to you. All you had to do was to bring a wide brush of paint slam-bang, and at random, across the face of that painting and it would be destroyed forever, and you would be safe. But suppose, instead, that if you studied the painting carefully, and added just a touch of paint here, a speck there, scraped off a minute portion in a third place and so on, you would alter the painting enough to avoid death, and yet leave it a masterpiece. Naturally, the revision couldn't be done except with the most painstaking care. It would take time, but surely, if that time existed, you would try to save the painting as well as your life.'

Trevize said, 'Perhaps. But in the end you destroyed the painting past redemption. The wide paintbrush came down and wiped out all the wonderful little touches of colour and subtleties of form and shape. And you did that instantly when a little hermaphrodite was at risk, where our danger and your own had not moved you.'

'We Outworlders were still not at *immediate* risk, while Fallom, it seemed to me, suddenly was. I had to choose between the Guardian robots and Fallom, and, with no time to lose, I had to choose Fallom.'

'Is that what it was, Bliss? A quick calculation weighing one mind against another, a quick judging of the greater complexity and the greater worth?'

'Yes.'

Trevize said, 'Suppose I tell you, it was just a child that was standing before you, a child threatened with death. An instinctive maternalism gripped you then, and you saved it where earlier you were all calculation when only three adult lives were at stake.'

Bliss reddened slightly. 'There might have been something like that in it; but it was not after the fashion of the mocking way in which you say it. It had rational thought behind it, too.'

'I wonder. If there had been rational thought behind it, you might have considered that the child was meeting the common fate inevitable in its own society. Who knows how many thousands of children had been cut down to maintain the low number these Solarians think suitable to their world?'

'There's more to it than that, Trevize. The child would be killed because it was too young to be a Successor, and that was because it had a parent who had died prematurely, and *that* was because I had killed that parent.'

'At a time when it was kill or be killed.'

'Not important. I killed the parent. I could not stand by and allow the child to be killed for my deed. – Besides, it offers for study a brain of a kind that has never been studied by Gaia.'

'A child's brain.'

'It will not remain a child's brain. It will further develop the two transducer-lobes on either side of the brain. Those lobes give a Solarian abilities that all of Gaia cannot match. Simply to keep a few lights lit, just to activate a device to open a door, wore me out. Bander could have kept all the power going over an estate as great in complexity and greater in size than that city we saw on Comporellon – and do it even while sleeping.'

Trevize said, 'Then you see the child as an important bit of fundamental brain research.'

'In a way, yes.'

'That's not the way I feel. To me, it seems we have taken danger aboard. Great danger.'

'Danger in what way? It will adapt perfectly – with my help. It is highly intelligent, and already shows signs of feeling affection for us. It will eat what we eat, go where we go, and I/we/Gaia will gain invaluable knowledge concerning its brain.'

'What if it produces young? It doesn't need a mate. It is its own mate.'

'It won't be of child-bearing age for many years. The Spacers lived for centuries and the Solarians had no desire to increase their numbers. Delayed reproduction is probably bred into the population. Fallom will have no children for a long time.'

'How do you know this?'

'I don't *know* it. I'm merely being logical.'

'And I tell you Fallom will prove dangerous.'

'You don't know that. And you're not being logical, either.'

'I feel it, Bliss, without reason. – At the moment. And it is you, not I, who insists my intuition is infallible.'

And Bliss frowned and looked uneasy.

59

Pelorat paused at the door to the pilot-room and looked inside in a rather ill-at-ease manner. It was as though he were trying to decide whether Trevize was hard at work or not.

Trevize had his hands on the table, as he always did when he made himself part of the computer, and his eyes were on the viewscreen. Pelorat judged, therefore, he was at work, and he waited patiently, trying not to move or, in any way, disturb the other.

Eventually, Trevize looked up at Pelorat. It was not a matter of total awareness. Trevize's eyes always seemed a bit glazed and unfocused when he was in computer-communion, as though he were looking, thinking, living in some other way than a person usually did.

But he nodded slowly at Pelorat, as though the sight, penetrating with difficulty, did, at last, sluggishly impress itself on the optic lobes. Then, after a while, he lifted his hands and smiled and was himself again.

Pelorat said apologetically, 'I'm afraid I'm getting in your way, Golan.'

'Not seriously, Janov. I was just testing to see if we were ready for the Jump. We are, just about, but I think I'll give it a few more hours, just for luck.'

'Does luck – or random factors – have anything to do with it?'

'An expression only,' said Trevize, smiling, 'but random factors do have something to do with it, in theory. – What's on your mind?'

'May I sit down?'

'Surely, but let's go into my room. How's Bliss?'

'Very well.' He cleared his throat. 'She's sleeping again. She must have her sleep, you understand.'

'I understand perfectly. It's the hyperspatial separation.'

'Exactly, old chap.'

'And Fallom?' Trevize reclined on the bed, leaving Pelorat the chair.

'Those books out of my library that you had your computer print up for me? The folk tales? It's reading them. Of course, it understands very little Galactic, but it seems to enjoy sounding out the words. He's – I keep wanting to use the masculine pronoun for him. Why do you suppose that is, old fellow?'

Trevize shrugged. 'Perhaps because you're masculine yourself.'

'Perhaps. It's fearfully intelligent, you know.'

'I'm sure.'

Pelorat hesitated. 'I gather you're not very fond of Fallom.'

'Nothing against it personally, Janov. I've never had children and I've never been particularly fond of them generally. You've had children, I seem to remember.'

'One son. – It was a pleasure, I recall, having my son when he was a little boy. Maybe *that's* why I want to use the masculine pronoun for Fallom. It takes me back a quarter of a century or so.'

'I've no objection to your liking it, Janov.'

'You'd like him, too, if you gave yourself a chance.'

'I'm sure I would, Janov, and maybe some day I will give myself a chance to do so.'

Pelorat hesitated again. 'I also know that you must get tired of arguing with Bliss.'

'Actually, I don't think we'll be arguing much, Janov. She and I are actually getting along quite well. We even had a reasonable discussion just the other day – no shouting, no recrimination – about her delay in inactivating the Guardian robots. She keeps saving our lives, after all, so I can't very well offer her less than friendship, can I?'

'Yes, I see that, but I don't mean arguing, in the sense of quarrelling. I mean this constant wrangle about Galaxia as opposed to individuality.'

'Oh, that! I suppose that will continue – politely.'

'Would you mind, Golan, if I took up the argument on her behalf?'

'Perfectly all right. Do you accept the idea of Galaxia on your own, or is it that you simply feel happier when you agree with Bliss?'

'Honestly, on my own. I think that Galaxia is what should be forthcoming. You yourself chose that course of action and I am constantly becoming more convinced that that is correct.'

'Because I chose it? That's no argument. Whatever Gaia says, I may be wrong, you know. So don't let Bliss persuade you into Galaxia on that basis.'

'I don't think you are wrong. Solaria showed me that, not Bliss.'

'How?'

'Well, to begin with, we are Isolates, you and I.'

'*Her* term, Janov. I prefer to think of us as individuals.'

'A matter of semantics, old chap. Call it what you will, we are enclosed in our private skins surrounding our private thoughts, and we think first and foremost of ourselves. Self-defence is our first law of nature, even if that means harming everyone else in existence.'

'People have been known to give their lives for others.'

'A rare phenomenon. Many more people have been known to sacrifice the dearest needs of others to some foolish whim of their own.'

'And what has that to do with Solaria?'

'Why, on Solaria, we see what Isolates – or individuals, if you prefer – can become. The Solarians can hardly bear to divide a whole world among themselves. They consider living a life of complete isolation to be perfect liberty. They have no yearning for even their own offspring, but kill them if there are too many. They surround themselves with robot slaves to which they supply the power, so that if they die, their whole huge estate symbolically dies as well. Is this admirable, Golan? Can you compare it in decency, kindness, and mutual concern with Gaia? – Bliss has not discussed this with me at all. It is my own feeling.'

Trevize said, 'And it is like you to have that feeling, Janov. I share it. I think Solarian society is horrible, but it wasn't always like that. They are descended from Earthmen, and, more immediately, from Spacers who lived a much more normal life. The Solarians chose a path, for one reason or another, which led to an extreme, but you can't judge by extremes. In all the Galaxy, with its millions of inhabited worlds, is there one you know that now, or in the past, has had a society like that of Solaria, or even *remotely* like that of Solaria. And would even Solaria have such a society if it were not riddled with robots? Is it conceivable that a society of individuals could evolve to such a pitch of Solarian horror without robots.'

Pelorat's face twitched a little. 'You punch holes in everything, Golan – or at least I mean you don't ever seem to be at a loss in defending the type of Galaxy you voted against.'

'I won't knock down everything. There *is* a rationale for Galaxia and when I find it, I'll know it, and I'll give in. Or perhaps, more accurately, *if* I find it.'

'Do you think you might not?'

Trevize shrugged. 'How can I say. – Do you know why I'm waiting a few hours to make the Jump, and why I'm in danger of talking myself into waiting a few days?'

'You said it would be safer if we waited.'

'Yes, that's what I said, but we'd be safe enough now. What I really fear is that those Spacer worlds for which we have the co-ordinates will fail us altogether. We have only three, and we've already used up two, narrowly escaping death each time. In doing so, we have still not gained any hint as to Earth's location, or even, in actual fact, Earth's existence. Now I face the third and last chance, and what if it, too, fails us?'

Pelorat sighed. 'You know there are old folk tales – one, in fact, exists among those I gave Fallom to practise upon – in which someone is allowed three wishes, but only three. Three seems to be a significant number in these things, perhaps because it is the first odd number so that it is the smallest decisive number. You know, two out of three wins. – The point is that in these stories, the wishes are of no use. No one ever wishes correctly, which, I have always supposed, is ancient wisdom to the effect that the satisfaction of your wants must be earned, and not –'

He fell suddenly silent and abashed. 'I'm sorry, old man, but I'm wasting your time. I do tend to rattle on when I get started on my hobby.'

'I find you always interesting, Janov. I am willing to see the analogy. We have been given three wishes, and we have had two and they have done us no good. Now only one is left. Somehow, I am sure of failure again and so I wish to postpone it. That is why I am putting off the Jump as long as possible.'

'What will you do if you do fail again? Go back to Gaia? To Terminus?'

'Oh no,' said Trevize in a whisper, shaking his head. 'The search must continue – if I only knew how.'

14

Dead Planet

60

Trevize felt depressed. What few victories he had had since the search began had never been definitive; they had merely been the temporary staving off of defeat.

Now he had delayed the Jump to the third of the Spacer worlds till he had spread his unease to the others. When he finally decided that he simply must tell the computer to move the ship through hyperspace, Pelorat was standing solemnly in the doorway to the pilot-room, and Bliss was just behind him and to one side. Even Fallom was standing there, gazing at Trevize owlishly, while one hand gripped Bliss's hand tightly.

Trevize had looked up from the computer and had said, rather churlishly, 'Quite the family group!' but that was only his own discomfort speaking.

He instructed the computer to Jump in such a way as to re-enter space at a further distance from the star in question than was absolutely necessary. He told himself that that was because he was learning caution as a result of events on the first two Spacer worlds, but he didn't believe that. Well underneath, he knew, he was hoping that he would arrive in space at a great enough distance from the star to be uncertain as to whether it did or did not have a habitable planet. That would give him a few more days of in-space travel before he could find out, and (perhaps) have to stare bitter defeat in the face.

So now, with the 'family group' watching, he drew a deep breath, held it, then expelled it in a between-the-lips whistle as he gave the computer its final instruction.

The star-pattern shifted in a silent discontinuity and the viewscreen became barer, for he had been taken into a region in which the stars were somewhat sparser. And there, nearly in the centre, was a brightly gleaming star.

Trevize grinned broadly, for this was a victory of sorts. After all, the third set of co-ordinates might have been wrong and there might have been no appropriate G-type star in sight. He glanced towards the other three, and said, 'That's it. Star number three.'

'Are you sure?' asked Bliss softly.

'Watch!' said Trevize. 'I will switch to the equi-centred view in the computer's Galactic map, and if that bright star disappears, it's not recorded on the map, and it's the one we want.'

The computer responded to his command, and the star blinked out without any prior dimming. It was as though it had never been, but the rest of the star-field remained as it was, in sublime indifference.

'We've got it,' said Trevize.

And yet he sent the *Far Star* forward at little more than half the speed he might easily have maintained. There was still the question of the presence or absence of a habitable planet, and he was in no hurry to find out. Even after three days of approach, there was still nothing to be said about that, either way.

Or, perhaps, not quite nothing. Circling the star was a large gas giant. It was very far from its star and it gleamed a very pale yellow on its daylight side, which they could see, from their position, as a thick crescent.

Trevize did not like its looks, but he tried not to show it and spoke as matter-of-factly as a guidebook. 'There's a big gas giant out there,' he said. 'It's rather spectacular. It has a thin pair of rings and two sizeable satellites that can be made out at the moment.'

Bliss said, 'Most systems include gas giants, don't they?'

'Yes, but this is a rather large one. Judging from the distance of its satellites, and their periods of revolution, that gas giant is almost two thousand times as massive as a habitable planet would be.'

'What's the difference?' said Bliss. 'Gas giants are gas giants and it doesn't matter what size they are, does it? They're always present at great distances from the star they circle, and none of them are habitable, thanks to their size and distance. We just have to look closer to the star for a habitable planet.'

Trevize hesitated, then decided to place the facts on the table. 'The thing is,' he said, 'that gas giants tend to sweep a volume of planetary space clean. What material they don't absorb into their own structures will coalesce into fairly large bodies that come to make up their satellite system. They prevent other coalescences at even a considerable distance from themselves, so that the larger the gas giant, the more likely it is to be the only sizeable planet of a particular star. There'll just be the gas giant and asteroids.'

'You mean there is no habitable planet here?'

'The larger the gas giant, the smaller the chance of a habitable planet and that gas giant is so massive it is virtually a dwarf star.'

Pelorat said, 'May we see it?'

All three now stared at the screen (Fallom was in Bliss's room with the books).

The view was magnified till the crescent filled the screen. Crossing that crescent a distance above centre was a thin dark line, the shadow of the ring system which could itself be seen a small distance beyond the planetary surface as a gleaming curve that stretched into the dark side a short distance before it entered the shadow itself.

Trevize said, 'The planet's axis of rotation is inclined about 35 degrees to its plane of revolution, and its ring is in the planetary equatorial plane, of course, so that the star's light comes in from below, at this point in its orbit, and casts the ring's shadow well above the equator.'

Pelorat watched, raptly. 'Those are thin rings.'

'Rather above average size, actually,' said Trevize.

'According to legend, the rings that circle a gas giant in Earth's planetary system are much wider, brighter, and more elaborate than this one. The rings actually dwarf the gas giant by comparison.'

'I'm not surprised,' said Trevize. 'When a story is handed on from person to person for thousands of years, do you suppose it shrinks in the telling?'

Bliss said, 'It's beautiful. If you watch the crescent it seems to writhe and wriggle before your eyes.'

'Atmospheric storms,' said Trevize. 'You can generally see that more clearly if you choose an appropriate wavelength of light. Here, let me try.' He placed his hands on the desk and ordered the computer to work its way through the spectrum, and stop at the appropriate wavelength.

The mildly-lit crescent went into a wilderness of colour that shifted so rapidly it almost dazed the eyes that tried to follow. Finally, it settled into a red-orange, and, within the crescent, clear spirals drifted, coiling and uncoiling as they moved.

'Unbelievable,' muttered Pelorat.

'Delightful,' said Bliss.

Quite believable, thought Trevize bitterly, and anything but delightful. Neither Pelorat nor Bliss, lost in the beauty, bothered to think that the planet they admired lowered the chances of solving the mystery Trevize was trying to unravel. But then, why should they? Both were satisfied that Trevize's decision had been correct, and they accompanied him in his search for certainty without an emotional bond to it. It was useless to blame them for that.

He said, 'The dark side seems dark, but if our eyes were sensitive to the range just a little beyond the usual long-wave limit, we would see it as a dull, deep, angry red. The planet is pouring infrared radiation out into space in great quantities because it is massive enough to be almost red-hot. It's more than a gas giant; it's a sub-star.'

He waited a little longer and then said, 'And now let's put that object out of our mind and look for the habitable planet that *may* exist.'

'Perhaps it does,' said Pelorat, smiling. 'Don't give up, old fellow.'

'I haven't given up,' said Trevize, without true conviction. 'The formation of planets is too complicated a matter for rules to be hard and fast. We speak only of probabilities. With that monster out in space, the probabilities decrease, but not to zero.'

Bliss said, 'Why don't you think of it this way? Since the first two sets of co-ordinates each gave you a habitable planet of the Spacers, then this third set, which has already given you an appropriate star, should give you a habitable planet as well. Why speak of probabilities?'

'I certainly hope you're right,' said Trevize, who did not feel at all consoled. 'Now we will shoot out of the planetary plane and in towards the star.'

The computer took care of that almost as soon as he had spoken his intention. He sat back in his pilot's chair and decided, once again, that the one evil of piloting a gravitic ship with a computer so advanced was that one could never – *never* – pilot any other type of ship again.

Could he ever again bear to do the calculations himself? Could he bear to have to take acceleration into account, and limit it to a reasonable level? – In all likelihood, he would forget and pour on the energy till he and everyone on board were smashed against one interior wall or another.

Well, then, he would continue to pilot this one ship – or another

exactly like it, if he could even bear to make so much of a change
– always.

And because he wanted to keep his mind off the question of the
habitable planet, yes or no, he mused on the fact that he had directed
the ship to move above the plane, rather than below. Barring any
definite reason to go below a plane, pilots almost always chose to
go above. Why?

For that matter, why be so intent on considering one direction
above and the other below? In the symmetry of space that was pure
convention.

Just the same, he was always aware of the direction in which any
planet under observation rotated about its axis and revolved about
its star. When both were counterclockwise, then the direction of
one's raised arm was north, and the direction of one's feet was south.
And throughout the Galaxy, north was pictured as above and south
as below.

It was pure convention, dating back into the primeval mists,
and it was followed slavishly. If one looked at a familiar map with
south above, one didn't recognize it. It had to be turned about to
make sense. And all things being equal, one turned north – and
'above'.

Trevize thought of a battle fought by Bel Riose, the Imperial
general of three centuries before, who had veered his squadron below
the planetary plane at a crucial moment, and caught a squadron of
vessels, waiting and unprepared. There were complaints that it had
been an unfair manœuvre – by the losers, of course.

A convention, so powerful and so primordially old, must have
started on Earth – and that brought Trevize's mind, with a jerk, back
to the question of the habitable planet.

Pelorat and Bliss continued to watch the gas giant as it slowly
turned on the viewscreen in a slow, slow back-somersault. The sunlit
portion spread and, as Trevize kept its spectrum fixed in the
orange-red wavelengths, the storm-writhing of its surface became
ever madder and more hypnotic.

Then Fallom came wandering in and Bliss decided it must take a nap and that so must she.

Trevize said to Pelorat, who remained, 'I have to let go of the gas-giant, Janov. I want to have the computer concentrate on the search for a gravitational blip of the right size.'

'Of course, old fellow,' said Pelorat.

But it was more complicated than that. It was not just a blip of the right size that the computer had to search for, it was one of the right size and at the right distance. It would still be several days before he could be sure.

61

Trevize walked into his room, grave, solemn – indeed sombre – and started perceptibly.

Bliss was waiting for him and immediately next to her was Fallom, with its loin cloth and robe bearing the unmistakable fresh odour of steaming and vacu-pressing. The youngster looked better in that than in one of Bliss's foreshortened nightgowns.

Bliss said, 'I didn't want to disturb you at the computer, but now listen. – Go on, Fallom.'

Fallom said, in its high-pitched musical voice, 'I greet you, Protector Trevize. It is with great pleasure that I am ap – ad – accompanying you in this ship through space. I am happy, too, for the kindness of my friends, Bliss and Pel.'

Fallom finished and smiled prettily, and once again Trevize thought to himself: Do I think of it as a boy or as a girl or as both or as neither?

He nodded his head. 'Very well memorized. Almost perfectly pronounced.'

'Not at all memorized,' said Bliss, warmly. 'Fallom composed this itself and asked if it would be possible to recite it to you. I didn't even know what Fallom would say till I heard it said.'

Trevize forced a smile, 'In that case, very good indeed.' He noticed Bliss avoided pronouns when she could.

Bliss turned to Fallom and said, 'I told you Trevize would like it. – Now go to Pel and you can have some more reading if you wish.'

Fallom ran off, and Bliss said, 'It's really astonishing how quickly Fallom is picking up Galactic. The Solarians must have a special aptitude for languages. Think how Bander spoke Galactic merely from hearing it on hyperspatial communications. Those brains may be remarkable in ways other than energy transduction.'

Trevize grunted.

Bliss said, 'Don't tell me you still don't like Fallom.'

'I neither like nor dislike. The creature simply makes me uneasy. For one thing, it's a grisly feeling to be dealing with a hermaphrodite.'

Bliss said, 'Come, Trevize, that's ridiculous. Fallom is a perfectly acceptable living creature. To a society of hermaphrodites, think how disgusting you and I must seem – males and females generally. Each is half of a whole and, in order to reproduce, there must be a temporary and clumsy union.'

'Do you object to that, Bliss?'

'Don't pretend to misunderstand. I am trying to view us from the hermaphroditic standpoint. To them, it must seem repellent in the extreme; to us, it seems natural. So Fallom seems repellent to you, but that's just a shortsighted parochial reaction.'

'Frankly,' said Trevize, 'it's annoying not to know the pronoun to use in connection with the creature. It impedes thought and conversation to hesitate forever at the pronoun.'

'But that's the fault of our language,' said Bliss, 'and not of Fallom. No human language has been devised with hermaphroditism in mind. And I'm glad you brought it up, because I've been thinking about it myself. – Saying "it", as Bander himself insisted on doing, is no solution. That is a pronoun intended for objects to which sex is irrelevant, and there is no pronoun at all for objects that are sexually active in both senses. Why not just pick one of the pronouns arbitrarily, then? I think of Fallom as a girl. She has the high voice of one, for one thing, and she has the capacity of producing young, which is the vital definition of femininity. Pelorat has agreed; why don't you do so, too? Let it be "she" and "her".'

Trevize shrugged. 'Very well. It will sound peculiar to point out that *she* has testicles, but very well.'

Bliss sighed. 'You do have this annoying habit of trying to turn everything into a joke, but I know you are under tension and I'll make allowance for that. Just use the feminine pronoun for Fallom, please.'

'I will.' Trevize hesitated, then, unable to resist, said, 'Fallom seems more your surrogate-child every time I see you together. Is it that you want a child and don't think Janov can give you one?'

Bliss's eyes opened wide. 'He's not there for children! Do you think I use him as a handy device to help me have a child? It is not time for me to have a child, in any case. And when it is time, it will have to be a Gaian child, something for which Pel doesn't qualify.'

'You mean Janov will have to be discarded?'

'Not at all. A temporary diversion only. It might even be brought about by artificial insemination.'

'I presume you can only have a child when Gaia's decision is that one is necessary; when there is a gap produced by the death of an already-existing Gaian human fragment.'

'That is an unfeeling way of putting it, but it is true enough. Gaia must be well-proportioned in all its parts and relationships.'

'As in the case of the Solarians.'

Bliss's lips pressed together and her face grew a little white. 'Not at all. The Solarians produce more than they need and destroy the excess. We produce just what we need and there is never a necessity of destroying – as you replace the dying outer layers of your skin by just enough new growth for renewal and by not one cell more.'

'I see what you mean,' said Trevize. 'I hope, by the way, that you are considering Janov's feelings.'

'In connection with a possible child for me? That has never come up for discussion; nor will it.'

'No, I don't mean that. – It strikes me you are becoming more
and more interested in Fallom. Janov may feel neglected.'

'He's not neglected, and he is as interested in Fallom as I am.
She is another point of mutual involvement that draws us even closer
together. Can it be that *you* are the one who feels neglected.'

'*I?*' He was genuinely surprised.

'Yes, you. I don't understand Isolates any more than you understand Gaia, but I have a feeling that you enjoy being the central
point of attention on this ship, and you may feel cut out by Fallom.'

'That's foolish.'

'No more foolish than your suggestion that I am neglecting Pel.'

'Then let's declare a truce and stop. I'll try to view Fallom as a
girl, and I shall not worry excessively about you being inconsiderate
of Janov's feelings.'

Bliss smiled. 'Thank you. All is well, then.'

Trevize turned away, and Bliss then said, 'Wait!'

Trevize turned back and said, just a bit wearily, 'Yes?'

'It's quite clear to me, Trevize, that you're sad and depressed. I
am not going to probe your mind, but you might be willing to tell
me what's wrong. Yesterday, you said there was an appropriate planet
in this system and you seemed quite pleased. – It's still there, I hope.
The finding hasn't turned out to be mistaken, has it?'

'There's an appropriate planet in the system, and it's still there,'
said Trevize.

'Is it the right size?'

Trevize nodded. 'Since it's appropriate, it's of the right size. And
it's at the right distance from the star as well.'

'Well, then, what's wrong?'

'We're close enough now to analyse the atmosphere. It turns out
that it has none to speak of.'

'No atmosphere?'

'None to speak of. It's a non-habitable planet, and there is no
other circling the sun that has even the remotest capacity for habitability. We have come up with zero on this third attempt.'

62

Pelorat, looking grave, was clearly unwilling to intrude on Trevize's unhappy silence. He watched from the door of the pilot-room, apparently hoping that Trevize would initiate a conversation.

Trevize did not. If ever a silence seemed stubborn, his did.

And finally, Pelorat could stand it no longer, and said, in a rather timid way, 'What are we doing?'

Trevize looked up, stared at Pelorat for a moment, turned away, and then said, 'We're zeroing in on the planet.'

'But since there's no atmosphere –'

'The computer *says* there's no atmosphere. Till now, it's always told me what I've wanted to hear and I've accepted it. Now it has told me something I *don't* want to hear, and I'm going to check it. If the computer is ever going to be wrong, this is the time I want it to be wrong.'

'Do you think it's wrong?'

'No, I don't.'

'Can you think of any reason that might make it wrong?'

'No, I can't.'

'Then why are you bothering, Golan?'

And Trevize finally wheeled in his seat to face Pelorat, his face twisted in near-despair, and said, 'Don't you see, Janov, that I can't think of anything else to do? We drew blanks on the first two worlds as far as Earth's location is concerned, and now this world is a blank. What do I do now? Wander from world to world, and peer about and say, "Pardon me. Where's Earth?" Earth has covered its tracks too well. Nowhere has it left any hint. I'm beginning to think that it will see to it that we're incapable of picking up a hint even if one exists.'

Pelorat nodded, and said, 'I've been thinking along those lines myself. Do you mind if we discuss it? I know you're unhappy, old chap, and don't want to talk, so if you want me to leave you alone, I will.'

'Go ahead, discuss it,' said Trevize, with something that was remarkably like a groan. 'What have I got better to do than listen?'

Pelorat said, 'That doesn't sound as though you really want me to talk, but perhaps it will do us good. Please stop me at any time if you decide you can stand it no longer. – It seems to me, Golan, that Earth need not take only passive and negative measures to hide itself. It need not merely wipe out references to itself. Might it not plant false evidence and work actively for obscurity in that fashion?'

'How do you mean?'

'Well, we've heard of Earth's radioactivity in several places, and that sort of thing would be designed to make anyone break off any attempt to locate it. If it were truly radioactive, it would be totally unapproachable. In all likelihood, we would not even be able to set foot on it. Even robot explorers, if we had any, might not survive the radiation. So why look? And if it is not radioactive, it remains inviolate, except for accidental approach, and even then it might have other means of masking itself.'

Trevize managed a smile. 'Oddly enough, Janov, that thought has occurred to me. It has even occurred to me that that improbable giant satellite has been invented and planted in the world's legends. As for the gas giant with the monstrous ring-system, that is equally improbable and may be equally planted. It is all designed, perhaps, to have us look for something that doesn't exist, so that we go right through the correct planetary system, staring at Earth and dismissing it because, in actual fact, it lacks a large satellite or a triple-ringed cousin or a radioactive crust. We don't recognize it, therefore, and don't dream we are looking at it. – I imagine worse, too.'

Pelorat looked downcast. 'How can there be worse?'

'Easily – when your mind gets sick in the middle of the night and begins searching the vast realm of fantasy for anything that can deepen despair. What if Earth's ability to hide is ultimate? What if our minds can be clouded? What if we can move right past Earth, *with* its giant satellite and *with* its distant ringed gas giant, and never see any of it? What if we have already done so?'

'But if you believe that, why are we –'

'I don't say I believe that. I'm talking about mad fancies. We'll keep on looking.'

Pelorat hesitated, then said, 'For how long, Trevize? At some point, surely, we'll have to give up.'

'Never,' said Trevize fiercely. 'If I have to spend the rest of my life going from planet to planet and peering about and saying, "Please, sir, where's Earth?" then that's what I'll do. At any time, I can take you and Bliss and even Fallom, if you wish, back to Gaia and then take off on my own.'

'Oh, no. You know I won't leave you, Golan, and neither will Bliss. We'll go planet-hopping with you, if we must. But why?'

'Because I *must* find Earth, and because I will. I don't know how, but I will. – Now, look, I'm trying to reach a position where I can study the sunlit side of the planet without its sun being too close, so just let me be for a while.'

Pelorat fell silent, but did not leave. He continued to watch while Trevize studied the planetary image, more than half in daylight, on the screen. To Pelorat, it seemed featureless, but he knew that Trevize, bound to the computer, saw it under enhanced circumstances.

Trevize whispered, 'There's a haze.'

'Then there must be an atmosphere,' blurted out Pelorat.

'Not necessarily much of one. Not enough to support life, but enough to support a thin wind that will raise dust. It's a well-known characteristic of planets with thin atmospheres. There may even be small polar ice caps. A little water-ice condensed at the poles, you know. This world is too warm for solid carbon dioxide. – I'll have to switch to radar-mapping. And if I do that I can work more easily on the night side.'

'Really?'

'Yes. I should have tried at first, but with a virtually airless and, therefore, cloudless planet, the attempt with visible light seems so natural.'

Trevize was silent for a long time, while the viewscreen grew fuzzy with radar-reflections that produced almost the abstraction of a planet, something that an artist of the Cleonian period might have produced. Then he said, 'Well –' emphatically, holding the sound for a while, and was silent again.

Pelorat said, at last, 'What's the "well" about?'

Trevize looked at him briefly. 'No craters that I can see.'

'No craters? Is that good?'

'Totally unexpected,' said Trevize. His face broke into a grin. 'And *very* good. In fact, possibly magnificent.'

63

Fallom remained with her nose pressed against the ship's porthole, where a small segment of the Universe was visible in the precise form in which the eye saw it, without computer enlargement or enhancement.

Bliss, who had been trying to explain it all, sighed and said in a low voice to Pelorat, 'I don't know how much she understands, Pel dear. To her, her father's mansion and a small section of the estate it stood upon was all the Universe. I don't think she was ever out at night, or ever saw the stars.'

'Do you really think so?'

'I really do. I didn't dare show her any part of it until she had enough vocabulary to understand me just a little – and how fortunate it was that you could speak with her in her own language.'

'The trouble is I'm not very good at it,' said Pelorat, apologetically. 'And the universe *is* rather hard to grasp if you come at it suddenly. She said to me that if those little lights are giant worlds, each one just like Solaria – they're much larger than Solaria, of course – that they couldn't hang in nothing. They ought to fall, she says.'

'And she's right, judging by what she knows. She asks sensible questions, and little by little, she'll understand. At least she's curious and she's not frightened.'

'The thing is, Bliss, I'm curious, too. Look how Golan changed as soon as he found out there were no craters on the world we're heading for. I haven't the slightest idea what difference that makes. Do you?'

'Not a bit. Still he knows much more planetology than we do. We can only assume he knows what he's doing.'

'I wish *I* knew.'

'Well, ask him.'

Pelorat grimaced. 'I'm always afraid I'll annoy him. I'm sure he thinks I ought to know these things without being told.'

Bliss said, 'That's silly, Pel. He has no hesitation in asking you about any aspect of the Galaxy's legends and myths which he thinks might be useful. You're always willing to answer and explain, so why shouldn't he be? You go ask him. If it annoys him, then he'll have a chance to practise sociability, and that will be good for him.'

'Will you come with me?'

'No, of course not. I want to stay with Fallom and continue to try to get the concept of the Universe into her head. You can always explain it to me afterwards – once he explains it to you.'

64

Pelorat entered the pilot-room diffidently. He was delighted to note that Trevize was whistling to himself and was clearly in a good mood.

'Golan,' he said, as brightly as he could.

Trevize looked up. 'Janov! You're always tiptoeing in as though you think it's against the law to disturb me. Close the door and sit down. Sit down! Look at that thing.'

He pointed to the planet on the viewscreen, and said, 'I haven't found more than two or three craters, each quite small.'

'Does that make a difference, Golan? Really?'

'A difference? Certainly. How can you ask?'

Pelorat gestured helplessly. 'It's all a mystery to me. I was a history major at college. I took sociology and psychology in addition to history, also languages and literature, mostly ancient, and specialized in mythology in graduate school. I never came near planetology, or any of the physical sciences.'

'That's no crime, Janov. I'd rather you know what you know. Your facility in ancient languages and in mythology has been of enormous use to us. You know that. – And when it comes to a matter of planetology, I'll take care of that.'

He went on, 'You see, Janov, planets form through the smashing together of smaller objects. The last few objects to collide leave crater marks. Potentially, that is. If the planet is large enough to be a gas giant, it is essentially liquid under a gaseous atmosphere and the final collisions are just splashes and leave no marks.

'Smaller planets which are solid, whether icy or rocky, *do* show crater marks, and these remain indefinitely unless an agency for removal exists. There are three types of removals.

'First, a world may have an icy surface overlying a liquid ocean. In that case, any colliding object breaks through the ice and splashes water. Behind it the ice re-freezes and heals the puncture, so to speak. Such a planet, or satellite, would have to be cold, and would not be what we would consider a habitable world.

'Second, if a planet is intensely active, volcanically, then a perpetual lava flow or ash fallout is forever filling in and obscuring any craters that form. However, such a planet or satellite is not likely to be habitable either.

'That brings us to habitable worlds as a third case. Such worlds may have polar ice-caps, but most of the ocean must be freely liquid. They may have active volcanoes, but these must be sparsely distributed. Such worlds can neither heal craters, nor fill them in. There are, however, erosion effects. Wind and flowing water will erode craters, and if there is life, the actions of living things are strongly erosive as well. See?'

Pelorat considered that, then said, 'But, Golan, I don't understand you at all. This planet we're approaching –'

'We'll be landing tomorrow,' said Trevize, cheerfully.

'This planet we're approaching doesn't have an ocean.'

'Only some thin polar ice caps.'

'Or much of an atmosphere.'

'Only a hundredth the density of the atmosphere on Terminus.'

'Or life.'

'Nothing I can detect.'

'Then what could have eroded away the craters?'

'An ocean, an atmosphere, and life,' said Trevize. 'Look, if this planet had been airless and waterless from the start, any craters that had been formed would still exist and the whole surface would be cratered. The absence of craters proves it can't have been airless and waterless from the start, and may even have had a sizeable atmosphere and ocean in the near past. Besides, there are huge basins, visible on this world, that must have held seas and oceans once, to say nothing of the marks of rivers that are now dry. So you see there *was* erosion and that erosion has ceased so short a time ago, that new cratering has not yet had time to accumulate.'

Pelorat looked doubtful. 'I may not be a planetologist, but it seems to me that if a planet is large enough to hang on to a dense atmosphere for perhaps billions of years, it isn't going to suddenly lose it, is it?'

'I shouldn't think so,' said Trevize. 'But this world undoubtedly held life before its atmosphere vanished, probably human life. My guess is that it was a terraformed world as almost all the human-inhabited worlds of the Galaxy are. The trouble is that we don't really know what its condition was before human life arrived, or what was done to it in order to make it comfortable for human beings, or under what conditions, actually, life vanished. There may have been a catastrophe that sucked off the atmosphere and that brought about the end of human life. Or there may have been some strange imbalance on this planet that human beings controlled as long as they were here and that went into a vicious cycle of atmospheric reduction once they were gone. Maybe we'll find the answer when we land, or maybe we won't. It doesn't matter.'

'But surely neither does it matter if there was life here once, if there isn't now. What's the difference if a planet has always been uninhabitable, or is only uninhabitable now?'

'If it is only uninhabitable now, there will be ruins of the one-time inhabitants.'

'There were ruins on Aurora –'

'Exactly, but on Aurora there had been twenty thousand years of rain and snow, freezing and thawing, wind and temperature change. And there was also life – don't forget life. There may not have been human beings there, but there was plenty of life. Ruins can be eroded just as craters can. Faster. And in twenty thousand years, not enough was left to do us any good. – Here on this planet, however, there has been a passage of time, perhaps twenty thousand years, perhaps less, without wind, or storm, or life. There has been temperature change, I admit, but that's all. The ruins will be in good shape.'

'Unless,' murmured Pelorat doubtfully, 'there are no ruins. Is it possible that there was never any life on the planet, or never any human life at any rate, and that the loss of the atmosphere was due to some event that human beings had nothing to do with.'

'No, no,' said Trevize. 'You can't turn pessimist on me, because it won't work. Even from here, I've spotted the remains of what I'm sure was a city. – So we land tomorrow.'

65

Bliss said, in a worried tone, 'Fallom is convinced we're going to take her back to Jemby, her robot.'

'Umm,' said Trevize, studying the surface of the world as it slid back under the drifting ship. Then he looked up as though he had heard the remark only after a delay. 'Well, it was the only parent she knew, wasn't it?'

'Yes, of course, but she thinks we've come back to Solaria.'

'Does it look like Solaria?'

'How would she know?'

'Tell her it's not Solaria. Look, I'll give you one or two reference book-films with graphic illustrations. Show her closeups of a number of different inhabited worlds and explain that there are millions of them. You'll have time for it. I don't know how long Janov and I will have to wander around, once we pick a likely target and land.'

'You and Janov?'

'Yes. Fallom can't come with us, even if I wanted her to, which I would only want if I were a madman. This world requires space-suits, Bliss. There's no breathable air. And we don't have a spacesuit that would fit Fallom. So she and you stay on the ship.'

'Why I?'

Trevize's lips stretched into a humourless smile. 'I admit,' he said, 'I would feel safer if you were along, but we can't leave Fallom on this ship alone. She can do damage even if she doesn't mean to. I must have Janov with me because he might be able to make out whatever archaic writing they have here. That means you will have to stay with Fallom. I should think you would want to.'

Bliss looked uncertain.

Trevize said, 'Look. You wanted Fallom along, when I didn't. I'm convinced she'll be nothing but trouble. So – her presence introduces constraints, and you'll have to adjust yourself to that. She's here, so you'll have to be here, too. That's the way it is.'

Bliss sighed. 'I suppose so.'

'Good. Where's Janov?'

'He's with Fallom.'

'Very well. Go and take over. I want to talk to him.'

Trevize was still studying the planetary surface when Pelorat walked in, clearing his throat to announce his presence. He said, 'Is anything wrong, Golan?'

'Not exactly wrong, Janov. I'm just uncertain. This is a peculiar world and I don't know what happened to it. The seas must have been extensive, judging from the basins left behind, but they were shallow. As nearly as I can tell from the traces left behind, this was a world of desalinization and canals – or perhaps the seas weren't very salty. If they weren't very salty, that would account for the absence of extensive salt flats in the basins. Or else, when the ocean was lost, the salt content was lost with it – which certainly makes it look like a human deed.'

Pelorat said hesitantly, 'Excuse my ignorance about such things,

Golan, but does any of this matter as far as what we are looking for is concerned?'

'I suppose not, but I can't help being curious. If I knew just how this planet was terraformed into human habitability and what it was like before terraforming, then perhaps I would understand what has happened to it after it was abandoned – or just before, perhaps. And if we did know what happened to it, we might be forewarned against unpleasant surprises.'

'What kind of surprises? It's a dead world, isn't it?'

'Dead enough. Very little water; thin, unbreathable atmosphere; and Bliss detects no signs of mental activity.'

'That should settle it, I should think.'

'Absence of mental activity doesn't necessarily imply lack of life.'

'It must surely imply lack of dangerous life.'

'I don't know. – But that's not what I want to consult you about. There are two cities that might do for our first inspection. They seem to be in excellent shape; all the cities do. Whatever destroyed the air and oceans did not seem to touch the cities. Anyway, those two cities are particularly large. The larger, however, seems to be short on empty space. There are spaceports far in the outskirts but nothing in the city itself. The one not so large does have empty formal spaceports – but then, who would care about that?'

Pelorat grimaced. 'Do you want *me* to make the decision, Golan?'

'No, I'll make the decision. I just want your thoughts.'

'For what they're worth, a large sprawling city is likely to be a commercial or manufacturing centre. A smaller city with open space is likely to be an administrative centre. It's the administrative centre we'd want. Does it have monumental buildings?'

'What do you mean by a monumental building?'

Pelorat smiled his tight little stretching of the lips. 'I scarcely know. Fashions change from world to world and from time to time. I suspect, though, that they always look large, useless, and expensive. – Like the place where we were on Comporellon.'

Trevize smiled in his turn. 'It's hard to tell looking straight down, and when I get a sideways glance as we approach or leave, it's too confusing. Why do you prefer the administrative centre?'

'That's where we're likely to find the planetary museum, library, archives, university, and so on.'

'Good. That's where we'll go, then; the smaller city. And maybe we'll find something. We've had two misses, but maybe we'll find something this time.'

'Perhaps it will be three times lucky.'

Trevize raised his eyebrows. 'Where did you get that phrase?'

'It's an old one,' said Pelorat. 'I found it in an ancient legend. It means success on the third try, I should think.'

'That sounds right,' said Trevize. 'Very well, then – Three times lucky, Janov.'

15

Moss

66

Trevize looked grotesque in his space suit. The only part of him that remained outside were his holsters – not the ones that he strapped around his hips ordinarily, but more substantial ones that were part of his suit. Carefully, he inserted the blaster in the right hand holster, the neuronic whip in the left. Again, they had been recharged and this time, he thought grimly, *nothing* would take them away from him.

Bliss smiled. 'Are you going to carry weapons even on a world without air or – Never mind! I won't question your decisions.'

Trevize said, 'Good!' and turned to help Pelorat adjust his helmet, before donning his own.

Pelorat, who had never worn a space suit before, said, rather plaintively, 'Will I really be able to breathe in this thing, Golan?'

'I promise you,' said Trevize.

Bliss watched as the final joints were sealed, her arm about Fallom's shoulder. The young Solarian stared at the two space-suited figures in obvious alarm. She was trembling, and Bliss's arm squeezed her gently and reassuringly.

The airlock door opened, and the two stepped inside, their bloated arms waving a farewell. It closed. The main-lock door opened and they stepped clumsily on to the soil of a dead world.

It was dawn. The sky was clear, of course, and purplish in colour, but the sun had not yet risen. Along the lighter horizon where the sun would come, there was a slight haze.

Pelorat said, 'It's cold.'

'Do you feel cold?' said Trevize, with surprise. The suits were well insulated and if there was a problem, now and then, it was with the need for getting rid of body heat.

Pelorat said, 'Not at all, but look –' His radioed voice sounded clear in Trevize's ear, and his finger pointed.

In the purplish light of dawn, the crumbling stone front of the building they were approaching was sheathed in hoar frost.

Trevize said, 'With a thin atmosphere, it would get colder at night than you would expect, and warmer in the day. Right now it's the coldest part of the day and it should take several hours before it gets too hot for us to remain in the sun.'

As though the word had been a cabalistic incantation, the rim of the sun appeared above the horizon.

'Don't look at it,' said Trevize conversationally. 'Your face-plate is reflective and ultraviolet-opaque, but it would still be dangerous.'

He turned his back to the rising sun and let his long shadow fall on the building. The sunlight was causing the frost to disappear, even as he watched. For a few moments, the wall looked dark with dampness and then that disappeared, too.

Trevize said, 'The buildings don't look as good down here as they looked from the sky. They're cracked and crumbling. That's the result of the temperature change, I suppose, and of having the water-traces freeze and melt each night and day for maybe as much as twenty thousand years.'

Pelorat said, 'There are letters engraved in the stone above the entrance, but crumbling has made them difficult to read.'

'Can you make it out, Janov?'

'A financial institution of some sort. At least I make out a word which may be "bank".'

'What's that?'

'A building in which assets were stored, withdrawn, traded, invested, loaned – if it's what I think it is.'

'A whole building devoted to it? No computers?'

'Without computers taking over altogether.'

Trevize shrugged. He did not find the details of ancient history inspiring.

They moved about, with increasing haste, spending less time at each building. The silence, the *deadness*, was completely depressing. The slow millennial-long collapse into which they had intruded made the place seem like the skeleton of a city, with everything gone but the bones.

They were well up in the temperate zone, but Trevize imagined he could feel the heat of the sun on his back.

Pelorat, about a hundred metres to his right, said sharply, 'Look at that.'

Trevize's ears rang. He said, 'Don't shout, Janov. I can hear your whispers clearly no matter how far away you are. What is it?'

Pelorat, his voice moderating at once, said, 'This building is the "Hall of the Worlds". At least, that's what I think the inscription reads.'

Trevize joined him. Before them was a three-storey structure, the line of its roof irregular and loaded with large fragments of rock, as though some sculptured object that had once stood there had fallen to pieces.

'Are you sure?' said Trevize.

'If we go in, we'll find out.'

They climbed five low, broad steps, and crossed a space-wasting plaza. In the thin air, their metal-shod footsteps made a whispering vibration rather than a sound.

'I see what you mean by "large, useless, and expensive",' muttered Trevize.

They entered a wide and high hall, with sunlight shining through tall windows and illuminating the interior too harshly where it struck and yet leaving things obscure in the shadow. The thin atmosphere scattered little light.

In the centre was a larger than life-size human figure in what seemed to be a synthetic stone. One arm had fallen off. The other arm was cracked at the shoulder and Trevize felt that if he tapped it sharply that arm, too, would break off. He stepped back as though getting too near might tempt him into such unbearable vandalism.

'I wonder who that is,' said Trevize. 'No markings anywhere. I suppose those who set it up felt that his fame was so obvious he needed no identification, but now –' He felt himself in danger of growing philosophical and turned his attention away.

Pelorat was looking up, and Trevize's glance followed the angle of Pelorat's head. There were markings – carvings – on the wall which Trevize could not read.

'Amazing,' said Pelorat. 'Twenty thousand years old, perhaps, and, in here, protected somewhat from sun and damp, they're still legible.'

'Not to me,' said Trevize.

'It's in old script and ornate even for that. Let's see now – seven – one – two –' His voice died away in a mumble, and then he spoke up again. 'There are fifty names listed and there are supposed to have been fifty Spacer worlds and this is "The Hall of the Worlds". I assume those are the names of the fifty Spacer worlds, probably in the order of establishment. Aurora is first and Solaria is last. If you'll notice, there are seven columns, with seven names in the first six columns and then eight names in the last. It is as though they had planned a seven by seven grid and then added Solaria after the fact. My guess, old chap, is that that list dates back to before Solaria was terraformed and populated.'

'And which one is this planet we're standing on? Can you tell?'

Pelorat said, 'You'll notice that the fifth one down in the third column, the nineteenth in order, is inscribed in letters a little larger than the others. The listers seem to have been self-centred enough to give themselves some pride of place. Besides –'

'What does the name read?'

'As near as I can make out, it says Melpomenia. It's a name I'm totally unfamiliar with.'

'Could it represent Earth?'

Pelorat shook his head vigorously, but that went unseen inside his helmet. He said, 'There are dozens of words used for Earth in the old legends. Gaia is one of them, as you know. So is Terra, and Erda, and so on. They're all short. I don't know of any long name used for it, or anything even resembling a short version of Melpomenia.'

'Then we're standing on Melpomenia, and it's not Earth.'

'Yes. And besides – as I started to say earlier – an even better indication than the larger lettering is that the co-ordinates of Melpomenia are given as 0, 0, 0, and you would expect co-ordinates to be referred to one's own planet.'

'Co-ordinates?' Trevize sounded dumbfounded. 'That list gives the co-ordinates, too?'

'They give three figures for each and I presume those are co-ordinates. What else can they be?'

Trevize did not answer. He opened a small compartment in the portion of the space suit that covered his right thigh and took out a compact device with wire connecting it to the compartment. He put it up to his eyes and carefully focused it on the inscription on the wall, his sheathed fingers making a difficult job out of something that would ordinarily have been a moment's work.

'Camera?' said Pelorat unnecessarily.

'It will feed the image directly into the ship's computer,' said Trevize.

He took several photographs from different angles, then said, 'Wait! I've got to get higher. Help me, Janov.'

Pelorat clasped his hands together, stirrup-fashion, but Trevize shook his head. 'That won't support my weight. Get on your hands and knees.'

Pelorat did so, laboriously, and, as laboriously, Trevize, having tucked the camera into its compartment again, stepped on Pelorat's shoulders and from them on to the pedestal of the statue. He tried to rock the statue carefully to judge its firmness, then placed his foot on one bent knee and used it as a base for pushing himself upwards and catching the armless shoulder. Wedging his toes against some unevenness at the chest, he lifted himself and, finally, after several grunts, managed to sit on the shoulder. To those long-dead who had revered the statue and what it represented, what Trevize did would have seemed blasphemy, and Trevize was sufficiently influenced by that thought to try to sit lightly.

'You'll fall and hurt yourself,' Pelorat called out, anxiously.

'I'm not going to fall and hurt myself, but *you* might deafen me.' Trevize unslung his camera and focused once more. Several more photographs were taken and then he replaced the camera yet again and carefully lowered himself till his feet touched the pedestal. He jumped to the ground and the vibration of his contact was apparently the final push, for the still intact arm crumbled, and produced a small heap of rubble at the foot of the statue. It made virtually no noise as it fell.

Trevize froze, his first impulse being that of finding a place to hide before the watchman came and caught him. Amazing, he thought afterwards, how quickly one relives the days of one's childhood in a situation like that – when you've accidentally broken something that looks important. It lasted only a moment, but it cut deeply.

Pelorat's voice was hollow, as befitted one who had witnessed and even abetted an act of vandalism, but he managed to find words of comfort. 'It's – it's all right, Golan. It was about to come down by itself, anyway.'

He walked over to the pieces on the pedestal and floor as though he were going to demonstrate the point, reached out for one of the larger fragments and then said, 'Golan, come here.'

Trevize approached and Pelorat, pointing at a piece of stone that had clearly been the portion of the arm that had been joined to the shoulder, said, 'What is this?'

Trevize stared. There was a patch of fuzz, bright green in colour. Trevize rubbed it gently with his suited finger. It scraped off without trouble.

'It looks a lot like moss,' he said.

'The life-without-mind that you mentioned?'

'I'm not completely sure how far without mind. Bliss, I imagine, would insist that this had consciousness, too – but she would claim this stone also had it.'

Pelorat said, 'Do you suppose that moss stuff is what's crumbling the rock?'

Trevize said, 'I wouldn't be surprised if it helped. The world has plenty of sunlight and it has some water. Half what atmosphere it has is water vapour. The rest is nitrogen and inert gases. Just a trace of carbon dioxide, which would lead one to suppose there's no plant life – but it could be that the carbon dioxide is low because it is virtually all incorporated into the rocky crust. Now if this rock has some carbonate in it, perhaps this moss breaks it down by secreting acid, and then makes use of the carbon dioxide generated. This may be the dominant remaining form of life on this planet.'

'Fascinating,' said Pelorat.

'Undoubtedly,' said Trevize, 'but only in a limited way. The co-ordinates of the Spacer worlds are rather more interesting but what we really want are the co-ordinates of *Earth*. If they're not here, they may be elsewhere in the building – or in another building. Come, Janov.'

'But you know –' began Pelorat.

'No, no,' said Trevize impatiently. 'We'll talk later. We've got to see what else, if anything, this building can give us. It's getting warmer.' He looked at the small temperature reading on the back of his left glove. 'Come, Janov.'

They tramped through the rooms, walking as gently as possible, not because they were making sounds in the ordinary sense, or that there was anyone to hear them, but because they were a little shy of doing further damage through vibration.

They kicked up some dust, which moved a short way upwards and settled quickly through the thin air, and they left footmarks behind them.

Occasionally, in some dim corner, one or the other would silently point out more samples of moss that were growing. There seemed a little comfort in the presence of life, however low in the scale, something that lifted the deadly, suffocating feel of walking through a dead world, especially one in which artifacts all about showed that once, long ago, it had been an elaborately-living one.

And then, Pelorat said, 'I think this must be a library.'

Trevize looked about curiously. There were shelves and, as he looked more narrowly, what the corner of his eye had dismissed as mere ornamentation, seemed as though they might well be book-films. Gingerly, he reached for one. They were thick and clumsy and then he realized they were only cases. He fumbled with his thick fingers to open one, and inside he saw several discs. They were thick, too, and seemed brittle, though he did not test that.

He said, 'Unbelievably primitive.'

'Thousands of years old,' said Pelorat, apologetically, as though defending the old Melpomenians against the accusation of retarded technology.

Trevize pointed to the spine of the film where there were dim curlicues of the ornate lettering that the ancients had used. 'Is that the title? What does it say?'

Pelorat studied it. 'I'm not really sure, old man. I think one of the words refers to microscopic life. It's a word for "micro-organism", perhaps. I suspect these are technical microbiological terms which I wouldn't understand even in Standard Galactic.'

'Probably,' said Trevize morosely. 'And, equally probably, it wouldn't do us any good even if we could read it. We're not interested in germs. – Do me a favour, Janov. Glance through some of these books and see if there's anything there with an interesting title. While you're doing that, I'll look over these book-viewers.'

'Is that what they are?' said Pelorat, wondering. They were squat, cubical structures, topped by a slanted screen and a curved extension at the top that might serve as an elbow rest or a place on which to put an electro-notepad – if they had had such on Melpomenia.

Trevize said, 'If this is a library, they must have book-viewers of one kind or another, and this seems as though it might suit.'

He brushed the dust off the screen very gingerly and was relieved that the screen, whatever it might be made of, did not crumble at his touch. He manipulated the controls lightly, one after another. Nothing happened. He tried another book-viewer, then another, with the same negative results.

He wasn't surprised. Even if the device were to remain in working order for twenty millennia in a thin atmosphere and was resistant to water vapour, there was still the question of the power source. Stored energy had a way of leaking, no matter what was done to stop it. That was another aspect of the all-embracing, irresistible second law of thermodynamics.

Pelorat was behind him. 'Golan?'

'Yes.'

'I have a book-film here –'

'What kind?'

'I think it's a history of space flight.'

'Perfect – but it won't do us any good if I can't make this viewer work.' His hands clenched in frustration.

'We could take the film back to the ship.'

'I wouldn't know how to adapt it to our viewer. It wouldn't fit and our scanning system is sure to be incompatible.'

'But is all that really necessary, Golan. If we –'

'It is really necessary, Janov. Now don't interrupt me. I'm trying to decide what to do. I can try adding power to the viewer. Perhaps that is all it needs.'

'Where would you get the power?'

'Well –' Trevize drew his weapons, looked at them briefly, then settled his blaster back into its holster. He cracked open his neuronic whip, and studied the energy-supply level. It was at maximum.

Trevize threw himself prone upon the floor and reached behind the viewer (he kept assuming that was what it was) and tried to push it forward. It moved a small way and he studied what he found in the process.

One of those cables had to carry the power supply and surely it was the one that came out of the wall. There was no obvious plug or joining. (How does one deal with an alien and ancient culture where the simplest taken-for-granted matters are made unrecognizable?)

He pulled gently at the cable, then harder. He turned it one way, then the other. He pressed the wall in the vicinity of the cable, and the cable in the vicinity of the wall. He turned his attention, as best he could, to the half-hidden back of the viewer and nothing he could do there worked, either.

He pressed one hand against the floor to raise himself and, as he stood up, the cable came with him. What he had done that had loosened it, he hadn't the slightest idea.

It didn't look broken or torn away. The end seemed quite smooth and it had left a smooth spot in the wall where it had been attached.

Pelorat said, softly, 'Golan, may I –'

Trevize waved a peremptory arm at the other, 'Not now, Janov. Please!'

He was suddenly aware of the green material caking the creases on his left glove. He must have picked up some of the moss behind the viewer and crushed it. His glove had a faint dampness to it, but it dried as he watched, and the greenish stain grew brown.

He turned his attention towards the cable, staring at the detached end carefully. Surely there were two small holes there. Wires could enter.

He sat on the floor again and opened the power unit of his neuronic whip. Carefully, he depolarized one of the wires and clicked it loose. He then, slowly and delicately, inserted it into the hole, pushing it in until it stopped. When he tried gently to withdraw it again, it remained put, as though it had been seized. He suppressed his first impulse to yank it out again by force. It was conceivable that that would close the circuit and supply the viewer with power.

'Janov,' he said, 'you've played about with book-films of all kinds. See if you can work out a way of inserting that book into the viewer.'

'Is it really nece –'

'Please, Janov, you keep trying to ask unnecessary questions. We only have so much time. I don't want to have to wait far into the night for the building to cool off to the point where we can return.'

'It must go in this way,' said Janov, 'but –'

'Good,' said Trevize. 'If it's a history of space flight, then it will have to begin with Earth, since it was on Earth that space flight was invented. Let's see if this thing works now.'

Pelorat, a little fussily, placed the book-film into the obvious receptacle and then began studying the markings on the various controls for any hint as to direction.

Trevize spoke in a low voice, while waiting, partly to ease his own tension. 'I suppose there must be robots on this world, too – here and there – in reasonable order to all appearances – glistening in the near-vacuum. The trouble is their power supply would long since have been drained, too, and, even if repowered, what about their brains? Levers and gears might withstand the millennia, but what about whatever microswitches or sub-atomic gizmos they had in their brains? They would have to have deteriorated, and even if it had not, what would they know about Earth. What would they –'

Pelorat said, 'The viewer is working, old chap. See here.'

In the dim light, the book-viewer screen began to flicker. It was only faint, but Trevize turned up the power slightly in his neuronic whip and it grew brighter. The thin air about them kept the area outside the shafts of sunlight comparatively dim, so that the room was faded and shadowy, and the screen seemed the brighter by contrast.

It continued to flicker, with occasional shadows drifting across the screen.

'It needs to be focused,' said Trevize.

'I know,' said Pelorat, 'but this seems the best I can do. The film itself must have deteriorated.'

The shadows came and went rapidly now, and periodically there seemed something like a faint caricature of print. Then, for a moment, there was sharpness and it faded again.

'Get that back and hold it, Janov,' said Trevize.

Pelorat was already trying. He passed it going backwards, then again forwards, and then got it and held it.

Eagerly, Trevize tried to read it, then said, in frustration, 'Can *you* make it out, Janov?'

'Not entirely,' said Pelorat, squinting at the screen. 'It's about Aurora. I can tell that much. I think it's dealing with the first hyperspatial expedition – the "prime outpouring", it says.'

He went forward, and it blurred and shadowed again. He said, finally, 'All the pieces I can get seem to deal with the Spacer worlds, Golan. There's nothing I can find about Earth.'

Trevize said bitterly, 'No, there wouldn't be. It's all been wiped out on this world as it has on Trantor. Turn the thing off.'

'But it doesn't matter –' began Pelorat, turning it off.

'Because we can try other libraries? It will be wiped out there, too. Everywhere. Do you know –' He had looked at Pelorat as he spoke, and now he stared at him with a mixture of horror and revulsion. 'What's wrong with your face-plate?' he asked.

67

Pelorat automatically lifted his gloved hand to his face-plate and then took it away and looked at it.

'What is it?' he said, puzzled. Then he looked at Trevize and went on, rather squeakily, 'There's something peculiar about *your* face-plate, Golan.'

Trevize looked about automatically for a mirror. There was none and he would need a light if there were. He muttered, 'Come into the sunlight, will you?'

He half-led, half-pulled Pelorat into the shaft of sunlight from the nearest window. He could feel its warmth upon his back despite the insulating effect of the space suit.

He said, 'Look towards the sun, Janov, and close your eyes.'

It was at once clear what was wrong with the face-plate. There was moss growing luxuriantly where the glass of the face-plate met the metallized fabric of the suit itself. The face-plate was rimmed with green fuzziness and Trevize knew his own was, too.

He brushed a finger of his glove across the moss on Pelorat's face-plate. Some of it came off, the crushed green staining the glove. Even as he watched it glisten in the sunlight, however, it seemed to grow stiffer and drier. He tried again, and this time, the moss crackled off. It was turning brown. He brushed the edges of Pelorat's faceplate again, rubbing hard.

'Do mine, Janov,' he said. Then, later, 'Do I look clean? Good, so do you. – Let's go. I don't think there's more to do here.'

The sun was uncomfortably hot in the deserted airless city. The stone buildings gleamed brightly, almost achingly. Trevize squinted as he looked at them and, as far as possible, walked on the shady side of the thoroughfares. He stopped at a crack in one of the building fronts, one wide enough to stick his little finger into, gloved as it was. He did just that, looked at it, muttered, 'Moss', and deliberately walked to the end of the shadow and held that finger out in the sunlight for a while.

He said, 'Carbon dioxide is the bottleneck. Anywhere they can get carbon dioxide – decaying rock – anywhere – it will grow. We're a good source of carbon dioxide, you know, probably richer than anything else on this nearly dead planet, and I suppose traces of the gas leak out at the boundary of the face-plate.'

'So the moss grows there.'

'Yes.'

It seemed a long walk back to the ship, much longer and, of course, hotter than the one they had taken at dawn. The ship was still in the shade when they got there, however; that much Trevize had calculated correctly, at least.

Pelorat said, 'Look!'

Trevize saw. The boundaries of the mainlock were outlined in green moss.

'More leakage?' said Pelorat.

'Of course. Insignificant amounts, I'm sure, but this moss seems to be a better indicator of trace amounts of carbon dioxide than anything I ever heard of. Its spores must be everywhere and wherever a few molecules of carbon dioxide are to be found, they sprout.' He adjusted his radio for ship's wavelength and said, 'Bliss, can you hear me.'

Bliss's voice sounded in both sets of ears. 'Yes. Are you ready to come in? Any luck?'

'We're just outside,' said Trevize, 'but *don't* open the lock. We'll open it from out here. Repeat, *don't* open the lock.'

'Why not?'

'Bliss, just do as I ask, will you? We can have a long discussion afterwards.'

Trevize brought out his blaster and carefully lowered its intensity to minimum, then gazed at it uncertainly. He had never used it at minimum. He looked about him. There was nothing suitably fragile to test it on.

In sheer desperation, he turned it on the rocky hillside in whose shadow the *Far Star* lay. – The target didn't turn red-hot. Automatically, he felt the spot he had hit. Did it feel warm? He couldn't tell with any degree of certainty through the insulated fabric of his suit.

He hesitated again, then thought that the hull of the ship would be as resistant, within an order of magnitude at any rate, as the hillside. He turned the blaster on the rim of the lock and flicked the contact briefly, holding his breath.

Several centimetres of the moss-like growth browned at once. He waved his hand in the vicinity of the browning and even the mild breeze set up in the thin air in this way sufficed to set the light skeletal remnants that made up the brown material to scattering.

'Does it work?' said Pelorat anxiously.

'Yes, it does,' said Trevize. 'I turned the blaster into a mild heat ray.'

He sprayed the heat all around the edge of the lock and the green vanished at the touch. All of it. He struck the mainlock to create a vibration that would knock off what remained and a brown dust fell to the ground – a dust so fine that it even lingered in the thin atmosphere, buoyed up by wisps of gas.

'I think we can open it now,' said Trevize, and, using his wrist controls, he tapped out the emission of the radio-wave combination that activated the opening mechanism from inside. The lock gaped and had not opened more than half-way when Trevize said, 'Don't dawdle, Janov, get inside. – Don't wait for the steps. Climb in.'

Trevize followed, sprayed the rim of the lock with his toned-down blaster. He sprayed the steps, too, once they had lowered. He then signalled the close of the lock and kept on spraying till they were totally enclosed.

Trevize said, 'We're in the lock, Bliss. We'll stay here a few minutes. Continue to do nothing!'

Bliss's voice said, 'Give me a hint. Are you all right? How is Pel?'

Pel said, 'I'm here, Bliss, and perfectly well. There's nothing to worry about.'

'If you say so, Pel, but there'll have to be explanations later. I hope you know that.'

'It's a promise,' said Trevize, and activated the lock light.

The two space-suited figures faced each other.

Trevize said, 'We're pumping out all the planetary air we can, so let's just wait till that's done.'

'What about the ship air? Are we going to let that in?'

'Not for a while. I'm as anxious to get out of the space suit as you are, Janov. I just want to make sure that we get rid of any spores that have entered with us – or upon us.'

By the not entirely satisfactory illumination of the lock light, Trevize turned his blaster on the inner meeting of lock and hull, spraying the heat methodically along the floor, up and around, and back to the floor.

'Now you, Janov.'

Pelorat stirred uneasily, and Trevize said, 'You may feel warm. It shouldn't be any worse than that. If it grows uncomfortable, just say so.'

He played the invisible beam over the face-plate, the edges particularly, then, little by little, over the rest of the space suit.

He muttered, 'Lift your arms, Janov.' Then, 'Rest your arms on my shoulder, and lift one foot – I've got to do the soles – now the other. – Are you getting too warm?'

Pelorat said, 'I'm not exactly bathed in cool breezes, Golan.'

'Well, then, give me a taste of my own medicine. Go over me.'

'I've never held a blaster.'

'You *must* hold it. Grip it so, and, with your thumb, push that little knob – and squeeze the holster tightly. Right. – Now play it over my face-plate. Move it steadily, Janov, don't let it linger in one place too long. Over the rest of the helmet, then down the cheek and neck.'

He kept up the directions, and when he had been heated everywhere and was in an uncomfortable perspiration as a result, he took back the blaster and studied the energy level.

'More than half gone,' he said, and sprayed the interior of the lock methodically, back and forth over the wall, till the blaster was emptied of its charge, having itself heated markedly through its rapid and sustained discharge. He then restored it to its holster.

Only then did he signal for entry into the ship. He welcomed the hiss and feel of air coming into the lock as the inner door opened. Its coolness and its convective powers would carry off the warmth of the space suit far more quickly than radiation alone would do. It might have been imagination, but he felt the cooling effect at once. Imagination or not, he welcomed that, too.

'Off with your suit, Janov, and leave it out here in the lock,' said Trevize.

'If you don't mind,' said Pelorat, 'a shower is what I would like to have before anything else.'

'Not before anything else. In fact, before that, and before you can empty your bladder even, I suspect you will have to talk to Bliss.'

Bliss was waiting for them, of course, and with a look of concern on her face. Behind her, peeping out, was Fallom, with her hands clutching firmly at Bliss's left arm.

'What happened?' Bliss asked severely. 'What's been going on?'

'Guarding against infection,' said Trevize, drily, 'so I'll be turning on the ultraviolet radiation. Break out the dark glasses. Please don't delay.'

With ultraviolet added to the wall illumination, Trevize took off his moist garments one by one and shook them out, turning them in one direction and another.

'Just a precaution,' he said. 'You do it, too, Janov. – And Bliss, I'll have to peel altogether. If that will make you uncomfortable, step into the next room.'

Bliss said, 'It will neither make me uncomfortable, nor embarrass me. I have a good notion of what you look like, and it will surely present me with nothing new. – What infection?'

'Just a little something that, given its own way,' said Trevize, with a deliberate air of indifference, 'could do great damage to humanity, I think.'

68

It was all done. The ultraviolet light had done its part. Officially, according to the complex films of information and instructions that had come with the *Far Star* when Trevize had first gone aboard back on Terminus, the light was there precisely for purposes of disinfection. Trevize suspected, however, that the temptation was always there, and sometimes yielded to, to use it for developing a fashionable tan for those who were from worlds where tans were fashionable. The light was, however, disinfecting, however used.

They took the ship up into space and Trevize manœuvred it as close to Melpomenia's sun as he might without making them all unpleasantly uncomfortable, turning and twisting the vessel so as to make sure that its entire surface was drenched in ultraviolet.

Finally, they rescued the two space suits that had been left in the lock and examined them until even Trevize was satisfied.

'All that,' said Bliss, at last, 'for moss. Isn't that what you said it was, Trevize? Moss?'

'I call it moss,' said Trevize, 'because that's what it reminded me of. I'm not a botanist, however. All I can say is that it's intensely green and can probably make do on very little light-energy.'

'Why very little?'

'The moss is sensitive to ultraviolet and can't grow, or even survive in direct illumination. Its spores are everywhere and it grows in hidden corners, in cracks in statuary, on the bottom surface of structures, feeding on the energy of scattered photons of light wherever there is a source of carbon dioxide.'

Bliss said, 'I take it you think they're dangerous.'

'They might well be. If some of the spores were clinging to us when we entered, or swirled in with us, they would find illumination in plenty without the harmful ultraviolet. They would find ample water and an unending supply of carbon dioxide.'

'Only 0.03 per cent of our atmosphere,' said Bliss.

'A great deal to them – and 4 per cent in our exhaled breath. What if spores grew in our nostrils, and on our skin. What if they decomposed and destroyed our food? What if they produced toxins that killed us? Even if we laboured to kill them but left some spores alive, they would be enough, when carried to another world by us, to infest it, and from there be carried to other worlds. Who knows what damage they might do?'

Bliss shook her head. 'Life is not necessarily dangerous because it is different. You are so ready to kill.'

'That's Gaia speaking,' said Trevize.

'Of course it is, but I hope I make sense, nevertheless. The moss is adapted to the conditions of this world. Just as it makes use of light in small quantities but is killed by large; it makes use of occasional tiny whiffs of carbon dioxide and may be killed by large amounts. It may not be capable of surviving on any world but Melpomenia.'

'Would you want me to take a chance on that?' demanded Trevize.

Bliss shrugged. 'Very well. Don't be defensive. I see your point. Being an Isolate, you probably had no choice but to do what you did.'

Trevize would have answered, but Fallom's clear high-pitched voice broke in, in her own language.

Trevize said to Pelorat, 'What's she saying?'

Pelorat began, 'What Fallom is saying –'

Fallom, however, as though remembering a moment too late that her own language was not easily understood, began again, 'Was there Jemby there where you were?'

The words were pronounced meticulously, and Bliss beamed. 'Doesn't she speak Galactic well? And in almost no time.'

Trevize said, in a low voice, 'I'll mess it up if I try, but you explain to her, Bliss, that we found no robots on the planet.'

'I'll explain it,' said Pelorat. 'Come, Fallom.' He placed a gentle arm about the youngster's shoulders. 'Come to our room and I'll get you another book to read.'

'A book? About Jemby?'

'Not exactly –' and the door closed behind them.

'You know,' said Trevize, looking after them impatiently, 'we waste our time playing nursemaid to that child.'

'Waste? In what way does it interfere with your search for Earth, Trevize? – In no way. Playing nursemaid establishes communication, however, allays fear, supplies love. Are these achievements nothing?'

'That's Gaia speaking again.'

'Yes,' said Bliss. 'Let us be practical, then. We have visited three of the old Spacer worlds and we have gained nothing.'

Trevize nodded. 'True enough.'

'In fact, we have found each one dangerous, haven't we? On Aurora, there were feral dogs; on Solaria, strange and dangerous human beings; on Melpomenia, a threatening moss. Apparently, then, when a world is left to itself, whether it contains human beings or not, it becomes dangerous to the interstellar community.'

'You can't consider that a general rule.'

'Three out of three certainly seems impressive.'

'And how does it impress you, Bliss?'

'I'll tell you. Please listen to me with an open mind. If you have millions of interacting worlds in the Galaxy, as is, of course, the actual case, and if each is made up entirely of Isolates, as they are, then on each world, human beings are dominant and can force their will on non-human lifeforms, on the inanimate geological background, and even on each other. The Galaxy is, then, a very primitive and fumbling and misfunctioning Galaxia. The beginnings of a unit. Do you see what I mean?'

'I see what you're trying to say – but that doesn't mean I'm going to agree with you when you're done saying it.'

'Just listen to me. Agree or not, as you please, but listen. The only way the Galaxy will work is as a proto-Galaxia, and the less proto and the more Galaxia, the better. The Galactic Empire was an attempt at a strong proto-Galaxia, and when it fell apart, times grew rapidly worse and there was the constant drive to strengthen the proto-Galaxia concept. The Foundation Confederation is such an attempt. So was the Mule's Empire. So is the Empire the Second Foundation is planning. But even if there were no such Empires or Confederations, even if the entire Galaxy were in turmoil, it would be a connected turmoil, with each world interacting, even if only hostilely, with each other. That would, in itself, be a kind of union and it would not yet be the worst case.'

'What would be the worst, then?'

'You know the answer to that, Trevize. You've seen it. If a human-inhabited world breaks up completely, is truly Isolate, and if it loses all interaction with other human worlds, it develops – malignantly.'

'A cancer, then?'

'*Yes.* Isn't Solaria just that. Its hand is against all worlds. And on it, the hand of each individual is against those of all others. You've seen it. And if human beings disappear altogether, the last trace of discipline goes. The each-against-each becomes unreasoning, as with the dogs, or is merely an elemental force as with the moss. You see, I suppose, that the closer we are to Galaxia, the better the society. Why, then, stop at anything short of Galaxia?'

For a while, Trevize stared silently at Bliss. 'I'm thinking about it. But why this assumption that dosage is a one-way thing; that if a little is good, a lot is better, and all there is is best of all? Didn't you yourself point out that it's possible the moss is adapted to very little carbon dioxide so that a plentiful supply might kill it? A human being two metres tall is better off than one who is one metre tall; but is also better off than one who is three metres tall. A mouse isn't better off, if it is expanded to the size of an elephant. He wouldn't live. Nor would an elephant be better off reduced to the size of a mouse.

'There's natural size, a natural complexity, some optimum quality for everything, whether star or atom, and it's certainly true of living things and living societies. I don't say the old Galactic Empire was ideal, and I can certainly see flaws in the Foundation Confederation, but I'm not prepared to say that because total Isolation is bad, total Unification is good. The extremes may both be equally horrible, and an old-fashioned Galactic Empire, however imperfect, may be the best we can do.'

Bliss shook her head. 'I wonder if you believe yourself, Trevize. Are you going to argue that a virus and a human being are equally unsatisfactory, and wish to settle for something in between – like a slime mould?'

'No. But I might argue that a virus and a superhuman being are equally unsatisfactory, and wish to settle for something in between – like an ordinary person. – There is, however, no point in arguing. I will have my solution when I find Earth. On Melpomenia, we found the co-ordinates of forty-seven other Spacer worlds.'

'And you'll visit them all?'

'Every one, if I have to.'

'Risking the dangers on each.'

'Yes, if that's what it takes to find Earth.'

Pelorat had emerged from the room within which he had left Fallom, and seemed about to say something when he was caught up in the rapid-fire exchange between Bliss and Trevize. He stared from one to the other as they spoke in turn.

'How long would it take?' asked Bliss.

'However long it takes,' said Trevize, 'and we might find what we need on the next one we visit.'

'Or on none of them.'

'That we cannot know till we search.'

And now, at last, Pelorat managed to insert a word. 'But why look, Golan. We have the answer.'

Trevize waved an impatient hand in the direction of Pelorat, checked the motion, turned his head and said blankly, 'What?'

'I said we have the answer. I tried to tell you this on Melpomenia at least five times, but you were so wrapped up in what you were doing –'

'What answer do we have? What are you talking about?'

'About *Earth*. I think we know where Earth is.'

Part VI

Alpha

16

The Centre of the Worlds

69

Trevize stared at Pelorat for a long moment, and with an expression of clear displeasure. Then he said, 'Is there something you saw that I did not, and that you did not tell me about?'

'No,' answered Pelorat mildly. 'You saw it and, as I just said, I tried to explain, but you were in no mood to listen to me.'

'Well, try again.'

Bliss said, 'Don't bully him, Trevize.'

'I'm not bullying him. I'm asking for information. And don't you baby him.'

'Please,' said Pelorat, 'listen to me, will you, and not to each other. – Do you remember, Golan, that we discussed early attempts to discover the origin of the human species? Yariff's project? You know, trying to plot the times of settlement of various planets on the assumption that planets would be settled outwards from the world of origin in all directions alike. Then, as we moved from newer to older planets we would approach the world of origin from all directions.'

Trevize nodded impatiently. 'What I remember is that it didn't work because the dates of settlement were not reliable.'

'That's right, old fellow. But the worlds that Yariff was working with were part of the second expansion of the human race. By then, hyperspatial travel was far advanced, and settlement must have grown quite ragged. Leapfrogging very long distances was very simple and settlement didn't necessarily proceed outwards in radial symmetry.

That surely added to the problem of unreliable dates of settlement.

'But just think for a moment, Golan, of the Spacer worlds. They were in the first wave of settlement. Hyperspatial travel was less advanced, then, and there was probably little or no leapfrogging. Whereas millions of worlds were settled, perhaps chaotically, during the second expansion, only fifty were settled, probably in an orderly manner, in the first. Whereas the millions of worlds of the second expansion were settled over a period of twenty thousand years, the fifty of the first expansion were settled over a period of a few centuries – almost instantaneously, in comparison. Those fifty, taken together, should exist in roughly spherical symmetry about the world of origin.

'We have the co-ordinates of the fifty worlds. You photographed them, remember, from the statue. Whatever or whoever it is that is destroying information that concerns Earth, either overlooked those co-ordinates, or didn't stop to think that they would give us the information we need. All you have to do, Golan, is to adjust the co-ordinates to allow for the last twenty thousand years of stellar motions, then find the centre of the sphere. You'll end up fairly close to Earth's sun, or at least to where it was twenty thousand years ago.'

Trevize's mouth had fallen slightly open during the recital and it took a few moments for him to close it after Pelorat was done. He said, 'Now why didn't *I* think of that?'

'I tried to tell you while we were still on Melpomenia.'

'I'm sure you did. I apologize, Janov, for refusing to listen. The fact is it didn't occur to me that –' He paused in embarrassment.

Pelorat chuckled quietly, 'That I could have anything of importance to say. I suppose that ordinarily I wouldn't, but this was something in my own field, you see. I am sure that, as a general rule, you'd be perfectly justified in not listening to me.'

'Never,' said Trevize. 'That's not so, Janov. I feel like a fool, and I well deserve the feeling. My apologies again – and I must now get to the computer.'

He and Pelorat walked into the pilot-room, and Pelorat, as always, watched with a combination of marvelling and incredulity as Trevize's hands settled down upon the desk, and he became what was almost a single man/computer organism.

'I'll have to make certain assumptions, Janov,' said Trevize, rather blank-faced from computer-absorption. 'I have to assume that the first number is a distance in parsecs, and that the other two numbers are angles in radians, the first being up and down, so to speak, and the other, right and left. I have to assume that the use of plus and minus in the case of the angles is Galactic Standard and that the zero-zero-zero mark is Melpomenia's sun.'

'That sounds fair enough,' said Pelorat.

'Does it? There are six possible ways of arranging the numbers, four possible ways of arranging the signs, distances may be in light-years rather than parsecs, the angles in degrees, rather than radians. That's ninety-six different variations right there. Add to that, the point that if the distances are light-years, I'm uncertain as to the length of the year used. Add also the fact that I don't know the actual conventions used to measure the angles – from the Melpomenian equator in one case, I suppose, but what's their prime meridian?'

Pelorat frowned. 'Now you make it sound hopeless.'

'Not hopeless. Aurora and Solaria are included in the list, and I know where they are in space. I'll use the co-ordinates, and see if I can locate them. If I end up in the wrong place, I will adjust the co-ordinates until they give me the right place, and that will tell me what mistaken assumptions I am making as far as the standards governing the co-ordinates are concerned. Once my assumptions are corrected, I can look for the centre of the sphere.'

'With all the possibilities for change, won't it make it difficult to decide what to do?'

'What?' said Trevize. He was increasingly absorbed. Then, when Pelorat repeated the question, he said, 'Oh well, chances are that the co-ordinates follow the Galactic Standard and adjusting for an unknown prime meridian isn't difficult. These systems for locating points in space were worked out long ago, and most astronomers are pretty confident they even antedate interstellar travel. Human beings are very conservative in some ways and virtually never change numerical conventions once they grow used to them. They even come to mistake them for laws of nature, I think. – Which is just as well, for if every world had its own conventions of measurement that changed every century, I honestly think scientific endeavour would stall and come to a permanent stop.'

He was obviously working while he was talking, for his words came haltingly. And now he muttered, 'But quiet now.'

After that, his face grew furrowed and concentrated until, after several minutes, he leaned back and drew a long breath. He said, quietly, 'The conventions hold. I've located Aurora. There's no question about it. – See?'

Pelorat stared at the field of stars, and at the bright one near the centre and said, 'Are you sure?'

Trevize said, 'My own opinion doesn't matter. The *computer* is sure. We've visited Aurora, after all. We have its characteristics – its diameter, mass, luminosity, temperature, spectral details, to say nothing of the pattern of neighbouring stars. The computer says it's Aurora.'

'Then I suppose we must take its word for it.'

'Believe me, we must. Let me adjust the viewscreen and the computer can get to work. It has the fifty sets of co-ordinates and it will use them one at a time.'

Trevize was working on the screen as he spoke. The computer worked in the four dimensions of space-time routinely, but, for human inspection, the viewscreen was rarely needed in more than two dimensions. Now the screen seemed to unfold into a dark volume as deep as it was tall and broad. Trevize dimmed the room lights almost totally to make the view of the star-shine easier to observe.

'It will begin now,' he whispered.

A moment later, a star appeared – then another – then another.

The view on the screen shifted with every addition so that all might be included. It was as though space was moving backwards from the eye so that a more and more panoramic view could be taken. Combine that with shifts up or down, right or left –

Eventually, fifty dots of light appeared, hovering in three-dimensional space.

Trevize said, 'I would have appreciated a beautiful spherical arrangement, but this looks like the skeleton of a snowball that had been patted into shape in a big hurry, out of snow that was too hard and gritty.'

'Does that ruin everything?'

'It introduces some difficulties, but that can't be helped, I suppose. The stars themselves aren't uniformly distributed, and certainly habitable planets aren't, so there are bound to be unevennesses in the establishment of new worlds. The computer will adjust each of those dots to its present position, allowing for its likely motion in the last twenty-thousand years – even in that time it won't mean much of an adjustment – and then fit them all into a "best-sphere". It will find a spherical surface, in other words, from which the distance of all the dots is a minimum. Then we find the centre of the sphere, and Earth should be fairly close to that centre. Or so we hope. – It won't take long.'

70

It didn't. Trevize, who was used to accepting miracles from the computer, found himself astonished at how little time it took.

Trevize had instructed the computer to sound a soft, reverberating note upon deciding the co-ordinates of the best-centre. There was no reason for that, except for the satisfaction of hearing it and knowing that perhaps the search had been ended.

The sound came in a matter of minutes, and was like the gentle stroking of a mellow gong. It swelled till they could feel the vibration physically, and then slowly faded.

Bliss appeared at the door almost at once. 'What's that?' she asked, her eyes big. 'An emergency?'

Trevize said, 'Not at all.'

Pelorat added, eagerly, 'We may have located Earth, Bliss. That sound was the computer's way of saying so.'

She walked into the room. 'I might have been warned.'

Trevize said, 'I'm sorry, Bliss. I didn't mean it to be quite that loud.'

Fallom had followed Bliss into the room and said, 'Why was there that sound, Bliss?'

'I see she's curious, too,' said Trevize. He sat back, feeling drained. The next step was to try the finding on the real Galaxy, to focus on the co-ordinates of the centre of the Spacer worlds and see if a G-type star was actually present. Once again, he was reluctant to take the obvious step, unable to make himself put the possible solution to the actual test.

'Yes,' said Bliss. 'Why shouldn't she be? She's as human as we are.'

'Her parent wouldn't have thought so,' said Trevize abstractedly. 'I worry about the kid. She's bad news.'

'In what way has she proven so?' demanded Bliss.

Trevize spread his arms. 'Just a feeling.'

Bliss gave him a disdainful look, and turned to Fallom. 'We are trying to locate Earth, Fallom.'

'What's Earth?'

'Another world, but a special one. It's the world our ancestors came from? Do you know what the word "ancestors" means from your reading, Fallom?'

'Does it mean——?' But the last word was not in Galactic.

Pelorat said, 'That's an archaic word for "ancestors", Bliss. Our word "forebears" is closer to it.'

'Very well,' said Bliss, with a sudden brilliant smile. 'Earth is the world where our forebears came from, Fallom. Yours and mine and Pel's and Trevize's.'

'Yours, Bliss – and mine also.' Fallom sounded puzzled. 'Both of them?'

'There's just one set of forebears,' said Bliss. 'We had the same forebears, all of us.'

Trevize said, 'It sounds to me as though the child knows very well that she's different from us.'

Bliss said to Trevize in a low voice, 'Don't say that. She must be made to see she isn't. Not in essentials.'

'Hermaphrodism is essential, I should think.'

'I'm talking about the mind.'

'Transducer-lobes are essential, too.'

'Now, Trevize, don't be difficult. She's intelligent and human regardless of details.'

She turned to Fallom, her voice rising to its normal level. 'Think quietly about this, Fallom, and see what it means to you. Your forebears and mine were the same. All the people on all the worlds – many, many worlds – all had the same forebears, and those forebears lived originally on the world named Earth. That means we're all relatives, doesn't it? – Now go back to our room and think of that.'

Fallom, after bestowing a thoughtful look on Trevize, turned and ran off, hastened on by Bliss's affectionate slap on her backside.

Bliss turned to Trevize, and said, 'Please, Trevize, promise me you won't make any comments in her hearing that will lead her to think she's different from us.'

Trevize said, 'I promise. I have no wish to impede or subvert the education procedure, but, you know, she *is* different from us.'

'In ways. As I'm different from you, and as Pel is.'

'Don't be naïve, Bliss. The differences in Fallom's case are much greater.'

'A *little* greater. The similarities are vastly more important. She, and her people, will be part of Galaxia some day, and a very useful part, I'm sure.'

'All right. We won't argue.' He turned to the computer with clear reluctance. 'And meanwhile, I'm afraid I have to check the supposed position of Earth in real space.'

'Afraid?'

'Well,' Trevize lifted his shoulders in what he hoped was a half-humorous way. 'What if there's no suitable star near the place?'

'Then there isn't,' said Bliss.

'I'm wondering if there's any point in checking it out now. We won't be able to make a Jump for several days.'

'And you'll spend them agonizing over the possibilities. Find out now. Waiting won't change matters.'

Trevize sat there with his lips compressed for a moment, then said, 'You're right. Very well, then – here goes.'

He turned to the computer, placed his hands on the hand-marks on the desk and the viewscreen went dark.

Bliss said, 'I'll leave you, then. I'll make you nervous if I stay.' She left, with a wave of her hand.

'The thing is,' he muttered, 'that we're going to be checking the computer's Galactic map first and even if Earth's sun is in the calculated position, the map should not include it. But we'll then –'

His voice trailed off in astonishment as the viewscreen flashed with a background of stars. These were fairly numerous and dim, with an occasional brighter one sparkling here and there, well scattered over the face of the screen. But quite close to the centre was a star that was brighter than all the rest.

'We've done it,' said Pelorat jubilantly. 'We've got it, old chap. Look how bright it is.'

'Any star at centred co-ordinates would look bright,' said Trevize, clearly trying to fight off any initial jubilation that might prove unfounded. 'The view, after all, is presented from a distance of a parsec from the centred co-ordinates. Still, that centred star certainly isn't a red dwarf, or a red giant, or a hot blue-white. Wait for information; the computer is checking its data banks.'

There was silence for a few seconds and then Trevize said, 'Spectral class G-2.' Another pause, then, 'Diameter, 1,400,000 kilometres – mass,

1.02 times that of Terminus's sun – surface temperature, 6,000 absolute – rotation slow, just under 30 days – no unusual activity or irregularity.'

Pelorat said, 'Isn't all that typical of the kind of star about which habitable planets are to be found?'

'Typical,' said Trevize, nodding in the dimness. 'And, therefore, what we'd expect Earth's sun to be like. If that is where life developed, the sun of Earth would have set the original standard.'

'So there is a reasonable chance that there would be a habitable planet circling it.'

'We don't have to speculate about that,' said Trevize, who sounded puzzled indeed over the matter. 'The Galactic Map lists it as possessing a planet with human life – but with a question mark.'

Pelorat's enthusiasm grew. 'That's exactly what we would expect, Golan. The life-bearing planet is there, but the attempt to hide the fact obscures data concerning it and leaves the makers of the map the computer uses uncertain.'

'No, that's what bothers me,' said Trevize. 'That's *not* what we should expect. We should expect far more than that. Considering the efficiency with which data concerning Earth has been wiped out, the makers of the map should not have known that life exists in the system, let alone human life. They should not even have known Earth's sun exists. The Spacer worlds aren't on the map. Why should Earth's sun be?'

'Well, it's there, just the same. What's the use of arguing the fact? What other information about the star is given?'

'A name.'

'Ah! What is it?'

'Alpha.'

There was a short pause, then Pelorat said eagerly, 'That's it, old man. That's the final bit of evidence. Consider the meaning.'

'Does it have a meaning?' said Trevize. 'It's just a name to me, and an odd one. It doesn't sound Galactic.'

'It *isn't* Galactic. It's in a prehistoric language of Earth, the same one that gave us Gaia as the name of Bliss's planet.'

'What does Alpha mean, then?'

'Alpha is the first letter of the alphabet of that ancient language. That is one of the most firmly attested scraps of knowledge we have about it. In ancient times, "alpha" was sometimes used to mean the first of anything. To call a sun "Alpha", implies that it's the first sun. And wouldn't the first sun be the one around which a planet revolved that was the first planet to bear human life – Earth?'

'Are you sure of that?'

'Absolutely,' said Pelorat.

'Is there anything in early legends – you're the mythologist, after all – that gives Earth's sun some very unusual attribute?'

'No, how can there be? It has to be standard by definition, and the characteristics the computer has given us are as standard as possible, I imagine. Aren't they?'

'Earth's sun is a single star, I suppose?'

Pelorat said, 'Well, of course! As far as I know, all inhabited worlds orbit single stars.'

'So I would have thought myself,' said Trevize. 'The trouble is that that star in the centre of the viewscreen is not a single star; it is a binary. The brighter of the two stars making up the binary is indeed standard and it is that one for which the computer supplied us with data. Circling that star with a period of roughly eighty years, however, is another star with a mass four fifths that of the brighter one. We can't see the two as separate stars with the unaided eye, but if I were to enlarge the view, I'm sure we would.'

'Are you certain of that, Golan,' said Pelorat, taken aback.

'It's what the computer is telling me. And if we are looking at a binary star, then it's not Earth's sun. It can't be.'

71

Trevize broke contact with the computer, and the lights brightened.

That was the signal, apparently, for Bliss to return, with Fallom tagging after her. 'Well, then, what are the results?' she asked.

Trevize said tonelessly, 'Somewhat disappointing. Where I

expected to find Earth's sun, I found a binary star, instead. Earth's sun is a single star, so the one centred is not it.'

Pelorat said, 'Now what, Golan?'

Trevize shrugged. 'I didn't really expect to see Earth's sun centred. Even the Spacers wouldn't settle worlds in such a way as to set up an exact sphere. Aurora, the oldest of the Spacer worlds, might have sent out settlers of its own and that may have distorted the sphere, too. Then, too, Earth's sun may not have moved at precisely the average velocity of the Spacer worlds.'

Pelorat said, 'So the Earth can be anywhere. Is that what you're saying?'

'No. Not quite "anywhere". All these possible sources of error can't amount to much. Earth's sun must be in the *vicinity* of the co-ordinates. The star we've spotted almost exactly at the co-ordinates must be a neighbour of Earth's sun. It's startling that there should be a neighbour that so closely resembles Earth's sun – except for being a binary – but that must be the case.'

'But we would see Earth's sun on the map, then, wouldn't we? I mean, near Alpha?'

'No, for I'm certain Earth's sun isn't on the map at all. It was that which shook my confidence when we first spied Alpha. Regardless of how much it might resemble Earth's sun, the mere fact that it was on the map made me suspect it was not the real thing.'

'Well, then,' said Bliss. 'Why not concentrate on the same co-ordinates in real space? Then, if there is any bright star close to the centre, a star that does not exist in the computer's map, and if it is very much like Alpha in its properties, but is single, might it not be Earth's sun?'

Trevize sighed. 'If all that were so, I'd be willing to wager half my fortune, such as it is, that circling that star you speak of would be the planet Earth. – Again, I hesitate to try.'

'Because you might fail?'

Trevize nodded. 'However,' he said, 'just give me a moment or two to catch my breath, and I'll force myself to do so.'

And while the three adults looked at each other, Fallom approached the computer-desk and stared curiously at the handmarks upon it. She reached out her own hand tentatively towards the markings, and Trevize blocked the motion with a swift outthrusting of his own arm and a sharp, 'Mustn't touch, Fallom.'

The young Solarian seemed startled, and retreated to the comfort of Bliss's encircling arm.

Pelorat said, 'We must face it, Golan. What if you find nothing in real space?'

'Then we will be forced to go back to the earlier plan,' said Trevize, 'and visit each of the forty-seven Spacer worlds in turn.'

'And if that yields nothing, Golan?'

Trevize shook his head in annoyance, as though to prevent that thought from taking too deep a root. Staring down at his knees, he said abruptly, 'Then I will think of something else.'

'But what if there is no world of forebears at all?'

Trevize looked up sharply at the treble voice, 'Who said that?' he asked.

It was a useless question. The moment of disbelief faded, and he knew very well who the questioner was.

'I did,' said Fallom.

Trevize looked at her with a slight frown. 'Did you understand the conversation?'

Fallom said, 'You are looking for the world of forebears, but you haven't found it yet. Maybe there isn't no such world.'

'*Any* such world,' said Bliss softly.

'No, Fallom,' said Trevize seriously. 'There has been a very big effort to hide it. To try so hard to hide something means there is something there to hide. Do you understand what I am saying?'

'Yes,' said Fallom. 'You do not let me touch the hands on the desk. Because you do not let me do that means it would be interesting to touch them.'

'Ah, but not for you, Fallom. – Bliss, you are creating a monster that will destroy us all. Don't ever let her in here unless I'm at the desk. And even then, think twice, will you?'

The small byplay, however, seemed to have shaken him out of his irresolution. He said, 'Obviously, I had better get to work. If I just sit here, uncertain as to what to do, that little fright will take over the ship.'

The lights dimmed, and Bliss said in a low voice, 'You promised, Trevize. Do not call her a monster or a fright in her hearing.'

'Then keep an eye on her, and teach her some manners. Tell her children should be never heard and seldom seen.'

Bliss frowned. 'Your attitude towards children is simply appalling, Trevize.'

'Maybe, but this is not the time to discuss the matter.'

Then he said, in tones in which satisfaction and relief were equally represented, 'There's Alpha again in real space. – And to its left, and slightly upwards, is almost as bright a star and one that isn't in the computer's Galactic map. *That* is Earth's sun. I'll wager *all* my fortune on it.'

72

'Well, now,' said Bliss, 'we won't take any part of your fortune if you lose, so why not settle the matter in a forthright manner? Let's visit the star as soon as you can make the Jump.'

Trevize shook his head. 'No. This time it's not a matter of irresolution or fear. It's a matter of being careful. Three times we've visited an unknown world and three times we've come up against something unexpectedly dangerous. And three times, moreover, we've had to leave that world in a hurry. This time the matter is ultimately crucial and I will not play my cards in ignorance again, or at least in any more ignorance than I can help. So far, all we have are vague stories about radioactivity, and that is not enough. By an odd chance that no one could have anticipated, there is a planet with human life about a parsec from Earth –'

'Do we really know that Alpha has a planet with human life on it?' put in Pelorat. 'You said the computer placed a question mark after that.'

'Even so,' said Trevize, 'it's worth trying. Why not take a look at it? If it does indeed have human beings on it, let us find out what they know about Earth. For them, after all, Earth is not a distant thing of legend; it is a neighbour world, bright and prominent in their sky.'

Bliss said thoughtfully, 'It's not a bad idea. It occurs to me that if Alpha is inhabited and if the inhabitants are not your thoroughly typical Isolates, they may be friendly, and we might be able to get some decent food for a change.'

'And meet some pleasant people,' said Trevize. 'Don't forget that. Will it be all right with you, Janov?'

Pelorat said, 'You make the decision, old chap. Wherever you go, I will go, too.'

Fallom said suddenly, 'Will we find Jemby?'

Bliss said, hastily, before Trevize could answer, 'We will look for it, Fallom.'

And then Trevize said, 'It's settled then. On to Alpha.'

73

'Two big stars,' said Fallom, pointing to the viewscreen.

'That's right,' said Trevize. 'Two of them. – Bliss, do keep an eye on her. I don't want her fiddling with anything.'

'She's fascinated by machinery,' said Bliss.

'Yes, I know she is,' said Trevize, 'but I'm not fascinated by her fascination. – Though to tell you the truth, I'm as fascinated as she is at seeing two stars that bright in the viewscreen at the same time.'

The two stars were bright enough to seem to be on the point of showing a disc – each of them. The screen had automatically increased filtration density in order to remove the hard radiation and dim the light of the bright stars so as to avoid retinal damage.

As a result, few other stars were bright enough to be noticeable, and the two that did reigned in haughty near-isolation.

'The thing is,' said Trevize, 'I've never been this close to a binary system before.'

'You haven't?' said Pelorat, open astonishment in his voice. 'How is that possible?'

Trevize laughed. 'I've been around, Janov, but I'm not the Galactic rover you think I am.'

Pelorat said, 'I was never in space at all till I met you, Golan, but I always thought that anyone who did manage to get into space –'

'Would go everywhere. I know. That's natural enough. The trouble with planet-bound people is that no matter how much their mind may tell them otherwise, their imaginations just can't take in the true size of the Galaxy. We could travel all our lives and leave most of the Galaxy unpenetrated and untouched. Besides, no one ever goes to binaries.'

'Why not?' said Bliss, frowning. 'We on Gaia know little astronomy compared to the travelling Isolates of the Galaxy, but I'm under the impression that binaries aren't rare.'

'They're not,' said Trevize. 'There are substantially more binaries than there are single stars. However, the formation of two stars in close association upsets the ordinary processes of planetary formation. Binaries have less planetary material than single stars do. Such planets as do form about them often have relatively unstable orbits and are very rarely of a type that is reasonably habitable.

'Early explorers, I imagine, studied many binaries at close range but, after a while, for settlement purposes, they sought out only singles. And, of course, once you have a densely settled Galaxy, virtually all travel involves trade and communications and is carried on between inhabited worlds circling single stars. In periods of military activity, I suppose bases were sometimes set up on small, otherwise uninhabited worlds circling one of the stars of a binary that happen to be strategically placed, but as hyperspatial travel came to be perfected, such bases were no longer necessary.'

Pelorat said humbly, 'It's amazing how much I don't know.'

Trevize merely grinned. 'Don't let that impress you, Janov. When I was in the Navy, we listened to an incredible number of lectures on outmoded military tactics that no one ever planned, or intended to use, and were just talked about out of inertia. I was just rattling off a bit of one of them. – Consider all you know about mythology, folklore, and archaic languages that I don't know, and that only you and a very few others do know.'

Bliss said, 'Yes, but those two stars make up a binary system and one of them has an inhabited planet circling it.'

'We hope it does, Bliss,' said Trevize. 'Everything has its exceptions. And with an official question mark in this case, which makes it more puzzling. – No, Fallom, those knobs are not toys. – Bliss, either keep her in handcuffs, or take her out.'

'She won't hurt anything,' said Bliss defensively, but pulled the Solarian youngster to herself just the same. 'If you're so interested in that habitable planet, why aren't we there already?'

'For one thing,' said Trevize, 'I'm just human enough to want to see this sight of a binary system at close quarters. Then, too, I'm just human enough to be cautious. As I've already explained, nothing has happened since we left Gaia that would encourage me to be anything but cautious.'

Pelorat said, 'Which one of those stars is Alpha, Golan?'

'We won't get lost, Janov. The computer knows exactly which one is Alpha, and, for that matter, so do we. It's the hotter and yellower of the two because it's the larger. Now the one on the right has a distinct orange tinge to its light, rather like Aurora's sun, if you recall. Do you notice?'

'Yes, now that you call it to my attention.'

'Very well. That's the smaller one. – What's the second letter of that ancient language you speak of.'

Pelorat thought a moment, and said, 'Beta.'

'Then let's call the orange one Beta and the yellow-white is Alpha, and it's Alpha we're heading for right now.'

17

New Earth

74

'Four planets,' muttered Trevize. 'All are small, plus a trailing off of asteroids. No gas giants.'

Pelorat said, 'Do you find that disappointing?'

'Not really. It's expected. Binaries that circle each other at small distances can have no planets circling one of the stars. Planets can circle the centre of gravity of both, but it's very unlikely that they would be habitable – too far away.

'On the other hand if the binaries are reasonably separate, there can be planets in stable orbits about each, if they are close enough to one or the other of the stars. These two stars, according to the computer's data bank, have an average separation of 3.5 billion kilometres and even at periastron, when they are closest together, are about 1.7 billion kilometres apart. A planet in an orbit of less than 200 million kilometres from either star would be stably situated, but there can be no planet with a larger orbit. That means no gas giants since they would have to be further away from a star, but what's the difference? Gas giants aren't habitable, anyway.'

'But one of those four planets might be habitable.'

'Actually the second planet is the only real possibility. For one thing, it's the only one of them large enough to have an atmosphere.'

They approached the second planet rapidly and over a period of two days its image expanded; at first with a majestic and measured swelling. And then, when there was no sign of any ship emerging to intercept them, with increasing and almost frightening speed.

The *Far Star* was moving swiftly along a temporary orbit a thousand kilometres above the cloud cover, when Trevize said grimly, 'I see why the computer's memory banks put a question mark after the notation that it was inhabited. There's no clear sign of radiation, either light in the night-hemisphere, or radio anywhere.'

'The cloud cover seems pretty thick,' said Pelorat.

'That should not blank out radio radiation.'

They watched the planet wheeling below them, a symphony in swirling white clouds, through occasional gaps of which a bluish wash indicated ocean.

Trevize said, 'The cloud level is fairly heavy for an inhabited world. It might be a rather gloomy one. – What bothers me most,' he added, as they plunged once more into the night-shadow, 'is that no space stations have hailed us.'

'The way they did back at Comporellon, you mean?' said Pelorat.

'The way they would in any inhabited world. We would have to stop for the usual checkup on papers, freight, length of stay and so on.'

Bliss said, 'Perhaps we missed the hail for some reason.'

'Our computer would have received it at any wavelength they might have cared to use. And we've been sending out our own signals, but have roused no one and nothing as a result. Dipping under the cloud layer without communicating with station officials violates space courtesy, but I don't see that we have a choice.'

The *Far Star* slowed, and strengthened its antigravity accordingly, so as to maintain its height. It came out into the sunlight again, and slowed further. Trevize, in co-ordination with the computer, found a sizeable break in the clouds. The ship sank and passed through it. Beneath them heaved the ocean in what must have been a fresh breeze. It lay, wrinkled, several kilometres below them, faintly striped in lines of froth.

They flew out of the sunlit patch and under the cloud cover. The expanse of water immediately beneath them turned a slate-grey, and the temperature dropped noticeably.

Fallom, staring at the viewscreen, spoke in her own consonant-rich language for a few moments, then shifted to Galactic. Her voice trembled. 'What is that which I see beneath?'

'That is an ocean,' said Bliss soothingly. 'It is a very large mass of water.'

'Why does it not dry up?'

Bliss looked at Trevize, who said, 'There's too much water for it to dry up.'

Fallom said in a half-choked manner, 'I don't want all that water. Let us go away.' And then she shrieked, thinly, as the *Far Star* moved through a patch of storm clouds so that the viewscreen turned milky and was streaked with the mark of raindrops.

The lights in the pilot-room dimmed and the ship's motion became slightly jerky.

Trevize looked up in surprise and cried out, 'Bliss, your Fallom is old enough to transduce. She's using electric power to try to manipulate the controls. Stop her!'

Bliss put her arms about Fallom, and hugged her tightly. 'It's all right, Fallom, it's all right. There's nothing to be afraid of. It's just another world, that's all. There are many like this.'

Fallom relaxed somewhat but continued to tremble.

Bliss said to Trevize, 'The child has never seen an ocean, and perhaps, for all I know, never experienced fog or rain. Can't you be sympathetic?'

'Not if she tampers with the ship. She's a danger to all of us, then. Take her into your room and calm her down.'

Bliss nodded curtly.

Pelorat said, 'I'll come with you, Bliss.'

'No, no, Pel,' she responded. 'You stay here. I'll soothe Fallom and you soothe Trevize.' And she left.

'I don't need soothing,' growled Trevize to Pelorat. 'I'm sorry if I flew off the handle, but we can't have a child playing with the controls, can we?'

'Of course we can't,' said Pelorat, 'but Bliss was caught by surprise.

She can control Fallom, who is really remarkably well behaved for a child taken from her home and her – her robot, and thrown, willy-nilly, into a life she doesn't understand.'

'I know. It wasn't I who wanted to take her along, remember. It was Bliss's idea.'

'Yes, but the child would have been killed if we hadn't taken her.'

'Well, I'll apologize to Bliss later on. To the child, too.'

But he was still frowning, and Pelorat said gently, 'Golan, old chap, is there anything else bothering you?'

'The ocean,' said Trevize. They had long emerged from the rain storm, but the clouds persisted.

'What's wrong with it?' asked Pelorat.

'There's too much of it, that's all.'

Pelorat looked blank, and Trevize said, with a snap, 'No land. We haven't seen any land. The atmosphere is perfectly normal, oxygen and nitrogen in decent proportions, so the planet has to be engineered, and there has to be plant life to maintain the oxygen level. In the natural state, such atmospheres do not occur – except, presumably, on Earth, where it developed, who knows how. But, then, on engineered planets there are always reasonable amounts of dry land, up to one third of the whole, and never less than a fifth. So how can this planet be engineered, and lack land.'

Pelorat said, 'Perhaps, since this planet is part of a binary system, it is completely atypical. Maybe it wasn't engineered, but evolved an atmosphere in ways that never prevail on planets about single stars. Perhaps life developed independently here, as it once did on Earth, but only sea life.'

'Even if we were to admit that,' said Trevize, 'it would do us no good. There's no way life in the sea can develop a technology. Technology is always based on fire, and fire is impossible in the sea. A life-bearing planet without technology is not what we're looking for.'

'I realize that, but I'm only considering ideas. After all, as far as we know, technology only developed once – on Earth. Everywhere else, the Settlers brought it with them. You can't say technology is "always" anything, if you only have one case to study.'

'Travel through the sea requires streamlining. Sea life cannot have irregular outlines and appendages such as hands.'

'Squids have tentacles.'

Trevize said, 'I admit we are allowed to speculate, but if you're thinking of intelligent squid-like creatures evolving independently somewhere in the Galaxy, and developing a technology not based on fire, you're supposing something not at all likely, in my opinion.'

'In your *opinion*,' said Pelorat gently.

Suddenly, Trevize laughed. 'Very well, Janov. I see you're logic-chopping in order to get even with me for speaking harshly to Bliss, and you're doing a good job. I promise you that if we find no land, we will examine the sea as best we can to see if we can find your civilized squids.'

As he spoke, the ship plunged into the night-shadow again, and the viewscreen turned black.

Pelorat winced. 'I keep wondering,' he said. 'Is this safe?'

'Is what safe, Janov?'

'Racing through the dark like this. We might dip, and dive into the ocean, and be destroyed instantly.'

'Quite impossible, Janov. Really! The computer keeps us travelling along a gravitational line of force. In other words, it remains always at a constant intensity of the planetary gravitational force which means it keeps us at a nearly constant height above sea level.'

'But how high?'

'Nearly five kilometres.'

'That doesn't really console me, Golan. Might we not reach land and smash into a mountain we don't see?'

'*We* don't see, but ship's radar will see it, and the computer will guide the ship around or over the mountain.'

'What if there's level land, then? We'll miss it in the dark.'

'No, Janov, we won't. Radar reflected from water is not at all like radar reflected from land. Water is essentially flat; land is rough.

For that reason, reflection from land is substantially more chaotic than reflection from water. The computer will know the difference and it will let me know if there's land in view. Even if it were day and the planet were sun-lit, the computer might well detect land before I would.'

They fell silent and, in a couple of hours, they were back in daylight, with an empty ocean again rolling beneath them monotonously, but occasionally invisible when they passed through one of the numerous storms. In one storm, the wind drove the *Far Star* out of its path. The computer gave way, Trevize explained, in order to prevent an unnecessary waste of energy and to minimize the chance of physical damage. Then, when the turbulence had passed, the computer eased the ship back into its path.

'Probably the edge of a hurricane,' said Trevize.

Pelorat said, 'See here, old chap, we're just travelling west to east – or east to west. All we're examining is the equator.'

Trevize said, 'That would be foolish, wouldn't it? We're following a great-circle route northwest-southeast. That takes us through the tropics and both temperate zones and each time we repeat the circle, the path moves westward, as the planet rotates on its axis beneath us. We're methodically criss-crossing the world. By now, since we haven't hit land, the chances of a sizeable continent are less than one in ten, according to the computer, and of a sizeable island less than one in four, with the chances going down each circle we make.'

'You know what I would have done' said Pelorat slowly, as the night hemisphere engulfed them again. 'I'd have stayed well away from the planet and swept the entire hemisphere facing me with radar. The clouds wouldn't have mattered, would they?'

Trevize said, 'And then zoom to the other side and do the same there. Or just let the planet turn once. – That's hindsight, Janov. Who would expect to approach a habitable planet without stopping at a station and being given a path – or being excluded? And if one went under the cloud layer without stopping at a station, who

would expect not to find land almost at once? Habitable planets
are – land!'

'Surely not all land,' said Pelorat.

'I'm not talking about that,' said Trevize, in sudden excitement.
'I'm saying we've found land! Quiet!'

Then, with a restraint that did not succeed in hiding his excitement, Trevize placed his hands on the desk and became part of the
computer. He said, 'It's an island about 250 kilometres long and 65
kilometres wide, more or less. Perhaps 15,000 square kilometres in
area, or thereabouts. Not large, but respectable. More than a dot
on the map. Wait –'

The lights in the pilot-room dimmed and went out.

'What are we doing?' said Pelorat, automatically whispering as
though darkness were something fragile that must not be shattered.

'Waiting for our eyes to undergo dark-adaptation. The ship is
hovering over the island. Just watch. Do you see anything?'

'No – Little specks of light, maybe. I'm not sure.'

'I see them, too. Now I'll throw in the telescopic lens.'

And there was light! Clearly visible. Irregular patches of it.

'It's inhabited,' said Trevize. 'It may be the only inhabited portion
of the planet.'

'What do we do?'

'We wait for daytime. That gives us a few hours in which we can
rest.'

'Might they not attack us?'

'With what? I detect almost no radiation except visible light and
infrared. It's inhabited and the inhabitants are clearly intelligent.
They have a technology, but obviously a pre-electronic one, so I
don't think there's anything to worry about up here. If I should be
wrong, the computer will warn me in plenty of time.'

'And once daylight comes?'

'We'll land, of course.'

75

They came down when the first rays of the morning sun shone through a break in the clouds to reveal part of the island – freshly green, with its interior marked by a line of low, rolling hills stretching into the purplish distance.

As they dropped closer, they could see isolated copses of trees and occasional orchards, but for the most part there were well-kept farms. Immediately below them, on the south-eastern shore of the island was a silvery beach backed by a broken line of boulders, and beyond it was a stretch of lawn. They caught a glimpse of an occasional house, but these did not cluster into anything like a town.

Eventually, they made out a dim network of roads, sparsely lined by dwelling places, and then, in the cool morning air, they spied an air-car in the far distance. They could only tell it was an air-car, and not a bird, by the manner of its manoeuvring. It was the first indubitable sign of intelligent life in action they had yet seen on the planet.

'It could be an automated vehicle, if they could manage that without electronics,' said Trevize.

Bliss said, 'It might well be. It seems to me that if there were a human being at the controls, it would be heading for us. We must be quite a sight – a vehicle sinking downwards without the use of braking jets of rocket fire.'

'A strange sight on any planet,' said Trevize thoughtfully. 'There can't be many worlds that have ever witnessed the descent of a gravitic space-vessel. – The beach would make a fine landing place, but if the winds blow I don't want the ship inundated. I'll make for the stretch of grass on the other side of the boulders.'

'At least,' said Pelorat, a gravitic ship won't scorch private property in descending.'

Down they came gently on the four broad pads that had moved slowly outwards during the last stage. These pressed down into the soil under the weight of the ship.

Pelorat said, 'I'm afraid we'll leave marks, though.'

'At least,' said Bliss, and there was that in her voice that was not entirely approving, 'the climate is evidently equable. – I would even say, warm.'

A human being was on the grass, watching the ship descend and showing no evidence of fear or surprise. The look on her face showed only rapt interest.

She wore very little, which accounted for Bliss's estimate of the climate. Her sandals seemed to be of canvas, and about her hips was a wrap-around skirt with a flowered pattern. There were no leg-coverings and there was nothing above her waist.

Her hair was black, long, and very glossy, descending almost to her waist. Her skin colour was a pale brown and her eyes were narrow.

Trevize scanned the surroundings and there was no other human being in sight. He shrugged and said, 'Well, it's early morning and the inhabitants may be mostly indoors, or even asleep. Still, I wouldn't say it was a well-populated area.'

He turned to the others and said, 'I'll go out and talk to the woman, if she speaks anything comprehensible. The rest of you –'

'I should think,' said Bliss firmly, 'that we might as well all step out. That woman looks completely harmless and, in any case, I want to stretch my legs and breathe planetary air, and perhaps arrange for planetary food. I want Fallom to get the feel of the world again, too, and I think Pel would like to examine the woman at closer range.'

'Who? I?' said Pelorat, turning faintly pink. 'Not at all, Bliss, but I *am* the linguist of our little party.'

Trevize shrugged. 'Come one, come all. Still, though she may look harmless, I intend to take my weapons with me.'

'I doubt,' said Bliss, 'that you will be much tempted to use them on that young woman.'

Trevize grinned. 'She is attractive, isn't she?'

Trevize left the ship first, then Bliss, with one hand swung back-wards to enclose Fallom's, who carefully made her way down the ramp after Bliss. Pelorat was last.

The black-haired young woman continued to watch with interest. She did not back away an inch.

Trevize muttered, 'Well, let's try.'

He held his arms away from his weapons and said, 'I greet you.'

The young woman considered that for a moment, and said, 'I greet thee and I greet thy companions.'

Pelorat said, joyfully, 'How wonderful! She speaks Classical Galactic and with a correct accent.'

'I understand her, too,' said Trevize, oscillating one hand to indicate his understanding wasn't perfect. 'I hope she understands me.'

He said, smiling, and assuming a friendly expression, 'We come from across space. We come from another world.'

'That is well,' said the young woman, in her clear soprano. 'Comes thy ship from the Empire?'

'It comes from a far star, and the ship is named *Far Star*.'

The young woman looked up at the lettering on the ship. 'Is that what that sayeth? If that be so, and if the first letter is an F, then, behold, it is imprinted backwards.'

Trevize was about to object, but Pelorat, in an ecstasy of joy, said, 'She's right. The letter F did reverse itself about two thousand years ago. What a marvellous chance to study classical Galactic in detail and as a living language.'

Trevize studied the young woman carefully. She was not much more than 1.5 metres in height, and her breasts, though shapely, were small. Yet she did not seem unripe. The nipples were large and the areolae dark, though that might be the result of her brownish skin colour.

He said, 'My name is Golan Trevize; my friend is Janov Pelorat; the woman is Bliss; and the child is Fallom.'

'Is it the custom, then, on the far star from which you come, that the men be given a double name? I am Hiroko, daughter of Hiroko.'

'And your father?' interposed Pelorat suddenly.

To which Hiroko replied with an indifferent shrug of her shoulder,

'His name, so sayeth my mother, is Smool, but it is of no importance. I know him not.'

'And where are the others?' asked Trevize. 'You seem to be the only one to be here to greet us.'

Hiroko said, 'Many men are aboard the fishboats; many women are in the fields. I take holiday these last two days and so am fortunate enough to see this great thing. Yet people are curious and the ship will have been seen as it descended, even from a distance. Others will be here soon.'

'Are there many others on this island?'

'There are more than a score and five thousand,' said Hiroko with obvious pride.

'And are there other islands in the ocean?'

'Other islands, good sir?' she seemed puzzled.

Trevize took that as answer enough. This was the one spot on the entire planet that was inhabited by human beings.

He said, 'What do you call your world?'

'It is Alpha, good sir. We are taught that the whole name is Alpha Centauri, if that has more meaning to thee, but we call it Alpha only and, see, it is a fair-visaged world.'

'A *what* world,' said Trevize, turning blankly to Pelorat.

'A beautiful world, she means,' said Pelorat.

'That it is,' said Trevize, 'at least here, and at this moment.' He looked up at the mild blue morning sky, with its occasional drift of clouds. 'You have a nice sunny day, Hiroko, but I imagine there aren't many of those on Alpha.'

Hiroko stiffened. 'As many as we wish, sir. The clouds may come when we need rain, but on most days it seemeth good to us that the sky is fair above. Surely a goodly sky and a quiet wind are much to be desired on those days when the fishboats are at sea.'

'Do your people control the weather then, Hiroko?'

'Did we not, sir Golan Trevize, we would be soggy with rain.'

'But how do you do that?'

'Not being a trained engineer, sir, I cannot tell thee.'

'And what might be the name of this island on which you and your people live?' said Trevize, finding himself trapped in the ornate sound of Classical Galactic (and wondering desperately if he had the conjugations right).

Hiroko said, 'We call our heavenly island in the midst of the vast sea, New Earth.'

At which Trevize and Pelorat stared at each other with surprise and delight.

76

There was no time to follow up on the statement. Others were arriving. Dozens. They must consist of those, Trevize thought, who were not on the ships or in the fields, and who were not from too far away. They came on foot for the most part, though two ground-cars were in evidence – rather old and clumsy.

Clearly, this was a low-technology society, and yet they controlled the weather.

It was well known that technology was not necessarily all of a piece; that lack of advance in some directions did not necessarily exclude considerable advance in others – but surely this example of uneven development was unusual.

Of those who were now watching the ship, at least half were elderly men and women; there were also three or four children. Of the rest, more were women than men. None showed any fear or uncertainty whatever.

Trevize said in a low voice to Bliss, 'Are you manipulating them. They seem – serene.'

'I'm not in the least manipulating them,' said Bliss. 'I never touch minds unless I must. It's Fallom I'm concerned with.'

Few as the newcomers were to anyone who had experienced the crowds of curiosity-seekers on any normal world in the Galaxy, they were a mob to Fallom, to whom the three adults on the *Far Star* had been something to grow accustomed to. Fallom was breathing rapidly and shallowly, and her eyes were half-closed. Almost, she seemed in shock

Bliss was stroking her hair, softly and rhythmically, and making soothing sounds. Trevize was certain that she was delicately accompanying it all by an infinitely gentle rearrangement of mental fibrils.

Fallom took in a sudden deep breath, almost a gasp, and shook herself, in what was perhaps an involuntary shudder. She raised her head and looked at those present with something approaching normality and then buried her head in the space between Bliss's arm and body.

Bliss let her remain so, while her arm, encircling Fallom's shoulder, tightened periodically as though to indicate her own protective presence over and over.

Pelorat seemed rather awestruck, as his eyes went from one Alphan to another. He said, 'Golan, they differ so among themselves.'

Trevize had noticed that, too. There were various shades of skin and hair colour, including one brilliant redhead with blue eyes and freckled skin. At least three apparent adults were as short as Hiroko, and one or two were taller than Trevize. A number of both sexes had eyes resembling those of Hiroko, and Trevize remembered that on the teeming commercial planets of the Fili sector, such eyes were characteristic of the population, but he had never visited that sector.

All the Alphans wore nothing above their waist and among the women the breasts all seemed to be small. That was the most nearly uniform of all the bodily characteristics that he could see.

Bliss said suddenly, 'Miss Hiroko, my youngster is not accustomed to travel through space and she is absorbing more novelty than she can easily manage. Would it be possible for her to sit down and, perhaps, have something to eat and drink?'

Hiroko looked puzzled, and Pelorat repeated what Bliss had said in the more ornate Galactic of the mid-Imperial period.

Hiroko's hand then flew to her mouth and she sank to her knees, gracefully. 'I crave your pardon, respected madam,' she said. 'I have not thought of this child's needs, nor of thine. The strangeness of this event has too occupied me. Wouldst thou – would you all – as visitors and guests, enter the refectory for morning meal. May we join you and serve as hosts?'

Bliss said, 'That is kind of you.' She spoke slowly and pronounced the words carefully, hoping to make them easier to understand. 'It would be better, though, if you alone served as hostess, for the sake of the comfort of the child who is unaccustomed to being with many people at once.'

Hiroko rose to her feet. 'It shall be as thou hast said.'

She led them, in leisurely manner, across the grass. Other Alphans edged closer. They seemed particularly interested in the clothing of the newcomers. Trevize removed his light jacket, and handed it to a man who had sidled towards him and had laid a questing finger upon it.

'Here,' he said, 'look it over, but return it.' Then he said to Hiroko, 'See that I get it back, Miss Hiroko.'

'Of a surety, it will be backhanded, respected sir.' She nodded her head gravely.

Trevize smiled and walked on. He was more comfortable without the jacket in the light, mild breeze.

He had detected no visible weapons on the persons of any of those about him, and he found it interesting that no one seemed to show any fear or discomfort over Trevize's. They did not even show curiosity concerning them. It might well be that they were not aware of the objects as weapons at all. From what Trevize had so far seen, Alpha might well be a world utterly without violence.

A woman, having moved rapidly forward, so as to be a little ahead of Bliss, turned to examine her blouse minutely, then said, 'Hast thou breasts, respected madam?'

And, as though unable to wait for an answer, she placed her hand lightly on Bliss's chest.

Bliss smiled and said, 'As thou hast discovered, I have. They are perhaps not as shapely as thine, but I hide them not for that reason. On my world, it is not fitting that they be uncovered.'

She whispered in an aside to Pelorat, 'How do you like the way I'm getting the hang of Classic Galactic?'

'You did that very well, Bliss,' said Pelorat.

The dining room was a large one with long tables to which were attached long benches on either side. Clearly, the Alphans ate community-fashion.

Trevize felt a pang of conscience. Bliss's request for privacy had reserved this space for five people and forced the Alphans generally to remain in exile outside. A number, however, placed themselves at a respectful distance from the windows (which were no more than gaps in the wall, unfilled even by screens), presumably so that they might watch the strangers eat.

Involuntarily, he wondered what would happen if it were to rain. Surely, the rain would come only when it was needed, light and mild, continuing without significant wind till enough had fallen. Moreover, it would always come at known times so that the Alphans would be ready for it, Trevize imagined.

The window he was facing looked out to sea, and far out at the horizon it seemed to Trevize that he could make out a bank of clouds similar to those that so nearly filled the skies everywhere but over this little spot of Eden.

There were advantages to weather control.

Eventually, they were served by a young woman on tiptoeing feet. They were not asked for their choice, but were merely served. There was a small glass of milk, a larger of grape juice, a still larger of water. Each diner received two large poached eggs, with slivers of white cheese on the side. Each also had a large platter of broiled fish and small roasted potatoes, resting on cool, green lettuce leaves.

Bliss looked with dismay at the quantity of food before her and was clearly at a loss where to begin. Fallom had no such trouble. She drank the grape juice thirstily and with clear evidence of approval, then chewed away at the fish and potatoes. She was about to use her fingers for the purpose, but Bliss held up a large spoon with tined ends that could serve as a fork as well, and Fallom accepted it.

Pelorat smiled his satisfaction and cut into the eggs at once.

Trevize, saying, 'Now to be reminded what real eggs taste like,' followed suit.

Hiroko, forgetting to eat her own breakfast in her delight at the manner in which the others ate (for even Bliss finally began, with obvious relish) said, at last, 'Is it well?'

'It is well,' said Trevize, his voice somewhat muffled. 'This island has no shortage of food, apparently. – Or do you serve us more than you should, out of politeness?'

Hiroko listened with intent eyes, and seemed to grasp the meaning for she said, 'No, no, respected sir. Our land is bountiful, our sea even more so. Our ducks give eggs, our goats both cheese and milk. And there are our grains. Above all, our sea is filled with countless varieties of fish in numberless quantity. The whole Empire could eat at our tables and consume not the fish of our sea.'

Trevize smiled discreetly. Clearly, the young Alphan had not the smallest idea of the true size of the Galaxy.

He said, 'You call this island New Earth, Hiroko. Where, then, might Old Earth be?'

She looked at him in bewilderment. '*Old* Earth, say you? I crave pardon, respected sir. I take not thy meaning.'

Trevize said, 'Before there was a New Earth, your people must have lived elsewhere. Where was this elsewhere from which they came?'

'I know naught of that, respected sir,' she said, with troubled gravity. 'This land has been mine all my life, and my mother's and grandmother's before me; and, I doubt not, their grandmother's and great-grandmother's before them. Of any other land, I know naught.'

'But,' said Trevize, descending to gentle argumentation, 'you speak of this land as *New* Earth. Why do you call it that?'

'Because, respected sir,' she replied, equally gentle, 'that is what it is called by all since the mind of woman goeth not to the contrary.'

'But it is *New* Earth, and therefore, a later Earth. There must be an *Old* Earth, a former one, for which it was named. Each morning there is a new day, and that implies that earlier there had existed an old day. Don't you see that this must be so?'

'Nay, respected sir. I know only what this land is called. I know of naught else, nor do I follow this reasoning of thine which sounds very much like what we call here chop-logic. I mean no offence.'

And Trevize shook his head and felt defeated.

77

Trevize leaned towards Pelorat, and whispered, 'Wherever we go, whatever we do, we get no information.'

'We know where Earth is, so what does it matter?' said Pelorat, doing little more than move his lips.

'I want to know something *about* it.'

'She's very young. Scarcely a repository of information.'

Trevize thought about that, then nodded, 'Right, Janov.'

He turned to Hiroko and said, 'Miss Hiroko, you haven't asked us why we are here in your land.'

Hiroko's eyes fell, and she said, 'That would be but scant courtesy until you have all eaten and rested, respected sir.'

'But we have eaten, or almost so, and we have recently rested, so I shall tell you why we are here. My friend, Dr Pelorat, is a scholar on our world, a learned man. He is a mythologist. Do you know what that means?'

'Nay, respected sir, I do not.'

'He studies old tales as they are told on different worlds. Old tales are known as myths or legends and they interest Dr Pelorat. Are there learned ones on New Earth who know the old tales of this world?'

Hiroko's forehead creased slightly into a frown of thought. She said, 'This is not a matter in which I am myself skilled. We have an old man in these parts who loves to talk of ancient days. Where he may have learned these things, I know not, and methinks he may have spun his notions out of air, or heard them from others who did so spin. This is perhaps the material which thy learned companion would hear, yet I would not mislead thee. It is in my mind,' she looked to right and left as though unwilling to be overheard, 'that the old man is but a prater, though many listen willingly to him.'

Trevize nodded. 'Such prating is what we wish. Would it be possible for you to take my friend to this old man –'

'Monolee he calls himself.'

'– to Monolee, then. And do you think Monolee would be willing to speak to my friend?'

'He? Willing to speak?' said Hiroko scornfully. 'Thou must ask, rather, if he be ever ready to cease from speaking. He is but a man, and will therefore speak, if allowed, till a fortnight hence, with no pause. I mean no offence, respected sir.'

'No offence taken. Would you lead my friend to Monolee now?'

'That may anyone do at any time. The ancient is ever home and ever ready to greet an ear.'

Trevize said, 'And perhaps an older woman would be willing to come and sit with Madam Bliss. She has the child to care for and can not move about too much. It would please her to have company, for women, as you know, are fond of –'

'Prating?' said Hiroko, clearly amused. 'Why, so men say, although I have observed that men are always the greater babblers. Let the men return from their fishing, and one will vie with another in telling greater flights of fancy concerning their catches. None will mark them nor believe, but this will not stop them, either. But enough of my prating, too. – I will have a friend of my mother's, one whom I can see through the window, stay with Madam Bliss and the child, and before that she will guide your friend, the respected doctor, to the aged Monolee. If your friend will hear as avidly as Monolee will prate, thou wilt scarcely part them in this life. Wilt thou pardon my absence a moment?'

When she had left, Trevize turned to Pelorat and said, 'Listen, get what you can out of the old man, and Bliss, you find out what you can from whoever stays with you. What you want is anything about Earth.'

'And you?' said Bliss. 'What will you do?'

'I will remain with Hiroko, and try to find a third source.'

Bliss smiled, 'Ah yes. Pel will be with this old man; I with an old woman. You will force yourself to remain with this fetchingly unclad young woman. It seems a reasonable division of labour.'

'As it happens, Bliss, it *is* reasonable.'

'But you don't find it depressing that the reasonable division of labour should work out so, I suppose.'

'No, I don't. Why should I?'

'Why should you, indeed?'

Hiroko was back, and sat down again. 'It is all arranged. The respected Dr Pelorat will be taken to Monolee; and the respected Madam Bliss, together with her child, will have company. May I be granted, then, respected sir Trevize, the boon of further conversation with thee, may-hap of this Old Earth of which thou –'

'Pratest?' asked Trevize.

'Nay,' said Hiroko, laughing. 'But thou dost well to mock me. I showed thee but discourtesy ere now in answering thy question on this matter. I would fain make amends.'

Trevize turned to Pelorat. 'Fain?'

'Be eager,' said Pelorat, softly.

Trevize said, 'Miss Hiroko, I felt no discourtesy, but if it will make you feel better, I will gladly speak with you.'

'Kindly spoken. I thank thee,' said Hiroko, rising.

Trevize rose, too. 'Bliss,' he said, 'make sure Janov remains safe.'

'Leave that to me. As for you, you nave your –' She nodded towards his holsters.

'I don't think I'll need them,' said Trevize uncomfortably.

He followed Hiroko out of the dining room. The sun was higher in the sky now and the temperature was still warmer. There was an other-worldly smell as always. Trevize remembered it had been faint on Comporellon, a little musty on Aurora, and rather delightful on Solaria. (On Melpomenia, they were in space suits where one is only aware of the smell of one's own body.) In every case, it disappeared in a matter of hours as the osmic centres of the nose grew saturated.

Here, on Alpha, the odour was a pleasant grassy fragrance under the warming effect of the sun, and Trevize felt a bit annoyed, knowing that this, too, would soon disappear.

They were approaching a small structure that seemed to be built of a pale pink plaster.

'This,' said Hiroko, 'is my home. It used to belong to my mother's younger sister.'

She walked in and motioned Trevize to follow. The door was open or, Trevize noticed as he passed through, it would be more accurate to say there was no door.

Trevize said, 'What do you do when it rains.'

'We are ready. It will rain two days hence, for three hours ere dawn, when it is coolest, and when it will moisten the soil most powerfully. Then I have but to draw this curtain, both heavy and water repellent, across the door.'

She did so as she spoke. It seemed made of a strong canvas-like material.

'I will leave it in place now,' she went on. 'All will then know I am within but not available, for I sleep or am occupied in matters of importance.'

'It doesn't seem much of a guardian of privacy.'

'Why should it not be? See, the entrance is covered.'

'But anyone could shove it aside.'

'With disregard of the wishes of the occupant?' Hiroko looked shocked. 'Are such things done on thy world? It would be barbarous.'

Trevize grinned. 'I only asked.'

She led him into the second of two rooms, and, at her invitation, he seated himself in a padded chair. There was something claustrophobic about the blockish smallness and emptiness of the rooms, but the house seemed designed for little more than seclusion and rest. The window openings were small and near the ceiling, but there were dull mirror strips in a careful pattern along the walls, which reflected light diffusely. There were slits in the floor from which a gentle, cool breeze uplifted. Trevize saw no signs of artificial lighting and wondered if Alphans had to wake at sunrise and go to bed at sunset.

He was about to ask, but Hiroko spoke first, saying, 'Is Madam Bliss thy woman companion?'

Trevize said cautiously, 'Do you mean by that, is she my sexual partner?'

Hiroko coloured. 'I pray thee, have regard for the decencies of polite conversation, but I *do* mean private pleasantry.'

'No, she is the woman companion of my learned friend.'

'But thou art the younger, and the more goodly.'

'Well, thank you for your opinion, but it is not Bliss's opinion. She likes Dr Pelorat much more than she does me.'

'That much surprises me. Will he not share?'

'I have not asked him whether he would, but I'm sure he wouldn't. Nor would I want him to.'

Hiroko nodded her head wisely. 'I know. It is her fundament.'

'Her fundament?'

'Thou knowest. This.' And she slapped her own dainty rear end.

'Oh, that! I understand you. Yes, Bliss is generously proportioned in her pelvic anatomy.' He made a curving gesture with his hands and winked. (And Hiroko laughed.)

Trevize said, 'Nevertheless, a great many men enjoy that kind of generosity of figure.'

'I cannot believe so. Surely it would be a sort of gluttony to wish excess of that which is pleasant in moderation. Wouldst thou think more of me if my breasts were massive and dangling, with nipples pointing to toes? I have, in good sooth, seen such, yet have I not seen men flock to them. The poor women so afflicted must needs cover their monstrosities – as Madam Bliss does.'

'Such oversize wouldn't attract me, either, though I am sure that Bliss doesn't cover her breasts for any imperfection they may have.'

'Thou does not, then, disapprove of my visage or form?'

'I would be a madman to do so. You are beautiful.'

'And what dost thou for pleasantries on this ship of thine, as thou flittest from one world to the next – Madam Bliss being denied thee?'

'Nothing, Hiroko. There's nothing to do. I think of pleasantries on occasion and that has its discomforts, but we who travel through space know well that there are times when we must do without. We make up for it at other times.'

'If it be a discomfort, how may that be removed?'

'I experience considerably more discomfort since you've brought up the subject. I don't think it would be polite to suggest how I might be comforted.'

'Would it be discourtesy, were I to suggest a way?'

'It would depend entirely on the nature of the suggestion.'

'I would suggest that we be pleasant with each other.'

'Did you bring me here, Hiroko, that it might come to this?'

Hiroko said, with a pleased smile, 'Yes. It would be both my hostess-duty of courtesy, and it would be my wish, too.'

'If that's the case, I will admit it is my wish, too. In fact, I would like very much to oblige you in this. I would be – uh – *fain* to do thee pleasure.'

18

The Music Festival

78

Lunch was in the same dining room in which they had had breakfast. It was full of Alphans, and with them were Trevize and Pelorat, made thoroughly welcome. Bliss and Fallom ate separately, and more or less privately, in a small annex.

There were several varieties of fish, together with soup in which there were strips of what might well have been boiled kid. Loaves of bread were there for the slicing, butter and jam for the spreading. A salad, large and diffuse, came afterwards, and there was a notable absence of any dessert, although fruit juices were passed about in apparently inexhaustible pitchers. Both Foundationers were forced to be abstemious after their heavy breakfast, but everyone else seemed to eat freely.

'How do they keep from getting fat?' wondered Pelorat in a low voice.

Trevize shrugged. 'Lots of physical labour, perhaps.'

It was clearly a society in which decorum at meals was not greatly valued. There was a miscellaneous hubbub of shouting, laughing, and thumping on the table with thick, obviously unbreakable, cups. Women were as loud and raucous as men, albeit in higher pitch.

Pelorat winced, but Trevize, who now (temporarily, at least) felt no trace of the discomfort he had spoken of to Hiroko, felt both relaxed and good-natured.

He said, 'Actually, it has its pleasant side. These are people who appear to enjoy life and who have few, if any, cares. Weather is what they make it and food is unimaginably plentiful. This is a golden age for them that simply continues and continues.'

He had to shout to make himself heard, and Pelorat shouted back, 'But it's so noisy.'

'They're used to it.'

'I don't see how they can understand each other in this riot.'

Certainly, it was all lost on the two Foundationers. The queer pronunciation and the archaic grammar and word order of the Alphan language made it impossible to understand at the intense sound levels. To the Foundationers, it was like listening to the sounds of a zoo in fright.

It was not till after lunch that they rejoined Bliss in a small structure, which Trevize found to be rather inconsiderably different from Hiroko's quarters, and which had been assigned them as their own temporary living quarters. Fallom was in the second room, enormously relieved to be alone, according to Bliss, and attempting to nap.

Pelorat looked at the door-gap in the wall and said uncertainly, 'There's very little privacy here. How can we speak freely?'

'I assure you,' said Trevize, 'that once we pull the canvas barrier across the door, we won't be disturbed. The canvas makes it impenetrable by all the force of social custom.'

Pelorat glanced at the high, open windows. 'We can be overheard.'

'We need not shout. The Alphans won't eavesdrop. Even when they stood outside the windows of the dining room at breakfast, they remained at a respectful distance.'

Bliss smiled. 'You've learned so much about Alphan customs in the time you spent alone with gentle little Hiroko, and you've gained such confidence in their respect for privacy. What happened?'

Trevize said, 'If you're aware that the tendrils of my mind have undergone a change for the better and can guess the reason, I can only ask you to leave my mind alone.'

'You know very well that Gaia will not touch your mind under any circumstances short of life-crisis, and you know why. Still, I'm not mentally blind. I could sense what happened a kilometre away. Is this your invariable custom on space voyages, my erotomaniac friend?'

'Erotomaniac? Come, Bliss. Twice on this entire trip. Twice!'

'We were only on two worlds that had functioning human females on them. Two out of two, and we had only been a few hours on each.'

'You are well aware I had no choice on Comporellon.'

'That makes sense. I remember what she looked like.' For a few moments, Bliss dissolved in laughter. Then she said, 'Yet I don't think Hiroko held you helpless in her mighty grip, or inflicted her irresistible will on your cringing body.'

'Of course not. I was perfectly willing. But it was her suggestion, just the same.'

Pelorat said, with just a tinge of envy in his voice, 'Does this happen to you all the time, Golan?'

'Of course it must, Pel,' said Bliss. 'Women are helplessly drawn to him.'

'I wish that were so,' said Trevize, 'but it isn't. And I'm glad it isn't – I do have other things I want to do in life. Just the same, in this case I *was* irresistible. After all, we were the first people from another world that Hiroko had ever seen or, apparently, that anyone now alive on Alpha had ever seen. I gathered from things she let slip, casual remarks, that she had the rather exciting notion that I might be different from Alphans, either anatomically or in my technique. Poor thing. I'm afraid she was disappointed.'

'Oh?' said Bliss. 'Were you?'

'No,' said Trevize. 'I have been on a number of worlds and I have had my experiences. And what I had discovered is that people are people and sex is sex, wherever one goes. If there are noticeable differences, they are usually both trivial and unpleasant. The perfumes I've encountered in my time! I remember when a young woman simply couldn't manage unless there was music loudly played, music that consisted of a desperate screeching sound. So she played the music and then *I* couldn't manage. I assure you – if it's the same old thing, then I'm satisfied.'

'Speaking of music,' said Bliss, 'we are invited to a musicale after dinner. A very formal thing, apparently, that is being held in our honour. I gather the Alphans are very proud of their music.'

Trevize grimaced. 'Their pride will in no way make the music sound better to our ears.'

'Hear me out,' said Bliss. 'I gather that their pride is that they play expertly on very archaic instruments. *Very* archaic. We may get some information about Earth by way of them.'

Trevize's eyebrows shot up. 'An interesting thought. And that reminds me that both of you may already have information. Janov, did you see this Monolee that Hiroko told us about?'

'Indeed I did,' said Pelorat. 'I was with him for three hours and

Hiroko did not exaggerate. It was a virtual monologue on his part and when I left to come to lunch, he clung to me and would not let me go until I promised to return whenever I could in order that I might listen to him some more.'

'And did he say anything of interest?'

'Well, he, too – like everybody else – insisted that Earth was thoroughly and murderously radioactive; that the ancestors of the Alphans were the last to leave and that if they hadn't, they would have died. – And Golan, he was so emphatic that I couldn't help believing him. I'm convinced that Earth *is* dead, and that our entire search is, after all, useless.'

79

Trevize sat back in his chair, staring at Pelorat, who was sitting on a narrow cot. Bliss, having risen where she had been sitting next to Pelorat, looked from one to the other.

Finally, Trevize said, 'Let me be the judge as to whether our search is useless or not, Janov. Tell me what the garrulous old man had to say to you – in brief of course.'

Pelorat said, 'I took notes as Monolee spoke. It helped reinforce my role as scholar, but I don't have to refer to them. He was quite stream-of-consciousness in his speaking. Each thing he said would remind him of something else, but, of course, I have spent my life trying to organize information in the search of the relevant and significant, so that it's second nature for me now to be able to condense a long and incoherent discourse –'

Trevize said gently, 'Into something just as long and incoherent? To the point, dear Janov.'

Pelorat cleared his throat uneasily. 'Yes, certainly, old chap. I'll try to make a connected and chronological tale out of it. Earth was the original home of humanity and of millions of species of plants and animals. It continued so for countless years until hyperspatial travel was invented. Then the Spacer worlds were founded. They broke away from Earth, developed their own cultures, and came to despise and oppress the mother planet.

'After a couple of centuries of this, Earth managed to regain its freedom, though Monolee did not explain the exact manner in which this was done, and I dared not ask questions, even if he had given me a chance to interrupt, which he did not, for that might merely have sent him into new byways. He did mention a culture-hero named Elijah Baley, but the references were so characteristic of the habit of attributing to one figure the accomplishments of generations that there was little value in attempting to –'

Bliss said, 'Yes, Pel dear, we understand that part.'

Again, Pelorat paused in midstream and reconsidered. 'Of course. My apologies. Earth initiated a second wave of settlements, founding many new worlds in a new fashion. The new group of Settlers proved more vigorous than the Spacers, outpaced them, defeated them, outlasted them, and eventually, established the Galactic Empire. During the course of the wars between the Settlers and the Spacers – no, not wars, for he used the word "conflict", being very careful about that – the Earth became radioactive.'

Trevize said, with clear annoyance, 'That's ridiculous, Janov. How can a world *become* radioactive? Every world is very slightly radioactive to one degree or another from the moment of formation, and that radioactivity slowly decays. It doesn't *become* radioactive.'

Pelorat shrugged. 'I'm only telling you what he said. And he was only telling me what he had heard – from someone who only told him what *he* had heard – and so on. It's folk-history, told and retold over the generations, with who knows what distortions creeping in at each retelling.'

'I understand that, but are there no books, documents, ancient histories which have frozen the story at an early time and which could give us something more accurate than the present tale?'

'Actually, I managed to ask that question, and the answer is no. He said vaguely that there were books about it in ancient times and that they had long ago been lost, but that what he was telling us was what had been in those books.'

'Yes, well distorted. It's the same story. In every world we go to, the records of Earth have, in one way or another, disappeared. – Well, how did he say the radioactivity began on Earth?'

'He didn't, in any detail. The closest he came to saying so was that the Spacers were reasonable, but then I gathered that the Spacers were the demons on whom the people of Earth blamed all misfortune. The radioactivity –'

A clear voice overrode him here. 'Bliss, am I a Spacer?'

Fallom was standing in the narrow doorway between the two rooms, hair tousled and the nightgown she was wearing (designed to fit Bliss's more ample proportions) having slid off one shoulder to reveal an undeveloped breast.

Bliss said, 'We worry about eavesdroppers outside and we forget the one inside. – Now, Fallom, why do you say that?' She rose and walked towards the youngster.

Fallom said, 'I don't have what they have,' she pointed at the two men, 'or what you have, Bliss. I'm different. Is that because I'm a Spacer?'

'You are, Fallom,' said Bliss, soothingly, 'but little differences don't matter. Come back to bed.'

Fallom became submissive as she always did when Bliss willed her to be so. She turned and said, 'Am I a demon? What is a demon?'

Bliss said over her shoulder, 'Wait one moment for me. I'll be right back.'

She was, within five minutes. She was shaking her head. 'She'll be sleeping now till I wake her. I should have done that before, I suppose, but any modification of the mind must be the result of necessity.' She added defensively, 'I can't have her brood on the differences between her genital equipment and ours.'

Pelorat said, 'Some day she'll have to know she's hermaphroditic.'

'Some day,' said Bliss, 'but not now. Go on with the story, Pel.'

'Yes,' said Trevize, 'before something else interrupts us.'

'Well, Earth became radioactive, or at least its crust did. At that time, Earth had had an enormous population that was centred in huge cities that existed for the most part underground –'

'Now that,' put in Trevize, 'is surely not so. It must be local patriotism glorifying the golden age of a planet, and the details were simply a distortion of Trantor in *its* golden age, when it was the Imperial capital of a Galaxy-wide system of worlds.'

Pelorat paused, then said, 'Really, Golan, you mustn't teach me my business. We mythologists know very well that myths and legends contain borrowings, moral lessons, nature cycles, and a hundred other distorting influences, and we labour to cut them away and get to what might be a kernel of truth. In fact, these same techniques must be applied to the most sober histories for no one writes the clear and apparent truth – if such a thing can even be said to exist. For now, I'm telling you more or less what Monolee told me, though I suppose I am adding distortions of my own, try as I might not to do so.'

'Well, well,' said Trevize. 'Go on, Janov. I meant no offence.'

'And I've taken none. The huge cities, assuming they existed, crumbled and shrank as the radioactivity slowly grew more intense until the population was but a remnant of what it had been, clinging precariously to regions that were relatively radiation-free. The population was kept down by rigid birth control and by the euthanasia of people over sixty.'

'Horrible,' said Bliss indignantly.

'Undoubtedly,' said Pelorat, 'but that is what they did, according to Monolee, and that might be true for it is certainly not complimentary to the Earthpeople and it is not likely that an uncomplimentary lie would be made up. The Earthpeople, having been despised and oppressed by the Spacers, were now despised and oppressed by the Empire, though here we may have exaggeration out of self-pity, which is a very seductive emotion. There is the case –'

'Yes, yes, Pelorat, another time. Please go on with Earth.'

'I beg your pardon. The Empire, in a fit of benevolence, agreed to substitute imported radiation-free soil and to cart away the contaminated soil. Needless to say, that was an enormous task which the Empire soon tired of, especially as this period (if my guess is right) coincided with the fall of Kandar V, after which the Empire had many more things to worry about than Earth.

'The radioactivity continued to grow more intense, the population continued to fall, and finally the Empire, in another fit of benevolence, offered to transport the remnant of the population to a new world of their own – to *this* world, in short.

'At an earlier period, it seems an expedition had stocked the ocean so that by the time the plans for the transplantation of Earthpeople were being developed, there was a full oxygen atmosphere and an ample supply of food on Alpha. Nor did any of the worlds of the Galactic Empire covet this world because there is a certain natural antipathy to planets that circle stars of a binary system. There are so few suitable planets in such a system, I suppose, that even suitable ones are rejected because of the assumption that there must be something wrong with them. This is a common thought-fashion. There is the well-known case, for instance, of –'

'Later with the well-known case, Janov,' said Trevize. 'On with the transplantation.'

'What remained,' said Pelorat, hurrying his words a little, 'was to prepare a land-base. The shallowest part of the ocean was found and sediment was raised from deeper parts to add to the shallow sea-bottom and, finally, to produce the island of New Earth. Boulders and coral were dredged up and added to the island. Land plants were seeded so that root-systems might help make the new land firm. Again, the Empire had set itself an enormous task. Perhaps continents were planned at first, but by the time this one island was produced, the Empire's moment of benevolence had passed.

'What was left of Earth's population was brought here. The Empire's fleets carried off its men and machinery, and they never returned. The Earthpeople, living on New Earth, found themselves in complete isolation.'

Trevize said, 'Complete? Did Monolee say that no one from elsewhere in the Galaxy has ever come here till we did?'

'Almost complete,' said Pelorat. 'There is nothing to come here for, I suppose, even if we set aside the superstitious distaste for binary systems. Occasionally, at long intervals, a ship would come, as ours did, but it would eventually leave and there has never been a follow-up. And that's it.'

Trevize said, 'Did you ask Monolee where Earth was located?'

'Of course I asked that. He didn't know.'

'How can he know so much about Earth's history without knowing where it is located?'

'I asked him specifically, Golan, if the star that was only a parsec or so distant from Alpha might be the sun about which Earth revolved. He didn't know what a parsec was, and I said it was a short distance, astronomically speaking. He said, short or long, he did not know where Earth was located and he didn't know anyone who knew, and, in his opinion, it was wrong to try to find it. It should be allowed, he said, to move endlessly through space in peace.'

Trevize said, 'Do you agree with him?'

Pelorat shook his head sorrowfully, 'Not really. But he said that at the rate the radioactivity continued to increase, the planet must have become totally uninhabitable not long after the transplantation took place and that by now it must be burning intensely so that no one can approach.'

'Nonsense,' said Trevize firmly. 'A planet cannot become radio-active and, having done so, continuously increase in radioactivity. Radioactivity can only decrease.'

'But Monolee is so sure of it. So many people we've talked to on various worlds unite in this – that Earth is radioactive. Surely, it is useless to go on.'

80

Trevize drew a deep breath, then said, in a carefully controlled voice, 'Nonsense, Janov. That's not true.'

Pelorat said, 'Well now, old chap, you mustn't believe something just because you want to believe it.'

'My wants have nothing to do with it. In world after world we find all records of Earth wiped out. Why should they be wiped out if there is nothing to hide; if Earth is a dead, radioactive world that cannot be approached?'

'I don't know, Golan.'

'Yes, you do. When we were approaching Melpomenia, you said that the radioactivity might be the other side of the coin. Destroy records to remove accurate information; supply the tale of radioactivity to insert inaccurate information. Both would discourage any attempt to find Earth, and we mustn't be deluded into discouragement.'

Bliss said, 'Actually, you seem to think the nearby star is Earth's sun. Why, then, continue to argue the question of radioactivity? What does it matter? Why not simply go to the nearby star and see if it is Earth, and, if so, what it is like?'

Trevize said, 'Because those on Earth must be, in their way, extraordinarily powerful, and I would prefer to approach with some knowledge of the world and its inhabitants. As it is, since I continue to remain ignorant of Earth, approaching it is dangerous. It is my notion that I leave the rest of you here in Alpha and that I proceed to Earth by myself. One life is quite enough to risk.'

'No, Golan,' said Pelorat earnestly. 'Bliss and the child might wait here, but I must go with you. I have been searching for Earth since before you were born and I cannot stay behind when the goal is so close, whatever dangers might threaten.'

'Bliss and the child will *not* wait here,' said Bliss. 'I am Gaia, and Gaia can protect us even against Earth.'

'I hope you're right,' said Trevize gloomily, 'but Gaia could not prevent the elimination of all early memories of Earth's role in its founding.'

'That was done in Gaia's early history when it was not yet well organized, not yet advanced. Matters are different now.'

'I hope that is so. – Or is it that you have gained information about Earth this morning that we don't have? I did ask that you speak to some of the older women that might be available here.'

'And so I did.'

Trevize said, 'And what did you find out?'

'Nothing about Earth. There is a total blank there.'

'Ah.'

'But they are advanced biotechnologists.'

'Oh?'

'On this small island, they have grown and tested innumerable strains of plants and animals and designed a suitable ecological balance, stable and self-supporting, despite the few species with which they began. They have improved on the species of ocean life that they found when they arrived here a few thousand years ago, increasing their nutritive value and improving their taste. It is their biotechnology that has made this world such a cornucopia of plenty. They have plans for themselves, too.'

'What kind of plans?'

Bliss said, 'They know perfectly well they cannot reasonably expect to expand their range under present circumstances, confined as they are to the one small patch of land that exists on their world, but they dream of becoming amphibious.'

'Of becoming *what*?'

'Amphibious. They plan to develop gills in addition to lungs. They dream of being able to spend substantial periods of time underwater; of finding shallow regions and building structures on the ocean bottom. My informant was quite glowing about it but she admitted that this had been a goal of the Alphans for some centuries now and that little, if any, progress had been made.'

Trevize said, 'That's two fields in which they might be more advanced than we are; weather control and biotechnology. I wonder what their techniques are.'

'We'd have to find specialists,' said Bliss, 'and they might not be willing to talk about it.'

Trevize said, 'It's not *our* primary concern here, but it would clearly pay the Foundation to attempt to learn from this miniature world.'

Pelorat said, 'We manage to control the weather fairly well on Terminus, as it is.'

'Control is good on many worlds,' said Trevize, 'but always it's a matter of the world as a whole. Here the Alphans control the weather of a small portion of the world and they must have techniques we don't have. – Anything else, Bliss.'

'Social invitations. These appear to be a holiday-making people, in whatever time they can take from farming and fishing. After dinner, tonight there'll be a music festival. I told you about that already. Tomorrow, during the day, there will be a beach festival. Apparently, all around the rim of the island there will be a congregation of everyone who can get away from the fields in order that they might enjoy the water and celebrate the sun, since it will be raining for the next day or two. Then the next morning, the fishing fleet will come back, beating the rain, and by evening there will be a food festival, sampling the catch.'

Pelorat groaned. 'The meals are ample enough as it is. What would a food festival be like?'

'I gather that it will feature not quantity, but variety. In any case, all four of us are invited to participate in all the festivals, especially the music festival tonight.'

'On the antique instruments?' asked Trevize.

'That's right.'

'What makes them antique, by the way? Primitive computers?'

'No, no. That's the point. It isn't electronic music at all, but mechanical. They described it to me. They scrape strings, blow in tubes, and bang on surfaces.'

'I hope you're making that up,' said Trevize, appalled.

'No, I'm not. And I understand that your Hiroko will be blowing on one of the tubes – I forget its name – and you ought to be able to endure that.'

'As for myself,' said Pelorat, 'I would love to go. I know very little about primitive music and I would like to hear it.'

'She is not "my Hiroko",' said Trevize coldly. 'But are the instruments of the type once used on Earth, do you suppose?'

'So I gathered,' said Bliss. 'At least the Alphan women said they were designed long before their ancestors came here.'

'In that case,' said Trevize, 'it may be worth listening to all that scraping, tootling, and banging, for whatever information it might conceivably yield concerning Earth.'

81

Oddly enough, it was Fallom who was most excited at the prospect of a musical evening. She and Bliss had bathed in the small outhouse behind their quarters. It had a bath with running water, hot and cold (or, rather, warm and cool), a washbowl, and a commode. It was totally clean and usable and, in the late afternoon sun, it was even well lit and cheerful.

As always, Fallom was fascinated with Bliss's breasts and Bliss was reduced to saying (now that Fallom understood Galactic) that on her world that was the way people were. To which Fallom said, inevitably, 'Why?' and Bliss, after some thought, deciding there was no sensible way of answering, returned the universal reply, 'Because!'

When they were done, Bliss helped Fallom put on the undergarment supplied them by the Alphans and worked out the system whereby the skirt went on over it. Leaving Fallom unclothed from the waist up seemed reasonable enough. She herself, while making use of Alphan garments below the waist (rather tight about the hips), put on her own blouse. It seemed silly to be too inhibited to expose breasts in a society where all women did, especially since her own were not large and were as shapely as any she had seen but – there it was.

The two men took their turn at the outhouse next, Trevize muttering the usual male complaint concerning the time the women had taken.

Bliss turned Fallom about to make sure the skirt would hold in place over her boyish hips and buttocks. She said, 'It's a very pretty skirt, Fallom. Do you like it?'

Fallom stared at it in a mirror and said, 'Yes, I do. Won't I be cold with nothing on, though?' and she ran her hands down her bare chest.

'I don't think so, Fallom. It's quite warm on this world.'

'*You* have something on.'

'Yes, I do. That's how it is on my world. Now, Fallom, we're going to be with a great many Alphans during dinner and afterwards. Do you think you can bear that?'

Fallom looked distressed, and Bliss went on, 'I will sit on your right side and I will hold you. Pel will sit on the other side, and Trevize will sit across the table from you. We won't let anyone talk to you, and you won't have to talk to anyone.'

'I'll try, Bliss,' Fallom piped in her highest tones.

'Then afterwards,' said Bliss, 'some Alphans will make music for us in their own special way. Do you know what music is?' She hummed in the best imitation of electronic harmony that she could.

Fallom's face lit up. 'You mean——' The last word was in her own language, and she burst into song.

Bliss's eyes widened. It was a beautiful tune, even though it was wild, and rich in trills. 'That's right. Music,' she said.

Fallom said excitedly, 'Jemby made' (she hesitated then decided to use the Galactic word) 'music all the time. It made music on a—' Again a word in her own language.

Bliss repeated the word doubtfully, 'On a feefal?'

Fallom laughed, 'Not feeful,——'

With both words juxtaposed like that, Bliss could hear the

difference, but she despaired of reproducing the second. She said, 'What does it look like?'

Fallom's as yet limited vocabulary in Galactic did not suffice for an accurate description, and her gestures did not produce any shape clearly in Bliss's mind.

'He showed me how to use the—', Fallom said proudly. 'I used my fingers just the way Jemby did, but it said that soon I wouldn't have to.'

'That's wonderful, dear,' said Bliss. 'After dinner, we'll see if the Alphans are as good as your Jemby was.'

Fallom's eyes sparkled and pleasant thoughts of what was to follow carried her through a lavish dinner despite the crowds and laughter and noise all about her. Only once, when a dish was accidentally upset, setting off shrieks of excitement fairly close to them, did Fallom look frightened, and Bliss promptly held her close in a warm and protective hug.

'I wonder if we can arrange to eat by ourselves,' she muttered to Pelorat. 'Otherwise, we'll have to get off this world. It's bad enough eating all this Isolate animal protein, but I *must* be able to do it in peace.'

'It's only high spirits,' said Pelorat, who would have endured anything within reason that he felt came under the heading of primitive behaviour and beliefs.

– And then the dinner was over, and the announcement came that the music festival would soon begin.

82

The hall in which the music festival was to be held was about as large as the dining room, and there were folding seats (rather uncomfortable, Trevize found out) for about a hundred and fifty people. As honoured guests, the visitors were led to the front row, and various Alphans commented politely and favourably on their clothes.

Both men were bare above the waist and Trevize tightened his abdominal muscles whenever he thought of it and stared down, on occasion, with complacent self-admiration at his dark-haired chest. Pelorat, in his ardent observation of everything about him, was indifferent to his own appearance. Bliss's blouse drew covert stares of puzzlement but nothing was said concerning it.

Trevize noted that the hall was only about half-full and that the large majority of the audience were women, since, presumably, so many men were out to sea.

Pelorat nudged Trevize and whispered, 'They have electricity.'

Trevize looked at the vertical tubes on the walls, and at others on the ceiling. They were softly luminous.

'Fluorescence,' he said. 'Quite primitive.'

'Yes, but they do the job, and we've got those things in our rooms and in the outhouse. I thought they were just decorative. If we can find out how to work them, we won't have to stay in the dark.'

Bliss said, irritably, 'They might have told us.'

Pelorat said, 'They thought we'd know; that anyone would know.'

Four women now emerged from behind screens and seated themselves in a group in the space at the front. Each held an instrument of varnished wood of a similar shape, but one that was not easily describable. The instruments were chiefly different in size. One was quite small, two somewhat larger, and the fourth considerably larger. Each woman also held a long rod in the other hand.

The audience whistled softly as they came in, in response to which the four women bowed. Each had a strip of gauze bound fairly tightly across their breasts as though to keep them from interfering with the instrument.

Trevize, interpreting the whistles as signs of approval, or of pleased anticipation, felt it only polite to add his own. At that, Fallom added a trill that was far more than a whistle and that was beginning to attract attention when pressure from Bliss's hand stopped her.

Three of the women, without preparation, put their instruments under their chins, while the largest of the instruments remained between the legs of the fourth woman and rested on the floor. The long rods in the right hand of each was sawed across the strings stretching nearly the length of the instrument, while the fingers of the left hand shifted rapidly along the upper ends of those strings.

This, thought Trevize, was the 'scraping' he had expected, but it didn't sound like scraping at all. There was a soft and melodious succession of notes; each instrument doing something of its own and the whole fusing pleasantly.

It lacked the infinite complexity of electronic music ('real music' as Trevize could not help but think of it) and there was a distinct sameness to it. Still, as time passed, and his ear grew accustomed to this odd system of sound, he began to pick out subtleties. It was wearisome to have to do so, and he thought, longingly, of the clamour and mathematical precision and purity of the real thing, but it occurred to him that if he listened to the music of these simple wooden devices long enough he might well grow to like it.

It was not till the concert was some forty-five minutes old that Hiroko stepped out. She noticed Trevize in the front row at once and smiled at him. He joined the audience in the soft whistle of approval with a whole heart. She looked beautiful in a long and most elaborate skirt, a large flower in her hair, and nothing at all over her breasts since (apparently) there was no danger of their interference with the instrument.

Her instrument proved to be a dark wooden tube about two thirds of a metre long and nearly two centimetres thick. She lifted the instrument to her lips and blew across an opening near one end, producing a thin, sweet note that wavered in pitch as her fingers manipulated metal objects along the length of the tube.

At the first sound, Fallom clutched at Bliss's arm, and said, 'Bliss, that's a——' and the word sounded like 'feeful' to Bliss.

Bliss shook her head firmly at Fallom, who said, in a lower voice, 'But it is!'

Others were looking in Fallom's direction. Bliss put her hand firmly over Fallom's mouth, and leaned down to mutter an almost subliminally forceful, 'Quiet!' into her ear.

Fallom listened to Hiroko's playing quietly thereafter, but her fingers moved spasmodically, as though they were operating the objects along the length of the instrument.

The final player in the concert was an elderly man who had an instrument with fluted sides suspended over his shoulders. He pulled it in and out while one hand flashed across a succession of white and dark objects at one end, pressing them down in groups.

Trevize found this sound particularly wearing, rather barbaric, and unpleasantly like the memory of the barking of the dogs on Aurora – not that the sound was like barking, but the emotions it gave rise to were similar. Bliss looked as though she would like to place her hands over her ears, and Pelorat had a frown on his face. Only Fallom seemed to enjoy it for she was tapping her foot lightly and Trevize, when he noticed that, realized, to his own surprise, that there was a beat to the music that matched Fallom's footfall.

It came to an end at last and there was a perfect storm of whistling, with Fallom's trill clearly heard above it all.

Then the audience broke up into small conversational groups and became as loud and raucous as Alphans seemed to be on all public occasions. The various individuals who had played in the concert stood about in front of the room and spoke to those people who came up to congratulate them.

Fallom evaded Bliss's grasp and ran up to Hiroko.

'Hiroko,' she cried out, gaspingly, 'let me see the——'

'The what, dear one?' said Hiroko.

'The thing you made the music with.'

'Oh.' Hiroko laughed. 'That's a flute, little one.'

'May I see it?'

'Well.' Hiroko opened a case and took out the instrument. It was in three parts, but she put it together quickly, held it towards Fallom with the mouthpiece near her lips, and said, 'There, blow thou thy breath across this.'

'I know. I know,' said Fallom eagerly, and reached for the flute.

Automatically, Hiroko snatched it away and held it high. 'Blow, child, but touch not.'

Fallom seemed disappointed. 'May I just look at it, then? I won't touch it.'

'Certainly, dear one.'

She held out the flute again and Fallom stared at it earnestly.

And then, the fluorescent lighting in the room dimmed very slightly, and the sound of a flute's note, a little uncertain and wavering, made itself heard.

Hiroko, in surprise, nearly dropped the flute, and Fallom cried out, 'I did it. I did it. Jemby said someday I could do it.'

Hiroko said, 'Was it thou that made the sound?'

'Yes, I did. I did.'

'But how didst thou do so, child?'

Bliss said, red with embarrassment, 'I'm sorry, Hiroko. I'll take her away.'

'No,' said Hiroko. 'I wish her to do it again.'

A few of the nearest Alphans had gathered to watch. Fallom furrowed her brow as though trying hard. The fluorescents dimmed rather more than before, and again there was the note of the flute, this time pure and steady. Then it became erratic as the metal objects along the length of the flute moved of their own accord.

'It's a little different from the——' Fallom said, a little breathlessly, as though the breath that had been activating the flute had been her own instead of power-driven air.

(Pelorat said to Trevize, 'She must be getting the energy from the electric current that feeds the fluorescents.')

'Try again,' said Hiroko in a choked voice.

Fallom closed her eyes. The note was softer now and under firmer control. The flute played by itself, manoeuvred by no fingers, but moved by distant energy, transduced through the still immature lobes of Fallom's brain. The notes which began as almost random settled into a musical succession and now everyone in the hall had gathered around Hiroko and Fallom, as Hiroko held the flute gently with thumb and forefinger at either end, and Fallom, eyes closed, directed the current of air and the movement of the keys.

'It's the piece I played,' whispered Hiroko.

'I remember it,' said Fallom, nodding her head slightly, trying not to break her concentration.

'Thou didst not miss a note,' said Hiroko, when it was done.

'But it's not right, Hiroko. You didn't do it right.'

Bliss said, 'Fallom! That's not polite. You mustn't –'

'Please,' said Hiroko peremptorily, 'do not interfere. Why is it not right, child?'

'Because I would play it differently.'

'Show me, then.'

Again the flute played, but in more complicated fashion, for the forces that pushed the keys did so more quickly, in more rapid succession and in more elaborate combinations than before. The music was more complex, and infinitely more emotional and moving. Hiroko stood rigid and there was not a sound to be heard anywhere in the room.

Even after Fallom had finished playing, there was not a sound until Hiroko drew a deep breath and said, 'Little one, hast thou ever played that before?'

'No,' said Fallom, 'before this I could only use my fingers, and I can't do my fingers like that.' Then, simply and with no trace of vaunting, 'No one can.'

'Canst thou play anything else?'

'I can make something up.'

'Dost thou mean – improvise?'

Fallom frowned at the word and looked towards Bliss. Bliss nodded and Fallom said, 'Yes.'

'Please do so, then,' said Hiroko.

Fallom paused and then thought for a minute or two, then began slowly, in a very simple succession of notes, the whole being rather dreamy. The fluorescent lights dimmed and brightened as the amount of power exerted intensified and faded. No one seemed to notice, for it seemed to be the effect of the music rather than the cause, as though a ghostly electrical spirit were obeying the dictates of the sound waves.

The combination of notes then repeated itself a bit more loudly, then a bit more complexly, then in variations that, without ever losing the clearly heard basic combination, became more stirring and more exciting until it was almost impossible to breathe. And finally, it descended much more rapidly than it had ascended and did so with the effect of a swooping dive that brought the listeners to ground level even while they still retained the feeling they were high in the air.

There followed sheer pandemonium that split the air, and even Trevize, who was used to a totally different kind of music, thought sadly, 'And now I'll never hear that again.'

When a most reluctant quiet had returned, Hiroko held out her flute. 'Here, Fallom, this is thine!'

Fallom reached for it eagerly, but Bliss caught hold of the child's outstretched arm and said, 'We can't take it, Hiroko. It's a valuable instrument.'

'I have another, Bliss. Not quite as good, but that is how it should be. This instrument belongeth to the person who playeth it best. Never have I heard such music and it would be wrong for me to own an instrument I cannot use to full potential. Would that I knew how the instrument could be made to play without being touched.'

Fallom took the flute and, with an expression of deep content, held it tightly to her chest.

83

Each of the two rooms of their quarters were lit by one fluorescent light. The outhouse had a third. The lights were dim, and were uncomfortable to read by, but at least the rooms were no longer dark.

Yet they now lingered outside. The sky was full of stars, something that was always fascinating to a native of Terminus, where the night sky was all but starless and in which only the faint foreshortened cloud of the Galaxy was prominent.

Hiroko had accompanied them back to their chambers for fear they would get lost in the dark, or that they would stumble. All the way back, she held Fallom's hand, and then, after lighting the fluorescents for them, remained outside with them, still clutching at the youngster.

Bliss tried again, for it was clear to her that Hiroko was in a state of a difficult conflict of emotions, 'Really, Hiroko, we cannot take your flute.'

'No, Fallom must have it.' But she seemed on edge just the same.

Trevize continued to look at the sky. The night was truly dark, a darkness that was scarcely affected by the trickle of light from their own chambers; and much less so by the tiny sparks of other houses farther off.

He said, 'Hiroko, do you see that star that is so bright? What is it called?'

Hiroko looked up casually and said, with no great appearance of interest, 'That's the Companion.'

'Why is it called that?'

'It circleth our Sun every eighty Standard Years. It is an evening star at this time of year. Thou canst see it in daytime, too, when it lieth above the horizon.'

Good, thought Trevize. She's not totally ignorant of astronomy. He said, 'Do you know that Alpha has another companion, a very small, dim one that's much further away than that bright star. You can't see it without a telescope.' (He hadn't seen it himself, hadn't bothered to search for it, but the ship's computer had the information in its memory banks.)

She said indifferently, 'We are told that in school.'

'But now what about that one? You see those six stars in a zigzag line?'

Hiroko said, 'That is Cassiopeia.'

'Really?' said Trevize, startled. 'Which star?'

'All of them. The whole zigzag. It is Cassiopeia.'

'Why is it called that?'

'I lack the knowledge. I know nothing of astronomy, respected Trevize.'

'Do you see the lowermost star in the zigzag, the one that's brighter than the other stars? What is that?'

'It is a star. I know not its name.'

'But except for the two companion stars, it's the closest of all the stars to Alpha. It is only a parsec away.'

Hiroko said, 'Sayest thou so? I know that not.'

'Might it not be the star about which Earth revolves?'

Hiroko looked at the star with a faint flash of interest. 'I know not. I have never heard any person say so.'

'Don't you think it might be?'

'How can I say? None knoweth where Earth might be. I – I must leave thee, now. I will be taking my shift in the fields tomorrow morning before the beach festival. I'll see you all there, right after lunch. Yes? Yes?'

'Certainly, Hiroko.'

She left suddenly, half-running in the dark. Trevize looked after her, then followed the others into the dimly lit cottage.

He said, 'Can you tell whether she was lying about Earth, Bliss?'

Bliss shook her head. 'I don't think she was. She is under enormous tension, something I was not aware of until after the concert. It existed before you asked her about the stars.'

'Because she gave away her flute, then?'

'Perhaps. I can't tell.' She turned to Fallom. 'Now, Fallom, I want you to go into your room. When you're ready for bed, go to the outhouse, use the potty, then wash your hands, your face, and your teeth.'

'I would like to play the flute, Bliss.'

'Just for a little while, and *very* quietly. Do you understand, Fallom? And you must stop when I tell you to.'

'Yes, Bliss.'

The three were now alone; Bliss in the one chair and the men sitting each on his cot.

Bliss said, 'Is there any point in staying on this planet any longer?'

Trevize shrugged, 'We never did get to discuss Earth in connection with the ancient instruments, and we might find something there. It might also pay to wait for the fishing fleet to return. The men might know something the stay-at-homes don't.'

'*Very* unlikely, I think,' said Bliss. 'Are you sure it's not Hiroko's dark eyes that hold you?'

Trevize said impatiently. 'I don't understand, Bliss. What have you to do with what I choose to do? Why do you seem to arrogate to yourself the right of sitting in moral judgement on me?'

'I'm not concerned with your morals. The matter affects our expedition. You want to find Earth so that you can finally decide whether you are right in choosing Galaxia over Isolate worlds. I want you to so decide. You say you need to visit Earth to make the decision and you seem to be convinced that Earth revolves about that bright star in the sky. Let us go there, then. I admit it would be useful to have some information about it before we go, but it is clear to me that the information is not forthcoming here. I do not wish to remain simply because you enjoy Hiroko.'

'Perhaps we'll leave,' said Trevize. 'Let me think about it, and Hiroko will play no part in my decision, I assure you.'

Pelorat said, 'I feel we ought to move on to Earth, if only to see whether it is radioactive or not. I see no point in waiting longer.'

'Are you sure it's not Bliss's dark eyes that drive you?' said Trevize, a bit spitefully, then, almost at once, 'No, I take that back, Janov. I was just being childish. Still – this is a charming world, quite apart from Hiroko, and I must say that under other circumstances I would be tempted to remain indefinitely. – Don't you think, Bliss, that Alpha destroys your theory about Isolates.'

'In what way?' asked Bliss.

'You've been maintaining that every truly isolated world turns dangerous and hostile.'

'Even Comporellon,' said Bliss evenly, 'which is rather out of the main current of Galactic activity for all that it is, in theory, an Associated Power of the Foundation Federation.'

'But *not* Alpha. This world is totally isolated, but can you complain of their friendliness and hospitality? They feed us, clothe us, shelter us, put on festivals in our honour, urge us to stay on. What fault is there to find with them?'

'None, apparently. Hiroko even gives you her body.'

Trevize said angrily, 'Bliss, what bothers you about that? She didn't give me her body. We gave each other our bodies. It was entirely mutual, entirely pleasurable. Nor can you say that you hesitate to give your body as it suits you.'

'Please, Bliss,' said Pelorat. 'Golan is entirely right. There is no reason to object to his private pleasures.'

'As long as they don't affect us,' said Bliss obdurately.

'They do not affect us,' said Trevize. 'We will leave, I assure you. A delay to search further for information will not be long.'

'Yet I don't trust Isolates,' said Bliss, 'even when they come bearing gifts.'

Trevize flung up his arms. 'Reach a conclusion, then twist the evidence to fit. How like a –'

'Don't say it,' said Bliss, dangerously. 'I am not a woman. I am Gaia. It is Gaia, not I, who is uneasy.'

'There is no reason to –' and at that point there was a scratching at the door.

Trevize froze. 'What's that?' he said, in a low voice.

Bliss shrugged lightly. 'Open the door and see. You tell us this is a kindly world that offers no danger.'

Nevertheless, Trevize hesitated, until a soft voice from the other side of the door called out softly, 'Please. It is I!'

It was Hiroko's voice. Trevize threw the door open.

Hiroko entered quickly. Her cheeks were wet.

'Close the door,' she gasped.

'What is it?' asked Bliss.

Hiroko clutched at Trevize. 'I could not stay away. I tried, but I endured it not. Go thou, and all of you. Take the youngster with you quickly. Take the ship away – away from Alpha – while it is yet dark.'

'But why?' asked Trevize.

'Because else wilt thou die; and all of you.'

84

The three Outworlders stared frozenly at Hiroko for a long moment. Then Trevize said, 'Are you saying your people will kill us.'

Hiroko said, as the tears rolled down her cheeks. 'Thou art already on the road to death, respected Trevize. And the others with you. – Long ago, those of learning devised a virus, harmless to us, but deadly to Outworlders. We have been made immune.' She shook Trevize's arm in distraction. 'Thou art infected.'

'How?'

'When we had our pleasure. It is one way.'

Trevize said, 'But I feel entirely well.'

'The virus is as yet inactive. It will be made active when the fishing fleet returns. By our laws, all must decide on such a thing – even the men. All will surely decide it must be done, and we keep you here till that time, two mornings hence. Leave now while it is yet dark and none suspects.'

Bliss said sharply, 'Why do your people do this?'

'For our safety. We are few and have much. We do not wish Outworlders to intrude. If one cometh and then reporteth our lot, others will come, and so when, once in a long while, a ship arriveth, we must make certain it leaveth not.'

'But then,' said Trevize, 'why do you warn us away?'

'Ask not the reason. – Nay, but I will tell you, since I hear it again. Listen –'

From the next room, they could hear Fallom playing softly – and infinitely sweetly.

Hiroko said, 'I cannot bear the destruction of that music, for the young one will also die.'

Trevize said sternly, 'Is that why you gave the flute to Fallom? Because you knew you would have it once again when she was dead?'

Hiroko looked horrified. 'Nay, that was not in my mind. And when it came to mind at length, I knew it must not be done. Leave with the child, and with her, take the flute that I may never see it more. Thou wilt be safe back in space and, left inactive, the virus now in thy body will die after a time. In return, I ask that none of you ever speak of this world, that none else may know of it.'

'We will not speak of it,' said Trevize.

Hiroko looked up. In a lower voice, she said, 'May I not kiss thee once ere thou leavest?'

Trevize said, 'No. I have been infected once and surely that is enough.' And then, a little less roughly, he added, 'Don't cry. People will ask why you are crying and you'll be unable to reply. – I'll forgive what you did to me in view of your present effort to save us.'

Hiroko straightened, carefully wiped her cheeks with the back of her hands, took a deep breath, and said, 'I thank thee for that,' and left quickly.

Trevize said, 'We will put out the light, and we will wait a while, and then we will leave. – Bliss, tell Fallom to stop playing her instrument. Remember to take the flute, of course. – Then we will make our way to the ship, if we can find it in the dark.'

'I will find it,' said Bliss. 'Clothing of mine is on board and, however dimly, that, too, is Gaia. Gaia will have no trouble finding Gaia.' And she vanished into her room to collect Fallom.

Pelorat said, 'Do you suppose that they've managed to damage our ship in order to keep us on the planet.'

'They lack the technology to do it,' said Trevize grimly. When Bliss emerged, holding Fallom by the hand, Trevize put out the lights.

They sat quietly in the dark for what seemed half the night, and might have been half an hour. Then Trevize slowly and silently opened the door. The sky seemed a bit more cloudy, but stars shone. High in the sky now was Cassiopeia, with what might be Earth's sun burning brightly at its lower tip. The air was still and there was no sound.

Carefully, Trevize stepped out, motioning the others to follow. One of his hands dropped, almost automatically, to the butt of his neuronic whip. He was sure he would not have to use it, but –

Bliss took the lead, holding Pelorat's hand, who held Trevize. Bliss's other hand held Fallom, and Fallom's other hand held the flute. Feeling gently with her feet in the nearly total darkness, Bliss guided the others towards where she felt, very weakly, the Gaia-ness of her clothing on board the *Far Star*.

Part VII

Earth

19

Radioactive?

85

The *Far Star* took off quietly, rising slowly through the atmosphere, leaving the dark island below. The few faint dots of light beneath them dimmed and vanished, and as the atmosphere grew thinner with height, the ship's speed grew greater, and the dots of light in the sky above them grew more numerous and brighter.

Eventually, they looked down upon the planet Alpha, with only a crescent illuminated and that crescent largely wreathed in clouds.

Pelorat said, 'I suppose they don't have an active space technology. They can't follow us.'

'I'm not sure that that cheers me up much,' said Trevize, his face dour, his voice disheartened. 'I'm infected.'

'But with an inactive strain,' said Bliss.

'Still, it can be made active. They had a method. What is the method?'

Bliss shrugged. 'Hiroko said the virus, left inactive, would eventually die in a body unadapted to it – as yours is.'

'Yes?' said Trevize angrily. 'How does she know that? For that matter, how do I know that Hiroko's statement wasn't a self-consoling lie? And isn't it possible that the method of activation, whatever it is, might not be duplicated naturally? A particular chemical, a type of radiation, a – a – who knows what? I may sicken suddenly, and then the three of you would die, too. Or if it happens after we have reached a populated world, there may be a vicious pandemic which fleeing refugees would carry to other worlds.'

He looked at Bliss. 'Is there something you can do about it?'

Slowly, Bliss shook her head. 'Not easily. There are parasites making up Gaia – micro-organisms, worms. They are a benign part of the ecological balance. They live and contribute to the world conscious-ness, but never overgrow. They live without doing noticeable harm. The trouble is, Trevize, the virus that affects you is not part of Gaia.'

'You say "not easily",' said Trevize, frowning. 'Under the circum-stances, can you take the trouble to do it even though it might be difficult? Can you locate the virus in me and destroy it? Can you, failing that, at least strengthen my defences?'

'Do you realize what you ask, Trevize? I am not acquainted with the microscopic flora of your body. I might not easily tell a virus in the cells of your body from the normal genes inhabiting them. It would be even more difficult to distinguish between viruses your body is accustomed to and those with which Hiroko infected you. I will try to do it, Trevize, but it will take time and I may not succeed.'

'Take time,' said Trevize. 'Try.'

'Certainly,' said Bliss.

Pelorat said, 'If Hiroko told the truth, Bliss, you might be able to find viruses that seem to be already diminishing in vitality, and you could accelerate their decline.'

'I could do that,' said Bliss. 'It is a good thought.'

'You won't weaken?' said Trevize. 'You will have to destroy precious bits of life when you kill those viruses, you know.'

'You are being sardonic, Trevize,' said Bliss coolly, 'but, sardonic or not, you are pointing out a true difficulty. Still, I can scarcely fail to put you ahead of the virus. I will kill them if I have the chance, never fear. After all, even if I fail to consider you,' and her mouth twitched as though she were repressing a smile, 'then certainly Pelorat and Fallom are also at risk, and you might feel more confi-dence in my feeling for them than in my feeling for you. You might even remember that I myself am at risk.'

'I have no faith in your self-love,' muttered Trevize. 'You're perfectly ready to give up your life for some high motive. I'll accept your concern for Pelorat, however.' Then, he said, 'I don't hear Fallom's flute. Is anything wrong with her?'

'No,' said Bliss. 'She's asleep. A perfectly natural sleep that I had nothing to do with. And I would suggest that, after you work out the Jump to the star we think is Earth's sun, we all do likewise. I need it badly and I suspect you do, too, Trevize.'

'Yes, if I can manage. – You were right, you know, Bliss.'

'About what, Trevize?'

'About Isolates. New Earth was not a paradise, however much it might have seemed like one. That hospitality – all that outgoing friendliness at first – was to put us off our guard, so that one of us might be easily infected. And all the hospitality afterwards, the festivals of this and that, were designed to keep us there till the fishing fleet returned and the activation could be carried through. And it would have worked but for Fallom and her music. It might be you were right there, too.'

'About Fallom?'

'Yes, I didn't want to take her along, and I've never been happy with her being on the ship. It was your doing, Bliss, that we have her here and it was she who, unwittingly, saved us. And yet –'

'And yet what?'

'Despite that, I'm *still* uneasy at Fallom's presence. I don't know why.'

'If it will make you feel better, Trevize, I don't know that we can lay all the credit at Fallom's feet. Hiroko advanced Fallom's music as her excuse for committing what the other Alphans would surely consider to be an act of treason. She may even have believed this, but there was something in her mind in addition, something that I vaguely detected but could not surely identify, something that perhaps she was ashamed to let emerge into her conscious mind. I am under the impression that she felt a warmth for you, and would not willingly see you die, regardless of Fallom and her music.'

'Do you really think so?' said Trevize, smiling slightly for the first time since they had left Alpha.

'I think so. You must have a certain proficiency at dealing with women. You persuaded Minister Lizalor to allow us to take our ship and leave Comporellon, and you helped influence Hiroko to save our lives. Credit where it's due.'

Trevize smiled more broadly. 'Well if you say so. – On to Earth, then.' He disappeared into the pilot-room with a step that was almost jaunty.

Pelorat lingering behind, said, 'You soothed him after all, didn't you, Bliss?'

'No, Pelorat, I never touched his mind.'

'You certainly did when you pampered his male vanity so outrageously.'

'Entirely indirect,' said Bliss, smiling.

'Even so, thank you, Bliss.'

86

After the Jump, the star that might well have been Earth's sun was still a tenth of a parsec away. It was the brightest object in the sky by far, but it was still no more than a star.

Trevize kept its light filtered for ease of viewing, and studied it sombrely.

He said, 'There seems no doubt that it is the virtual twin of Alpha, the star that new Earth circles. Yet Alpha is in the computer map and this star is not. We don't have a name for this star, we aren't given its statistics, we lack any information concerning its planetary system, if it has one.'

Pelorat said, 'Isn't that what we would expect if Earth circles this sun. Such a blackout of information would fit with the fact that all information about Earth seems to have been eliminated.'

'Yes, but it could also mean that it's a Spacer world that just happened not to be on the list on the wall of the Melpomenian building. We can't be altogether sure that that list was complete. Or this star could be without planets and therefore perhaps not worth listing on a computer map which is primarily used for military and commercial purposes. – Janov, is there any legend that tells of Earth's sun being a mere parsec or so from a twin of itself.'

Pelorat shook his head. 'I'm sorry, Golan, but no such legend occurs to me. There may be one, though. My memory isn't perfect. I'll search for it.'

'It's not important. Is there any name given to Earth's sun?'

'Some different names are given. I imagine there must be a name in each of the different languages.'

'I keep forgetting that Earth had many languages.'

'It must have had. It's the only way of making sense out of many of the legends.'

Trevize said peevishly, 'Well, then, what do we do? We can't tell anything about the planetary system from this distance, and we have to move closer. I would like to be cautious, but there's such a thing as excessive and unreasoning caution, and I see no evidence of possible danger. Presumably anything powerful enough to wipe the Galaxy clean of information about Earth may be powerful enough to wipe us out even at this distance if they seriously did not wish to be located, but nothing's happened. It isn't rational to stay here forever on the mere possibility that something might happen if we move closer, is it?'

Bliss said, 'I take it the computer detects nothing that might be interpreted as dangerous.'

'When I say I see no evidence of possible danger, it's the computer I'm relying on. I certainly can't see anything with the unaided eye. I wouldn't expect to.'

'Then I take it you're just looking for support in making what you consider a risky decision. All right, then. I'm with you. We haven't come this far in order to turn back for no reason, have we?'

'No,' said Trevize. 'What do you say, Pelorat?'

Pelorat said, 'I'm willing to move on, if only out of curiosity. It would be unbearable to go back without knowing if we have found Earth.'

'Well, then,' said Trevize, 'we're all agreed.'

'Not all,' said Pelorat. 'There's Fallom.'

Trevize looked astonished. 'Are you suggesting we consult the child? Of what value would her opinion be even if she had one? Besides, all she would want would be to get back to her own world.'

'Can you blame her for that?' asked Bliss, warmly.

And because the matter of Fallom had arisen, Trevize became aware of her flute, which was sounding in a rather stirring march rhythm.

'Listen to her,' he said, 'where has she ever heard anything in march rhythm?'

'Perhaps Jemby played marches on the flute for her.'

Trevize shook his head. 'I doubt it. Dance rhythms, I should think, lullabies. – Listen, Fallom makes me uneasy. She learns too quickly.'

'I *help* her,' said Bliss. 'Remember that. And she's *very* intelligent and she has been extraordinarily stimulated in the time she's been with us. New sensations have flooded her mind. She's seen space, different worlds, many people, all for the first time.'

Fallom's march music grew wilder and more richly barbaric.

Trevize sighed and said, 'Well, she's here, and she's producing music that seems to breathe optimism, and delight in adventure. I'll take that as her vote in favour of moving in more closely. Let us do so cautiously, then, and check this sun's planetary system.'

'If any,' said Bliss.

Trevize smiled thinly. 'There's a planetary system. It's a bet. Choose your sum.'

87

'You lose,' said Trevize abstractedly. 'How much money did you decide to bet.'

'None. I never accepted the wager,' said Bliss.

'Just as well. I wouldn't like to accept the money, anyway.'

They were some 10 billion kilometres from the Sun. It was still star-like, but it was nearly 1/4000 as bright as the average sun would have been when viewed from the surface of a habitable planet.

'We can see two planets under magnification, right now,' said Trevize. 'From their measured diameters and from the spectrum of the reflected light, they are clearly gas giants.'

The ship was well outside the planetary plane, and Bliss and Pelorat, staring over Trevize's shoulder at the viewscreen, found themselves looking at two tiny crescents of greenish light. The smaller was in the somewhat thicker phase of the two.

Trevize said, 'Janov! It is correct, isn't it, that Earth's sun is supposed to have four gas giants.'

'According to the legends. Yes,' said Pelorat.

'The nearest of the four to the sun is the largest, and the second nearest has rings. Right?'

'Large prominent rings, Golan. Yes. Just the same, old chap, you have to allow for exaggeration in the telling and retelling of a legend. If we should not find a planet with an extraordinary ring system, I don't think we ought to let that count seriously against this being Earth's star.'

'Nevertheless, the two we see may be the furthest, and the two nearer ones may well be on the other side of the Sun and too far to be easily located against the background of stars. We'll have to move still closer – and beyond the sun to the other side.'

'Can that be done in the presence of the star's nearby mass?'

'With reasonable caution, the computer can do it, I'm sure. If it judges the danger to be too great, however, it will refuse to budge us, and we can then move in cautious, smaller steps.'

His mind directed the computer – and the starfield on the viewscreen changed. The star brightened sharply and then moved off the viewscreen as the computer, following directions, scanned the sky for another gas giant. It did so successfully.

All three onlookers stiffened and stared, while Trevize's mind, almost helpless with astonishment, fumbled at the computer to direct further magnification.

'Incredible,' gasped Bliss.

88

A gas giant was in view, seen at an angle that allowed most of it to be sunlit. About it, there curved a broad and brilliant ring of material, tipped so as to catch the sunlight on the side being viewed. It was brighter than the planet itself and along it, one third of the way in towards the planet was a narrow, dividing line.

Trevize threw in a request for maximum enhancement and the ring became ringlets, narrow and concentric, glittering in the sunlight. Only a portion of the ring system was visible on the viewscreen and the planet itself had moved off. A further direction from Trevize and one corner of the screen marked itself off and showed, within itself, a miniature of the planet and rings under lesser magnification.

'Is that sort of thing common?' asked Bliss, awed.

'No,' said Trevize. 'Almost every gas giant has rings of debris, but they tend to be faint and narrow. I once saw one in which the rings were narrow, but quite bright. But I never saw anything like this; or heard of it, either.'

Pelorat said, 'That's clearly the ringed giant the legends speak of. If this is really unique –'

'Really unique, as far as I know, or as far as the computer knows,' said Trevize.

'Then this *must* be the planetary system containing Earth. Surely, no one could invent such a planet. It would have had to have been seen to be described.'

Trevize said, 'I'm prepared to believe just about anything your legends say now. This is the sixth planet and Earth would be the third?'

'Right, Golan.'

'Then I would say we are less than 1.5 billion kilometres from Earth, and we haven't been stopped. Gaia stopped us when we approached.'

Bliss said, 'You were closer to Gaia when you were stopped.'

'Ah,' said Trevize, 'but it's my opinion Earth is more powerful than Gaia, and I take this to be a good sign. If we are not stopped, it may be that Earth does not object to our approach.'

'Or that there is no Earth,' said Bliss.

'Do you care to bet this time?' asked Trevize, grimly.

'What I think Bliss means,' put in Pelorat, 'is that Earth may be radioactive as everyone seems to think, and that no one stops us because there is no life on Earth.'

'No,' said Trevize, violently. 'I'll believe everything that's said about Earth, *but* that. We'll just close in on Earth and see for ourselves. And I have the feeling we won't be stopped.'

89

The gas giants were well behind. An asteroid belt lay just inside the gas giant nearest the sun. (It was the largest and most massive, just as the legends said.)

Inside the asteroid belt were four planets.

Trevize studied them carefully. 'The third is the largest. The size is appropriate and the distance from the Sun is appropriate. It could be habitable.'

Pelorat caught what seemed to be a note of uncertainty in Trevize's words.

He said, 'Does it have an atmosphere?'

'Oh, yes,' said Trevize. 'The second, third, and fourth planets all have atmospheres. And, as in the old children's tale, the second's is too dense, the fourth's is not dense enough, but the third's is just right.'

'Do you think it might be Earth, then?'

'Think?' said Trevize almost explosively. 'I don't have to think. It *is* Earth. It has the giant satellite you told me of.'

'It has?' and Pelorat's face broke into a wider smile than any that Trevize had ever seen upon it.

'Absolutely! Here, look at it under maximum magnification.'

Pelorat saw two crescents, one distinctly larger and brighter than the other.

'Is that smaller one the satellite?' he asked.

'Yes. It's rather farther from the planet than one might expect but it's definitely revolving about it. It's only the size of a small planet; in fact, it's smaller than any of the four inner planets circling the Sun. Still, it's large for a satellite. It's at least two thousand kilometres in diameter, which makes it in the size range of the large satellites that revolve about gas giants.'

'No larger?' Pelorat seemed disappointed. 'Then it's not a giant satellite?'

'Yes, it is. A satellite with a diameter of two to three thousand kilometres that is circling an enormous gas giant is one thing. That same satellite circling a small, rocky habitable planet is quite another. That satellite has a diameter roughly a quarter that of Earth. Where have you heard of such near-parity involving a habitable planet?'

Pelorat said timidly, 'I know very little of such things.'

Trevize said, 'Then take my word for it, Janov. It's unique. We're looking at something that is practically a double planet, and there are few habitable planets that have anything more than pebbles orbiting them. – Janov, if you consider that gas giant with its enormous ring system in sixth place, and this planet with its enormous satellite in third – both of which your legends told you about, against all credibility, before you ever saw them – then that world you're looking at *must* be Earth. It cannot conceivably be anything else. We've found it, Janov; we've found it.'

90

They were on the second day of their coasting progress towards Earth, and Bliss yawned over the dinner meal. She said, 'It seems to me we've spent more time coasting towards and away from planets than anything else. We've spent weeks at it, literally.'

'Partly,' said Trevize, 'that's because Jumps are dangerous *too* close to a star. And in *this* case, we're moving very slowly because I do not wish to advance into possible danger too quickly.'

'I thought you said you had the feeling we would not be stopped.'

'So I do, but I don't want to stake everything on a feeling.' Trevize looked at the contents of the spoon before putting it into his mouth and said, 'You know, I miss the fish we had on Alpha. We only had three meals there.'

'A pity,' agreed Pelorat.

'Well,' said Bliss, 'we visited five worlds and had to leave each one of them so hurriedly that we never had time to add to our food supplies and introduce variety. Even when the world had food to offer, as did Comporellon and Alpha, and, presumably –'

She did not complete the sentence, for Fallom, looking up quickly, finished it for her. 'Solaria? Could you get no food there? There is plenty of food there. As much as on Alpha. And better, too.'

'I know that, Fallom,' said Bliss. 'There was just no time.'

Fallom stared at her, solemnly. 'Will I ever see Jemby again, Bliss? Tell me the truth.'

Bliss said, 'You may, if we return to Solaria.'

'Will we ever return to Solaria?'

Bliss hesitated. 'I cannot say.'

'Now we go to Earth, is that right? Isn't that the planet where you say we all originated?'

'Where our *forebears* originated,' said Bliss.

'I can say "ancestors",' said Fallom.

'Yes, we are going to Earth.'

'Why?'

Bliss said lightly, 'Wouldn't anyone wish to see the world of their ancestors?'

'I think there's more to it. You all seem so concerned.'

'But we've never been there before. We don't know what to expect.'

'I think it is more than that.'

Bliss smiled. 'You've finished eating, Fallom dear, so why not go to the room and let us have a little serenade on your flute. You're playing it more beautifully all the time. Come, come.' She gave Fallom an accelerating pat on the rear end, and off Fallom went, turning only once to give Trevize a thoughtful look.

Trevize looked after her with clear distaste. 'Does that thing read minds?'

'Don't call her a "thing", Trevize,' said Bliss sharply.

'Does she read minds? You ought to be able to tell.'

'No, she doesn't. Nor can Gaia. Nor can the Second Foundationers. Reading minds in the sense of overhearing a conversation, or making out precise ideas is not something that can be done now, or in the foreseeable future. We can detect, interpret, and, to some extent, manipulate emotions, but that is not the same thing at all.'

'How do you know she can't do this thing that supposedly can't be done?'

'Because as you have just said, I ought to be able to tell.'

'Perhaps she is manipulating you so that you remain ignorant of the fact that she can.'

Bliss rolled her eyes upwards. 'Be reasonable, Trevize. Even if she had unusual abilities, she could do nothing with me for I am not Bliss, I am Gaia. You keep forgetting. Do you know the mental inertia represented by an entire planet? Do you think one Isolate, however talented, can overcome that?'

'You don't know everything, Bliss, so don't be overconfident,' said Trevize, sullenly. 'That th – *She* has been with us not very long. I couldn't learn anything but the rudiments of a language in that time, yet she already speaks Galactic perfectly and with virtually a full vocabulary. Yes, I know you've been helping her, but I wish you would stop.'

'I told you I was helping her, but I also told you she's fearfully intelligent. Intelligent enough so that I would like to have her part of Gaia. If we can gather her in; if she's still young enough; we might learn enough about the Solarians to absorb that entire world eventually. It might well be useful to us.'

'Does it occur to you that the Solarians are pathological Isolates even by *my* standards?'

'They wouldn't stay so as part of Gaia.'

'I think you're wrong, Bliss. I think that Solarian child is dangerous and that we should get rid of her.'

'How? Dump her through the air-lock? Kill her, chop her up, and add her to our food supply.'

Pelorat said, 'Oh, Bliss.'

And Trevize said, 'That's disgusting, and completely uncalled for.' He listened for a moment. The flute was sounding without flaw or waver, and they had been talking in half-whispers. 'When this is all over, we've got to return her to Solaria, and make sure that Solaria is forever cut off from the Galaxy. My own feeling is that it should be destroyed. I distrust and fear it.'

Bliss thought awhile and said, 'Trevize, I know that you have the knack of coming to a right decision, but I also know you have been antipathetic to Fallom from the start. I suspect that may just be because you were humiliated on Solaria and have taken a violent hatred to the planet and its inhabitants as a result. Since I must not tamper with your mind, I can't tell that for sure. Please remember that if we had not taken Fallom with us, we would be on Alpha right now – dead and, I presume, buried.'

'I know that, Bliss, but even so –'

'And her intelligence is to be admired, not envied.'

'I do not envy her. I fear her.'

'Her intelligence?'

Trevize licked his lips thoughtfully. 'No, not quite.'

'What, then?'

'I don't know. Bliss, if I knew what I feared, I might not have to fear it. It's something I don't quite understand.' His voice lowered, as though he were speaking to himself. 'The Galaxy seems to be crowded with things I don't understand. Why did I choose Gaia? Why must I find Earth? Is there a missing assumption in psycho-history? If there is, what is it? And on top of all that, why does Fallom make me uneasy?'

Bliss said, 'Unfortunately, I can't answer those questions.' She rose, and left the room.

Pelorat looked after her, then said, 'Surely things aren't totally black, Golan. We're getting closer and closer to Earth and once we reach it all mysteries may be solved. And so far nothing seems to be making any effort to stop us from reaching it.'

Trevize's eyes flickered towards Pelorat and he said in a low voice, 'I wish something would.'

Pelorat said, 'You do? Why should you want that?'

'Frankly, I'd welcome a sign of life.'

Pelorat's eyes opened wide. 'Have you found that Earth is radioactive after all?'

'Not quite. But it is warm. A bit warmer than I would have expected.'

'Is that bad?'

'Not necessarily. It may be rather warm but that wouldn't make it necessarily uninhabitable. The cloud cover is thick and it is definitely water vapour, so that those clouds, together with a copious water ocean could tend to keep things livable despite the temperature we calculated from microwave emission. I can't be sure, yet. It's just that –'

'Yes, Golan?'

'Well, if Earth *were* radioactive, that might well account for its being warmer than expected.'

'But that doesn't argue the reverse, does it? If it's warmer than expected that doesn't mean it *must* be radioactive.'

'No. No, it doesn't.' Trevize managed to force a smile. 'No use brooding, Janov. In a day or two, I'll be able to tell more about it and we'll know for sure.'

91

Fallom was sitting on the cot in deep thought when Bliss came into the room. Fallom looked up briefly, then down again.

Bliss said quietly, 'What's the matter, Fallom?'

Fallom said, 'Why does Trevize dislike me so much, Bliss?'

'What makes you think he dislikes you.'

'He looks at me impatiently – Is that the word?'

'It might be the word.'

'He looks at me impatiently when I am near him. His face always twists a little.'

'Trevize is having a hard time, Fallom.'

'Because he's looking for Earth?'

'Yes.'

Fallom thought awhile, then said, 'He is particularly impatient when I think something into moving.'

Bliss's lips tightened. 'Now, Fallom, didn't I tell you you must not do that, especially when Trevize is present?'

'Well, it was yesterday, right here in this room, and he was in the doorway and I didn't notice. I didn't know he was watching. It was just one of Pel's book-films, anyway, and I was trying to make it stand on one tip. I wasn't doing any harm.'

'It makes him nervous, Fallom, and I want you not to do it, whether he's watching or not.'

'Does it make him nervous because he can't do it?'

'Perhaps.'

'Can you do it?'

Bliss shook her head slowly, 'No, I can't.'

'It doesn't make *you* nervous when I do it. It doesn't make Pel nervous, either.'

'People are different.'

'I know,' said Fallom, with a sudden hardness that surprised Bliss and caused her to frown.

'What do you know, Fallom?'

'*I'm* different.'

'Of course, I just said so. People are different.'

'My shape is different. I can move things.'

'That's true.'

Fallom said, with a shade of rebelliousness, 'I *must* move things. Trevize should not be angry with me for that, and you should not stop me.'

'But why must you move things?'

'It is practice. Exerceez. – Is that the right word?'

'Not quite. Exercise.'

'Yes. Jemby always said I must train my – my –'

'Transducer-lobes?'

'Yes. And make them strong. Then, when I was grown up, I could power all the robots. Even Jemby.'

'Fallom, who did power all the robots if you did not?'

'Bander.' Fallom said it very matter-of-factly.

'Did you know Bander?'

'Of course. I viewed it many times. I was to be the next estate-head. The Bander estate would become the Fallom estate. Jemby told me so.'

'You mean Bander came to your –'

Fallom's mouth made a perfect O of shock. She said in a choked voice, 'Bander would never come to –' The youngster ran out of breath and panted a bit, then said, 'I *viewed* Bander's image.'

Bliss asked hesitantly, 'How did Bander treat you?'

Fallom looked at Bliss with a faintly puzzled eye. 'Bander would ask me if I needed anything; if I was comfortable. But Jemby was always near me so I never needed anything and I was always comfortable.'

Her head bent and she stared at the floor. Then she placed her hands over her eyes and said, 'But Jemby stopped. I think it was because Bander – stopped, too.'

Bliss said, 'Why do you say that?'

'I've been thinking about it. Bander powered all the robots, and if Jemby stopped, and all the other robots, too, it must be that Bander stopped. Isn't that so?'

Bliss was silent.

Fallom said, 'But when you take me back to Solaria I will power Jemby and all the rest of the robots, and I will be happy again.'

She was sobbing.

Bliss said, 'Aren't you happy with us, Fallom? Just a little? Sometimes?'

Fallom lifted her tear-stained face to Bliss and her voice trembled as she shook her head and said, 'I want Jemby.'

In an agony of sympathy, Bliss threw her arms about the youngster. 'Oh, Fallom, how I wish I could bring you and Jemby together again,' and was suddenly aware that she was weeping, too.

92

Pelorat entered and found them so. He halted in mid-step and said, 'What's the matter?'

Bliss detached herself and fumbled for a small tissue so that she might wipe her eyes. She shook her head, and Pelorat at once said, with heightened concern, 'But what's the *matter*?'

Bliss said, 'Fallom, just rest a little. I'll think of something to make things a little better for you. Remember – I love you just the same way that Jemby did.'

She seized Pelorat's elbow and rushed him out into the living room, saying, 'It's nothing, Pel – Nothing.'

'It's Fallom, though, isn't it? She still misses Jemby.'

'Terribly. And there's nothing we can do about it. I can tell her that I love her – and, truthfully, I do. How can you help loving a child so intelligent and gentle? – Fearfully intelligent. Trevize thinks *too* intelligent. She's seen Bander in her time, you know – or viewed it, rather, as a holographic image. She's not moved by that memory, however; she's very cold and matter-of-fact about it, and I can understand why. There was only the fact that Bander was owner of the estate and that Fallom would be the next owner that bound them. No other relationship at all.'

'Does Fallom understand that Bander is her father.'

'Her *mother*. If we agree that Fallom is to be regarded as feminine, so is Bander.'

'Either way, Bliss dear. Is Fallom aware of the parental relationship?'

'I don't know that she would understand what that is. She may, of course, but she gave no hint. However, Pel, she has reasoned out that Bander is dead, for it's dawned on her that Jemby's inactivation must be the result of power loss and since Bander supplied the power – that frightens me.'

Pelorat said thoughtfully, 'Why should it, Bliss? It's only a logical inference, after all.'

'Another logical inference can be drawn from that death. Deaths must be few and far distant on Solaria with its long-lived and isolated Spacers. Experience of natural death must be a limited one for any of them, and probably absent altogether for a Solarian child of Fallom's age. If Fallom continues to think of Bander's death, she's going to begin to wonder *why* Bander died, and the fact that it happened when we strangers were on the planet will surely lead her to the obvious cause and effect.'

'That we killed Bander?'

'It wasn't we who killed Bander, Pel. It was *I*.'

'She couldn't guess that.'

'But I would have to tell her that. She is annoyed with Trevize as it is, and he is clearly the leader of the expedition. She would take it for granted that it would be he who would have brought about the death of Bander, and how could I allow Trevize to bear the blame unjustly?'

'What would it matter, Bliss? The child feels nothing for her fath – mother. Only for her robot, Jemby.'

'But the death of the mother meant the death of her robot, too. I almost did own up to my responsibility. I was strongly tempted.'

'Why?'

'So I could explain it my way. So I could soothe her, forestall her own discovery of the fact in a reasoning process that would work it out in a way that would offer no justification for it.'

'But there *was* justification. It was self-defence. In a moment, we all would have been dead, if you had not acted.'

'It's what I would have said, but I could not bring myself to explain. I was afraid she wouldn't believe me.'

Pelorat shook his head. He said, sighing, 'Do you suppose it might have been better if we had not brought her. The situation makes you so unhappy.'

'No,' said Bliss angrily, 'don't say that. It would have made me infinitely more unhappy to have to sit here right now and remember that we had left an innocent child behind to be slaughtered mercilessly because of what *we* had done.'

'It's the way of Fallom's world.'

'Now, Pel, don't fall into Trevize's way of thinking. Isolates find it possible to accept such things and think no more about it. The way of Gaia is to save life, however, not destroy it – or to sit idly by while it is destroyed. Life of all kinds must, we all know, constantly be coming to an end in order that other life might endure, but never uselessly, never to no end. Bander's death, though unavoidable, is hard enough to bear; Fallom's would have been past all bounds.'

'Ah, well,' said Pelorat, 'I suppose you're right. – And in any case, it is not the problem of Fallom concerning which I've come to see you. It's Trevize.'

'What about Trevize?'

'Bliss, I'm worried about him. He's waiting to determine the facts about Earth, and I'm not sure he can withstand the strain.'

'I don't fear for him. I suspect he has a sturdy and stable mind.'

'We all have our limits. Listen, the planet Earth is warmer than he expected it to be; he told me so. I suspect that he thinks it may be too warm for life, though he's clearly trying to talk himself into believing that's not so.'

'Maybe he's right. Maybe it's *not* too warm for life.'

'Also, he admits it's possible that the warmth might possibly arise from a radioactive crust, but he is refusing to believe that also. – In a day or two, we'll be close enough so that the truth of the matter will be unmistakable. What if Earth *is* radioactive?'

'Then he'll have to accept the fact.'

'But – I don't know how to say this, or how to put it in mental terms. What if his mind –'

Bliss waited, then said, wryly, 'Blows a fuse?'

'Yes. Blows a fuse. Shouldn't you do something now to strengthen him? Keep him level and under control, so to speak?'

'No, Pel. I can't believe he's that fragile, and there is a firm Gaian decision that his mind must not be tampered with.'

'But that's the very point. He has this unusual "rightness", or whatever you want to call it. The shock of his entire project falling to nothingness at the moment when it seems successfully concluded may not destroy his brain, but it may destroy his "rightness". It's a very unusual property he has. Might it not be unusually fragile, too?'

Bliss remained for a moment in thought. Then she shrugged. 'Well, perhaps I'll keep an eye on him.'

93

For the next thirty-six hours, Trevize was vaguely aware that Bliss and, to a lesser degree, Pelorat, tended to dog his footsteps. Still, that was not utterly unusual in a ship as compact as theirs, and he had other things on his mind.

Now, as he sat at the computer, he was aware of them standing just inside the doorway. He looked up at them, his face blank.

'Well?' he said, in a very quiet voice.

Pelorat said, rather awkwardly, 'How are you, Golan?'

Trevize said, 'Ask Bliss. She's been staring at me intently for hours. She must be poking through my mind. – Aren't you, Bliss?'

'No, I am not,' said Bliss, evenly, 'but if you feel the need for my help, I can try. – Do you want my help?'

'No, why should I? Leave me alone. Both of you.'

Pelorat said, 'Please tell us what's going on.'

'Guess!'

'Is Earth –'

'Yes, it is. What everyone insisted on telling us, is perfectly true.' Trevize gestured at the viewscreen, where Earth presented its night side and was eclipsing the Sun. It was a solid circle of black against the starry sky, its circumference outlined by a broken orange curve.

Pelorat said, 'Is that orange the radioactivity?'

'No. Just refracted sunlight through the atmosphere. It would be a solid orange circle if the atmosphere weren't so cloudy. We can't see the radioactivity. The various radiations, even the gamma rays, are absorbed by the atmosphere. However, they do set up secondary radiations, comparatively feeble ones, but the computer can detect them. They're still invisible to the eye, but the computer can produce a photon of visible light for each particle or wave of radiation it receives and put Earth into false colour. Look.'

And the black circle glowed with a faint, blotchy blue.

'How much radioactivity is there?' asked Bliss, in a low voice. 'Enough to signify that no human life can exist there?'

'No life of any kind,' said Trevize. 'The planet is uninhabitable. The last bacterium, the last virus, is long gone.'

'Can we explore it?' said Pelorat. 'I mean, in space suits.'

'For a few hours – before we come down with irreversible radiation sickness.'

'Then what do we do, Golan?'

'Do?' Trevize looked at Pelorat with that same expressionless face. 'Do you know what I would like to do? I would like to take you and Bliss – and the child – back to Gaia and leave you all there forever. Then I would like to go back to Terminus and hand back the ship. Then I would like to resign from the Council, which ought to make Mayor Branno very happy. Then I would like to live on my pension and let the Galaxy go as it will. I won't care about the Seldon Plan, or about the Foundation, or about the Second Foundation, or about Gaia. The Galaxy can choose its own path. It will last my time and why should I care a snap as to what happens afterwards.'

'Surely, you don't mean it, Golan,' said Pelorat urgently.

Trevize stared at him for a while, and then he drew a long breath. 'No, I don't, but, oh, how I wish I could do exactly what I have just outlined to you.'

'Never mind that. What *will* you do?'

'Keep the ship in orbit about the Earth, rest, get over the shock of all this, and think of what to do next. Except that –'

'Yes?'

And Trevize blurted out, '*What* can I do next? What is there further to look for? What is there further to find?'

20

The Nearby World

94

For four successive meals, Pelorat and Bliss had seen Trevize only *at* meals. During the rest of the time, he was either in the pilot-room or in his bedroom. At mealtimes, he was silent. His lips remained pressed together and he ate little.

At the fourth meal, however, it seemed to Pelorat that some of the unusual gravity had lifted from Trevize's countenance. Pelorat cleared his throat twice, as though preparing to say something and then retreating.

Finally, Trevize looked up at him and said, 'Well?'

'Have you – have you thought it out, Golan?'

'Why do you ask?'

'You seem less gloomy.'

'I'm not less gloomy, but I *have* been thinking. Heavily.'

'May we know what?' asked Pelorat.

Trevize glanced briefly in Bliss's direction. She was looking firmly

at her plate, maintaining a careful silence, as though certain that
Pelorat would get further than she at this sensitive moment.

Trevize said, 'Are you also curious, Bliss?'

She raised her eyes for a moment. 'Yes. Certainly.'

Fallom kicked a leg of the table moodily, and said, 'Have we found
Earth?'

Bliss squeezed the youngster's shoulder. Trevize paid no attention.

He said, 'What we must start with is a basic fact. All information
concerning Earth has been removed on various worlds. That is bound
to bring us to an inescapable conclusion. Something on Earth is
being hidden. And yet, by observation, we see that Earth is radioactively deadly, so that anything on it is automatically hidden. No
one can land on it, and from this distance, when we are quite near
the outer edge of the magnetosphere and would not care to approach
Earth any more closely, there is nothing for us to find.'

'Can you be sure of that?' asked Bliss, softly.

'I have spent my time at the computer, analysing Earth in every
way it and I can. There is nothing. What's more, I *feel* there is
nothing. Why, then, has data concerning the Earth been wiped out?
Surely, whatever must be hidden is more effectively hidden now
than anyone can easily imagine, and there need be no human gilding
of this particular piece of gold.'

'It may be,' said Pelorat, 'that there was indeed something hidden
on Earth at a time when it had not yet grown so severely radioactive
as to preclude visitors. People on Earth may then have feared that
someone might land and find this whatever-it-is. It was *then* that
Earth tried to remove information concerning itself. What we have
now is a vestigial remnant of that insecure time.'

'No, I don't think so,' said Trevize. 'The removal of information
from the Galactic Library at Trantor seems to have taken place very
recently.' He turned suddenly to Bliss, 'Am I right?'

Bliss said evenly, 'I/we/Gaia gathered that much from the troubled
mind of the Second Foundationer Gendibal, when he, you and I
had the meeting with the Mayor of Terminus.'

Trevize said, 'So whatever must have had to be hidden because there existed the chance of finding it must still be in hiding *now*, and there must be danger of finding it *now* despite the fact that Earth is radioactive.'

'How is that possible?' asked Pelorat anxiously.

'Consider,' said Trevize. 'What if what was on Earth is no longer on Earth, but was removed when the radioactive danger grew greater? Yet though the secret is no longer on Earth, it may be that if we can find Earth, we would be able to reason out the place where the secret has been taken. If that were so, Earth's whereabouts would still have to be hidden.'

Fallom's voice piped up again. 'Because if we can't find Earth, Bliss says you'll take me back to Jemby.'

Trevize turned towards Fallom and glared – and Bliss said, in a low voice, 'I told you we *might*, Fallom. We'll talk about it later. Right now, go to your room and read, or play the flute, or anything else you want to do. Go – go.'

Fallom, frowning sulkily, left the table.

Pelorat said, 'But how can you say that, Golan. Here we are. We've located Earth. Can we now deduce where whatever it is might be if it isn't on Earth?'

It took a moment for Trevize to get over the moment of ill humour Fallom had induced. Then, he said, 'Why not? Imagine the radioactivity of Earth's crust growing steadily worse. The population would be decreasing steadily through death and emigration, and the secret, whatever it is, would be in increasing danger. Who would remain to protect it? Eventually, it would have to be shifted to another world, or the use of – whatever it was – would be lost to Earth. I suspect there would be reluctance to move it and it is likely that it would be done more or less at the last minute. Now, then, Janov, remember the old man on New Earth who filled your ears with his version of Earth's history?'

'Monolee?'

'Yes. He. Did he not say in reference to the establishment of New

Earth that what was left of Earth's population was brought to the planet?'

Pelorat said, 'Do you mean, old chap, that what we're searching for is now on New Earth? Brought there by the last of Earth's population to leave?'

Trevize said, 'Might that not be so? New Earth is scarcely better known to the Galaxy in general than Earth is, and the inhabitants are suspiciously eager to keep all Outworlders away.'

'We were there,' put in Bliss. 'We didn't find anything.'

'We weren't looking for anything but the whereabouts of Earth.'

Pelorat said, in a puzzled way, 'But we're looking for something with a high technology; something that can remove information from under the nose of the Second Foundation itself, and even from under the nose – excuse me, Bliss – of Gaia. Those people on New Earth may be able to control their patch of weather and may have some techniques of biotechnology at their disposal, but I think you'll admit that their level of technology is, on the whole, quite low.'

Bliss nodded. 'I agree with Pel.'

Trevize said, 'We're judging from very little. We never did see the men of the fishing fleet. We never saw any part of the island but the small patch we landed on. What might we have found if we had explored more thoroughly? After all, we didn't recognize the fluorescent lights till we saw them in action, and if it appeared that the technology was low, *appeared*, I say –'

'Yes?' said Bliss, clearly convinced.

'That could be part of the veil intended to obscure the truth.'

'Impossible,' said Bliss.

'Impossible? It was you who told me, back on Gaia, that at Trantor, the larger civilization was deliberately held at a level of low technology in order to hide the small kernel of Second Foundationers. Why might not the same strategy be used on New Earth?'

'Do you suggest, then, that we return to New Earth and face infection again – this time to have it activated? Sexual intercourse is undoubtedly a particularly pleasant mode of infection, but it may not be the only one.'

Trevize shrugged. 'I am not eager to return to New Earth, but we may have to.'

'*May?*'

'May! After all, there is another possibility.'

'What is that?'

'New Earth circles the star the people call Alpha. But Alpha is part of a binary system. Might there not be a habitable planet circling Alpha's companion as well?'

'Too dim, I should think,' said Bliss, shaking her head. 'The companion is only a quarter as bright as Alpha.'

'Dim, but not too dim. If there is a planet fairly close to the star, it might do.'

Pelorat said, 'Does the computer say anything about any planets for the companion?'

Trevize smiled grimly. 'I checked that. There are five planets of moderate size. No gas giants.'

'And are any of the five planets habitable?'

'The computer gives no information at all about the planets, other than their number, and the fact that they aren't large.'

'Oh,' said Pelorat deflated.

Trevize said, 'That's nothing to be disappointed about. None of the Spacer worlds are to be found in the computer at all. The information on Alpha itself is minimal. These things are hidden deliberately and if almost nothing is known about Alpha's companion, that might almost be regarded as a good sign.'

'Then,' said Bliss, in a business-like manner, 'what you are planning to do is this – visit the companion and, if that draws a blank, return to Alpha itself.'

'Yes. And this time when we reach the island of New Earth, we will be prepared. We will examine the entire island meticulously before landing and, Bliss, I expect you to use your mental abilities to shield –'

And at that moment, the *Far Star* lurched slightly, as though it had undergone a ship-sized hiccup, and Trevize cried out, half-way between anger and perplexity, 'Who's at the controls?'

And even as he asked, he knew very well who was.

95

Fallom, at the computer console, was completely absorbed. Her small, long-fingered hands were stretched wide in order to fit the faintly gleaming handmarks on the desk. Fallom's hands seemed to sink into the material of the desk, even though it was clearly felt to be hard and slippery.

She had seen Trevize hold his hands so on a number of occasions, and she hadn't seen him do more than that, though it was quite plain to her that in so doing he controlled the ship.

On occasion, Fallom had seen Trevize close his eyes, and she closed hers now. After a moment or two, it was almost as though she heard a faint, far-off voice – far off, but sounding in her own head, through (she dimly realized) her transducer-lobes. They were even more important than her hands. She strained to make out the words.

Instructions, it said, almost pleadingly. *What are your instructions?*

Fallom didn't say anything. She had never witnessed Trevize saying anything to the computer – but she knew what it was that she wanted with all her heart. She wanted to go back to Solaria, to the comforting endlessness of the mansion, to Jemby – Jemby – Jemby –

She wanted to go there and, as she thought of the world she loved, she imagined it visible on the viewscreen as she had seen other worlds she didn't want. She opened her eyes and stared at the viewscreen willing some other world there than this hateful Earth, then staring at what she saw, imagined it to be Solaria. She hated the empty Galaxy to which she had been introduced against her will. Tears came to her eyes, and the ship trembled.

She could feel that tremble, and she swayed a little in response.

And then she heard loud steps in the corridor outside and, when she opened her eyes, Trevize's face, distorted, filled her vision, blocking out the viewscreen which held all she wanted. He was shouting something, but she paid no attention. It was he who had taken her from Solaria by killing Bander, and it was he who was preventing her from returning by thinking only of Earth, and she was not going to listen to him.

She was going to take the ship to Solaria, and, with the intensity of her resolve, it trembled again.

96

Bliss clutched wildly at Trevize's arm. 'Don't! Don't!'

She clung strongly, holding him back, while Pelorat stood, confused and frozen, in the background.

Trevize was shouting, 'Take your hands off the computer! – Bliss, don't get in my way. I don't want to hurt you.'

Bliss said, in a tone that seemed almost exhausted, 'Don't offer violence to the child. I'd have to hurt *you* – against all instructions.'

Trevize's eyes darted wildly from Fallom to Bliss. He said, 'Then you get her off, Bliss. Now!'

Bliss pushed him away with surprising strength (drawing it, Trevize thought afterwards, from Gaia, perhaps).

'Fallom,' she said, 'lift your hands.'

'No,' shrieked Fallom. 'I want the ship to go to Solaria. I want it to go there. There.' She nodded towards the viewscreen with her head, unwilling to let even one hand release its pressure on the desk for the purpose.

But Bliss reached for the child's shoulders and, as her hands touched Fallom, the youngster began to tremble.

Bliss's voice grew soft. 'Now, Fallom, tell the computer to be as it was and come with me. Come with me.' Her hands stroked the child, who collapsed in an agony of weeping.

Fallom's hands left the desk, and Bliss, catching her under the armpits, lifted her into a standing position. She turned her, held her firmly against her breast, and allowed the child to smother her wrenching sobs there.

Bliss said to Trevize, who was now standing dumbly in the doorway, 'Step out of the way, Trevize, and don't touch either of us as we pass.'

Trevize stepped quickly to one side.

Bliss paused a moment, saying in a low voice to Trevize, 'I had to get into her mind for a moment. If I've caused any damage, I won't forgive you easily.'

It was Trevize's impulse to tell her he didn't care a cubic millimetre of vacuum for Fallom's mind; that it was the computer for which he feared. Against the concentrated glare of Gaia, however (surely it wasn't only Bliss whose sole expression could inspire the moment of cold terror he felt), he kept silent.

He remained silent for a perceptible period, and motionless as well, after Bliss and Fallom had disappeared into their room. He remained so, in fact, until Pelorat said softly, 'Golan, are you all right? She didn't hurt you, did she?'

Trevize shook his head vigorously, as though to shake off the touch of paralysis that had afflicted him. 'I'm all right. The real question is whether *that*'s all right.' He sat down at the computer console, his hands resting on the two handmarks which Fallom's hands had so recently covered.

'Well?' said Pelorat anxiously.

Trevize shrugged. 'It seems to respond normally. I might conceivably find something wrong later on, but there's nothing that seems off now.' Then, more angrily, 'The computer should not combine effectively with any hands other than mine, but in that hermaphrodite's case, it wasn't the hands alone. It was the transducer-lobes, I'm sure –'

'But what made the ship shake? It shouldn't do that, should it?'

'No. It's a gravitic ship and we shouldn't have these inertial effects. But that she-monster –' He paused, looking angry again.

'Yes?'

'I suspect she faced the computer with two self-contradictory demands, and each with such force that the computer had no choice but to attempt to do both things at once. In the attempt to do the impossible, the computer must have released the inertia-free condition of the ship, momentarily. At least that's what I think happened.'

And then, somehow, his face smoothed. 'And that might be a good thing, too, for it occurs to me now that all my talk about Alpha Centauri and its companion was flapdoodle. I know now where Earth must have transferred its secret.'

97

Pelorat stared, then ignored the final remark and went back to an earlier puzzle. 'In what way did Fallom ask for two self-contradictory things?'

'Well, she said she wanted the ship to go to Solaria.'

'Yes. Of course, she would.'

'But what did she mean by Solaria? She can't recognize Solaria from space. She's never really seen it from space. She was asleep when we left that world in a hurry. And despite her readings in your library, together with whatever Bliss has told her, I imagine she can't really grasp the truth of a Galaxy of hundreds of billions of stars and millions of populated planets. Brought up, as she was, underground and alone, it is all she can do to grasp the bare concept that there are different worlds – but how many? Two? Three? Four? To her any world she sees is likely to be Solaria, and given the strength of her wishful thinking, *is* Solaria. And since I presume Bliss has tried to quiet her by hinting that if we don't find Earth, we'll take her back to Solaria, she may even have worked up the notion that Solaria is close to Earth.'

'But how can you tell this, Golan? What makes you think it's so?'

'She as much as told us so, Janov, when we burst in upon her. She cried out that she wanted to go to Solaria and then added "there – there", nodding her head at the viewscreen. And what is on the viewscreen? Earth's satellite. It wasn't there when I left the machine before dinner; Earth was. But Fallom must have pictured the satellite in her mind when she asked for Solaria, and the computer, in response, must therefore have focused on the satellite. Believe me, Janov, I know how this computer works. Who would know better?'

Pelorat looked at the thick crescent of light on the viewscreen and said thoughtfully, 'It was called "moon" in at least one of Earth's languages; "Luna", in another language. Probably many other names too. – Imagine the confusion, old chap, on a world with numerous languages – the misunderstandings, the complications, the –'

'Moon?' said Trevize. 'Well, that's simple enough. – Then, too, come to think of it, it may be that the child tried, instinctively, to move the ship by means of its transducer-lobes, using the ship's own energy-source, and that may have helped produce the momentary inertial confusion. – But none of that matters, Janov. What does matter is that all this has brought this moon – yes I like the name – to the screen and magnified it, and there it still is. I'm looking at it now, and wondering.'

'Wondering what, Golan?'

'At the size of it. We tend to ignore satellites, Janov. They're such little things, when they exist at all. This one is different, though. It's a *world*. It has a diameter of about 3,500 kilometres.'

'A world? Surely you wouldn't call it a world. It can't be habitable. Even a 3,500-kilometre diameter is too small. It has no atmosphere. I can tell that just looking at it. No clouds. The circular curve against space is sharp, so is the inner curve that bounds the light and dark hemisphere.'

Trevize nodded, 'You're getting to be a seasoned space traveller, Janov. You're right. No air. No water. But that only means the moon's not habitable on its unprotected surface. What about underground?'

'Underground?' said Pelorat doubtfully.

'Yes. Underground. Why not? Earth's cities were underground, you tell me. We know that Trantor was underground. Comporellon has much of its capital city underground. The Solarian mansions were almost entirely underground. It's a very common state of affairs.'

'But, Golan, in every one of these cases, people were living on a habitable planet. The surface was habitable, too, with an atmosphere and with an ocean. Is it possible to live underground when the surface is uninhabitable?'

'Come, Janov, think! Where are we living right now? The *Far Star* is a tiny world that has an uninhabitable surface. There's no air or water on the outside. Yet we live in perfect comfort. The Galaxy is full of space stations and space settlements all uninhabitable except for the interior. Consider the moon a gigantic spaceship.'

'With a crew inside?'

'Yes. Millions of people, for all we know; and plants and animals; and an advanced technology. – Look, Janov, doesn't it make sense? If Earth, in its last days, could send out a party of Settlers to a planet orbiting Alpha Centauri, and if, possibly with Imperial help, they could attempt to terraform it, seed its oceans, build dry land where there was none; could Earth not also send a party to its satellite and terraform its interior?'

Pelorat said reluctantly, 'I suppose so.'

'It *would* be done. If Earth has something to hide, why send it over a parsec away, when it could be hidden on a world less than a hundred millionth the distance to Alpha. And the moon would be a more efficient hiding place from the psychological standpoint. No one would think of satellites in connection with life. For that matter I didn't. With the moon an inch before my nose, my thoughts went haring off to Alpha. If it hadn't been for Fallom –' His lips tightened, and he shook his head. 'I suppose I'll have to credit her for that. Bliss surely will if I don't.'

Pelorat said, 'But see here, old man, if there's something hiding under the surface of the moon, how do we find it? There must be millions of square kilometres of surface –'

'Roughly forty million.'

'And we would have to inspect all of that, looking for what? An opening? Some sort of airlock?'

Trevize said, 'Put that way, it would seem rather a task, but we're not just looking for objects, we're looking for life; and for intelligent life at that. And we've got Bliss, and detecting intelligence is her talent, isn't it?'

98

Bliss looked at Trevize accusingly. 'I've finally got her to sleep. I had the hardest time. She was *wild*. Fortunately, I don't think I've damaged her.'

Trevize said coldly, 'You might try removing her fixation on Jemby, you know, since I certainly have no intention of ever going back to Solaria.'

'Just remove her fixation, is that it? What do you know about such things, Trevize? You've never sensed a mind. You haven't the faintest idea of its complexity. If you knew anything at all about it, you wouldn't talk about removing a fixation as though it were just a matter of scooping jam out of a jar.'

'Well, weaken it at least.'

'I might weaken it a bit, after a month of careful dethreading.'

'What do you mean, dethreading?'

'To someone who doesn't know, it can't be explained.'

'What are you going to do with the child, then?'

'I don't know yet; it will take a lot of consideration.'

'In that case,' said Trevize, 'let me tell you what we're going to do with the ship.'

'I know what you're going to do. It's back to New Earth and another try at the lovely Hiroko, if she'll promise not to infect you this time.'

Trevize kept his face expressionless. He said, 'No, as a matter of fact. I've changed my mind. We're going to the moon – which is the name of the satellite, according to Janov.'

'The satellite? Because it's the nearest world at hand? I hadn't thought of that.'

'Nor I. Nor would anyone have thought of it. Nowhere in the Galaxy is there a satellite worth thinking about – but this satellite, in being large, is unique. What's more, Earth's anonymity covers it as well. Anyone who can't find the Earth can't find the moon, either.'

'Is it habitable?'

'Not on the surface, but it is not radioactive, not at all, so it isn't absolutely uninhabitable. It may have life – it may be teeming with life, in fact – under the surface. And, of course, you'll be able to tell if that's so, once we get close enough.'

Bliss shrugged. 'I'll try. – But, then, what made you suddenly think of trying the satellite?'

Trevize said, quietly, 'Something Fallom did when she was at the controls.'

Bliss waited, as though expecting more, then shrugged again, 'Whatever it was, I suspect you wouldn't have got the inspiration if you had followed your own impulse and killed her.'

'I had no intention of killing her, Bliss.'

Bliss waved her hand. 'All right. Let it be. Are we moving towards the moon now?'

'Yes. As a matter of caution, I'm not going too fast, but if all goes well, we'll be in its vicinity in thirty hours.'

99

The moon was a wasteland. Trevize watched the bright daylit portion drifting past them below. It was a monotonous panorama of crater rings and mountainous areas, and of shadows black against the sunlight. There were subtle colour changes in the soil and occasional sizeable stretches of flatness, broken by small craters.

As they approached the night side, the shadows grew longer and finally fused together. For a while, behind them, peaks glittered in the sun, like fat stars, far outshining their brethren in the sky.

Then they disappeared and below was only the fainter light of Earth in the sky, a large bluish-white sphere, a little more than half full. The ship finally outran Earth, too, which sank beneath the horizon so that under them was unrelieved blackness, and above only the faint powdering of stars, which, to Trevize, who had been brought up on the starless world of Terminus, was always miracle enough.

Then, new bright stars appeared ahead, first just one or two, then others, expanding and thickening and finally coalescing. And at once they passed the terminator into the daylit side. The Sun rose with infernal splendour, while the viewscreen shifted away from it at once and polarized the glare of the ground beneath.

Trevize could see quite well that it was useless to hope to find any way into the inhabited interior (if that existed) by mere eye inspection of this perfectly enormous world.

He turned to look at Bliss, who sat beside him. She did not look at the viewscreen; indeed, she kept her eyes closed. She seemed to have collapsed into the chair rather than to be sitting in it.

Trevize, wondering if she were asleep, said softly, 'Do you detect anything else?'

Bliss shook her head very slightly. 'No,' she whispered. 'There was just that faint whiff. You'd better take me back there. Do you know where that region was?'

'The computer knows.'

It was like zeroing in on a target, shifting this way and that and then finding it. The area in question was still deep in the night side and, except that the Earth shone fairly low in the sky and gave the surface a ghostly ashen glow between the shadows, there was nothing to make out, even though the light in the pilot-room had been blacked out for better viewing.

Pelorat had approached and was standing anxiously in the doorway. 'Have we found anything?' he asked, in a husky whisper.

Trevize held up his hand for silence. He was watching Bliss. He knew it would be days before sunlight would return to this spot on the moon, but he also knew that for what Bliss was trying to sense, light of any kind was irrelevant.

She said, 'It's there.'

'Are you sure?'

'Yes.'

'And it's the only spot?'

'It's the only spot I've detected. Have you been over every part of the moon's surface?'

'We've been over a respectable fraction of it.'

'Well, then, in that respectable fraction, this is all I have detected. It's stronger now, as though *it* has detected *us*, and it doesn't seem dangerous. The feeling I get is a welcoming one.'

'Are you sure?'

'It's the feeling I get.'

Pelorat said, 'Could it be faking the feeling?'

Bliss said, with a trace of hauteur, 'I would detect a fake, I assure you.'

Trevize muttered something about overconfidence, then said, 'What you detect is intelligence, I hope.'

'I detect strong intelligence. Except –' And an odd note entered her voice.

'Except what?'

'Ssh. Don't disturb me. Let me concentrate.' The last word was a mere motion of her lips.

Then she said, in faint elated surprise, 'It's not human.'

'Not human,' said Trevize, in much stronger surprise. 'Are we dealing with robots again? As on Solaria?'

'No.' Bliss was smiling. 'It's not quite robotic, either.'

'It has to be one or the other.'

'Neither.' She actually chuckled. 'It's not human, and yet it's not like any robot I've detected before.'

Pelorat said, 'I would like to see that.' He nodded his head vigorously, his eyes wide with pleasure. 'It would be exciting. Something new.'

'Something new,' muttered Trevize with a sudden lift of his own spirits – and a flash of unexpected insight seemed to illuminate the interior of his skull.

100

Down they sank to the Moon's surface, in what was almost jubilation. Even Fallom had joined them now and, with the abandonment of a youngster, was hugging herself with unbearable joy as though she were truly returning to Solaria.

As for Trevize, he felt within himself a touch of sanity telling him that it was strange that Earth – or whatever of Earth was on the moon – which had taken such measures to keep off all others, should now be taking measures to draw them in. Could the purpose be the same in either way? Was it a case of 'If you can't make them avoid you, draw them in and destroy them?' Either way, would not Earth's secret remain untouched?

But that thought faded and drowned in the flood of joy that deepened steadily as they came closer to the moon's surface. Yet over and beyond that, he managed to cling to the moment of illumination that had reached him just before they had begun their gliding dive to the surface of the Earth's satellite.

He seemed to have no doubts as to where the ship was going. They were just above the tops of the rolling hills now, and Trevize, at the computer, felt no need to do anything. It was as though he and the computer, both, were being guided, and he felt only an enormous euphoria at having the weight of responsibility taken away from him.

They were sliding parallel to the ground, towards a cliff that raised its menacing height as a barrier against them; a barrier glistening faintly in Earth-shine and in the light-beam of the *Far Star*. The approach of certain collision seemed to mean nothing to Trevize, and it was with no surprise whatever that he became aware that the section of cliff directly ahead had fallen away and that a corridor, gleaming in artificial light, had opened before them.

The ship slowed to a crawl, apparently of its own accord, and fitted neatly into the opening – entering – sliding along – The opening closed behind it, and another then opened before it. Through the second opening went the ship, into a gigantic hall that seemed the hollowed interior of a mountain.

The ship halted and all aboard rushed to the air-lock eagerly. It occurred to none of them, not even to Trevize, to check whether there might be a breathable atmosphere outside – or any atmosphere at all.

There *was* air, however. It was breathable and it was comfortable. They looked about themselves with the pleased air of people who had somehow come home and it was only after a while that they became aware of a man who was waiting politely for them to approach.

He was tall, and his expression was grave. His hair was bronze in colour, and cut short. His cheekbones were broad, his eyes were bright, and his clothing was rather after the fashion one saw in ancient history books. Although he seemed sturdy and vigorous there was, just the same, an air of weariness about him – not in anything that one could see, but rather in something appealing to no recognizable sense.

It was Fallom who reacted first. With a loud, whistling scream, she ran towards the man, waving her arms and crying, 'Jemby! Jemby!' in a breathless fashion.

She never slackened her pace, and when she was close enough, the man stooped and lifted her high in the air. She threw her arms about his neck, sobbing, and still gasping, 'Jemby!'

The others approached more soberly and Trevize said, slowly and distinctly (could this man understand Galactic?), 'We ask pardon, sir. This child has lost her protector and is searching for it desperately. How it came to fasten on you is a puzzle to us, since it is seeking a robot; a mechanical –'

The man spoke for the first time. His voice was utilitarian rather than musical, and there was a faint air of archaism clinging to it, but he spoke Galactic with perfect ease.

'I greet you all in friendship,' he said – and he seemed unmistakably friendly, even though his face continued to remain fixed in its expression of gravity. 'As for the child,' he went on, 'she shows perhaps a greater perceptivity than you think, for I am a robot. My name is Daneel Olivaw.'

21

The Search Ends

101

Trevize found himself in a complete state of disbelief. He had recovered from the odd euphoria he had felt just before and after the landing on the moon – a euphoria, he now suspected, that had been imposed on him by this self-styled robot who now stood before him.

Trevize was still staring, and in his now perfectly sane and untouched mind, he remained lost in astonishment. He had talked in astonishment, made conversation, scarcely understood what he said or heard as he searched for something in the appearance of this apparent man, in his behaviour, in his manner of speaking, that bespoke the robot.

No wonder, thought Trevize, that Bliss had detected something that was neither human nor robot but, that was, in Pelorat's words, 'something new'. Just as well, of course, for it had turned Trevize's thoughts into another and more enlightening channel – but even that was now crowded into the back of his mind.

Bliss and Fallom wandered off to explore the grounds. It had been Bliss's suggestion, but it seemed to Trevize that it came after a lightning-quick glance had been exchanged between herself and Daneel. When Fallom refused and asked to stay with the being she persisted in calling Jemby, a grave word from Daneel and a lift of the finger was enough to cause her to trot off at once. Trevize and Pelorat remained.

'They are not Foundationers, sirs,' said the robot, as though that explained it all. 'One is Gaia and one is a Spacer.'

Trevize remained silent while they were led to simply designed chairs under a tree. They seated themselves, at a gesture from the robot, and when he sat down, too, in a perfectly human movement, Trevize said, 'Are you truly a robot?'

'Truly, sir,' said Daneel.

Pelorat's face seemed to shine with joy. He said, 'There are references to a robot named Daneel in the old legends. Are you named in his honour?'

'I am that robot,' said Daneel. 'It is not a legend.'

'Oh no,' said Pelorat. 'If you are that robot, you would have to be thousands of years old.'

'Twenty thousand,' said Daneel quietly.

Pelorat seemed abashed at that, and glanced at Trevize, who said, with a touch of anger, 'If you are a robot, I order you to speak truthfully.'

'I do not need to be told to speak truthfully, sir. I *must* do so. You are faced then, sir, with three alternatives. Either I am a man who is lying to you; or I am a robot who has been programmed to believe that it is twenty thousand years old but, in fact, is not; or I am a robot who *is* twenty thousand years old. You must decide which alternative to accept.'

'The matter may decide itself with continued conversation,' said Trevize, drily. 'For that matter, it is hard to believe that this is the interior of the moon. Neither the light –' (he looked up as he said that, for the light was precisely that of soft, diffuse sunlight, though no sun was in the sky, and, for that matter, no sky was clearly visible) 'nor the gravity seems credible. This world should have a surface gravity of less than 0.2 g.'

'The normal surface gravity would be 0.15 g actually, sir. It is built up, however, by the same forces that give you, on your ship, the sensation of normal gravity, even when you are in free fall, or under acceleration. Other energy needs, including the light, are also met gravitically, though we use solar energy where that is convenient. Our material needs are all supplied by the moon's soil, except for the light elements – hydrogen, carbon, and nitrogen – which the moon does not possess. We obtain those by capturing an occasional comet. One such capture a century is more than enough to supply our needs.'

'I take it Earth is useless as a source of supply.'

'Unfortunately, that is so, sir. Our positronic brains are as sensitive to radioactivity as human proteins are.'

'You use the plural, and this mansion before us seems large, beautiful and elaborate – at least as seen from the outside. There are then other beings on the moon. Humans? Robots?'

'Yes, sir. We have a complete ecology on the moon and a vast and complex hollow within which the ecology exists. The intelligent beings are all robots, however, more or less like myself. You will see none of them, however. As for this mansion, it is used by myself only and it is an establishment that is modelled exactly on one I used to live in twenty thousand years ago.'

'Which you remember in detail, do you?'

'Perfectly, sir. I was manufactured, and existed for a time – how brief a time it seems to me, now – on the Spacer world of Aurora.'

'The one with the –' Trevize paused.

'Yes, sir. The one with the dogs.'

'You know about that?'

'Yes, sir.'

'How do you come to be here, then, if you lived at first on Aurora?'

'Sir, it was to prevent the creation of a radioactive Earth that I came here in the very beginnings of the settlement of the Galaxy. There was another robot with me, named Giskard, who could sense and adjust minds.'

'As Bliss can?'

'Yes, sir. We failed, in a way, and Giskard ceased to operate. Before the cessation, however, he made it possible for me to have his talent and left it to me to care for the Galaxy; for Earth, particularly.'

'Why Earth, particularly.'

'In part because of a man named Elijah Baley, an Earthman.'

Pelorat put in excitedly, 'He is the culture-hero I mentioned some time ago, Golan.'

'A culture-hero, sir?'

'What Dr Pelorat means,' said Trevize, 'is that he is a person to whom much was attributed, and who may have been an amalgamation of many men in actual history, or who may be an invented person altogether.'

Daneel considered for a moment, and then said, quite calmly, 'That is not so, sirs. Elijah Baley was a real man and he was one man. I do not know what your legends say of him, but in actual history, the Galaxy might never have been settled without him. In his honour, I did my best to salvage what I could of Earth after it began to turn radioactive. My fellow-robots were distributed over the Galaxy in an effort to influence a person here – a person there. At one time I manœuvred a beginning to the recycling of Earth's soil. At another much later time, I manœuvred a beginning to the terraforming of a world circling the nearby star now called Alpha. In neither case was I truly successful. I could never adjust human minds entirely as I wished, for there was always the chance that I might do harm to the various humans who were adjusted. I was bound, you see – and am bound to this day – by the Laws of Robotics.'

'Yes?'

It did not necessarily take a being with Daneel's mental power to detect uncertainty in that monosyllable.

'The First Law,' he said, 'is this, sir: "A robot may not injure a human being or, through inaction, allow a human being to come to harm." The Second Law: "A robot must obey the orders given it by human beings except where such order would conflict with the First Law." The Third Law: "A robot must protect its own existence as long as such protection does not conflict with the First or Second Laws." – Naturally, I give you these laws in the approximation of language. In actual fact they represent complicated mathematical configurations of our positronic brain-paths.'

'Do you find it difficult to deal with those Laws?'

'I must, sir. The First Law is an absolute that almost forbids the use of my mental talents altogether. When dealing with the Galaxy it is not likely that any course of action will prevent harm altogether. Always, some people, perhaps many people, will suffer so that a robot must choose minimum harm. Yet, the complexity of possibilities is such that it takes time to make that choice and one is, even then, never certain.'

'I see that,' said Trevize.

'All through Galactic history,' said Daneel, 'I tried to ameliorate the worst aspects of the strife and disaster that perpetually made itself felt in the Galaxy. I may have succeeded, on occasion, and to some extent, but if you know your Galactic history, you will know that I did not succeed often, or by much.'

'That much I know,' said Trevize, with a wry smile.

'Just before Giskard's end, he conceived of a robotic law that superseded even the first. We called it the "Zeroth Law" out of an inability to think of any other name that made sense. The Zeroth Law is: "A robot may not injure humanity or, through inaction, allow humanity to come to harm." This automatically means that the First Law must be modified to be: "A robot may not injure a human being, or, through inaction, allow a human being to come to harm, except where that would conflict with the Zeroth Law." And similar modifications must be made in the Second and Third Laws.'

Trevize frowned. 'How do you decide what is injurious, or not injurious, to humanity as a whole?'

'Precisely, sir,' said Daneel. 'In theory, the Zeroth Law was the answer to our problems. In practice, we could never decide. A human being is a concrete object. Injury to a person can be estimated and judged. Humanity is an abstraction. How do we deal with it?'

'I don't know,' said Trevize.

'Wait,' said Pelorat. 'You could convert humanity into a single organism. Gaia.'

'That is what I tried to do, sir. I engineered the founding of Gaia. If humanity could be made a single organism, it would become a concrete object, and it could be dealt with. It was, however, not as easy to create a super-organism as I had hoped. In the first place, it could not be done unless human beings valued the super-organism more than their individuality, and I had to find a mind-cast that would allow that. It was a long time before I thought of the Laws of Robotics.'

'Ah, then, the Gaians *are* robots. I had suspected that from the start.'

'In that case, you suspected incorrectly, sir. They are human beings, but they have brains firmly inculcated with the equivalent of the Laws of Robotics. They have to value life, *really* value it. – And even after that was done, there remained a serious flaw. A super-organism consisting of human beings only is unstable. It cannot be set up. Other animals must be added – then plants – then the inorganic world. The smallest super-organism that is truly stable is an entire world, and a world large enough and complex enough to have a stable ecology. It took a long time to understand this, and it is only in this last century that Gaia was *fully* established and that it became ready to move on towards Galaxia – and, even so, that will take a long time, too. Perhaps not as long as the road already travelled, however, since we now know the rules.'

'But you needed me to make the decision for you. Is that it, Daneel?'

'Yes, sir. The Laws of Robotics would not allow me, nor Gaia, to make the decision and chance harm to humanity. And meanwhile, five centuries ago, when it seemed that I would never work out methods for getting round all the difficulties that stood in the way of establishing Gaia, I turned to the second-best and helped bring about the development of the science of psychohistory.'

'I might have guessed that,' mumbled Trevize. 'You know, Daneel, I'm beginning to believe you *are* twenty thousand years old.'

'Thank you, sir.'

Pelorat said, 'Wait a while. I think I see something. Are you part of Gaia yourself, Daneel? Would that be how you knew about the dogs on Aurora? Through Bliss?'

Daneel said, 'In a way, sir, you are correct. I am associated with Gaia, though I am not part of it.'

Trevize's eyebrows went up. 'That sounds like Comporellon, the world we visited immediately after leaving Gaia. It insists it is not part of the Foundation Confederation, but is only associated with it.'

Slowly, Daneel nodded. 'I suppose that analogy is apt, sir. I can, as an associate of Gaia, make myself aware of what Gaia is aware of – in the person of the woman, Bliss, for instance. Gaia, however, cannot make itself aware of what I am aware of, so that I maintain my freedom of action. That freedom of action is necessary until Galaxia is well established.'

Trevize looked steadily at the robot for a moment, then said, 'And did you use your awareness through Bliss in order to interfere with events on our journey to mould them to your better liking?'

Daneel sighed in a curiously human fashion. 'I could not do much, sir. The Laws of Robotics always hold me back. – And yet, I lightened the load on Bliss's mind, taking a small amount of added responsibility on myself, so that she might deal with the wolves of Aurora and the Spacer on Solaria with greater dispatch and with less harm to herself. In addition, I influenced the woman on Comporellon and the one on New Earth, through Bliss, in order to have them look with favour on you, so that you might continue on your journey.'

Trevize smiled, half-sadly. 'I ought to have known it wasn't I.'

Daneel accepted the statement without its rueful self-deprecation. 'On the contrary, sir,' he said, 'it was you in considerable part. Each of the two women looked with favour upon you from the start. I merely strengthened the impulses already present – about all one can safely do under the strictures of the Laws of Robotics. Because of those strictures – and for other reasons as well – it was only with great difficulty that I brought you here, and only indirectly. I was in great danger at several points of losing you.'

'And now I *am* here,' said Trevize. 'What is it you want of me? To confirm my decision in favour of Galaxia?'

Daneel's face, always expressionless, somehow managed to seem despairing. 'No, sir. The mere decision is no longer enough. I brought you here, as best I could in my present condition, for something far more desperate. I am dying.'

102

Perhaps it was because of the matter-of-fact way in which Daneel said it; or perhaps because a lifetime of twenty thousand years made death seem no tragedy to one doomed to live less than half a per cent of that period; but, in any case, Trevize felt no stir of sympathy.

'Die? Can a machine die?'

'I can cease to exist, sir, call it by whatever word you wish. I am old. Not one sentient being in the Galaxy that was alive when I was first given consciousness is still alive today; nothing organic; nothing robotic. Even I myself lack continuity.'

'In what way?'

'There is no physical part of my body, sir, that has escaped replacement, not only once but many times. Even my positronic brain has been replaced on five different occasions. Each time the contents of my earlier brain were etched into the newer one to the last positron. Each time, the new brain had a greater capacity and complexity than the old, so that there was room for more memories, and for faster decision and action. But –'

'But?'

'The more advanced and complex the brain, the more unstable it is, and the more quickly it deteriorates. My present brain is a hundred thousand times as sensitive as my first, and has ten million times the capacity; but whereas my first brain endured for over ten thousand years, the present one is but six hundred years old and is unmistakably senescent. With every memory of twenty thousand years perfectly recorded and with a perfect recall mechanism in place, the brain is filled. There is a rapidly declining ability to reach decisions; an even more rapidly declining ability to test and influence minds at hyper-spatial distances. Nor can I design a sixth brain. Further miniaturization will run against the blank wall of the uncertainty principle, and further complexity will but assure decay almost at once.'

Pelorat seemed desperately troubled. 'But surely, Daneel, Gaia can carry on without you. Now that Trevize has judged and selected Galaxia –'

'The process simply took too long, sir,' said Daneel, as always betraying no emotion. 'I had to wait for Gaia to be fully established, despite the unanticipated difficulties that arose. By the time a human being – Mr Trevize – was located who was capable of making the key decision, it was too late. Do not think, however, that I took no measure to lengthen my life span. Little by little I have reduced my activities, in order to conserve what I could for emergencies. When I could no longer rely on active measures to preserve the isolation of the Earth-moon system, I adopted passive ones. Over a period of years, the humaniform robots that have been working with me have been, one by one, called home. Their last tasks have been to remove all references to Earth in the planetary archives. And without myself and my fellow-robots in full play, Gaia will lack the essential tools to carry through the development of Galaxia in less than an inordinate period of time.'

'And you knew all this,' said Trevize, 'when I made my decision?'

'A substantial time before, sir,' said Daneel. 'Gaia, of course, did not know.'

'But then,' said Trevize angrily, 'what was the use of carrying through the charade? What good has it been? Ever since my decision, I have scoured the Galaxy, searching for Earth and what I thought of as its "secret" – not knowing the secret was *you* – in order that I might confirm the decision. Well, I *have* confirmed it. I know now that Galaxia is absolutely essential – and it appears to be all for nothing. Why could you not have left the Galaxy to itself – and me to myself?'

Daneel said, 'Because, sir, I have been searching for a way out, and I have been carrying on in the hope that I might find one. I think I have. Instead of replacing my brain with yet another positronic one, which is impractical, I might merge it with a human brain instead; a human brain that is not affected by the Three Laws, and will not only add capacity to my brain, but add a whole new level of abilities as well. That is why I have brought you here.'

Trevize looked appalled. 'You mean you plan to merge a human brain into yours? Have the human brain lose its individuality so that you can achieve a two-brain Gaia?'

'Yes, sir. It would not make me immortal, but it might enable me to live long enough to establish Galaxia.'

'And you brought *me* here for that? You want my independence of the Three Laws and my sense of judgement made part of you at the price of my individuality? – No!'

Daneel said, 'Yet you said a moment ago that Galaxia is essential for the welfare of the human –'

'Even if it is, it would take a long time to establish, and I would remain an individual in my lifetime. On the other hand, if it were established rapidly, there would be a Galactic loss of individuality and my own loss would be part of an unimaginably greater whole. I would, however, certainly never consent to lose my individuality while the rest of the Galaxy retains theirs.'

Daneel said, 'It is then as I thought. Your brain would not merge well and, in any case, it would serve a better purpose if you retained an independent judgemental ability.'

'When did you change your mind? You said that it was for merging that you brought me here.'

'Yes, and only by using the fullest extent of my greatly diminished powers. Still, when I said, "That is why I have brought you here", please remember that in Galactic Standard, the word "you" represents the plural as well as the singular. I was referring to all of you.'

Pelorat stiffened in his seat. 'Indeed? Tell me then, Daneel, would a human brain that was merged with your brain share in all your memories – all twenty thousand years of it, back to legendary times?'

'Certainly, sir.'

Pelorat drew a long breath. 'That would fulfil a lifetime search, and it is something I would gladly give up my individuality for. Please let me have the privilege of sharing your brain.'

Trevize asked softly, 'And Bliss? What about her?'

Pelorat hesitated for no more than a moment. 'Bliss will understand,' he said. 'She will, in any case, be better off without me – after a while.'

Daneel shook his head. 'Your offer, Dr Pelorat, is a generous one, but I cannot accept it. Your brain is an old one and it cannot survive for more than two or three decades at best, even in a merger with my own. I need something else. – See!' He pointed and said, 'I've called her back.'

Bliss was returning, walking happily, with a bounce to her steps.

Pelorat rose convulsively to his feet. 'Bliss! Oh, no!'

'Do not be alarmed, Dr Pelorat,' said Daneel. 'I cannot use Bliss. That would merge me with Gaia, and I must remain independent of Gaia, as I have already explained.'

'But in that case,' said Pelorat, 'who –'

And Trevize, looking at the slim figure running after Bliss, said, 'The robot has wanted Fallom all along, Janov.'

103

Bliss returned, smiling, clearly in a state of great pleasure.

'We couldn't pass beyond the bounds of the estate,' she said, 'but it all reminded me very much of Solaria. Fallom, of course, is convinced it *is* Solaria. I asked her if she didn't think that Daneel had an appearance different from that of Jemby – after all, Jemby was metallic – and Fallom said, "No, not really." I don't know what she meant by "not really".'

She looked across to the middle distance where Fallom was now playing her flute for a grave Daneel, whose head nodded in time. The sound reached them, thin, clear, and lovely.

'Did you know she took the flute with her when we left the ship?' asked Bliss. 'I suspect we won't be able to get her away from Daneel for quite a while.'

The remark was met with a heavy silence, and Bliss looked at the two men in quick alarm. 'What's the matter?'

Trevize gestured gently in Pelorat's direction. It was up to him, the gesture seemed to say.

Pelorat cleared his throat and said, 'Actually, Bliss, I think that Fallom will be staying with Daneel permanently.'

'Indeed?' Bliss, frowning, made as though to walk in Daneel's direction, but Pelorat caught her arm. 'Bliss dear, you can't. He's more powerful than Gaia even now, and Fallom must stay with him if Galaxia is to come into existence. Let me explain – and Golan, please correct me if I get anything wrong.'

Bliss listened to the account, her expression sinking into something close to despair.

Trevize said, in an attempt at cool reason, 'You see how it is, Bliss. The child is a Spacer and Daneel was designed and put together by Spacers. The child was brought up by a robot and knew nothing else on an estate as empty as this one. The child has transductive powers which Daneel will need, and she will live for three or four centuries, which may be what is required for the construction of Galaxia.'

Bliss said, her cheeks flushed and her eyes moist, 'I suppose that the robot manœuvred our trip to Earth in such a way as to make us pass through Solaria in order to pick up a child for his use.'

Trevize shrugged. 'He may simply have taken advantage of the opportunity. I don't think his powers are strong enough at the moment to make complete puppets of us at hyperspatial distances.'

'No. It was purposeful. He made certain that I would feel strongly attracted to the child so that I would take her with me, rather than leave her to be killed; that I would protect her even against you when you showed nothing but resentment and annoyance at her being with us.'

Trevize said, 'That might just as easily have been your Gaian ethics, which Daneel could have strengthened a bit, I suppose. Come, Bliss, there's nothing to be gained. Suppose you *could* take Fallom away. Where could you then take her that would make her as happy as she is here? Would you take her back to Solaria where she would be killed quite pitilessly; to some crowded world where she would sicken and die; to Gaia, where she would wear her heart out longing for Jemby; on an endless voyage through the Galaxy, where she would think that every world we came across was her Solaria? And would you find a substitute for Daneel's use so that Galaxia could be constructed?'

Bliss was sadly silent.

Pelorat held out his hand to her, a bit timidly. 'Bliss,' he said, 'I volunteered to have my brain fused with Daneel's. He wouldn't take it because he said I was too old. I wish he had, if that would have saved Fallom for you.'

Bliss took his hand and kissed it. 'Thank you, Pel, but the price would be too high, even for Fallom.' She took a deep breath, and tried to smile. 'Perhaps, when we get back to Gaia, room will be found in the global organism for a child for me – and I will place Fallom in the syllables of its name.'

And now Daneel, as though aware that the matter was settled, was walking towards them, with Fallom skipping along at his side.

The youngster broke into a run and reached them first. She said to Bliss, 'Thank you, Bliss, for taking me home to Jemby again and for taking care of me while we were on the ship. I shall always remember you.' Then she flung herself at Bliss and the two held each other tightly.

'I hope you will always be happy,' said Bliss. 'I will remember you, too, Fallom dear,' and released her with reluctance.

Fallom turned to Pelorat, and said, 'Thank you, too. Pel, for letting me read your book-films.' Then, without an additional word, and after a trace of hesitation, the thin, girlish hand was extended to Trevize. He took it for a moment, then let it go.

'Good luck, Fallom,' he muttered.

Daneel said, 'I thank you all, sirs and madam, for what you have done, each in your own way. You are free to go now, for your search is ended. As for my own work, it will be ended, too, soon enough, and successfully now.'

But Bliss said, 'Wait, we are not quite through. We don't know yet whether Trevize is still of the mind that the proper future for humanity is Galaxia, as opposed to a vast conglomeration of Isolates.'

Daneel said, 'He has already made that clear a while ago, madam. He has decided in favour of Galaxia.'

Bliss's lips tightened. 'I'd rather hear that from him. – Which is it to be, Trevize?'

Trevize said calmly, 'Which do you want it to be, Bliss? If I decide against Galaxia, you may get Fallom back.'

Bliss said, 'I am Gaia. I must know your decision, and its reason, for the sake of the truth and nothing else.'

Daneel said, 'Tell her, sir. Your mind, as Gaia is aware, is untouched.'

And Trevize said, 'The decision is for Galaxia. There is no further doubt in my mind on that point.'

104

Bliss remained motionless for the time one might take to count to fifty at a moderate rate, as though she were allowing the information to reach all parts of Gaia, and then she said, 'Why?'

Trevize said, 'Listen to me. I knew from the start that there were two possible futures for humanity – Galaxia, or else the Second Empire of Seldon's Plan. And it seemed to me that those two possible futures were mutually exclusive. We couldn't have Galaxia unless, for some reason, Seldon's Plan had some fundamental flaw in it.

'Unfortunately, I knew nothing about Seldon's Plan except for the two axioms on which it is based: one, that there be involved a large enough number of human beings to allow humanity to be treated statistically as a group of individuals interacting randomly; and second, that humanity not know the results of psychohistorical conclusions before the results are achieved.

'Since I had already decided in favour of Galaxia, I felt I must be subliminally aware of flaws in Seldon's Plan, and those flaws could only be in the axioms, which were all I knew of the Plan. Yet I could see nothing wrong with the axioms. I strove, then, to find Earth, feeling that Earth could not be so thoroughly hidden for no purpose. I had to find out what that purpose was.

'I had no real reason to expect to find a solution once I found Earth, but I was desperate and could think of nothing else to do. – And perhaps Daneel's desire for a Solarian child helped drive me.

'In any case, we finally reached Earth, and then the moon, and Bliss detected Daneel's mind, which he, of course, was deliberately reaching out to her. She described that mind as neither quite human nor quite robotic. In hindsight, that proved to make sense, for Daneel's brain is far advanced beyond any robot that ever existed, and would not be sensed as simply robotic. Neither would it be sensed as human, however. Pelorat referred to it as "something new" and that served as a trigger for "something new" of my own; a new thought.

'Just as, long ago, Daneel and his colleague worked out a fourth law of robotics that was more fundamental than the other three, so I could suddenly see a third basic axiom of psychohistory that was more fundamental than the other two; a third axiom so fundamental that no one ever bothered to mention it.

'Here it is. The two known axioms deal with human beings, and they are based on the unspoken axiom that human beings are the *only* intelligent species in the Galaxy, and therefore the only organisms whose actions are significant in the development of society and history. That is the unstated axiom: that there is only one species of intelligence in the Galaxy and that it is *Homo sapiens*. If there were "something new", if there were other species of intelligence widely different in nature, then their behaviour would not be described accurately by the mathematics of psychohistory and Seldon's Plan would have no meaning. Do you see?'

Trevize was almost shaking with the earnest desire to make himself understood. 'Do you see?' he repeated.

Pelorat said, 'Yes, I see, but as devil's advocate, old chap –'

'Yes? Go on.'

'Human beings *are* the only intelligences in the Galaxy.'

'Robots?' said Bliss. 'Gaia?'

Pelorat thought awhile, then said hesitantly, 'Robots have played no significant role in human history since the disappearance of the Spacers. Gaia has played no significant role until very recently. Robots are the creation of human beings, and Gaia is the creation of robots – and both robots and Gaia, insofar as they must be bound by the Three Laws, have no choice but to yield to human will. Despite the twenty thousand years Daneel has laboured, and the long development of Gaia, a single word from Golan Trevize, a human being, would put an end to both those labours and that development. It follows, then, that humanity is the only significant species of intelligence in the Galaxy, and psychohistory remains valid.'

'The only form of intelligence in the Galaxy,' repeated Trevize slowly. 'I agree. Yet we speak so much and so often of the Galaxy that it is all but impossible for us to see that this is not enough. The Galaxy is not the Universe. There are other galaxies.'

Pelorat and Bliss stirred uneasily. Daneel listened with benign gravity, his hand slowly stroking Fallom's hair.

Trevize said, 'Listen to me again. Just outside the Galaxy are the Magellanic Clouds, where no human ship has ever penetrated. Beyond that are other small galaxies, and not very far away is the giant Andromeda Galaxy, larger than our own. Beyond that are galaxies by the billions.

'Our own Galaxy has developed only one species of an intelligence great enough to develop a technological society, but what do we know of the others? Ours may be atypical. In some of the others

– perhaps even all – there may be many competing intelligent species, struggling with each other, and each incomprehensible to us. Perhaps it is their mutual struggle that preoccupies them, but what if, in some Galaxy, one species gains domination over the rest and then has time to consider the possibility of penetrating other galaxies.

'Hyperspatially, the Galaxy is a point – and so is all the Universe. We have not visited any other galaxy, and, as far as we know, no intelligent species from another galaxy has ever visited us – but that state of affairs may end some day. And if the invaders come, they are bound to find ways of turning some human beings against other human beings. We have so long had only ourselves to fight that we are used to such internecine quarrels. An invader that finds us divided against ourselves will dominate us all, or destroy us all. The only true defence is to produce Galaxia, which cannot be turned against itself and which can meet invaders with maximum power.'

Bliss said, 'The picture you paint is a frightening one. Will we have time to form Galaxia?'

Trevize looked up, as though to penetrate the thick layer of moonrock that separated him from the surface and from space; as though to force himself to see those far distant galaxies, moving slowly through unimaginable vistas of space.

He said, 'In all human history, no other intelligence has impinged on us, to our knowledge. This need only continue a few more centuries, perhaps little more than one ten thousandth of the time civilization has already existed, and we will be safe. After all,' and here Trevize felt a sudden twinge of trouble, which he forced himself to disregard, 'it is not as though we had the enemy already here and among us.'

And he did not look down to meet the brooding eyes of Fallom – hermaphroditic, transductive, different – as they rested, unfathomably, on him.